I0604219

THE GAMES
OF OLYMPUS

THE GAMES OF OLYMPUS

THEOS BOOK 2

Arthur Wordsmith

Podium

To Mom and Dad,
You two are the best.

All rights reserved. No part of this publication may be reproduced, stored in a retrieval system, or transmitted in any form or by any means electronic, mechanical, photocopying, recording, or otherwise without prior written permission from Podium Publishing.

This is a work of fiction. Names, characters, places, and incidents are either products of the author's imagination or used fictitiously. Any resemblance to actual events, locales, or persons, living, dead, or undead, is entirely coincidental.

Copyright © 2024 by Arthur Wordsmith

Cover design by Dailen Ogden

ISBN: 978-1-0394-5536-8

Published in 2024 by Podium Publishing
www.podiumaudio.com

THE GAMES
OF OLYMPUS

CHAPTER 1

Aboard the Argo

Luke and Lukeus walked a half step behind Jason as he led them through the wooden halls of the *Argo* toward Rex's quarters in the stables. Luke marveled at his own presence aboard the mythical ship. Never would he have expected that freeing Heracles would lead to such an outcome. Then again, these days he never really knew what to expect, and hadn't from the moment he died.

Along with his awe, Luke felt another, less pleasant emotion gnawing at him. Worry for his missing—and rather valuable weapons—after some casual prodding about the location of their stuff, Heracles had divulged that Rex was the one who had made off with their things. Considering that Rex was a part of their party, and Lukeus's brother on top of that, none of the Argonauts had found a reason to deny him.

Luke wished that they had. He wanted nothing more than to not worry about anything, and to just play around with the new aspects of his powers and find his limits. See how fast he could fly and how much he could lift.

The universe, it seemed, wasn't that kind.

Glancing at Lukeus's face, Luke found him entirely unconcerned about his own missing belongings. It made sense, he realized. The emperor's grandson was unlikely to own anything that was truly hard for him to replace, and the one who had taken his things was his brother.

He carefully schooled his own expression in response. While he was both concerned and curious about why Rex had taken his stuff, he didn't want to let on that not all his belongings were anything more than what they appeared to be.

The boots are awesome, but strictly speaking, I don't really need them anymore. The sword and ring Cyzicus gave me are also nice, but the ring was a Warrior-tier artifact meant to help mortals develop their Arcana. I doubt it's even useful to me anymore, if it even works anymore. That was a lot of pressure I put it under, and it did get really hot. The sword, while cool and probably valuable for the average person, is also something I can live without and something that I can replace.

Bellerophon's Blade, though . . . that's an entirely different matter. As far as I know, it's unique, and cultivating with it is magnitudes easier than without. Maybe some gods have similar stuff that they hand out to their kids or something, but unless Prometheus gets himself free, I doubt I'll get similar treatment.

He suppressed a wince as he remembered the progenitor of his bloodline. Having divine ancestry was bound to be useful, and figuring out what his bloodline did and how it worked nearly had him salivating. It was the fact that Prometheus both looked insane and had admitted to being insane that made him nervous. Combined with the fact that apparently their bloodline connected them somehow was nerve-racking. Just remembering the vision, and the titan's pitifully gross form, his strange blue eyes and bloody stomach, nearly made him retch.

As if that wasn't enough, it wasn't long ago that Luke had witnessed Jax's death because his family had some way to track him. To learn that there was something like that, and now it might actually be something that he had to watch out for was . . . disconcerting.

I'll need to look into it. The blood compasses are supposed to be rare, so there's a chance that I'm worrying about nothing. Besides, even if one does exist, it doesn't necessarily mean that Prometheus has any ill intentions. He's not well, but at the same time . . . would he harm his family?

Luke discarded that train of thought. For the moment, at least, it wasn't an issue. Prometheus was still imprisoned, hopefully somewhere far, far away, and for a long time. If he ever did escape, Luke decided, he would worry about it then.

Besides, if nothing else, the Seed has proven to be somewhat reliable in getting out of these situations. Nefkha and Arke are proof of that. If there is something that will let Prometheus track me, there might also be something that will hide me from him. Once I get a quest telling me to do so, that's when I'll really need to be worried.

"Rex is through there," Jason said. Standing beside a large brass door, he pried it open. "I'll wait here."

"Is Nutbutter in there, too?" Lukeus asked eagerly.

"He is." Jason nodded, looking at the two of them with pity. "Good luck with that dreadglare. It was hard to even convince everyone to let him onboard. They all think your brother is insane. Heracles was adamant about not leaving him behind, though, and Rex wouldn't come unless we also let his pet demon aboard."

Lukeus frowned in confusion. "Since whe— Shit." He crossed his arms and turned to Luke. "Why didn't you tell me he hatched it?"

"I forgot." Luke shuddered slightly at the memory as he stared at the open door. "It did look like it was tamed, so there's that." Luke cupped the back of his neck, suddenly feeling chills running down his spine at the horror that awaited them past the door. "I think he was using it to fly when he shot Zeus."

Jason broke into a coughing fit. "Wait a minute . . . Rex *shot* Lord Zeus?"

"The arrow bounced off him," Luke clarified.

"How?" he sputtered. The mere idea of a mortal firing an arrow at, not just a god, but the king of gods himself, was ludicrous.

"Honestly"—Luke grinned—"I think Rex can do just about anything at this point."

Someone who attempts to suckle at the teat of a sheep won't ever be stopped by conventional limitations or sense. It's probably wise not to try.

Lukeus sighed and shook his head. "Can I borrow a sword? I'm not going in there without one."

"Me, too," Luke pitched in.

"Yeah." Jason nodded. One of his gold earrings glowed a dim white, and two bronze blades appeared in front of the pair.

Luke snatched it out of the air and felt its weight in his hands. It was heavy. Heavier even than his gold blades.

"They're basic Warrior-tier blades. They won't do anything special, but they cut admirably and have served me well. My teacher gave them to me when I awakened my mana. I want them back when you come out. I'm only giving them to you now because, well . . ." He nodded at the door.

"Thanks." Luke nodded gratefully. His eye lingered on Jason's earring. It was the first time he'd seen someone put a ring anywhere other than their fingers.

His thoughts drifted to Cyzicus's vault and all the treasures contained within. He wondered if the emperor had any storage rings lying around. So far every warrior he had seen possessed one, to the point that he would find it weird to meet one who didn't.

I bet I can convince him to give me one. Then, I can finally have a reason to randomly have stuff that I should have no business having.

All right. Focus. There's a monster and an idiot inside that door, and they have my stuff. Luke gulped. His eyes meeting Lukeus's, he tilted his head to the side, indicating for him to go first.

"Why me?"

"He's your brother."

Lukeus's mouth opened and closed as he tried to find some way out of it. Unfortunately for him, Luke wasn't Nel. "Fine," he said. Then, squaring his shoulders, he strode through the shadowy door with bravado. A moment later, Luke nodded solemnly to Jason and followed Lukeus into the hallway on the other side.

His sword drawn, he preemptively activated the minor stage of the First Truth of Death, on the lookout for any surprises.

"Rex," Lukeus called out. "Are you there?"

No one answered. Sharing a nervous glance, they traveled farther down the dimly lit wooden corridor.

Eventually it widened, revealing rows upon rows of stables and cages. Most of them were empty, but some were filled with all manner of strange and not-so-strange mounts—everything from lions and horses to large birds and even a few hybridized animals.

Luke stopped and stared at a particularly odd one, a beaver-looking thing with large and mesmerizing cobalt-blue butterfly wings jutting out from its side, flapping slowly.

It hissed quietly at him, displaying rows of sharp canine teeth and climbing onto its hind legs in an attempt to look menacing.

"This one's kind of cute." Luke grinned before stepping past the cage. He didn't want to provoke the animal needlessly.

"Nutbutter!" Lukeus gasped and took off toward the back of the room, having spotted his giant Pegasus's frame and distinctive chestnut coat. His feet lifted into the air and his body became parallel to the ground as he flew toward his steed as fast as he could.

"Careful."

Luke tensed, tightening his grip on his sword as he followed behind Lukeus on foot. More out of caution than to hide the fact that he too could fly or that he had become a warrior. He knew he didn't want to hide his breakthrough, and even if he did, he wouldn't be able to. Just the sheer inconvenience of it didn't make it worth it.

"It looks like they gave him a healing potion." Lukeus grinned as he flew over the gate and next to his familiar. He stroked his hands through his fur, making the creature neigh softly.

"Is Rex in there?"

"No." He shook his head.

Thought so. Luke sighed, briefly stopping in front of the pair before walking farther in. *That's heartwarming, but not what I came here for.*

The uncountable eyes of the dreadglare blinked at him nervously from a stall a few down from the Pegasus, its hairlike tendrils merging perfectly with the shadows, making them nearly impossible to see. It was . . . sitting, for a lack of a better term, pressed tightly against the corner of its stall.

His skill whispered in the back of his head, telling him exactly how to kill the thing—destroy each and every one of its eyes.

A single boot lay on its side right in front of it, and Luke could see the blue tassel attached to his sword poking out from within its mass, alongside the handle of Lukeus's own sword.

What the fuck! He resisted the urge to groan and forced himself to look through the rest of the stable for any signs of a human. *Where's Rex?* He gulped as the creature fidgeted. Taking that as his cue, he slowly stepped back and out of its sight. He did not want to go in there and try to pry his stuff loose. Not when there was literally any other option available. Nor did he think that Jason, the crew of the *Argo*, or even Rex himself would take kindly to him chucking a dozen explosive talismans into the stable and picking the remains of his belongings from the demon's dead corpse.

He knew it would work, too. It was likely because it had just been hatched, but the dreadglare was a lot smaller than the one they had killed in the desert—only the size of a horse, compared to the sprawling multistory monstrosity its parent had been.

"Lukeus," he whispered, "I found the eye monster. It has our stuff; do you think I could get a little help?"

"Is Rex not with it?" he asked, flying out of the stable and touching down softly next to Luke.

"No," Luke said as the emperor's grandson poked his head past the corner. He stepped back a moment later, his face pale.

"Well." Lukeus drummed his hands on the side of his legs. "I think it's pretty obvious what happened."

"It is?"

"Yep. That thing ate Rex, and our weapons are a lost cause. I say we just forget about them and let Heracles or Jason or whoever deal with it. It's not really my problem—they were stupid enough to let that thing on their ship, you know?" He began to march back out. "I'll just take Nutbutter and fly back to the capital, deliver the bad news, and you can just ride into town with them."

"Nope." Luke grabbed a fistful of Lukeus's robes and yanked him back. "Your brother did this, and it's your job to fix it."

"Is it really? I have a lot of family, Luke. I don't think it's fair for you to hold me personally accountable for everything that they do."

"Is it?"

"It is."

"Do you think I care?"

"Do you?"

Luke resisted the urge to yank his hair out and stab Lukeus. "Look, Rex isn't dead—there's no blood anywhere, and I really doubt that thing is a clean eater. Let's just go find him. That stuff has a lot of sentimental value to me, and I'm not going without it. Okay?"

"Would you two keep it down?" a voice echoed from behind them. A hatch, near flush and almost unnoticeable, opened up on the ground, and Rex climbed out of it, lethargically rubbing the sleep out of his eyes.

"No," Luke said. "I want my stuff."

Rex sighed. "Can't you just let Blinky play with them a little longer?"

What? Luke stared at him incomprehensibly.

CHAPTER 2

Ins and Outs

You named it Blinky?" Luke asked incredulously.

"I thought it fit," Rex mumbled, brushing past Luke and into the stable that contained the dreadglare. He came back a second later with the monstrosity latched onto the back of his neck and draped around him like a cape—one made of thousands of eyes, each one blinking at random, with mouths opening and closing around them.

A bead of nervous sweat rolled down Luke's face at how casually Rex seemed to handle the demon. Feeling a dull ache beginning to form behind his eyes from looking at it too long, Luke tore his gaze away from the pair.

He's insane. Absolutely insane. There's got to be some other powerful things that hatch from eggs—why not make one of them his familiar? His grandpa is literally an emperor of an entire continent-size island. Does he really need to resort to this? he thought, and, shaking his head, he walked past him and into the now-empty stable.

His shoulders sank slightly in relief at finding all his artifacts as well as Lukeus's and Rex's swords lying on the ground, and he reached down and grabbed the leather grip of his most valuable possession, only to drop it a moment later in disgust. It was wet. Bile crept up in his throat, and a mild burning sensation spread over his skin.

He closed his eyes, took a deep breath, and wiped his hand over his robe, all the while doing his best to ignore how his hand stuck to the fabric.

Rex better have a good reason for this, he thought darkly while he shrugged out of his robes. Using them as impromptu gloves, he gathered his things and marched out of the stable.

"Where's my manasink?"

"Oh, it broke. I tossed it out." Rex shrugged.

"I see. Bye." He walked straight out of the room, unwilling to stay in the uncomfortable presence of the dreadglare for a second longer.

"You got what you needed?" Jason asked as soon as Luke stepped through the brass door.

Frowning, Luke returned his borrowed blade. "I did. Do you have anywhere I can wash these?" he asked, miserably lifting the blue bundle into the air.

"Yeah, we do, actually." Jason nodded and stepped away from the brass door. "Follow me."

They walked back up through the wooden halls of the *Argo*, leaving the brothers behind, and toward the very back of the ship.

"What do you guys do on the *Argo*, anyways?"

"What do you mean?"

"Like . . . what's all this for?" Luke asked, gesturing around them vaguely. "Are you an army, mercenaries . . . pirates? And how did you even get a ship this big and awesome?" he asked, curiosity and a hint of desire burning in his eyes. A small part of him yearned for his own giant craft.

Jason laughed out loud. "I— We do have a goal, but at heart, all of us are adventurers. When I set sail, I didn't expect it to turn into what it did, or for so many people to join me. It kind of became its own thing after Heracles said he was coming with us. You may not have heard of him here, but back in Pelion he's . . . famous. Not just as a son of Zeus, but as a prodigy even among prodigies. As for the ship"—he ran his arms along its walls—"I won it."

"You did?"

"Mmm-hmm." He grunted. "In the Olympics, ten years ago."

Luke felt his heartbeat in anticipation. "I didn't know the prizes were—quite this impressive. Cyzicus mentioned an apple that sounded really cool, but this ship is . . . It won't help you cultivate but— Wow."

"The apple from the Evening Garden. I believe it was Lady Hera hosting that year. If I had the choice, though, I don't know what I'd pick. On one hand, you save years if not decades of effort, but the *Argo* is, well . . . the *Argo*. Anyway, the prizes usually aren't this grand," Jason admitted, immediately putting a damper on Luke's enthusiasm. "But it was Lord Poseidon who was hosting the games the year I participated. He's known to be generous. My mentor told me that it's usually something more . . . simple. Things like weapons, armor, and the like. Still amazing, but . . ." He trailed off.

Yeah, I kind of doubted a ship bigger than a supertanker is a common prize.

"What about Lord Hephaestus? I heard he's hosting this year," Luke asked.

"I don't know." He shrugged. "The tournament takes place once every ten years, and neither the prizes nor the challenges are the same. It's also been centuries since Lord Hephaestus hosted, and of all the Olympians, he is one of the most reclusive. There are likely some records of what prizes he's given before, but I don't remember reading them. You're thinking of competing?"

"I will be," Luke said, already making plans to ask Clite if she had a list of past prizes and winners. "What did you have to do to win?"

"Swim."

"Swim?"

"It was a little more complicated than that, I assure you, but essentially, yes."

"So you won the tournament, got the *Argo* as a prize, and have been on an adventure since?"

"Mmm-hmm."

"And there's nothing you want to do with an entire army at your back other than that?" Luke pried.

"What I want . . ." Jason trailed off, his voice losing some of its earlier cheer. "I'd be lying if I said I was doing all this for nothing more than the joy of seeing the world, but I'm afraid I can't tell you unless you join us. So what do you say?"

"Join you?" Luke's eyes widened in surprise.

"Mmm-hmm."

"I, uh, I don't know about that."

"Well, think about it. We'll stay until the games are over, so take at least until then to decide," he said, throwing open another brass door.

A golden fountain in the shape of a woman spewed hot water from her hands and into an array of waist-level aqueducts positioned around it. Each one was made of colorful clay—and vibrating, filling the room with the sounds of falling water and a quiet buzz.

In the far corner, Luke saw someone strip out of their clothes and armor and haphazardly chuck everything in before walking through a door deeper in the room.

"This is one of our cleaning rooms," Jason said, leading him over to one of the clay constructs. "Drop your weapons and clothes in there, and when you pull them back out, they'll be free of any stains," he explained enthusiastically. "The whole system is enchanted to clean basically everything."

A magic, communal washing machine . . . Luke looked at the contraption, amusement welling within him, as he carefully laid out his artifacts in the water. *Now I've seen everything.*

"It's impressive, right?" Jason asked eagerly.

"It is." Luke nodded to him. For a minute, they just stood there as small particles shook themselves free of his clothes, to be carried away by the water moments later. "Why do you want me to join you?"

"Why wouldn't I?" He turned to Luke. "Any man that can fight countless giants for hours on end, slay thousands of them without injury, and then survive an encounter with a foe many tiers higher is someone I want fighting beside me."

"Oh," Luke said.

I guess either Heracles or Rex has been talking. Still, when he puts it like that, even I would want me fighting by my side.

"Captain!" A door burst open, and a lean man with curly brown hair poked his head through. "There's trouble on deck. It's Atalanta again."

Jason cursed under his breath. "I have to go." He rose into the air and disappeared down the hallway.

"I'm Luke." He nodded toward the man.

"Maleager." The man nodded curtly before he, too, rose into the air and disappeared after Jason.

Collecting his clothes and weapons from the magical laundry, Luke wandered aimlessly around the *Argo* before finding his way back to the room he had awoken in. As much as he wanted to explore the ship, and meet the people on it, he couldn't delay exploring the changes in his status anymore.

Sitting cross-legged on his bed, he toggled the Seed and flipped through its tabs, intent on finding what had changed.

Status | Skills | Quests | Inventory

Name: Lukas King

Tier: Warrior

Bloodline: Eyes of Insight

Mana: 351 / 351

Rate: 17% per hour

Strength: 14

Agility: 11

Constitution: 18

Arcana: 39

Stat Points: 9

Charges: 7/10

Status | **Skills** | Quests | Inventory

First Truth of Death

Tier: Warrior

Progress: 0.1%

An expression of a Warrior-tier truth derived by Lukas King, from the Three Stances of Death created by Empress Alexia Xancrest. Gives users the ability to perceive the future of those that carry the desire to kill them.

First Stance of the Sword

Tier: Mortal

Progress: 100% [COMPLETED]

An expression of a Mortal-tier truth uncovered by the Hero Alexia Xancrest. Through centuries of battle and meditation, she perfected her understanding of the truth and infused it in the First Stance of the Sword, creating a sword style that draws out its complete potential. A technique that has since received the acknowledgment of the heavens and become permanently entwined within the eternal tapestry.

First Stance of the Shield

Tier: Mortal

Progress: 100% [COMPLETED]

[...]

First Stance of the Spear

Tier: Mortal

Progress: 100% [COMPLETED]

[...]

Status | Skills | **Quests** | Inventory

A Paragon's Path:

Over the eons, many gods have arisen, but few have trod the Path of Paragons, and fewer have succeeded.

Requirements:

—All attributes must be advanced to 1,000 at the same time to advance to the Hero tier.

—All incomplete techniques must be fully mastered to advance to the Hero tier.

*All attribute gains over 999 will be redirected as **Stat Points** until all conditions are met.

Status | Skills | Quests | **Inventory**

Capacity: 1,013.4 kg of 1,540,000 kg

Overall, the differences weren't unexpected.

The most notable change was that his paragon quest had been updated to reflect his new tier instead of vanishing from his status when the task was completed.

I kind of had a feeling it would be that way, too. It wouldn't really make sense to be a paragon at the Mortal tier and then decide not to be one later. No, for better or worse I'm locked in. And it's definitely for the better.

At least this time I don't need to gather an additional ten thousand points to unlock my bloodline. From what Lukeus said, he awakened his along with his mana. Obviously, mine is different. But why, though?

If the gods are real, and they really have as many kids as it seems like they do, then just by the sheer virtue of their age, everyone should have a bloodline. Assuming, of course, you even need to be a god make one. And I sincerely doubt that Lukeus's mother is a god. So is it just binary—either you unlock it or you don't?

Rex's is supposed to be weaker than Lukeus's and Nel's, so that could be it.

Or maybe some people unlock it at different tiers? And I would have been able to do it later even without the Seed. For now, though, it seems to be like another Arcana situation. I have it, but I'm still missing the impetus to actually make it work.

I'll have to figure that out, and hopefully without causing a scene. If it ever leaks out that I have one, though, I'll need to pretend that it's always been there. If I ever manage to use it, that is.

What else . . .

The formula for my inventory looks like it changed, too. It's definitely not just Strength multiplied by Constitution anymore . . . Unless it is, and it's just adjusted for my compressed stats. He closed his eyes and did some math in his head, grinning slightly at the obscenely large number. *Looks like it is.*

Still over a million kilograms—that's a lot. Or is it? If I look at it in terms of water, I can carry around basically a swimming pool's worth. It's more than I'd realistically need, but bound to be useful if I ever need to store a whole swimming pool's worth of stuff. Which . . . could happen.

I'll need to explore the limits of my inventory a little better, too. Not being able to stuff Heracles's ring in there was a surprise.

Sighing, he added his nine free points to his Arcana stat one at a time and closed his status, paying careful attention to how each point caused his mana to surge within him and become a little more vigorous.

Arcana should definitely be the stat I prioritize, but letting Constitution drag too far behind is a no-go, both because it's nonoptimal and because being squishy seems like a bad idea. I still have the boiling and freezing baths to increase it naturally, so it's not like I'm completely hung out to dry on that front, though. As for Agility and Strength, I should be able to improve them the normal way for now. Especially with my saturation point so high.

If I can max out my Arcana and get another manasink, though . . . I'll basically have free stat points as long as I'm willing to suffer a headache.

Grinning, he closed his eyes and focused on his mana. Circulating it around his body, he let some seep through his skin.

Just like when he was under the metal slab, he could feel it brushing against space itself.

How do I move now? He frowned. *I'm anchored here, in this spot, and if someone moved the bed out from under me, I'd float. Except floating isn't flying.*

Letting go of his mana, he climbed off his bed and looked around the room. Finding an empty spot, he jumped into the air. The moment his feet left the ground, he once again called his mana forward, and like he expected, he hung in the air.

How did Lukeus make it seem so easy? He frowned as he adjusted his mana into the soles of his feet and took a step forward. *As it is, I can imitate my boots, but that's not how everyone else does it. I've never seen anyone have to move their body at all.*

A light bulb went on in his head. Channeling mana into his hands, he held himself in the air with his palms alone. Then, slowly, he rotated the film of mana on his hands so that the mana at the back of his palm would glide forward while the mana on the tips of his fingers would seep back into him.

"Fuck yeah!" he yelled as he crawled an inch backward in the air.

Someone banged on the wall, and, startled, he fell out of the air.

"KEEP IT QUIET, ASSHOLE. I'M TRYING TO SLEEP."

"Sorry!" he yelled back. A wide grin plastered on his face as he covered his whole body in mana and darted through the room.

I should go outside. Flying in a room isn't that fun.

CHAPTER 3

Return to Cyzicus

Luke opened the door leading out to the main deck of the *Argo*. A streak of bright-red hair flashed in front of his eyes, and immediately a woman—the first he had seen the entire time he had been on the ship—collided into him with enough force to send him stumbling back into the hallway.

"Are you okay—"

"Fuck off." She planted a hand on his chest and pushed him into the wall before marching away, stomping her feet into the ground hard enough to make the wood groan.

Luke blinked in surprise, glancing between the spot on his chest where she had pushed him and her retreating figure before pulling himself forward.

"That was pretty rude, you know!" he called after her as she turned around the corner. She ignored him. He scoffed and absently rubbed his chest, but then pulled his hand away in mild surprise a second later. His mind lingered on the strange sensation of being hit hard enough to stumble and crash into a wall but still not take any damage—or even feel a sting, for that matter.

Weird, but not unexpected. I'm definitely getting to the point that my body is durable enough to withstand some decent force. He grinned.

Grip, though, might be an issue when I'm not actively using mana for traction, he thought as he dusted himself off. *Which makes sense—my weight didn't change when I broke through, so it's easy for people to throw me around when I'm not braced. Not the worst thing, but becoming a rag doll isn't ideal.*

Maybe I just need to keep channeling my mana constantly and have it wrapped around my body all the time—but the amount of practice I'll need to control my mana like that instinctually . . . He shook his head slightly. *It should be possible, but I'll have to match my mana drain so I'm not always running on empty, and, on top of that, do it in a way that still lets me focus on other things.*

Which, now that I think about it, will be necessary when fighting in the air is a very real thing. I guess with some practice it won't be too different than using an artifact. Then again, every artifact I have I just push mana in. Holding myself tethered to space and maneuvering around is a bit more complicated than that.

I'll try it out, but it's one more thing I'll need to ask Clite, or any experienced warrior, for that matter. The way mana interacts with space opens up way too many possibilities for me to fumble around with by myself. Not when I can learn the basic tricks and tips from someone else.

Besides, if I don't, I risk missing something important and having my ass handed to me. Cyzicus mentioned that a lot of the participants in the tournament are going to be important people—as in the children of gods and other high-level cultivators. Who knows what kind of tricks and bloodlines they're going to pull out of their asses?

Lukeus was a mortal when he broke through in the desert with me, and he already knew how to fly and make stuff float. For most people, I bet even breaking into the Warrior tier is a struggle, but for Lukeus and probably even Rex, it might as well be inevitable. It wouldn't be strange if their instructors had them doing exercises that would only be useful in the Warrior tier from the moment they unlocked their mana.

That's fine, though. With the tide, I'll have the instruction of an experienced tutor and no shortage of monsters to harvest points from. I can probably even ask Heracles for help. I did help free him, so it won't be too out of place asking for a couple pointers.

Scratching his chin in thought, he walked through the door, only to stop dead in his tracks.

What the . . . He blinked in surprise. *Did she do this?*

Lying on the floor of the deck were dozens of men covered in blood and cuts—a few even had arrows poking out of their arms and legs. He gulped and rose into the air and over the comatose form of an exceedingly hairy man who was lying right by the door. If it weren't for the slight rise and fall of his chest, Luke would have thought he was dead.

What happened here? He frowned, his earlier thoughts leaving his head.

Searching the deck, he found Jason standing at the very front of the ship, leaning forward with his hands on the rail and gazing deep into the water below. Luke glided through the air toward him.

A hand shot out from beneath him and grabbed his leg. A chill ran down Luke's spine.

"Wha—" Luke frowned and instinctively tried to tug his leg free. It didn't move an inch.

"Relax, it's me." Heracles smiled and winked from under him.

"What are you doing?" Luke asked.

"Hiding," the son of Zeus said, letting go of him and rising into the air so that he was floating alongside Luke.

"From?"

"Atalanta." He shivered. "Her wrath isn't worth facing, so whenever she goes off, I just lie down and pretend I'm unconscious."

"That . . . I guess that's smart. Is that what happened here?"

"Aye."

"Why was she mad?"

"Eh." He shrugged, and then looking at Luke's skeptical face as his eyes roamed the fallen bodies, he elaborated. "It's not as serious as it seems. They'll all be fine with a potion or two."

"But why?" *I've got to be missing something here.*

"I highly doubt anyone remembers. Anyway, I've been meaning to find you. We're almost at the Capital, and when I was talking to Rex earlier, he mentioned that you and Nel have been getting on well. Did she say anything about me?"

"What?"

Heracles blushed. "Just casually, you know. I, uh . . . Forget it, I was just . . . It's fine." He scratched his chin. "Did she?"

"No, sorry. No one talked about you, at least to me. Unless you count Lukeus, but that was when we were coming to get you, so . . ." Luke trailed off.

"Oh. I guess that's fine." Heracles deflated slightly and scratched his head. "I have to go check something down in the . . ." He pointed to the door and floated away. "I'll find you later."

"So, what was all that about?" Luke asked, landing gently behind Jason.

Jason scratched his chin. "Heracles has taken a fancy to Nel. From what I understand, they met a few years ago, and he's been besotted since. Half the reason he even joined my quest was so that he could woo her. You wouldn't believe the stink he made on Lemnos to get us to leave. He actuall—"

"I was asking about the bodies on the ground," Luke cut him off.

"Oh, that. It's something of a tradition now. Whenever Atalanta gets mad, she goads one fool after another into a battle."

"And they just line up?" Luke asked incredulously.

"She pays well, and most of the crew considers it training. We all spar with each other anyway, but fighting someone on her level is an experience. There's not many among us that can defeat her," the captain admitted.

"Huh." *Seems like a waste of potions, but at the same time, if you have them, might as well use them. It's not like I haven't been taking them to heal after training, and getting pierced by arrows and knocked unconscious is likely less painful than being boiled, so . . .*

"I smell blood," Jason said suddenly, pulling Luke out of his musings.

Luke sniffed the air. "Yeah, me, too. I think it's mostly that guy." Luke pointed to someone lying in a pool of his own blood right under the holographic map hovering near the ship's wheel. "Is he going to be okay?"

"I'm not talking about them." He pointed forward. "From up ahead. The wind is carrying it downstream. The scent has been getting stronger for the past hour."

Luke took a deep breath and shook his head slightly when he didn't smell anything but water. *Does he have a really good sense of smell, or is he just fucking with me?*

"Could it be the giants? If there's a town they cleared nearby?"

"No . . ." Jason frowned. "It doesn't smell like the giants you felled while freeing Heracles, but it doesn't smell human, either."

"Some kind of monster, then? Harpies?"

"No." He shook his head. The golden ring dangling from his ear glowed, and a key appeared in his hand. He flicked it forward, and it shot through the air and embedded itself in the ship's wheel. "We're much too close to the capital for that to be the case. They shy away from the bigger towns. This is something else."

The *Argo* shook, and all fifty of its sails suddenly fell to the side and hung horizontally over the ship's rails.

"Whoa, is that supposed to—" Luke's eyes widened in awe as the sails lifted up and then beat down again. The ship groaned as it took to the sky. "Whoa."

Of course it can fly. He grinned slightly, peered over the edge, and watched the shadow of the flying boat shrink rapidly on the water. A moment later, Jason made a gesture with his hands, and the ship's wheel started spinning to the right.

"Impressive, isn't it?" he said, directing the ship over the land and forgoing the river entirely in favor of a straight path toward the capital.

"Very." Luke nodded. He moved to the side as Jason stepped past him with a large frown on his face.

How much blood does he smell? Luke thought worriedly, watching as Jason knelt down in front of a brown-haired man and withdrew a potion from his ring.

Pinching the man's face, Jason forced his lips open and spilled the contents of the vial down his throat. The second he woke up, Jason started barking orders.

"Find Lukeus and send him here. Sound the alarm and tell everyone to prepare for battle. Once that's done, find a medic and have them treat all these bozos. I want them battle ready in ten!"

"Yes, sir." The revived man saluted Jason and ran off to do his bidding.

Luke gulped heavily. "Did the smell change?"

"I smell a lot more blood," Jason said grimly, walking over to the map displaying all the ships in the fleet and staring at it. His storage ring glowed softly, and one talisman after another appeared in the air in front of him. "Attention, all Argonauts, this is Jason. We may be entering a live conflict. Hold a perimeter around the island while the *Argo* investigates. Stand ready to assist, but do not act. I repeat, do not act until I've confirmed the tier of the enemy." He waved his hand, and every talisman flew off in a direction behind him.

"Why do you want them to stay?" Luke frowned. "If we're really going into a fight, then shouldn't the more people we have, the better?"

"No. The *Argo* has enough protections built in that you'd need to be very strong—at least at the Saint tier, maybe even higher—to break through our wards, and I've got a trick or two that lets us run fast if things go south. Most of the ships that are following us don't. They'll barely hold up to a hero. And anyone who's anyone won't attack this ship carelessly. Lady Hera blessed my voyage, and Lord Poseidon gave it to me. Both their symbols are on the side . . . The rest of the fleet doesn't carry similar protections."

Luke nodded in understanding and looked over the horizon, squinting as the faint outline of the capital of Sylcra, wrapped in a shimmering gold barrier, came into focus.

"Shit," Luke cursed as a shockwave traveled through the air and made the *Argo* shudder underneath his feet. Considering that the boat was enchanted, and that the entire time he had been on it he hadn't felt a single tremor, it worried him.

Who would attack the capital? Is it the Rebel? It can't be . . . Sophia should still be chasing her.

Jason rose into the air and sighed. "It looks like we're fine," he said, a hint of awe in his voice. "It appears Lord Cyzicus has already slain the monster."

"No," Luke said, his heart dropping in his chest. His eyes were just barely able to make out the form of a giant, many-story-tall decapitated head sitting outside the barrier. A head belonging to a woman, with blond hair and a single blue eye. "That's not a monster. That's Sophia, Cyzicus's fiancée."

CHAPTER 4

A Hero's Wrath

T his is bad," Luke said, his hand resting on the handle of his sword and his knuckles white with the strength of his grip. "Really *fucking* bad."

"If it's as you say, then . . . I agree." Jason nodded. "Someone intends to start a war."

Luke shook his head. "Cyzicus has been at war. This is going beyond that. It was already personal, but—" He sighed loudly. He hadn't known Cyzicus or Sophia that long, but the emperor had been good to him, and good to his people. *I can't even imagine what he's going through right now. Fuck,* Luke thought, feeling angry on the Emperor's behalf. Angry that someone would be cruel enough to come from who knew where and kill a man's family to steal from him. It was both despicable and an example of everything that was wrong with Theos.

"At war with who?" Jason asked.

"Another Hero-tier cultivator. They call her the Rebel, but her name is Tyrisa—Tyrisa of Peles. A few weeks ago, she killed one of his grandsons. Sophia and Cyzicus chased her for over a month, but Cyzicus had to come and power the teleportation altars when the tide began. Sophia kept up the chase, but . . ." He trailed off, wincing as he turned his head away from the sight.

"I see," Jason said darkly. "To stoop so low as to kill his family and then his lover . . ."

Another shock wave traveled through the air, rocking the *Argo* back violently as the ship pressed onward toward the city.

"Shit. Shit. Shit," Jason yelled, his face suddenly going pale. A bronze key left his ring and attached itself to the wheel. Suddenly the ship stopped moving, and a shimmering golden barrier engulfed it.

"What happened? Why did you stop?" Luke frowned.

On cue, a violent explosion detonated above the city, and a corona of electric fire bloomed out from a point high in the clouds. It splashed harmlessly across the city's shields but devastated all the trees and roads around it, throwing vast amounts of dust and other debris into the air. A moment later, the same wave, significantly diminished, collided with the *Argo*.

For a moment, his vision turned white and he flinched away from the light, but the ship's wards were more than capable of withstanding the energy. The only sign of the ring of fire even hitting them was the boat rocking back as if it had hit a wave of water.

Luke spilled small amounts of mana from his body and anchored himself in space to stay steady.

"That was . . ." Luke whispered in awe, eyeing Jason out of the corner of his eyes. Curiosity bubbled within him as he wondered how Jason had predicted the blast.

Does he know the same truth as me? No, I need to actually see the thing to react, and unless he can . . . Luke dismissed the thought. Now wasn't the time.

He squinted as he looked past the barrier surrounding the ship and strained his eyes to get a glimpse of the battle, or perhaps the result of it. He had a hard time imagining anyone surviving such a violent attack. If it turned out that Cyzicus that had lost, or worse . . . Luke frowned. That would be bad. Not just for him, but for everyone who relied upon the Emperor.

A few seconds later, a small ripple tore through the sparse clouds still hanging in the sky, and some tension left his body. They were still fighting.

Luke didn't know whether the emperor or the Rebel had unleashed that attack, but so long as the battle continued, Cyzicus lived. For now, Luke would take solace in that.

A few seconds later, the frequency of the shock waves picked up and almost became rhythmic, as if someone was striking a hammer onto an anvil.

"We need to move back," Jason said hurriedly, darting toward the wooden wheel in the center of the deck. He turned one of the keys embedded in it, and instantly, the sails hanging over the side of the ship changed direction, and the ship banked to the left.

"We should help," Luke said impatiently. "You said we can take Saint-tier attacks, right? Let's go and bash right into her or something."

"I—uhhh." A pained look came over Jason's face, and he shook his head. "No. We can't. Getting in between two Hero tiers is a terrible idea. We can stand up to something like that, but we won't be able to *do* anything other than run. Besides, all the weapons we have are still at the Warrior tier, and—"

A commotion behind him alerted him to Heracles and a dozen other Argonauts marching onto the deck. "Jason," Heracles said, his club slung over his shoulder and a savage grin on his face, his earlier embarrassment seemingly gone. "What's attacking!" he yelled, rising into the air.

"No one is—"

Luke zoned out, only listening with half an ear and letting Jason explain the situation. His eyes focused on the sky, hoping to see anything other than a faint ripple splitting the clouds, and occasionally darting toward the door whenever someone new wandered onto the deck.

His thoughts churned in his head as he wondered if there was anything he could do to help. Try as he might, though, he couldn't think of a single thing.

But, I don't have to be the one to do it, either.

"Heracles, do you have anything that can kill a hero?" Luke asked the blond son of Zeus, grinning slightly as his question was met with a savage smile.

"I have a few things that might do the trick." His ring glowed softly, and a bow appeared in one hand and a single black arrow in the other. An uncountable number of sickly red runes ran up the length of its shaft, glowing dimly in light.

Luke stepped away as the ominous aura originating from the arrow spread across the deck, and an unknown instinct warned him to get away and run as far as he could.

What tier is that? he thought, feeling his heart beating nervously in his chest.

"No! Don't get yourself killed." Jason shook his head. "We just got you back, and you know as well as I do that the difference in tiers isn't something you can solve with some talismans. This isn't a monster in a cave. You won't be able to hit her, and we can't have Lord Cyzicus caught in the crossfire, either."

"I can—"

"No, you can't." Jason shut him down. "Put that away."

"But—"

"Now, Heracles."

The son of Zeus glared at Jason, but his ring glowed once again, and both the arrow and the bow vanished.

Unconsciously, Luke let out a sigh of relief. *What kind of crazy-ass shit did Zeus give to him?*

"We wait," Jason said with finality, craning his neck as he looked to the sky with a frown.

The battle went on far longer than Luke thought it would. Another massive explosion like the one that spooked Jason never happened again, but even hours later, tremors could be felt.

At the four-hour mark, most of the ship's crew returned inside. Not that Luke could blame them.

No one could actually see the battle, and with Lukeus and Rex having climbed on to the deck with Blinky in tow, not many were eager to spend time in the creature's headache-inducing company.

At some point someone had suggested that Rex just leave the dreadglare in the stables and return without it, but no one was comfortable leaving it unsupervised, and neither did they want to tell him to go away when it was his own grandfather fighting to the death.

So they just stood there. Solemn and quiet, with their eyes trained to the sky.

Until, eventually—it happened.

A blood-soaked figure half tumbled and half flew through the air, directly toward the *Argo.* Luke's breath hitched as he tried to see if it was a friend or foe.

A golden crown glinted atop the figure's head, and an instant later, multiple people leaped into action.

Lukeus and Heracles both lifted off the deck of the ship and barreled toward him. Others let loose dozens of arrows. Some skillfully deposited protective talismans right behind Cyzicus and covered what looked to be his retreat, while others shot far into the sky and detonated with thunderous force in the direction he came from—hopefully forestalling the Rebel. If she had chased him.

Before any of them, though, it was the *Argo* itself that reached him, and Luke suppressed a wince as both Lukeus and Heracles slammed into its deck.

Cyzicus himself passed through the wards without resistance and came to a sudden stop as soon as he was within the boundary of the golden shield.

"YOU HIDE BEHIND THESE CHILDREN!" a bald, legless woman screamed as she whaled on the barrier with both of her blood-covered fists.

So that's her?

"Something like that . . ." the emperor muttered under his breath. "Saint tier, right?" he asked, turning to Jason.

"Y—"

The world flashed white, and then it *roared.*

Blood poured out of every orifice of Luke's face, and the control he had over his mana slipped entirely as he collided heavily with the ship's walls.

Ears ringing, and with blood pooling in his mouth, he desperately tried to hold on to consciousness. Instinctively, he reached into his inventory and poured a healing potion straight into his mouth, swallowing it with the blood already in there.

Cool, healing energy spread throughout his body.

"Sorry about that," Cyzicus said, his breath heavy. "It seems that this barrier doesn't defend against sound."

"It does," Jason said, climbing to his feet. "I just have it disabled. I didn't know that even the noise would be so devastating."

"Is she dead?" Luke asked, staggered forward while wiping blood from his mouth.

"She—" Cyzicus suddenly coughed blood and fell to his knees. Lukeus rushed to his side and poured a healing potion down his throat.

"Gramps. Stay with me! Come on," he yelled, but it was too late. Cyzicus was unconscious.

"She lives. I saw her flee," Heracles said, his hands clenching the brass rails of the *Argo.* "Jason, take Cyzicus back to the capital and see to it that he gets the care that he needs. From what I understand, he's been away from the teleportation altars too long as well. Use the *Argo* to power the system while he recovers."

"What are you thinking?" Jason asked tiredly.

"There's a hero out there who hurt someone important to me. She's weakened, and I have the means to kill her."

"Heracles . . . That's—"

"I won't be talked out of this, Jason. You saw the state she was in, even before she took a Saint-tier talisman to the face. If we give her the chance to recover, then . . ."

"Then she'll run and kill more of my family the next time she comes," Lukeus interrupted him. "I've had enough. Let's end it while she's weak." Lukeus drew his sword from its sheath and marched through the door to the ship, no doubt going to retrieve Nutbutter.

These fuckers. Are they serious? Luke grinned as his mind ground to a halt at the sheer audacity they were displaying. He already knew Heracles was insane, but for Lukeus to go along with it as well—it was truly outside his expectation.

"Are you stupid?" Jason yelled. "Lord Zeus won't bail you out every time, Heracles. Do you know how lucky you got with Arke? Do you know how many people died when we broke her blockade?"

"Three hundred and eleven," he said without skipping a beat.

"Then how can you even consider this?"

"Some things are worth dying for, Jason. Being meek and showing your belly like a good little dog is no way to live. Just because they're strong doesn't mean they deserve to be obeyed. Even if it means death. I'd rather die on my feet, with my club in my hand, then live in fear of those stronger than I."

"That's the stupidest thing I've ever heard," Jason ran his hands through his hair and screamed.

"That's why you'll never be a god," Heracles muttered. "Chiron taught us better than this."

"Chiron literally taught us the opposite of that!"

"Enough. I'm going," he said, and a moment later Lukeus landed on the deck of the *Argo*, his Pegasus harnessed to a cheap-looking chariot.

Luke blinked as a quest popped up in his vision.

Quest Alert: Kill a Hero

"I'll come with."

CHAPTER 5

The Chase Begins

<table>
<tr><td colspan="1">Status | Skills | Quests | Inventory</td></tr>
<tr><td>Kill a Hero:

Land the killing blow on Tyrisa of Peles, and as the light leaves her eyes, grant Bellerophon's Blade a name worthy of a weapon that will one day belong to a god.

Subquest: Claim her storage ring as a spoil of war.

*Killing an entity at the Hero tier is equivalent to killing a hundred warriors.</td></tr>
</table>

Luke quickly read through the description of the quest before dismissing it, wondering absently both why the Seed wanted him to name his sword and what was in the Rebel's ring that would help him become a god. A part of him already dreaded how that conversation would go over with the others, but he didn't linger on it. Future Luke could deal with being looked on as greedy, but as he scanned his eyes over his would-be companions, he realized that both of them were already rich. Lukeus probably wouldn't even care, and he sincerely doubted that the Rebel hero had anything worthy of a son of Zeus anyhow.

He grinned slightly at the look of defeat on Jason's face. He liked the guy, he really did, and what he was saying made a lot of sense. Caution should be prioritized. If it weren't for the quest, Luke would probably even agree with him. He knew how much stronger a hero was compared to a warrior. The effortless way Cyzicus had killed that giant was still burned into his memory.

But some small part of him couldn't help but wonder if the Seed had once again reacted to his desires.

He knew he shouldn't go—logically, it was just dangerous. Trying to kill a hero when he'd just broken through to the Warrior tier was ludicrous. Even more so, considering that the Rebel wasn't likely far from the Saint tier if she could keep up with Cyzicus, who was at the peak of the Hero tier.

Even so, he had *wanted* to go, even before the quest had been issued by the Seed. Just based on sheer principle alone, because fuck Tyrisa.

The lengths she was willing to go to for a throne were evil. An evil he would gladly expunge. One that would make him sleep better at night if it wasn't there. Since he'd learned about her, she had been a cloud hanging over his head, and he wanted it gone.

Nel might have killed Jax, but it was a decision made in fear of Tyrisa and what she would do to her family and her home.

He had only met Sophia for a handful of minutes, but she was *sweet*. The look of glee on her face when she read Cyzicus's letter had been both beautiful and happy. A breath of fresh air compared to the bleakness of the rest of the world and their journey toward her, and to see her decapitated head outside Cyzicus's home—it wasn't what she or Cyzicus deserved.

Not even counting the fact that he was a good and well-liked ruler, the emperor had done more for Luke than anyone else on all of Theos. Granted, he had his reasons, but there was more than one way he could have gotten Luke to obey him, and he had used none of them, choosing instead to just *ask* and trust. The Saint-tier marble in his inventory, the oath orb, proved that. The emperor hadn't known nor cared about what Luke had to hide; he had simply sworn himself to secrecy as a gesture of trust.

All that together was more than enough to make him want to see the Rebel dead.

Would he have actually volunteered to go without the quest, though, he didn't know, and now it didn't matter. He was going, and it was with confidence backed by the Seed. If the Primordial artifact thought he could do it, then he did, too, mostly.

An insidious thought tickled the back of his head. *Unless my theory about the Seed planning for my failure is true, I don't really have anything to worry about. I haven't failed a quest yet, and I don't plan to. That said, I'll have a better idea about the consequences when I actually do. If I had to guess, though, the Seed is probably relying on me using a charge if things go south. Which isn't ideal. Still, a quest is a quest.*

"You're going?" Rex asked incredulously, staring at Luke with a dumbfounded expression on his face.

I've done way too much reckless shit in front of him at this point. I don't even know why he's surprised.

"Yeah, why not." Luke shrugged with a grin, and, extending his mana around his body, he rose into the air and shot toward the chariot.

"HA-HA-HA! I knew you had a heart of steel," Heracles cheered and slapped Luke on the back as he climbed into the chariot.

"Since when are you a warrior?" Rex asked, his mouth dropping open in shock.

Luke blinked through a headache just from looking at him and grinned. "Sometimes in life, you only have two choices: to become stronger or die. I got stronger."

At that moment, Lukeus tugged the reins, and Nutbutter flew off the deck and in a wide circle around the giant ship.

"Where is she?" Lukeus asked, turning to Heracles.

The son of Zeus pointed toward the river, to a destination north of the capital. Luke strained his eyes, and his jaw clenched in determination. At the very edge of his vision, he saw her—a charred, legless figure flying unsteadily through the sky.

"It looks like she's retreating to Clan Skyscar territory," Luke said.

"Who are they?" Heracles asked.

"Traitors."

"Of course." Heracles grunted. "We'll have to try and keep her separated from any strongholds she has set up, then. It's unlikely that she has many resources, especially as a rogue cultivator. Whatever she does have, she will have depleted by now, and it will likely take her decades to replenish her stock, but if we let her retreat behind wards . . . You know what, never mind; it doesn't matter. If she hides, I have something that will break anything she may possess. She'll learn what it means to make an enemy of me."

Being rich has its perks, I guess. Luke grinned.

Nutbutter neighed, and the distance between them began to shrink rapidly. Injured as Tyrisa was, it seemed that she couldn't fly faster than their steed.

"Don't get too close to her yet," Heracles warned. His ring glowed as he retrieved a bow from his inventory. For a moment, Luke thought Heracles was going to fire that crazy red-and-black arrow, only to relax when it turned out not to be the case. It was a different bow, the same one he had used to kill a Warrior-tier giant. Taking aim, he pulled back the string, and an arrow made of blue energy appeared.

It flew through the air faster than Luke could even follow, but Tyrisa had no problem dodging it. The arrow sailed past her harmlessly and dissipated into the air.

"Let's see how long you can keep that up," Heracles muttered under his breath before firing one arrow after another at her.

"LEAVE ME, OR YOU SHALL REGRET THIS." She turned her head back and screeched, revealing the ugliest sight Luke had ever seen. The hero really hadn't escaped unscathed—the entire front of her face looked like it belonged in a horror movie. The flesh on her head was simply gone, leaving just two unblinking, bloodshot orbs lingering on charred bone. Her nose had vanished, and even her teeth could be seen through her holes in her cheeks.

How is she even alive? Luke thought incredulously. *She's basically just a charred torso.*

"FUCK YOU," Lukeus yelled back.

Resisting the urge to empty his stomach, Luke drew the sword Cyzicus had given him from its sheath and channeled mana into it. He frowned slightly when his heavier mana filled it more completely than it ever had before, touching mechanisms inside it that he didn't even know existed.

Right. It's a Warrior-tier artifact. Obviously it works best for a warrior, even if it was made to be used by a mortal.

Feeling around with his mana, Luke quickly learned the new limits of his weapon. He could still fire the same Mortal-tier attack he had been before, but the blade now defaulted to attacks with Warrior-tier potency, and he had some control over the shape of the arcs. More than that, there wasn't really a set amount of mana that he needed to fill the blade with anymore, either.

Back when he first got the sword, it drained nearly ninety percent of his mana pool. Granted, he'd had fewer than six thousand mana then. When he was at the peak of the Mortal tier, he'd possessed hundreds of times that amount, making the weapon much more useful.

Now, he suspected that he could unleash attacks at that level all day. His denser mana was both more efficient and more abundant, doing more of the work with less than a quarter of the effort.

A Mortal-tier attack won't do shit to her, though. He frowned and filled the blade with five points of mana. *Five points worth of my mana now was fifty thousand points of mana then. Let's see if that does anything,* he thought as he held out the glowing edge of the blade in front of him.

Then, remembering Heracles's missed attack, he began to enter the First Stance, the Mortal version of his Warrior-tier skill.

"Don't," the son of Zeus suddenly said, his hand darting out and pushing Luke's sword down.

"What?" Luke looked at him, confused.

"Don't use any techniques. Not unless you think you can kill her with one. Otherwise you'll just drain your mana uselessly. This isn't going to be like any fight you've been in before. So here's the plan." He swallowed nervously and ripped a talisman. A translucent white bubble spread out around them, and silence engulfed the chariot.

Right, super hearing is a thing, too.

"We're going to wear her down with countless cuts and deny her the opportunity to rest. But nothing we do will be more than a nuisance, and that's what we want. It's her injuries that are our biggest strength, and the longer she flees without addressing them, the better for us. Everyone at the Hero tier is durable, but not that durable. I think she's using either some artifact or a technique to keep her alive. The longer she keeps it up, the less mana she has," Heracles explained.

"Is that why she isn't attacking us?" Luke asked suddenly. "She can't spare the mana?"

"In part. I imagine whatever is keeping her alive is costly in more ways than one. Perhaps the focus required to maintain it is high. Her speed alone is proof of that. So remember, the longer we drag this out, the better. She is also in immense amounts of pain right now as well, and she'll make more mistakes the longer she suffers."

"Right." Luke nodded, paying careful attention to his words and idly wondering how the son of Zeus had even known he was planning to use a technique. "We let her exhaust herself before we move in for the kill."

"Yes. My arsenal is big, but Jason wasn't wrong. Hitting her with anything will require both immense luck and skill. Especially if we want to do it in a way that doesn't end with her throwing our attack back at us. We also won't have many chances. If she realizes that we have the means to end her, I suspect that she will either risk mana exhaustion and teleport away or try to kill us. We want her to try to kill us," he said.

The ring on his finger glowed, and a handful of talismans, both protective and explosive, appeared in front of Luke and Lukeus.

"Those are all at the Hero tier, but there's two Saint-tier protective talismans with them. I don't think she held anything back, considering her state, but in case she does, do not stray far from me."

"Thanks." Lukeus nodded gratefully before roughly stuffing them into his pocket, not taking his eyes off the Rebel for even a second.

Luke sorted his own out a bit more carefully before also stuffing them in his pocket.

Fuck, this plan is full of holes, but it's not garbage. Keep pestering her until she decides to deal with us. No biggie.

The bubble surrounding them vanished, and Luke took careful aim with his sword before slashing forward. He watched carefully as she tilted to the side, allowing it to glide harmlessly past her.

Five mana was too much, he realized. *If the goal is to just be annoying, then it doesn't matter how shallow the cut is if I do hit her.* He opened his status and watched his mana tick up. *Heracles is right, too—the real fight hasn't even started yet. I need to conserve as much as possible.*

In that case, if I attack with half a point worth of mana every thirty seconds, I'll match my regen.

Frowning in determination, he did just that, letting Heracles take the lead with his near endless rain of arrows while Luke loosed an attack once or twice a minute.

Tyrisa continued to dodge every single one. But with every attack that was fired, Luke imagined the expression on her face getting just a little more annoyed.

Hours later, as the nine suns of Theos began sinking over the horizon, one of Heracles's arrows finally struck her.

An aura of palpable rage emanated from her wretched figure.

Luke gulped as Nutbutter neighed.

It was time.

CHAPTER 6

On Death's Door

She turned and faced them, and the three of them looked back at her. It was dim outside and they were nearly a mile away, but Luke had no problem seeing her hate-filled glare.

His mouth felt dry, and he could feel his heart thumping in his chest, but he didn't look away. Instead he took a deep, calming breath, adjusted the grip on his sword, and returned her gaze with a blank stare. Then, just to put her off-kilter, he cocked his head to the side, smiled, and waved cheerfully with his free hand. As if she were a friend he hadn't seen in a long time.

Maybe it was arrogance, or perhaps apathy, but he found himself unafraid of her.

The Rebel's wretched and battered form combined with her despicable actions—something in him was just unwilling to let her inspire fear in him. He suspected, though, that he was just tired of living like that. He hadn't realized until Arke was gone just how exhausting being scared all the time truly was, how good it felt not to feel that, and even the idea of returning to that state of mind was repulsing.

So he wouldn't.

Heracles was right, he decided. It was better to die than to live at the mercy and in fear of those stronger than him. Not that he would actually challenge Arke to a fight anytime soon, but maybe there was a line he could toe between being stupid and getting himself killed and being meek. It didn't have to be one way or the other.

Kind of like Nefkha, or even Cyzicus. Do enough not to get killed out of hand, but no need to bend over backward and obey their every whim. Maybe even act against them when it suits me.

His smile turned a hint more genuine, and he chuckled. Out of the corner of his eyes, he saw both Heracles and Lukeus stiffen at his gesture.

Yeah, they probably think I'm insane. Whatever—any minute now, my sword is going to be buried in her chest, and I'll probably be hiding my agony as it drinks her Hero-tier mana. The thought unnerved him as much as it excited him.

As he looked at Tyrisa, he couldn't help but wonder how he was actually going to do that. He wondered how his sword would evolve and if it would gain any new abilities or not. Speculated on how many stat points he would gain and the leg up they would give him in the tournament.

He sighed deeply. *Yeah . . . that's all she is now—someone that I will step on to go higher. Couldn't have happened to a better person, but it still feels a little slimy. Sure, I suppose the real reason I'm doing this is because it's the right thing to do, and the world will be better without her. That's not even a question, but it does feel a little on the nose. Hunting monsters for gains is one thing, and hunting people, no matter how monstrous, is something else.*

"This is your last warning," Tyrisa yelled at them. "Leave me be, and I shall spare you. We have no quarrel."

No quarrel . . . Is she for real?

"I think I misheard you. What did you say?" Luke yelled, putting his hand behind his ear and leaning forward comically.

"We have no quar—"

He slashed lazily with the blade Cyzicus had given him, filling it with a single point of his mana. The world seemed to hold its breath as it cut through the air between them. She easily dodged to the side, and an ominous pressure filled the distance between them. Luke held back a grin.

She really doesn't want to fight, huh.

"What is the meaning of this? Does this"—she pointed at Luke—"buffoon speak for the two of you as well? If you give him to me and turn back, I shall consider sparing both your lives."

Wow. Straight for the divide-and-conquer strategy. Does she really think this is going to work, or is she just that desperate?

"I'm not a buffoon," Luke yelled back. "I thought I heard a mosquito buzzing right where your face is." He shrugged. "Promise."

Heracles chortled at his bad attempt at humor, and a wide grin stretched across his face. Almost lazily, he drew back the string on his bow and fired an energy arrow straight at her.

The charred remains of her lips stretched wide in displeasure as she dodged once again.

"I think I saw a mosquito, too," he called out as he fired another arrow, and then, chuckling, rapidly fired a dozen more. "Oh, wow, there's so many of them."

All right, that was kind of cheesy. Luke cringed internally. *It also kinda feels like kicking a dog . . . Yeah, I probably shouldn't be making fun of people when I plan to kill them. Not that she doesn't deserve it—she definitely does—but let's not turn into that guy, Luke. I should execute people with grace and seriousness. For real.*

His jaw set in determination as the reality of the situation suddenly dawned on him.

She's an asshole, but I'm still stealing her life. This isn't something I should let myself get used to, or something I can take lightly, and especially not joke about to the person I'm going to kill. Ever. That's entering megalomaniac territory, he thought solemnly as he watched the path of the arrows toward her.

She managed to dodge all but a single one, which grazed her shoulder, not that she seemed affected.

Then, with a snarl, she came barreling toward them faster than she had moved the entire time they'd chased after her.

She was too slow—or rather, Heracles was faster.

A golden barrier manifested around their chariot, barely big enough to hold all three of them and Nutbutter inside, a second before she reached them.

A thin silver blade appeared in her hand, and she swung downward. Nutbutter squealed and neighed as they were sent plummeting down to the forested ground underneath them from the force of the blow hitting the bubble. Luke held on to the chariot with a single hand and then slashed at her with his sword.

An arc of blue light flew out and through the barrier and collided with her before fizzling out.

A shallow line of blood appeared, traveling from her hip all the way to her shoulder.

I really can hurt her, then. Not much, but . . . I'll take it.

Out of the corner of his eyes, he saw Lukeus sneakily prepping an explosive talisman. Tearing off the perforated edge, he activated the talisman and then, counting down the seconds, flung it toward her.

The moment the talisman left the shield, her sword jabbed forward and sliced it in two.

"You didn't think it would be that easy, did you?" She grinned savagely, and just as Nutbutter managed to stabilize his flight, she slashed down with her sword again. The golden barrier undulated, and for a moment, Luke thought she might cut into it.

It held.

A pit formed in his stomach as they hurtled violently toward the ground, his attempt at catching himself with his mana failing entirely under her might. A moment later, he realized it was because Heracles had grabbed his ankle and forcibly broken his grasp on the fabric of space.

A drop of sweat fell down the side of his face. He had almost thrown himself out of the chariot with his actions. The shield was tethered to a slip of paper that either Lukeus or Heracles was holding; had he resisted falling with the chariot successfully, he would have left its protection.

That could have been really bad, he thought, careful not to panic, and with the lesson learned, he anchored his own mana to their vehicle.

Just when they were about to hit the earth, she appeared underneath them and slashed upward with her sword, sending them flying. Heracles activated another barrier just as their current one was about to fizzle away.

"I wonder," she said calmly as, appearing above them, she heaved her sword down on the bubble, sending them plummeting once again. "How many talismans do you have? Because you know, right?" Her eyes traced over them. "You know that once you run out, you're dead. One itty, tiny mistake, and I sever your heads from your necks, and Cyzicus can admire them with all the others I've left him."

Heracles activated another talisman as they hit the ground and dug a deep trench with their impact.

"I tried to be merciful, but you really thought you could do something that both Cyzicus and his pet cyclops failed at? HA." She wheezed as she battered their barrier into the ground. "I am three thousand years old. I have survived horrors beyond your imagination. I have killed more people than you have seen. I will not be bested by Three. Ignorant. Arrogant. Nobody. Warriors," she said, driving them farther and farther into the dirt with each strike.

All right, this may actually be bad. Think, think, think . . .

Luke ripped a tab off an explosive talisman and slid it outside the barrier and underneath them, simultaneously activating another protective barrier.

It detonated and sent them flying into the sky. The Rebel bounced off the surface of the bubble.

Heracles, capitalizing on the opportunity, shot her with what looked like a dozen arrows in the span of a second, most sinking into her torso and leaving marble-size rends in her blackened flesh. A single one pierced her eye, and blood splattered across her face as it blew up.

Lukeus held on to Nutbutter's reins, and the Pegasus's wings caught the air, rapidly trying to put some distance between them.

Seeing that she was distracted, Luke ripped the tab off three explosive talismans and threw them in Tyrisa's general vicinity.

She managed to cut through two before the third blew up beside her.

White blurred their vision as they were blown through the air once again, and they blinked the spots out of their eyes with bated breath, desperately raking their eyes across the sky in search of her.

Is she dead?

Heracles shuffled around and shot one arrow after another behind them. She cut through them with her sword and shoulder checked them back toward the ground.

Lukeus activated another protective barrier.

Luke frowned as he tried to assess the damage the single explosive talisman had done to her. It was harder than he expected. She already looked like she should be dead. Had looked like that before the battle even began, and as he was learning, there was only so wretched a single person could look.

With the exception of the eye and the few holes Heracles's arrows had poked, she looked the same.

How is that possible, though? If my Warrior-tier sword can leave cuts and Heracles's half-assed arrows can do the same, then an explosion that big should have torn her to bits.

Does she just have something that nullifies explosive talismans?

That would explain how she's still alive, but . . . if explosions don't wear her down, then this just got a lot harder. I don't know how much mana Heracles has, but he's been spamming the bow constantly.

He looked at the son of Zeus and opened his mouth before closing it.

Luke wanted to ask if he had a Saint-tier talisman he could try but decided not to. If she heard them talk and teleported away, that would end the battle right then and there and defeat the purpose entirely. It wasn't the worst possible outcome, but he really didn't want to learn what happened when he failed a quest.

Their battle continued for over an hour in the same vein. They would sneak in an attack every once in a while as she used her sword like a bat and tossed them through the air like they were toys.

Until, suddenly, a spear crackling with lightning pierced her stomach.

An eagle cried, and a golden blur shot through the air faster than Luke could even see. It flew right at her, and blood spurted from the hero as it passed her.

Something had torn her arm off.

Luke activated a protective talisman as he raked his eyes across the sky. He didn't have to search long to see who had come. There was only one person who had a steed that fast, and she was over a mile away and standing heroically atop it as her griffin casually tossed the Rebel's arm into the air and swallowed it whole.

"THAT'S FOR SOPHIA, YOU BITCH."

"AND FOR JAX!" a bald girl peeked her head out behind her and yelled.

"Agnella! It's so nice to see you again." Heracles waved at her with the goofiest grin Luke had ever seen.

"We're fighting for our lives, man. Can you take this seriously?" Lukeus snapped at him.

"I'm just saying hi," the son of Zeus grumbled, pulling back the string of his bow and starting to fire arrows again.

"I think Lukeus is right—that was a bit too flirty for a midcombat hi," Luke added, grinning slightly when the emperor's grandson leveled a glare at him.

CHAPTER 7

In Desperate Times

The Rebel glared at them. Her single remaining eye darted between the chariot ensconced within a golden bubble and the duo riding the griffin while she clutched the stump of her arm with her other hand. For a second, her storage ring flashed, and a bandage wrapped itself around her wound. Heracles, in response, savagely upped the frequency of his attacks.

Unease spread through the battlefield as they desperately tried to assess how the fight would now play out. With Nel's arrival having broken the stalemate, none of them quite knew what to make of it.

This could either be really good or really bad, Luke thought as he sent out another attack.

On one hand, Aura's speed was bound to be a massive advantage, one she had already proven by taking the Rebel's arm. That was the most substantial damage they had done to her since the start of the fight, discounting Heracles taking her eye hours ago.

On the other hand, while Nel no doubt had some means to protect herself, Luke wondered if that would be enough to stave off someone an entire tier higher. The only reason they themselves had hung on for as long as they had was because of Heracles's deep pockets. Without his nigh-endless talismans, Nel would simply lack the ability to withstand sustained serious attacks from Tyrisa, and try as he might, Luke couldn't see an easy way for them to give some to her.

Everything he could think of risked interference from their opponent, but leaving her potentially vulnerable was also a no-go. He had no doubt that neither Lukeus nor Heracles would stand by and let the Rebel so much as lay a hand on her—even if it meant that they would die.

Not that Nel seemed worried about her safety.

"Hey, Heracles," she yelled, waving excitedly to the son of Zeus. "It's nice to see you again."

Luke resisted the urge to palm his forehead as the man in question blushed, but he settled for shaking his head. Funneling a half point of mana to his sword, he sent another arc of energy racing toward their enemy.

His own sword light, as he had come to call it, traveled substantially slower than Heracles's arrows, allowing her to dodge them with little effort.

On occasion, though, he had been able to sneak an attack by her, albeit a lot less frequently than the elder warrior, and almost always when she risked a more major injury from one of Heracles's attacks.

Her griffin circling a mile above them, Nel adopted a stern expression, her gaze locking on to the other two riders on the chariot. "Lukeus, Luke—are you two insane? You two were literally mortals days ago, and now you're trying to kill a hero, one that almost killed Grandfather?" she admonished them. "Do you have any idea how much stronger she is than you?" She pointed to Tyrisa. "Luke I can understand; he's never sparred with Grandpa, but you? You should know better than this, Lukeus." Somehow, she managed to project her voice clearly through the air.

I need to learn how to do that.

"Nel—" her brother started to explain, only to give up when he saw her glare.

"Don't Nel me! Do you know how worried Mom is?"

"Can we talk about this later . . ."

Luke listened to their argument with half an ear and stared contemplatively at their target, activating another protective talisman while he waited for an opening.

For a brief moment, his eyes met Tyrisa's, and he couldn't help but be taken aback.

The Rebel, in spite of her terrible appearance, looked a mixture of angry, embarrassed, and, for the first time since the battle began—scared.

Luke thought he knew why, and like a shark, he smelled blood in the water.

It was already ridiculous that they, as mere warriors, had lasted as long as they had in a fight against her. The fact that two of them were freshly advanced rookies, just added insult to injury. On top of that, they had a seemingly inexhaustible supply of Hero-tier talismans, which she had still not been able to deplete. Instead she had been accruing countless small injuries as the battle wore on.

Now, a new arrival had joined, with a powerful steed that had already taken her arm.

She started this battle, likely thinking of us as a minor nuisance that she needed to take care of before she rode off into the sunset and licked her wounds. Instead, we've dragged this out for hours, and she's down an eye and an arm. So she's probably desperate to end it.

I don't see us running out of talismans anytime soon, and I bet at this point, neither does she. I don't know if they have an equivalent to the sunk-cost fallacy here, but if she's really as old as she is, she'll be considering cutting her losses and running.

Fucking hell, the way this battle is going, pretty soon she'll be an eyeless, limbless torso. If I were her, I would have run after an hour. This battle might as well be pointless to her.

I'm guessing she can't.

The Rebel's figure blurred and shot through the sky toward the griffin.

Luke's heart dropped in his chest, and, straining his eyes to keep up with her movement, he slashed his sword as fast as he could.

A hail of arrows and an arc of sharp light attempted to cut her path toward Nel, while Lukeus tugged on Nutbutter's reins and sent them climbing in the sky after her.

Their aid, however, wasn't needed. A single flap of the griffin's wings saw them retreat a mile away, leaving the Rebel to deflect their hasty attacks.

"YARHHHGG," she screamed in frustration and pain when the wave of energy from Luke's sword nicked her neck.

So she's going to try and get rid of Nel first, then. Luke frowned as he thumbed an explosive talisman before deciding to pocket it. Now would have been a good time to activate it, but they didn't do enough damage to make the risk to Nel worth it.

"She's going to run." Heracles cursed under his breath.

A moment later, the Rebel's storage ring flashed, and a clay plate appeared in her hand.

From her position in the sky, Nel unleashed a dozen of her lightning-covered spears straight toward Tyrisa. Before any of them could reach their, a portal opened up underneath the Rebel.

A large, fiery ring, within which they could see a single, run-down castle.

The Rebel's figure wobbled in the sky as she desperately tried to stave off unconsciousness. A spear struck her hand, dislodging her grip on the weapon and making it tumble through the sky and into the forest below.

Luke watched with rapt attention as her lone eye closed in exhaustion, and she tumbled through the portal, unconscious.

"Get there before it closes!" Heracles yelled urgently, and, not wasting a second, Lukeus tugged Nutbutter's reins.

"Shoot after her!" Luke barked at the son of Zeus, and immediately Heracles affixed an explosive talisman to an arrow. It wasn't to be, however; the moment she crossed through the hole, it closed behind her.

Leaving the five of them, and their two steeds flying alone over the scarred land they had battled on.

"SHIT," Heracles cursed.

"Lukeus, do you know where that castle is?" Luke asked.

"No," he said blankly, staring listlessly at the spot where the portal had closed. Not that Luke could blame him. They had spent long, nerve-racking hours being tossed around by the Rebel, only for her to escape.

Now she'll probably be back. As crazy as this world is, I wouldn't even be surprised if she manages to find a way to heal from all those injuries.

Fuck.

Luke sighed loudly as the golden bubble around them vanished, and for the first time in hours, he saw the world untainted by its golden hue.

Looking at the aftermath of the battle, he couldn't help but be even more disappointed.

All this destruction. All that wealth. All for nothing.

A gust of wind ruffled his sweat-covered robes as Nel maneuvered Aura beside them.

"Hi," she said, waving awkwardly and seeming less tense now that their foe had fled the battle.

"Hey, Nel, it's nice seeing you again," Luke said tiredly, his gaze darting between her and her passenger. "Who's your friend?" he asked heavily, his eyes lingering on the girl's bald head and her rounded, youngish facial features. He gulped heavily, fearing he already knew who she was. She looked just like him, after all.

She barely looks older than twelve. What's Nel doing bringing her here? he thought angrily. *All of Clan Skyscar will know where we are.*

"This is Eva. Eva of Clan Skyscar. She's . . . Jax's sister."

Eva seemed to shrink into herself as Luke gulped heavily. He already knew, had known since she yelled "for Jax" upon her arrival, but having it confirmed just made it all too real. Forgotten guilt and suppressed trauma formed a lead ball of anxiety in his stomach as his ears roared with the blood rushing into them.

"I'm sorry about your brother. I—" Luke started to say, only for a spear to appear in Nel's hand. She whacked him lightly in the head with it.

"Jax was my fault," Nel said resolutely. "I killed him." A look of regret crossed her face as the younger girl shied away from her. "Only I bear that responsibility. You need not be guilty, Luke."

"I—"

"Agnella told me what happened," Eva said suddenly, her fists clenching and unclenching. "She told me you tried to help him, that you could have killed him but you didn't. Not even when he attacked you."

Luke looked away from her. *Yeah, but I left him on the ground. I could have hidden him, and those guys were mortals. I could have fought them instead of hiding myself. Maybe then . . .* He stopped himself from thinking about what-ifs. At the end of the day, Jax had been slain after Nel killed the last of the attackers.

He knew that, but some part of him still couldn't help but feel responsible for his death. It was him telling her about the Rebel that had led them to joining Nel on her journey to Sophia.

"Right." Lukeus suddenly clapped his hands. "How's the old man?" he asked Nel.

"Unconscious. His wounds were heavy, and he overdrew his mana. Clite said he won't wake for another few days."

"But he's fine, right?" Luke asked.

"Yes. He'll make a full recovery." Nel nodded, and Luke sighed in relief.

"That's wonderful news. It's a shame that we will be unable to offer him the Rebel's head when he wakes, but knowing that he is well, that is a prize of its own," Heracles said awkwardly. "Was Jason able to power your teleportation altars with the ship's core?"

"He was, and we were fortunate that no Hero- or Warrior-tier giants attacked in the meantime."

"That's good." Luke nodded as he looked at the pair on the griffin. Something didn't feel right.

How did they even find us? I mean, yeah, we're not too far from the capital, and we've been dropping really big bombs for a long time, but still. Sylcra is big, and I don't think we were moving in a straight line the whole time.

And why did she bring a kid with her? I get that she's Jax's sister, but if anything, that makes it even worse.

"How did you find us?" Luke asked suddenly.

Nel shifted uncomfortably on her steed.

"Nel didn't find you," Eva said. Reaching into her pocket, she pulled out a fist-size glass orb. A single red needle inside it pointed toward the forest.

Don't tell me . . .

"Is that a blood compass?" Luke said, his mouth suddenly dry.

Heracles slapped him on his back, a wide grin stretched across his face. "You didn't find us did you? You found the Rebel," he said, immediately connecting the dots.

"We're returning to the capital," Nel said, glaring at Eva. "Put that away."

Eva just glared at her in response and held the orb higher for them to see.

"Nel. Tyrisa was unconscious when she fell through the portal . . . If we can get there fast enough . . ." Luke tried to convince her, leaving her to figure out what he meant.

CHAPTER 8

Entering Dangerous Territory

Nel opened and closed her mouth, her eyes darting between the three of them on the chariot. Her expression rapidly shifted from contemplative to uncertain.

"If we want to do this, we'll have to decide soon," Luke added. His eyes lingered on the orb in Eva's hands. A part of him really wanted to know what she was doing with them, but another, much bigger part of him was too concerned about making sure the quest continued.

"Do you really think we can kill her?"

"She's running from us." Luke crossed his arms over his chest. "She's also down to one arm and a single eye. I like our odds."

"What he said," Heracles chipped in. "If that thing can truly lead us to her, then I say we end this. The alternative is that she flees, recovers, and comes back here."

"We can wait for Grandfather to recover," said Nel.

"Or we can put her head on his nightstand and he can admire it when he wakes up," Luke insisted. "I mean, we don't have to do exactly that, but . . ." He made a spasming motion with his hands. "You know what I mean."

Nel sighed deeply. "Why do you want to kill her?"

Well, I have to kill her.

"Why don't you?" Luke asked in turn. She lifted an eyebrow and frowned at him.

Yeah, I didn't think it would be that easy.

"I like Cyzicus," Luke replied truthfully. "He's been good to me, and I want to be good to him. More than that, the Rebel's very existence makes me uncomfortable. It has since the day Jax told me about her. The fact that she's willing to sink so low scares the shit out of me, and if I'm being honest, so does this war lasting a second longer than it needs to. Sure, I guess we can retreat now and Cyzicus can kill her later, but how many people will die from now till then? We have a real shot at ending this, right now, without anyone else losing their lives, and I say we do."

"What he said," Lukeus chimed in.

Nel bit her lip. "Let's see where she is first."

The creeping ball of anxiety that had been gestating in Luke's stomach eased slightly.

The ring on Nel's finger flashed, and a giant map of Sylcra appeared in the air in front of her. They watched curiously as she lined the map up with the orientation of the island. Her gaze shifted between the compass still in Eva's hands and the map, and almost immediately a worried frown settled over her face.

"It's pointing straight toward the swamp," she said.

Luke scratched his chin as both Eva and Lukeus grew pale. *Rex said that place was scary, but honestly, we're all warriors. Unless there are Hero-tier monsters hiding in there, we should be fine, right?*

"That doesn't mean much—it could just be pointing to Skyscar territory. Does that thing tell us how deep we'll need to go?" Lukeus asked.

Nel shook her head. "The compass only points in the direction; it doesn't tell me how far."

"What manner of creatures lurk in the swamps that have you so frightened?" Heracles grumbled after seeing their reactions.

"It's not one thing in there; it's the whole . . . You'll see," Lukeus said.

Hmm. If we draw a line on the map here, and then another one from a different position, then we should—

"There's a way to find out exactly where a person is," Eva said, pulling Luke out of his thoughts.

He listened with half an ear as the twelve-year-old girl explained how to triangulate a target's exact position with the blood compass.

I wonder what the story there is? I do remember Cyzicus saying something about going and getting Jax's remaining family, but that still doesn't explain why she's flying around with Nel. And how would Nel have even gotten the compass? Is that what she was doing while we were freeing Heracles—sneaking into enemy territory and stealing important artifacts?

Even so . . . Eva seems a bit too comfortable with her. I don't care how good a reason Nel had to kill Jax, but if he was my brother, I wouldn't be able to forgive his killer. Probably not ever, and definitely not so easily. Nel doesn't seem the type to obscure the truth, either. If there's one thing I know about her, it's that she's straightforward.

Nel nodded to Eva, and, drawing a line on the map, they vanished with a single beat of the griffin's wings and appeared in the air miles away a few minutes later.

"So fast," Luke whispered to himself.

"It truly is. Griffins are powerful creatures, and that one seems to be a descendant from a particularly powerful line," Heracles said. "Your Pegasus is also good," he added hastily, after remembering Lukeus was still there. "Pegasi make for the finest steeds. Father has a—"

"Heracles, you don't have to explain why Pegasi are good. I have one," Lukeus cut him off.

"It was just that you—"

Nel chose that moment to return. Not wasting a second, she floated the map in front of them. Her face was set into a nervous frown. "Do you still want to go?"

Luke glanced at the narrow X she had drawn on the map. It marked the middle of the swampy region. Maybe a day's worth of travel on the Pegasus—less if they could all fit on her griffin.

If Cyzicus is going to be out for days, then I don't imagine the Rebel being up and running anytime soon. And if there's nothing of any real importance down there, Heracles probably has something that can level the whole area if it comes down to it. Although . . . avoiding widespread destruction is probably for the best if possible.

I have to kill her with my sword, anyway.

"I don't see a problem with it. Unless there're some Hero-tier monsters we need to be concerned about, I think we should be fine, but I also don't really know what you guys are scared of," Luke confessed.

Nel hesitated before answering. "There's not one thing in there that I can point to and say, that's what makes it dangerous. It's just that we don't know what could be in there. It's the only part of the island that Grandfather couldn't tame when he first settled here, and every expedition that goes into it and tries inevitably fails. It's also home to most of the island's monsters. Every strange, creepy, or disgusting creature that you'll find on Sylcra crawled out of there."

"Lukeus, what do you say?" Heracles turned to the emperor's grandson.

Luke held his breath and waited for him to respond.

I guess my quest, once again, rides on his shoulders. It should be fine.

In spite of his actions, Lukeus wasn't the lustful coward he portrayed himself as, but at the same time, Luke had seen him unabashedly run from prospective danger twice. Seeing it a third time wouldn't surprise him.

"We end this now," he said resolutely. "Someone needs to take the little girl back, though. We're not taking her with us. It's too dangerous."

"I'll be fine," Eva protested, punching Nel on the back. "And me and her have a dea—"

Nel turned around, put a hand over her mouth, and frowned. "I suppose I can fly back and—"

"No. Aura is faster than Nutbutter," he said reluctantly. "I'll take her back to the capital, and you take Heracles and Luke north. You said the *Argo* is able to power the teleportation altars, right?"

"It was," said Nel.

He nodded. "Okay. I'll—" He glanced at the map. "I'll see what I can do from the capital, gramps should have left an altar around the area, so . . . send me a talisman if you need anything."

"It's decided, then." Heracles clapped his hands together, a wide grin stretched across his face.

Luke scratched his chin. *I suppose that works. Killing the hero and risking our own lives is well and good, but bringing a kid with us is pretty stupid. She would probably be fine if we won, but if we lost . . . No, this is definitely for the best. Especially if there's more than one compass, which hopefully there isn't.*

"Be careful on your way back, and don't stop for anything," Luke warned him. "Not until you're back in the capital. I don't know how this blood-compass stuff works, but if they have more than one, they'll be able to find you."

"That shouldn't be a problem." Nel shook her head. "Eva has the only one."

"Oh. Never mind, then. Let's take that in case the Rebel starts to move, and we—"

"Mmmahifuodosonf," Eva mumbled.

"Biting my hand isn't going to work." Nel sighed. "And there's no point in taking it with us. Only descendants of the clan can use it."

"MMMMHHDOHIDF."

"Excuse me." Her ring flashed, and a small, translucent bubble appeared around the griffin. Confident that she wouldn't be heard, Nel lifted her hand off the girl's face.

Luke couldn't hear what they were arguing about, but if one thing was clear, it was that Eva was mad and Nel undeterred. After what felt like hours of watching their lips move, the bubble around them faded.

Nel nodded at Lukeus, and with the plan decided, Luke and Heracles both left the chariot, while Nel transferred the upset but reluctantly willing Eva to it.

Not wasting any time, Lukeus tugged the reins, and in seconds he was no more than a small speck in the sky.

"What's the deal with you two?" Luke asked her.

"It's none of your concern," Nel replied curtly, her tone making it clear that she didn't want to talk about it.

"Fair enough." Luke shrugged.

The next moment, she patted her griffin's neck, and they were comfortably shooting through the air. The forested ground rapidly contracted underneath them as they flew into danger.

"What have you been up to all this time?" Heracles asked casually.

"Um . . . just hanging around. Training."

"Training is good. I do quite a lot of it myself."

Luke stared impassively at his back. *This is going to be a long trip. Clearly being rich doesn't make you good at talking to girls. Not that I have any reason to judge—I've barely even looked at a girl since I came to Theos.*

Closing his eyes, he tuned out the son of Zeus's awkward attempts at flirting and meditated on his mana.

Taking one deep breath after another, he tried to be aware of it as it flowed within his body, paying particularly close attention to the area around his heart and the way it pulsed in tune with his body's natural rhythm. It was gentle but at the same time chaotic.

Tracing the resulting currents through his body, down his extremities, he just watched as it flowed back inward after hitting the barrier of his skin. The waves crashed with each other and folded back into themselves before another pulse from his heart temporarily washed away the chaos.

On a whim, he flexed his will and seized control of every drop of the energy within him. Letting it become completely still within him, he released his hold, enough to let a single pulse through before he stilled the mana around his heart alone. Preventing another pulse from escaping, he watched.

It wasn't long until he noticed a subtle difference in the way it moved in his eyes, compared to the rest of him, and immediately his heart sped up in excitement before he forcefully calmed himself down.

There's only one thing that would make a difference in the way my mana moves, and around my eyes in particular—my bloodline. Taking a deep breath, he quickly opened his eyes and made sure everything was fine before returning to his meditation.

It was such a minor difference that it would have been impossible to notice in his body's natural state, and even with him carefully calming his mana, it surprised even him that he'd noticed it. Once he did, though, it was impossible to unsee it.

If his mana was like water, then in the back of each of his eyes was a tiny pebble, minutely disturbing the way it flowed. Pebbles that would be undetectable if not for the minor way his mana formed a whirlpool around them. Taking a hold of his mana, he prepared to investigate before stopping himself.

I should probably wait, he thought reluctantly. *If this is anything like unlocking my mana was, I should hold off.*

On the other hand, do I really want to leave anything on the table when I'm about to potentially fight a foe in the Hero tier? There's no other way I'll be able to stick my sword in her.

Before he could make a decision, though, a loud shriek pulled him out of his thoughts. Opening his eyes, he gulped as a cloud of giant, winged serpents barreled through the sky and collided headfirst into their griffin.

Shit. Guess we're at the swamp.

CHAPTER 9

Some Quick Work

Luke drew a blade from its sheath, while Heracles tore the perforated tab off a protective talisman. A shimmering golden barrier took shape around them.

The bubble succeeded in repelling the vast majority of the flesh-colored, winged serpents, but its activation had been too slow. Three of the winged centipede serpents were close enough to Nel's steed that the talisman engulfed them as well.

It couldn't be helped, though. The serpents had been invisible before the would-be hero killers had encroached on their territory. Ambush predators that they were, they hung in the sky until something was unfortunate enough to wander in.

If it weren't for the fact that nearly every Warrior-tier creature he had seen until now could fly, Luke would have thought the practice impractical. As it was, he was reasonably sure that while humans weren't the intended prey, the tactic was incredibly potent.

In a matter of moments, it became pure chaos as one creature after another rammed into the barrier, while others wound themselves tightly around the bubble, seeming intent on crushing it. Heracles tossed something outside the area of the talisman, and white engulfed their vision. A violent explosion cleared away their immediate surroundings and sent them careening in a random direction.

Leaving the world outside their little bubble for Heracles to deal with, Luke eyed the monsters that had managed to get into their guard.

Jaw clenched, he locked eyes with the largest of the three creatures and, activating his technique, he sank dozens of points of mana into his blade and slashed over both Heracles and Nel.

An arc of brilliant blue light traveled toward the head of the snake. He grinned slightly when a bloody cut split the soft, fleshy, pink scales of its snout in two and left a shallow gash on its skull.

It stunned the monster, and it hissed in pain.

Rearing back, it flew out of the bubble and collided in a tangled mess with one of its brethren that had already filled the space made by the explosive talisman.

The remaining two serpents instantly became invisible, wound their long winged-bodies around Aura, and, before any of them could react, squeezed. A loud crunching noise sickened Luke to the stomach as he tried to direct his skill toward them. It wasn't to be, though.

However the sky serpents made themselves invisible, it seemed that it was enough to prevent the First Truth from working on them.

Any other time, Luke would have been fascinated by the idea that his skill wasn't as invincible as he thought it was, but as it was, a jolt of dread shot through him. The technique was perhaps his biggest advantage, and suddenly having it negated was not ideal. That opened an entirely new can of worms.

If these things can block it, then what else can? Luke thought worriedly.

"SCREEEEEEE," the griffin screeched as one of them bit into her throat and another one into her legs, all within a second of them colliding into the cloud of the monsters.

Both Nel's and Heracles's rings shined, and their respective weapons appeared in their hands—a spear and a club. Before either of them could make a single move, though, whatever skill or technique the griffin used to keep the wind at bay faltered and then failed entirely. Aura was unable to keep it activated through the pain.

The wind crashed into them with tremendous force. Luke didn't know how fast they were moving, but caught unprepared as he was, it succeeded in pulling the air from his lungs and sent him tumbling back and into the open air.

Shit. Shit. Shit. He cursed, for a moment fearing that he would be sent out of the bubble before he tamped down on the panic.

Reacting in the nick of time, he latched onto Aura's tail and cursed under his breath as he used her appendage like a rope and crawled back to the others. He kept his eyes carefully trained on the area where he thought the snakes were.

Carefully, he kept his mana contained with him so that he wouldn't accidentally lock himself in space as he inched forward. He hadn't been a warrior for long, but already the instinct to catch himself with his ability to hold on to space was strong.

He knew, though, that if he did, he would kill his own momentum, but not the griffin's, which would leave him alone to fend off the skyful of monsters. Even slowed down and in agony, with her movement more of a free fall than carefully controlled flight, Aura moved incredibly fast. Fast enough that Luke knew he wouldn't be able to keep up with her speed. Which would be incredibly bad.

Although the cloud of Warrior-tier creatures was ripe with points, they were both on a deadline, and he wasn't confident that he would even be able to win, making the prospect of battling them not only unappealing but scary and fraught with danger.

Warriors, even weak ones, weren't fodder. At least not to him, and not yet. Even with all the tools he had at his disposal, he knew that he wasn't a match for that many. Their number alone was overwhelming, even before factoring in their ability to turn invisible, which prevented him from using his own greatest asset.

I wouldn't stand a chance.

Blood splattered on his face from a wound on Aura's hind leg, and the griffin screeched once again as she completely lost control of her flight, and they began tumbling through the sky straight toward the ground.

This could be bad.

"Feed her a healing potion!" Luke yelled into the wind, hoping beyond hope that Heracles heard him, his eyes locked onto a faint shimmer creeping under her belly.

If this is what's in the sky, then I really don't want to know what's on the ground.

Frowning in determination, he hung onto the griffin's tail with one hand, clutching his blade with the other. Eyeing where the blood was spilling into the sky, he tried to activate his technique.

He failed.

I have to make it let go and fast. Heracles probably has a healing potion that will have Aura fixed up in no time, but none of that will mean shit if there's still a snake trying to eat her alive, and if she does die, then the whole quest is fucked.

Think. Think. Think.

Hitting its body won't do much. These things are definitely durable enough that they'll work through the pain, he thought, recalling how long Nel had had to batter the one they'd encountered when they were journeying to Sophia's forge. *But if pain can make it lose concentration . . .*

A plan began to take shape in his mind.

If pain can make Aura lose her ability to control the wind, then it should stop these things from staying invisible.

He filled the sword Cyzicus had given him with mana and swiped so that the arc of sword light would hit the monster as far away from the griffin as possible, lest he accidentally hurt Nel's familiar. And he let loose his attack.

A handful of the monster's wings separated from its body and fell through the air. It writhed in pain, and for a brief moment, its form became visible.

With it finally in sight, he activated the first layer of his technique. It whispered its deadly song for the shortest of moments before the creature once again activated its own technique, but it was enough. Luke knew what he needed to do.

He let loose another arc of sword light, this one precisely aimed toward the winged serpent's nose, at what he was fast suspecting was their weak spot. The monster hissed as it flickered into visibility, this time for a few seconds. All the time Luke needed.

It reared its head and, almost faster than Luke could perceive, shot toward him. So long as he could see the creature, though, its fate was sealed.

Another wave of energy escaped Luke's swords, but, wise to the danger, the monster ducked its head down in an attempt to get underneath him and ended up taking attack to its back.

Rivers of blood splattered from the wound, but the level of damage was nothing more than a nuisance to the creature. It was stronger than the one they had fought before, and Luke remembered well the punishment that one had endured under Nel's ministrations.

While the attacks would eventually drain its mana and weaken it, they didn't have that much time.

With his understanding of the First Truth, however, Luke didn't need time. The creature's every intention was bare before him, and it was with that knowledge that he struck again.

An arc of light escaped his sword, but this time the creature dodged the attack entirely, untangling itself from the griffin in favor of killing Luke.

Its maw opened wide, it sprang forward. Just like Luke knew it would.

For an instant Luke tore his gaze away from the monster and looked over the griffin's back, and, seeing that neither Nel nor Heracles had a clear line of sight toward him, he decided to take a small risk.

Wrapping Bellerophon's Blade with his mana, he for an instant sent both it and the blade Cyzicus had given him into his inventory.

It wasn't a requirement of the technique itself, but in mere moments the sword in his hand would kill the monster.

Luke decided that it might as well do it in a way that benefited him the most.

With where they were going, he would need every ounce of strength he could muster, and he was unwilling to let even a single point go to waste. Not when he needed to kill a hero. She was weakened, but by no means was she weak, and even the slightest increase in ability could mean life or death.

He didn't want to die. Not again. Not ever.

Holding his now-empty hand out in front of him, he felt the world slow down as it disappeared into the monster's gaping maw. Its warm breath tickled his skin.

He recalled Bellerophon's Blade back into existence and simultaneously returned his other blade to the sheath on his hip and, with every ounce of strength he could muster, slashed upward.

Like a hot knife through butter, the blade cut through the roof of the sky serpent's mouth, straight into its brain, and back out into the open air. He wrinkled his nose as splatters of blood arced through the air.

+ 8 Stat Points

Dead, the creature fell through the air, and Luke watched in grim satisfaction as another sky serpent took a bite out of its carcass moments later.

Grinning, Luke dashed back onto the griffin's back.

Heracles was bent over the griffin's head, pouring a vial of yellow liquid down her throat, while Nel ineffectually but relentlessly stabbed the last remaining sky serpent with a handful of lightning-covered spears.

Luke once again embraced the First Truth of Death, intending on helping her out, but before he could do anything, Heracles leaped toward the monster and grabbed it with his bare hands. His finger dug into its scaly hide, and Luke watched in awe as he made a bloody fist, and then, in a feat of disgusting strength, sank his entire arm into the creature's body.

The light faded from its eyes as, with a loud cry, the son of Zeus ripped his hand free and yanked out the sky serpent's still-beating heart.

Releasing the technique, Luke reached into his pocket and quickly activated another protective talisman, then took a moment to process what he had just seen.

Heracles, seeing his stupefied expression, grinned mischievously and tossed the bloody heart toward him.

Frowning in disgust, he swiped with his blade and cut it into two, sending each half of the twitching organ flying over the side of the griffin. It exploded in a curtain of blood, drenching his already-soaked robes even more.

Man—

+ 2 Stat Points

Huh. Would you look at that? Nasty, but for two stat points . . . I'll take it. But—

"That was gross." Luke crossed his arms over his chest.

"I think it was funny." The son of Zeus grinned.

"No. No, it wasn't." He turned to Nel. "Do you have any water . . . and maybe a change of clothes?"

She ignored him and rushed toward Aura's head. "Are you okay?" she asked her familiar, rubbing her hand through the griffin's feathers.

"I fed her a Hero-tier potion. She'll be fine."

"Do you have any extra robes?" Luke asked Heracles. "This is really gross."

CHAPTER 10

A Looming Castle

The population of the flying serpents thinned, but from the moment they first crashed into them, it never went away entirely.

Every ten to fifteen minutes they would crash into another one, but at that rate, it wasn't hard for them to deal with the creatures. Most they could escape, and the rest they killed. After combating their reduced numbers for a while, Heracles metaphorically put his foot down and decided that they shouldn't keep a talisman activated the entire time. A few minutes later, he cut the expenditure entirely, and they began to fly through the air without any protection.

Luke had mixed feelings about it.

On one hand, it made sense . . . they didn't need to use the talismans all the time, and having one activated every second was a waste of resources. In fact, not having one constantly activated meant that Luke had the chance to kill a handful of the more persistent sky serpents and in doing so collect some much-needed stat points.

On the other hand, he didn't like the way Heracles said it. It raised certain questions.

"How many talismans do you have left?" Luke asked after spending the past half hour agonizing over the thought. "Like . . . don't get me wrong, you've been incredibly generous with them so far, and I'm very grateful, but if there's a chance we're going to run out, we'll have to reassess some things. Not saying we turn back or anything, but if there's a chance we're going to run out, then letting the Rebel attack us while we hit her with Warrior-tier attacks sounds like a losing strategy."

The son of Zeus scratched the back of his head and shifted uncomfortably in his spot between Luke and Nel. He opened and closed his mouth for the better part of a minute before sighing audibly. "I can't say."

Well, that's concerning.

"What do you mean?" Nel asked.

"I'm not allowed to tell people what I have, and how much I have of it." He shrugged. "It was one of the conditions Dad gave me when he gave me the ring. I even had to swear an oath, so . . ."

"Huh . . . that's interesting," Luke hedged, carefully trying to keep his voice neutral so as not to let his doubt show or reveal how disappointed he was with the nonanswer.

It seemed strange to him that Heracles was willing to take things out of his ring and show them off, but not be able to tell people what he had. The oath itself made sense, though, he reasoned. If Luke were Zeus, he, too, would advise his son not to show off all the treasure he was carrying around with him. He knew all too well the consequences of greed, but then again, if the god had sworn his son to secrecy, it didn't make sense for him to just take stuff out and wave it around.

I suppose Zeus might have had provisions in it that lets Heracles take something out when he's thinking about using it . . . but hmm. He's acting suspicious, but if he says we're good, I'll trust him for now. He deserves the benefit, at least, and I really don't think he'd put us at risk by lying . . . but he was also okay with Arke killing a bunch of people.

Nope. Luke forcefully shut down that stream of thought. *Even if he's willing to risk our lives, it's not like I'm not willing to risk his, either. Or Nel's, for that matter, and my own cause is much more selfish than either of theirs,* he thought guiltily. *Hell, the only reason I even knew he needed to be saved was because of the Seed, and I'm only really here now because of the same. As much as I want to think otherwise, I probably wouldn't have done this without having a quest, either.*

Fuck . . . Talk about throwing stones when my own house is made of glass.

Besides . . . I really doubt he's ambivalent about our deaths. Maybe mine, but definitely not Nel's. Yeah, I'll be fine.

Heracles stiffened slightly, sensing something he didn't like in Luke's demeanor.

"It's nothing to worry about, I promise. I have what we need," he insisted. "Dealing with a single hero shouldn't be a problem, and this one is, like, half-dead anyway. If I can't kill her, I'll . . . change my name." He chuckled.

"Take this seriously, Heracles. Heroes aren't weak," Nel said quietly, her head on a constant swivel as she scanned for threats. "I know you'll be fine—you always are—but this is important. I know you have a habit of—"

"I am taking it seriously, Nel. Just because I'm confident in our chances doesn't mean that I'm—"

"I know," she cut him off. "Sorry, I'm just on edge." Her ring flashed, and a map appeared in her hand. "We're almost there."

Instantly Luke perked up and opened his status, for the moment letting go of his concerns. He had some points to spend. Forty-five of them, to be exact, and he knew exactly what he wanted to use them on.

It was an easy choice to make.

While improving his Strength and speed would be nice, the way he fought didn't stress those attributes. With his techniques guiding his actions, his attacks were precise and served to impose death on his target as efficiently as possible.

He didn't need to be strong if his blade never met his opponent's, and he didn't need to be fast when he knew what his foe was going to do before he did it. Nor would a handful of points in those stats make up for the difference in his Strength and that of an opponent who was a lot stronger than him. Glancing at Heracles, he shook his head. Not even a couple hundred points would bridge the gap between them in any reasonable way, and he could only imagine what it would be like with a hero.

Just based on his own observations, he had grown at least twice as strong as he was at the Mortal tier just by breaking through; if something similar happened when someone advanced to Hero, then even at the peak of the Warrior tier he wouldn't be a match for her.

What he did need was mana, and the best way to maximize that was to improve both Arcana and Constitution in step with each other.

Even so, ignoring Agility and Strength entirely seemed unwise. Biting the inside of his mouth, he finalized his choices and began to increase his stats by ones and twos, carefully watching both Heracles and Nel in front of him as he did so.

In the past, he had been worried about spending tens of points in front of just Nel, but now he was about to add the equivalent of 4,500.

In terms of aethereal mana, it was more than he had ever spent at one time before, but when weighed against the entirety of the Warrior tier, it was a small fraction of what he needed to progress through the entire level.

As long as no one touches me for a few days, it should be fine, and something tells me neither Heracles nor Nel is suspicious enough of me to actively try and feel it.

It was definitely strange how fast he grew, and he was fully cognizant of that fact. He still wouldn't do anything differently. Not being as strong as he could wasn't an option. He wouldn't half-ass a fight with a hero.

Twenty minutes later, he added the last of his stat points.

Status	Skills	Quests	Inventory

Name: Lukas King

Tier: Warrior

Bloodline: Eyes of Insight

Mana: 1,236 / 1,250

Rate: 17% per hour

Strength: 14 > 21

Agility: 11 > 15

Constitution: 18 > 50

Arcana: 48 > 50

Stat Points: 0

Charges: 7/10

Just in time, too, as Nel suddenly tapped her griffin on the shoulder, and they rapidly descended toward the ground.

"We're less likely to be seen if we go in low," she said.

"Right." Luke nodded and, rising a few feet into the air, he repositioned himself so that he was standing on the griffin. Then, adjusting himself once again, he lowered himself into a kneeling position. His swords scraped satisfyingly against his sheath as he drew the golden blades. He could feel his heart thumping nervously in chest, but he grinned. "Let's kill a bitch."

In front of him, Heracles did the same. His ring glowed softly, and a bow appeared in his hands. "Aye."

Aura broke through the tree line a moment later. Her wings folded into her sides, and she stopped her descent mere feet away from the ground and extended her legs. Her clawed, lionlike legs latched onto the air itself, and her powerful strides propelled them forward at blistering speed.

Luke slashed forward, and an arc of light leaped from his sword and cut away the trees and other shrubbery in their path.

Beasts beset them from all sides. Giant snakes, centipedes, and even alligators poked their heads out from the swampy ground of the Northern Marshes, while giant, iridescent dragonflies and birds emerged from the trees and shrubs.

Most were unable to keep up with them, but the few that were in their way or close enough to strike swiftly found one of Heracles's arrows lodged in their foreheads, and their bodies disintegrated.

Luke channeled his technique in quick bursts and split in half anything the son of Zeus missed with a precise arc of blue light.

At the edge of his mind, an unknown instinct warned him of the presence of greater monsters, but it seemed none of them were interested in challenging them.

"One minute," Nel said urgently. "How are we doing this?"

"We probably should have planned that before we got this close." Luke grinned.

Heracles shook his head. "Like I said before, a plan only works if we know what we're up against. All we know is that the Rebel is unconscious in a castle. Best case, we break in and stick a sword through her chest while she sleeps. Worst case—"

Aura came skidding to a halt. The foliage cleared away, and they stopped in a part of the marsh inches shy of a shimmering golden barrier. Within it stood a moss-covered stone castle. They were there.

"Shit," Nel cursed.

"Hmm," Heracles grunted.

The bow disappeared from his hand, and a spiked black club appeared in its place.

"Wai—" Nel tried to stop him, but it was too late. Flying forward, he heaved the club above his head and slammed it down. Sparks of golden light danced across the barrier, but it didn't so much as shimmer.

"Hero tier at minimum," he mumbled under his breath.

"She'll know we're here now," she said, and the griffin reared back, adding space between them and the barrier. On cue, shouts erupted from inside the barrier, and dozens of warriors flew from the castle and took to the sky inside the golden bubble.

"It's not a problem. She would have known regardless." Heracles shrugged. "This was never going to be a quiet affair."

"Can you get us through?" Luke asked.

"I can." The son of Zeus grinned savagely. His ring flashed, and two talismans appeared in his hand. "This one will destroy the barrier, and likely the castle, and this one will keep us alive through it all."

"NO," Nel yelled. "We're not killing them."

"What?" Heracles frowned, confusion dancing across his face. "They're traitors, are they not?"

"Some of them. Most of them are members of Clan Skyscar. The Rebel coerced them into obeying her with force, not willingly. When I rescued her, Eva told me Tyrisa took most of the clan's children hostage. We don't kill them," she said urgently, looking at the bald figures flying around the castle with worry.

"Obviously we're not killing kids. But . . . there're kids in there?" Luke asked incredulously.

Fucking hell. She couldn't have mentioned this sooner? Why the fuck was she sitting on this?

"I—I don't know for sure. The compass only works on people whose blood you have after they unlock their mana. That's why she took them. They might be, or she's keeping them somewhere else. I don't know, but if she is . . ."

"I see." Heracles clenched his fist tightly around his club. "It seems I underestimated how vile this woman is."

"Then it's agreed. We don't kill indiscriminately," Nel said resolutely. "I'm not doing that again. If they flee, let them run. If they fight, we fight back. But we're going to give them the option. Once she's dead, I'll ask Grandfather to summon them to the capital, and he can pass judgment. Not us."

The two talismans disappeared from Heracles's hand, and a single one appeared in their place. He looked at it reluctantly before sighing. "This one will get us in, too . . ."

"There," someone shouted. Luke glanced up and immediately ripped one of his Warrior-tier protective talismans. A moment later, wooden arrows began to rain down on them from the sky.

CHAPTER 11

The Aether's Dark

A shimmering golden bubble appeared around them as Heracles activated a protective talisman in response to the incoming attacks.

Just in time, too, as the next volley of arrows contained seemingly countless amount of explosive talismans attached to them. Each of the resulting explosions splashed harmlessly off their own barrier and sent dirt, mud, and bits of plants flying into the air.

Amid the barrage, dozens more hairless warriors spilled out from the castle and joined the offensive.

A man dressed in golden armor and holding a gilded spear rose higher in the air than the rest of his clan, almost escaping the barrier entirely, and immediately started barking orders.

Luke glanced at them nervously and tore his eyes away, ignoring them for the moment as he looked at the slip of paper in Heracles's hand. It looked like any other talisman, but the way the son of Zeus gazed at it longingly stoked his curiosity.

"So what does that one do?" he asked eagerly.

"It's a teleportation talisman. I don't know what tier it is, but we found two of them on Lemnos. Out of every talisman I have, this one is the most useful. It should take us anywhere I've seen with my own eyes . . . It's also the only one I have left, and I don't have the ability to get more." He frowned. "As far as I know, there's only a single god who knows the pattern to create them, and he . . . can't anymore." He took a deep, reluctant breath and started scanning the castle grounds in search of a place to enter. "I wanted to keep it for . . ." He shook his head. "Never mind."

That does sound useful . . . instantly going anywhere you want—that's . . . A single one of those is basically a get-out-of-jail-free card. I mean . . . it's not super useful to me personally—the only places I've been are Carim and now Sylcra—but for someone like Heracles, who's actually seen the world . . . He could move halfway across it in an instant. Unless . . . he mentioned a god . . . Could it take me back to Earth?

"Teleportation isn't impossible for heroes, though. Why would that be rare?" Nel looked at it skeptically.

"You're right, of course. But when I say anywhere, I mean it. With this, I could go to Olympus, Atlantis, Elysium, or even jump back to the *Argo*—all without any cost to me. The way heroes teleport doesn't compare, and it drains them. Most, like your grandfather, rely on artifacts that gather and store ambient mana to mitigate the cost, but even then it's quite difficult and the range is small. With help, they could probably make a network that spans the archipelago, but that's it. You have to be a god or something close to it to really travel the world freely. With this, I can. So long as I've been there before, I can be there again. Some wards might block it, but . . ." He trailed off and looked meaningfully at the barrier surrounding the castle. "Not that. A Rebel hero won't have anything that can stop this."

Nel's jaw practically dropped to the floor, and her eyes widened in surprise. "Maybe we shouldn't—"

Heracles tore the perforated tab.

The talisman flew through the air, and an ominous pressure emerged from it. Every instinct Luke had told him to get far away from it, and his knees buckled into the soft fur of the griffin's back. His mouth immediately went dry, and he took ahold of his mana and struggled back to his feet, nervously eyeing Nel's crumpled form resting against the griffin's neck.

"Steady," she yelled, and her familiar began bucking, threatening to throw them off and to the ground. Her wings stretched out to the side and began beating nervously while she screeched. "Stay," Nel yelled again, rubbing soothing circles on her neck.

What kind of talisman is that? Luke thought with horror.

Space itself seemed to fracture in every direction and formed a weblike black pattern from where the slip of paper anchored itself in the air.

Heracles roared, taking one strenuous step after another toward the talisman. Stretching an arm out in front of him, he tried to touch it.

The cracks surged forward and crept up to his arm. Blood sprayed from his hand and forearms. Undeterred, he gritted his teeth and kept pushing forward.

His ring glowed softly, and brilliant silver armor appeared around him, covering every inch of his body.

Luke didn't know how much it helped, as the cracks had no difficulty spreading through the armor, but it seemed to provide him enough relief to close the last few inches between him and the talisman.

The second his finger touched it, a black hole appeared in its place. A cloud of devastating pressure gusted forward, and instantly the griffin ceased its thrashing. Something *alien* emerged from the blackness and observed them.

Recognition spread across Luke's face before he carefully schooled his expression. He knew that inky blackness. He would never forget it. It was the same one he had been engulfed in when he died on Earth. It was the darkness of the Aether.

Where the fuck did Heracles get this thing?

Unable to tear his eyes away, he felt where the path was leading, too. Forcefully turning his gaze away from it, he could just *feel* the spot behind the castle where it would deposit them.

"GO NOW," Heracles yelled, breaking him free of a daze he didn't even know he was in. Luke winced at the blood pouring from the seams of Heracles's armor and looked to Nel. She nudged her griffin forward, but she reared back from the light-sucking hole in reality.

Before that moment, Luke hadn't known birds could look that scared.

"NO. AURA. NO," she yelled.

Shit. Shit. Shit. Luke panicked as the golden wings of the griffin started flapping in agitation as she inched back from the portal.

Knowing what was about to happen, he leaped from her back, and on cue, the griffin flapped her wings and disappeared into the sky with Nel still on it. A golden bubble appeared around them as they did, and Luke watched with despair as a handful of the warriors flew from the shielded castle in pursuit of her.

"NO TIME. GO," Heracles yelled again. "I'll be right behin—"

Face set in determination, Luke nodded, and, wrapping himself in a coat of his mana, he flew through the portal. The second he crossed through to the other side, he felt the hole in reality dissolve. The pressure disappeared entirely, and he was inside the barrier in a secluded spot on the opposite side of the castle for the moment, hidden for the moment, but separated from his allies and surrounded by enemies.

Instead of blood, he felt dread run through his veins.

Shit. Shit. Shit. He cursed over and over again in his mind. *Okay, it's not that bad. It seems like none of them noticed me come in. So, that's something.*

Forcibly calming himself down, he pressed himself clean against the wall and carefully peeked around the corner.

Heracles had flown high into the air, and Luke strained his eyes as he watched him down what looked like a healing potion. Their eyes briefly met, and Luke nodded to him.

Opening his mouth, he rested a finger across his lips. Imperceptibly, Heracles nodded at him, seeming to clue in to Luke's intentions.

What happened next stunned both him and each of the Clan Skyscar members. The son of Zeus rose high into the air and began to yell.

"I AM HERACLES, FAVORED SON OF ZEUS, KING OF GODS, AND A PRINCE OF OLYMPUS. AND YOU"—he pointed his club toward the flying warriors inside the barrier surrounding the decrepit castle—"ARE MY ENEMIES. SURRENDER NOW, AND I SHALL SPARE YOU MY JUDGMENT."

A hush fell over them, and immediately they stopped attacking. The man in golden armor flew to the very edge of the barrier and bowed to Heracles.

"Your Highness . . ." he said reluctantly. "Our families have been captured, and we are sworn by oath to serve the empress. We cannot do as you ask, but we humbly ask for your mercy. If you attack, we will be forced to die by your might."

Taking that as his cue, Luke scanned the castle walls and, finding a window, flew toward it.

Distantly, he heard Heracles demand for them to deliver him Tyrisa. A moment later, the world once again devolved into battle. They had refused.

If they really swore oaths, that was probably going to be the outcome from the start. All right. No problem. I just have to kill her, and it should work out.

Luke hyped himself up and peeked inside the castle.

Seeing that no one was there, he stuck his sword into the window's frame. Then, as quietly as he could, pried open the wooden panel and flew inside. Landing lightly on his feet, he took a deep breath and looked around the cobblestone interior, at the gas lamps illuminating the corridor, and began walking down it while channeling negligible amounts of mana into his boots so he was just an inch over the ground and not making any noise.

Idly, he peeked his head into the empty rooms as he passed one after another, carefully checking each as he did.

I'll need to find her fast, though. If I'm found, I'll likely have to fight, and getting into a fight would be bad.

Not only have I never fought a warrior before, but I don't want to kill any of them, either. More than that, most of them will probably be stronger than me and might even have techniques of their own. Any one of them could have an advantage that instantly wipes out my own.

That said, I also had a perfect ascension to the Warrior tier . . . It's possible that most of them still have attributes in the Mortal tier, but some of them may be centuries old. If that's the case . . . Shit.

Heracles is distracting them for the moment, but I doubt they'll focus on a threat outside their wards if they find one inside them.

Coming to a halt at a corner, he carefully poked his head around, withdrew it instantly, and then poked it back out.

There was no one there, but the hall opened up to a set of stairs—one side going up and the other going down.

If I was a Rebel, recovering from wounds, would I rest at the top of the castle or the bottom? Anyone that's a threat to her would be able to fly . . . so bottom it is.

Silently inching forward, he went around the corner and poked his head over. There was no one there, but Luke could hear two voices.

"I don't get it—why is fighting this Heracles guy such a big deal?" a gruff voice echoed through the second floor.

"Because if he's actually a son of a god, and we kill him . . . the empress won't be able to protect us. Or herself," a woman answered.

"He's gotta be lying, though, right? What would the child of a god be doing all the way out here, and why would he be trying to kill us? Do you think the empress killed someone he cares about or something?"

No, Heracles just isn't a fan of letting people with more power than restraint have their way, Luke thought dryly, straining his ears to make out the direction the voice came from.

"Look, it doesn't matter," the woman snapped. "We're stuck with the empress until she dies and the oath we swore breaks. Until then, wait here. I'm going to see what's taking the alchemists so long. The sooner we get her the potions, the sooner she can go and kill the bastard, whoever he is. Honestly I hope she does, and I hope he's actually the child of a god. Maybe one of those bastard Olympians will actually come down from their gilded paradise and kill her," she muttered under her breath.

Luke slid back as the woman quickly flew past the stairs and descended deeper into the castle.

Is she . . . Feeling his heartbeat in his chest, Luke sent both his swords and their sheaths into his inventory. Then, swapping out his robes for a fresh pair, he took a deep breath and strode forward, a vial of healing potion in each hand.

CHAPTER 12

Attempting an Assassination

Who are you?" a bald teen asked the second Luke rounded the corner.

"Rex," Luke said casually, and without skipping a beat, he lifted the vial of healing potion in his hand and gestured toward the door behind him. "I brought some potions for the empress."

The teen lifted an eyebrow and cocked his head to the side. Slowly raking his eyes up and down Luke's body, a confused expression settled over his face.

"I've never seen you before. Where are you from?" he asked.

Luke stilled his gaze and met the suspicious stare as calmly as he could. Very aware of the ring on the teen's hand, he activated the base version of the First Truth of Death. It would be enough to alert him if—or, more likely, when—the Clan Skyscar member turned hostile.

"I'm from Sixra," he said, cocking his own head to the side in faux confusion while his heart hammered in his chest. *That's where Jax wanted to go, so it should be fine—hopefully.*

The teen's eyebrows furrowed. "Me, too . . . Why do you have hair?"

"Huh?"

"Why do you have hair?" he repeated.

"Why don't you have hair?" A dumbfounded look appeared on his face. "Look, what's with these questions? I have to give the empress her medicine—if you haven't noticed we're in a bit of a situation right now."

Outside the castle, a particularly violent explosion went off, and even inside the barrier the resulting shock wave could be felt.

What is Heracles doing? Luke thought incredulously.

The bald teen didn't budge from the door.

"Listen, do you really want to stall me when a god's child is outside the barrier?"

"Um—" The teen looked between him and the door nervously. A look of resolve came over his face.

Luke's technique practically screamed at him, warning him of an attack to come.

Fuck. Luke shot through the air toward him.

His opponent's storage ring flashed.

With his fist extended, he punched the kid in the stomach as hard as he possibly could, wincing slightly as he felt the other warrior's rib crack under the force of his attack.

A dagger appeared in his foe's hand, and suddenly, the drain on Luke's mana exceeded his passive regeneration.

Alerted by the technique, he flew back a meter, causing the Skyscar teen's dagger to miss his throat by mere inches.

That was all Luke needed.

With his opponent overextended, he called Bellerophon's Blade from his inventory into his hands, and, in a quick motion, he slapped the Skyscar clan member with the flat of his blade, leaving a shallow cut on his temple that both dazed him and sent him stumbling back deeper into the hallway. Then, before he could recover, Luke sliced clean through his wrist. Both his storage ring and dagger tumbled to the ground along with his severed appendage.

A pained look came over his face, but the teen gritted his teeth and charged toward Luke.

He's not making any noise. Luke realized. *Why?* he thought, even though he already knew the answer. The teen's oath made him fight, but it didn't make him call for help. Nor did it make him fight *well.*

Kicking his foe in the chest, Luke knocked him down and pressed his blade against the bald teen's neck. A single drop of blood ran down the side of his throat.

A look of acceptance came over his foe's face, but Luke knew better than to believe it. He was scared.

Luke cursed under his breath, and with a quick gesture, impaled the teen's remaining wrist with his sword, robbing him the use of his hand while keeping it mostly intact. He'd inflicted enough damage to take his opponent out of the fight, but not enough to leave him permanently crippled. A small mercy.

He's weaker than me; he's eighteen, maybe nineteen, and I doubt he's been a warrior for long. He doesn't have a technique, so he's practically disarmed, and without the use of his hands, even if he does attack, I'll be fine.

With my technique, I should see it coming the moment he tries anything, and even my inventory isn't a secret I need to keep as strongly now. He doesn't know I don't have a storage ring, so . . .

"One move and you're dead, okay?" he said quietly, making the decision to keep his opponent alive. Then, slowly stepping backward, he picked up the teen's severed hand. Not breaking eye contact, he separated the ring from its finger and put it in his pocket. "Try anything, and you're dead. Make a single noise, and you're dead."

"Okay—"

Luke glared at him, and the boy's mouth immediately snapped shut.

He nodded slowly at that, and then, feeling the severed hand drip blood onto his boots, he frowned in disgust. Stepping forward, he leaned over the figure of his fallen foe and slid the hand into one of the teens pockets, using the opportunity to search him for any surprises. Not finding anything, he nodded in approval and straightened up.

"A healing potion should fix that. I have one that I'll give you, but before that, I need you to get up."

The teen looked at him, confused—no doubt wondering why Luke hadn't ended him. Nodding hastily, he rose into the air like a plank being lifted.

"Is she in there?"

The teen nodded.

"Good. Open the door," Luke instructed, lightly poking his neck with the tip of his sword.

The boy glanced down at his broken arms and back at Luke.

"What? It's not like I do this every day?" he said, feeling heat rise in his cheeks. "Never mind." Leaning forward, he turned the handle before stepping back.

Without needing instruction, the young warrior stepped through the door. His heart hammering in his chest, Luke followed him.

Lightly closing the door behind him, he tore his eyes away from his hostage and locked onto the broken form of the Rebel lying in her bed.

Already, she looked a lot better than when he had last seen her. Her limbs were still missing, and although her eyelids were shut, one socket was empty. Even still, she had shed her charred skin. In its place, smooth pink skin covered what was visible of her body.

Eyeing the slow rise and fall of her chest, Luke tore his eyes away from her and turned to the young Clan Skyscar member.

"I want you to stand in that corner with your arms raised behind your back," Luke instructed.

"I—" He opened and closed his mouth.

"What? Say what you want . . . just speak softly."

"If you are going to try and kill her, my oath will compel me to fend you off. You should tie me up first. I have restraints in my ring," he whispered.

"Why aren't you attacking me already, then?" Luke eyed him with suspicion.

"I'm compelled to obey her commands, but she didn't command me to fight suspected assassins. I don't know for sure if you are one, so—"

"That seems awfully convenient."

"I suppose." The teen shrugged. "If I were you, I'd hurry. If Cleo comes back . . ."

"Right." Luke nodded carefully. Keeping his eyes trained on his hostage, he fingered the ring. A nervous but somewhat eager look flashed across his opponent's face, and instantly Luke felt that something was off.

Unwittingly, he remembered something Lukeus had said when Rex told him that he had tried peering into Heracles's storage ring.

They were protected, and they came with defenses.

He's laying a trap.

"What are you waiting for? Hur—" He dashed toward the door and made to escape, only to stop in his tracks when he found a golden blade stopping him from passing.

What the fuck, man? Just make up your mind. Do you want to die or not? Luke thought miserably.

The teen stepped back. Luke stepped forward. His back pressed against the wall, the boy lifted both arms in the air. "It's the oath I can't resis—"

Frowning in resignation, Luke held his sword against his chest. He didn't want to kill him, and a small, callous part of him regretted showing mercy in the first place. It would have been easier in a way if his opponent had just died in combat. At least then he wouldn't have had to feel like an executioner.

It wasn't a role Luke was eager to play, to consign someone he knew nothing about to death . . . It was one thing with Tyrisa. She deserved it. Someone like the bald teen, though? His only sin was being weaker than her.

It would be wrong to kill him.

Luke didn't know what his oath made him do and what he did willingly. He didn't know if the Rebel was holding his family hostage or not. He didn't know a lot, but what he did know was that if he killed him, it would be final. His soul would be sucked into the Aether, and from there, not even Luke knew what would happen to it. At the same time, he couldn't risk having him around. Knocking out someone at the Warrior tier wasn't easy. Restraining him with ropes wouldn't work. Not when mana physically interacted with space.

Before he could make a decision one way or the other, the choice was taken out of his hands.

The First Truth of Death blazed in the back of his head, and with a sense of numbness, Luke let what he saw coming happen.

The bald teen kicked off the wall and impaled himself on Luke's sword. His mouth opened wide, he tried and failed to bite at Luke's neck. "I'll kill—" Luke twisted his blade in his chest. "Ghhrrk."

Stepping back, Luke watched with a frown as his foe stumbled to his knees. A wind suddenly drafted across the room, and a cyclone started to form around his form.

What the— A skill or a bloodline? he thought absently before erasing the thought from his mind. It didn't matter now.

Taking a deep breath, Luke stopped and, pulling his blade free from his torso, he slashed it horizontally and severed his foe's head from his body. A deep frown settled on his face as a message from the Seed flashed across his vision.

+ 5 Stat Points

He had to know that wasn't going to work, right? Luke thought miserably. *Now isn't the time to be upset about it, though.*

Shaking his head at having killed yet another person, he turned on his heel and walked toward the bed, toward the unmoving form of the would-be empress.

It was finally time to do what he had come here for. It hadn't been long since he had passed through the barrier, but he fully expected the other Warrior tier, Cleo, as the teen had called her, to be back any second.

He wanted to be gone by then. Out of the castle, and out past the wards. Where he could hopefully escape with Nel. Who he desperately wished had managed to calm down her griffin. Eyeing the golden storage ring on her finger, he quickly reached forward and pulled it free. Turning it over in his hand, he attempted to send it into his inventory, only to fail for the second time.

Are storage rings just incompatible with my inventory?

Frowning, he put the thought aside for the moment. It wasn't the time.

All this mana is going to hurt, he realized as he rose into the air above her and positioned his sword over her heart.

He had feared that she would have put up some manner of protection over herself, but if she'd really come here while she was unconscious, it wouldn't be strange for her unwilling conscripts to be lax with her security, and as his blade poked at her robe, he realized that they had been.

Finding his mouth suddenly growing dry, he reached into his inventory and pulled out a handful of Heracles's Hero-tier protective talismans. Ripping the tab off them all, he sent most to his inventory while leaving one between him and her.

He hoped that she wouldn't wake and would instead die in her sleep. As it was, though, he knew how unlikely that was going to be.

Taking one last deep breath, he heaved his sword into the air and plunged it down into the Rebel with every ounce of strength he could muster.

CHAPTER 13

What It Takes

Fuck, he thought with mounting horror. His blade had sunk into her flesh near effortlessly. Easier than he thought it would, if he was being honest, but not entirely unexpected.

It may have only been a Mortal-tier weapon at the moment, but it was still something that had once belonged to Bellerophon—a man struck down by the king of gods himself at the last moments of his ascent toward divinity. Which, Luke suspected, wasn't a common occurrence.

Even as diminished as it was, his blade, Luke's blade, would not fail to bite into flesh.

Unfortunately, that didn't necessarily mean that it would cut where he wanted it to.

The Rebel had moved at the last second, and she had moved fast. Faster than Luke's eyes could follow, and quicker than even the First Truth of Death could perceive.

His golden sword pinned her shoulder to the mattress. Blood spilled from her wound and stained the sheets and her clothes red with her blood, and her single remaining eye fluttered open and looked at him with confusion.

Hastily, he cut off the technique before it drained the last of his mana and tamped down on his panic with a ruthlessness that surprised even him. Being scared wasn't an acceptable response at that moment. No, it was time to take action.

His heart thumped involuntarily in his chest and blood drained from his face as her gaze hardened. An ominous pressure descended into the room and seemed to make his thoughts themselves heavy.

Her gaze traveled languidly across his form. If Luke didn't know better, he would think she didn't care about the sword sticking out of her.

Come on, Luke. Think. Think. Think.

"Let me get this for you—it looks uncomfortable."

He began pulling his sword out of her.

"This really isn't what it looks like," Luke said, smiling genially at her, as he rose higher into the air. Her gaze locked on his blade.

Taking comfort in the fact that for the moment, at least, he was safe in his protective bubble, his jaw set in resolve, he decided to milk that buffer as much as he could.

Reaching into his inventory, he gathered a bunch of pretorn explosive talismans onto the bottoms of his feet, and, hoping she wouldn't notice, let them drop out of his bubble and onto her mattress. All of them were Warrior tier, the same ones Lukeus and Rex had given him when they killed Blinky's mom. He could have included a Hero-tier talisman in the bunch but discarded the thought almost immediately.

He didn't want to pull his punches, but if he killed a bunch of forced conscripts in the process of killing her, it would haunt him for a long time to come. Especially if it was like Nel said and the Rebel was keeping kids hostage in the castle. He refused to sink that low.

Not that he expected the damage from an explosive talisman, even one at the Hero tier, to affect her anyhow.

Multiple times now, she had proven to be resistant to the damage caused by them—to the point that while both his swords were capable of drawing blood, the one Hero-tier explosion they had set off hadn't even made her stumble, and even the Saint-tier one Cyzicus had hit her with hadn't done more than char her skin.

The talismans were a good tool but not one he would trust to finish the job.

The Rebel opened her mouth to say something. What it was, Luke wouldn't know as blood spilled from her parted lips and dribbled down the side of her mouth.

Not intending to let the moment of weakness slide, he immediately brought down his blade over her heart again.

Coughing, she twitched her arm and backhanded him across the room, stopping its path and almost knocking it out of his hands with the force of her blow.

Even injured, her strength was great enough to send him crashing through the wall. He frowned in disgust as his protective bubble crushed the corpse of the Skyscar member he had killed earlier.

Shaking his head, he tore his eyes away from the boy's body and focused on the Rebel.

He watched with bated breath as she straightened on her bed.

Come on. Come on. Come on. He repeated the mantra over and over in his head. *Stay there for just a second longer . . .*

An arrow bounced off his shield as members of Clan Skyscar came crowding around the corner and poked their head through the doorway.

He ripped another Hero-tier protective talisman and stared intently at her. Ignoring them. They didn't matter. Not yet.

The collective talismans he had left for her burst in an eruption of debris and light.

The warriors at the door flinched away.

Luke shot toward the Rebel as she lazily used her single remaining hand to dust off her white robes.

For the first time, he fully activated the First Truth of Death. A ghostly apparition of the Rebel appeared in his vision, transposed above her actual body, and his mana levels began plummeting.

Their eyes met.

Her ghost slipped past her body, and warning bells rang in Luke's head. Dodging before she even moved, he held his sword out past his protective bubble and into what would be her path.

His blade sliced clean through a rib as she whooshed past him. A spurt of blood hung in the air as their eyes met again.

Holding out her hand, she frowned in confusion as her own sword failed to appear. Luke smirked and shot toward her once again.

Once again her apparition betrayed her intentions, and once again Bellerophon's Blade drew blood, this time biting into her elbow.

The Rebel didn't even flinch.

I have to end this . . . and fast, Luke realized as his mana levels had crept past the halfway mark. Adding the five points he had gained from killing the bald teen into his Constitution for a quick, if minor boost, to his capacity, he gritted his teeth and shot toward her again.

If the battle became that of attrition, he would lose. Unlike Heracles, he only had enough protective talismans to last him roughly half an hour, which would be enough to let him escape. Unfortunately, though, he only had enough mana to be a threat to her for a few more seconds at best.

Her ghost split from her body again, moving a lot slower and more cautiously than it had previously and even swaying as she lost control of her mana, betraying how poor her condition was, in spite of her up-till-now nonchalant expression.

Just a little more.

Jaw clenched in determination, Luke positioned himself so that she would run into his blade. Only this time, the apparition flickered out of sight and reappeared a foot away.

What the—

Before Luke could make sense of the situation, another volley of explosions went off underneath his bubble and propelled him away from her.

Dropping out of the technique, he activated another talisman and raked his eyes across the room as he assessed the situation.

A handful of Clan Skyscar members had come into the room, and Luke watched incredulously as one after another they unleashed rows and rows of arrows into the Rebel's chambers. On each arrow was affixed an explosive talisman.

Maybe a third of them reached him, while the rest missed him entirely, and he grinned as he realized what was going on.

They couldn't attack Tyrisa themselves, but they could, and evidently would, attack Luke as poorly as they could—even if he was surrounded by a protective talisman and most of the damage intended for him was absorbed by their leader.

Loyalty, it seemed, couldn't be forced.

Ignoring the bright pulses of flashing light, he scanned through the smoke and debris. Then, floating into the air, he once again charged the would-be empress, this time not even bothering with his technique.

It was true that it was the only real chance he had at taking her down, but almost embarrassingly, he remembered something Heracles had told him hours ago.

It was a waste of mana to use the technique unless he was confident that he could actually kill her, and he had lost that confidence.

Her speed and higher rank made it so that despite being able to see her movement and feel her rather limited intentions through her body language, he couldn't land a clean, fatal attack.

That in mind, he resolved to drag this out as much as possible.

A decision he came to regret when, in the next moment, she blurred and so did his vision.

Desperately clinging to the space around him with his mana, he crashed through at least four stone walls before he was able to kill his momentum, just barely managing to stay within the golden barrier surrounding the stronghold.

The sounds of battle ceased almost instantly, as all those who were firing at Heracles turned their attention toward him.

"Luke, come out!" the son of Zeus yelled as he resumed whaling on the barrier with his club. Each swing sent countless ripples dancing across its surface. "It's too dangerous—we'll find a way to break it and attack together."

Luke glanced at Heracles briefly before turning his attention back to the Rebel. The top of the castle blew off the walls as a handful of Clan Skyscar members came crashing through after him.

The very ones who had used the chaos of his attack to land potshots on the would-be empress.

Unlike Luke, they didn't fare nearly as well.

Gritting his teeth in determination, he shook his head.

"Not yet. She's already getting weaker!" he yelled back at Heracles. Staring nervously as the near-limbless form of the Rebel flew out of the castle, he activated another protective talisman.

"Who are you?" she asked, tilting her head to the side. The empty sleeves of her white robes flapped violently in the wind, and blood dripped from the wounds he had managed to inflict on her.

"Nobody important," he replied cautiously as she slowly inched her way through the air toward him.

"Why do you go to such lengths to see me dead? Did I do something to you? Kill your family, perhaps?"

"Are you really asking me that?"

She blinked at him expectantly, not saying a word.

"Let me put it this way—did Cyzicus ever do anything to you?"

She shrugged and disappeared, only to appear behind him a moment later.

"He hasn't," Luke heard her whisper. Something pushed against his barrier. The grip he had on the air shattered, and before he knew it, he was digging a deep trench into the earth.

Think. Think. Think, he repeated over and over to himself.

His thoughts churned in his mind as he tried to find a solution. Anything that could help him not only get out of this alive but succeed in his quest as well.

He couldn't think of a single thing.

His best chance would have been while she was still unconscious, but he still had no counter to her monstrous speed.

I have enough mana for two, maybe three, more seconds of the First Truth of Death before I run out of mana, and about twenty-five minutes of Hero-tier protective talismans left.

His eyes raked across the sky and darted from Heracles, desperately bashing into the barrier with his club, to the bald warriors looking at him with thinly veiled hope.

Hope that he increasingly felt he wouldn't be able to live up to.

The Rebel flew toward him and into the trench he had dug into the ground. Grinning, she raked her dirty nails across the surface of the bubble. It rippled and strained under her strength and sank even deeper under the ground.

Preemptively, he activated another talisman.

"Are you scared? Your friend can strike that barrier for days and it won't break. Those are days I have to wait until you run out of your little toys . . . and when you do"—she grinned widely—"I'm going to rip you apart one tiny piece at a time. Slices so thin it will—"

Luke blinked rapidly and looked past her head to the sky above them. A shadow covered the castle.

Is that . . . He grinned as a monster, made entirely out of hairlike tendrils and with more eyes than he could count, spread itself across the barrier. Its teeth clacked incessantly as its dreadful glare bored into every one of the dome's inhabitants. Above the monster, the form of the *Argo* could just barely be seen through the gaps between its tendrils.

CHAPTER 14

A Vulgar Ally

Hey, you limbless little bitch: surrender now and Blinky won't eat your corpse," a familiar voice echoed out from the deck of the ship.

"Rex . . ." Jason admonished, and, shaking his head, he flew over the *Argo's* railing, already encased in a protective talisman. Seemingly embarrassed, he smiled apologetically. Upon some unseen and unsaid command, the demon shifted its mass just enough so that Jason could be seen through its writhing flesh. "Sorry about him—Rex lacks both restraint and decorum, but if you could kindly do as he says, I'll make sure your corpse isn't fed to his pet . . . thing. We have some pigs that would be much more fitting for the occasion."

This guy . . . Luke shook his head in amusement, taking more pleasure than he probably should have as fifty different shades of anger flashed across the Rebel's face.

"Jason?" Heracles frowned and, ending his barrage on the barrier, flew toward him. "What are you doing here? Who's powering the teleportation altars in the capital?"

"I came to help; you didn't think I would leave you alone, now did you? As for the teleportation altars . . . they're all taken care of," he said dismissively. "What's Luke doing inside?"

"Oh, that." Heracles looked between both Luke and Jason nervously. "It . . . just kind of happened. I was supposed to be there with him, but . . ." Their voices petered away.

Activating another talisman, Luke strained to hear the rest of their conversation while the empress looked nervously at the abomination blotting out most of the sky and the ship above her.

Blinky's getting really big, really fast. She's already bigger than her mom was, and that's . . . actually insane. She hatched, what, a day ago? Is it a demon thing, or is Rex just feeding her really well? he wondered, tearing his eyes away from the dreadglare's headache-inducing form. The task proved to be futile as the creature spread even more and encompassed the rest of the barrier, artificially creating night in their small part of the world, leaving only the soft golden glow of the barrier to give them light.

"WHAT ARE YOU FOOLS WAITING FOR? KILL THE DEMON!" the Rebel barked, and Luke winced as, on cue, the Skyscar warriors unleashed a devastating number of attacks.

Blinky just blinked as one arrow after another destroyed her eyes and explosions sent bits of her scattering through the sky. Like her mother, she appeared entirely unconcerned by the damage being done to her.

Luke eyed the Rebel as she muttered curses under her breath and floated away from him. On cue, two warriors touched down in front of him.

"Don't let him escape—he has my storage ring. Once his bubble bursts, I expect it to be delivered back to me," she said to them and disappeared and emerged next to the man dressed in golden armor.

Which gave Luke some much needed time to think.

The arrival of the Argonauts was welcome but introduced another variable to the conflict. The battle was sure to get more chaotic, and Luke didn't know if that would end in his favor or not.

I gotta step up my act, and fast, but how?

He tightened his grip on his sword and discarded one bad idea after another.

Attacking wildly would get him nowhere but dead.

Using a Hero-tier explosive might give him the impetus he needed to sneak in an attack, but it would also fling him around and do more damage than he felt was acceptable. At the very least, it would kill the majority of people in the castle who didn't have a Hero-tier talisman of their own. Which, as far as he knew, may well be everybody. The one person it wouldn't kill, however, was the Rebel.

His quest required that he kill her—specifically with his sword—and while the arrival of the allies was reassuring in that it increased his odds of making it back to the capital alive, it also increased the odds of someone who wasn't him landing the precious last blow.

Luke was confident in his strength, but he also recognized that if Heracles had his chance with her, he would be hard-pressed not to get in the way, let alone find the opportunity to finish his own mission. Jason was also bound to be substantially stronger than the current him, and the rest of the Argonauts didn't seem like pushovers, either.

He had his technique, but there was no chance that some of the older warriors didn't have ones of their own. Adding any potential bloodlines, or artifacts that were also now present on the battlefield, made the dilemma even harder to solve.

No. I have to kill her before they find a way in, but how? They probably won't blow this place to bits considering I'm still inside, and once they find out about the kids somewhere in here, the chances of that go down even more, so I have some time . . . but.

Danger Detected.

Every thought in his head ground down to a halt.

"You're in quite the bind, huh," one of the two warriors guarding him said casually. Forcibly keeping his expression neutral, he turned to the cheerfully smiling woman next to him. She was bald, like every other Skyscar Clan member, and wearing the same type of robes every cultivator who wasn't an Argonaut seemed to wear. Hers were the traditional red of a warrior, but with bronze armor plated on top.

"It's Luke, isn't it? It's good to meet you."

"Is it?" he said carefully. "What's your name?"

In response, her face changed, rapidly shifting from one form to another—everything from an old man to a bearded and scarred warrior, a little kid, Luke's own face, and a dozen more.

"I'm whoever I want to be. That doesn't answer your question, though . . ." She tapped her chin with her index finger. "You can address me as Cybele."

Yeah, I have no idea who the fuck that is.

Luke felt his heart thump nervously in his chest. Avoiding panicking as best as he could, he glanced at the other warrior guarding him, only to see him staring dumbly off into space, oblivious to what was happening right next to him.

"Oh my!" Her face settled back into the form of the woman she was earlier, but this time with a head full of scarlet hair. "No need to worry about him. So long as I desire it, not one of those gathered here today will hear or see anything other than what I want them to, and I like to keep a low profile. Most people assume I'm dead, and I prefer to keep it that way."

"What do you want?"

She shrugged. "Truthfully, I don't want much of anything these days. I was on a walk, felt some moron make a breach in the fabric of reality and open a path through the Aether, and now I'm here. Originally I just wanted to make sure nothing came over from the other side—the last thing we need is another infestation."

What. The. Fuck.

"I, uh. Sorry? I'll make sure we don't do that again."

"Oh, no. Don't you worry about that. Honestly, I feel quite lucky to have stumbled upon this little kerfuffle. My, I can practically *feel* the ebbs and flows of fate gathering into a storm. Then again, I guess I shouldn't be surprised. Cursed land does tend to produce the most fascinating stories."

"Oh." Luke shifted in his bubble and activated another talisman, slightly, just slightly more at ease now that he knew what had drawn her to him. Or, more importantly, what hadn't drawn her to him.

Unless she's lying . . . but what can I even do about that? Even if she's not a god, she's not someone I can do anything about. Fuck.

She smiled mysteriously.

"Let's see," she said, turning away from Luke, her gaze locked onto the Rebel. "She's quite the mystery. I never imagined I'd find the last living inheritors of Ouranos's bloodline unwillingly enslaved by one of their own waging a war against some nobody emperor—and losing for that matter. Then again, if you knew Ouranos, you'd know it's exactly the type of thing he'd do, so . . . hmm. Still quite strange. I thought his line had been purged eons ago. I know quite a few people who would be interested to know what hole they crawled out of."

Ouranos? That was the original sky guy, right? That's who the Rebel's descended from? Damn, I thought I had it bad.

Turning toward the barrier, she stared at something past it. "The son of Zeus is rather interesting, but they have a tendency to show up no matter where you go in this world nowadays. A tame demon isn't quite as common, but considering that Epimetheus seems to have spread his seed on this island . . ." She shrugged. ". . . not entirely unexpected. He'll get a kick out of this kid if he shows his face again sometime this millennium. Even this island . . . I'd almost forgotten about it. The last time I was here, it was naught but charred rock. It has quite the story, in fact. Did you know it was here that Ouranos once imprisoned his queen?"

"I can't say that I did."

"Mmm-hmm." She wrinkled her nose. "I suppose that's not unexpected. Not many who remember the ancients still remain on Theos. Now, where was I?"

She grinned, and her hand sank into Luke's protective bubble without so much as a ripple.

"Wh—"

Faster than he could react, she reached into his pocket and pulled out the Rebel's storage ring. As she turned it between her fingers, it flashed briefly, and an unassuming circlet made of twine and roses appeared in her hands.

"—at—"

"You can have the rest," she said and flicked the ring back through his barrier and into his hands. "This, however . . . hmm. It would be quite funny if I let you have it, but I'm not quite that irresponsible. Now, it was nice talking to you. You're rather slow for one who carries Prometheus's blood, but not every child can live up to expectations. Hmm . . ." She tilted her head to the side, reached out, grabbed his chin, and turned his head around. "You do look an awful lot like Poseidon, though. If you have any of him in you, then it's only to be expected."

Releasing him, she patted him on the back and began to slowly, deliberately inch away.

Does she want me to—

"Wait . . ." Luke called after her.

She smiled. "Yes?"

"Um—"

She clapped, and the circlet vanished from her hand. "Of course! You need to be paid. I'm not a thief, I'll have you know. What is it that you want for selling it to me?"

"I c—"

"Oh, never mind." She cut him off the second he opened his mouth. "You kids never know what's best for you. I'll decide," she said impatiently. Her eyes raked across his form.

Feeling naked under her gaze, as if his every secret and every thought were laid bare, he shifted uncomfortably.

Finally, her eyes landed on his sword. Revealing a row of pristine white teeth, she held her hand out, and the blade ripped itself free from Luke's hand, passed through his protective bubble, and landed in her hands.

"Oh, my. This is quite the find you have here. It's . . ." She closed her eyes, and the sword lit up a brilliant blue. ". . . been funneling mana into you, hasn't it?"

"It has," Luke said, his mouth suddenly feeling very dry.

"I don't know whose or how long ago, but I can feel the traces of a higher being's mana . . . Well, higher than you. You lot came here to kill Tyrisa, yes?"

"We did."

"Good. Very good." She let go of the blade, and it flew from her hand and back to Luke. "This blade, he thirsts for death, and death I shall give you the means to deliver. Eat this."

A single pomegranate seed appeared inches in front of Luke. Inadvertently, his mouth began to water, and hunger unlike any he had ever experienced suffused his being. Every cell in his body came to life and began throbbing in desire. Swallowing the spit in his now too-wet mouth, he defied every instinct he had and turned away from it.

"What will this do?" he asked.

"Where's the fun in telling? Eat it and you'll find out, or don't and stay here until the demon chews through the shield and your friends come and rescue you. Either way"—the circlet once again appeared in her hands—"we're even."

CHAPTER 15

A Different Seed

T a-ta." The mysterious woman waved him goodbye, and then, before Luke's eyes, vanished into a warm gust of wind that washed over him, leaving behind a strong smell of popcorn and butter. It was not at all what he expected, and it left him feeling even hungrier. His stomach churned and grumbled loudly, like he hadn't eaten in days.

What the fuck just happened . . . What the fuck is happening?

Luke blinked slowly and wiped the drool escaping his mouth with the end of his sleeve, staring blankly at the ruby-colored pomegranate seed suspended in the air inches from him. It shimmered in the dim light of the barrier surrounding the castle, and the whole world seemed to be reflected in the vivid, juicy, gemlike red kernel.

It somehow looked more real than anything else in his surroundings—as if it possessed its own gravity.

With a tremendous effort of will, he shook his head and lightly slapped his own cheeks, doing his utmost to stay in control and not give in to his gluttony.

The moment he did, he felt his Arcana stat begin to steadily tick up, one point, then two. A few seconds later, it ticked up again, and gradually the draw of the seed on him began to weaken. Not by much, but enough to realize that he had been staring at it like an idiot for perhaps longer than was appropriate in an active battlefield. Even his protective talisman had expired.

Heart hammering in his chest, he scrambled and, fishing around his pockets, ripped the tab off another one.

What the actual fuck.

Tearing his eyes away from the seed, he looked at everyone in the barrier and beyond it, and just like Cybele had said, none of them were any wiser. Even the two guards standing beside him appeared completely indifferent to him having a minor panic attack in his bubble, and both were oblivious to the sinfully delicious seed hanging in the air an inch from his mouth.

He took a step back.

Is . . . is it getting closer?

And . . . wasn't she one of the guards? How are there two again? What's even real?

He took a deep breath, forcing himself to think rationally.

I've never heard of a Cybele before, but that doesn't mean she's not a god. Hell, I'd never heard of Aeolus, and he was a god, so I can't rule that out as a possibility. Yeah, that would be stupid. Let's just assume that whoever she is, she's a god. Or, at the very least, close enough to it that it doesn't matter to me at this point.

He scanned the castle grounds again. Whatever spell she had worked on the Skyscar clan and even the Argonauts, it appeared that it would hide the presence of the gift she had left him for a while longer.

If it was a gift at all.

Many times since he had come to Theos, Luke had come to regret his limited knowledge of mythology, and he suspected that he would continue to do so long into the future, but there were some things he did remember.

The story of how Persephone came to be the queen of the underworld was one such tale.

In the myth, she ate a single pomegranate seed, and because of it was eternally trapped in the underworld. Until her mom broke her out? There was also winter? Which . . . This isn't going to get me anywhere.

I have no clue whether the myth was Hades just being an asshole or if there's some esoteric rule about not eating food in the underworld or a combination of both. Either way, I haven't heard about anything other than an oathstone that can compel me to do anything, and the seed looks nothing like that. More than that, I'm not actually in the underworld—I think. It would really be fucking something if this is the afterlife, I'm still dead, and this is all a dream, but—NO. Fuck that, this is happening, focus, Luke. No spiraling.

He slapped his cheeks again and frowned in disgust as a string of thick saliva connected his hand to his face.

"Okay. That's enough. Thirty seconds before I drop my spell. I have places to be, and I'm not going to hide you from all these gazes forever. Eat it, stomp on it, put it in a storage ring, do something!" Cybele's voice rang out in his ear.

"Wha—" He snapped his head in the direction the voice had come from in search of her figure. A fruitless effort. She could be anyone, anywhere . . .

"Twenty-nine. Twenty-eight. Twenty-seven—" Her voice began counting down impatiently.

"Okay, okay . . . I'll—" Luke nodded to the air and lifted his hands in surrender, not even a little surprised that the woman was still lurking.

Cyzicus had long since disabused him of the idea that he would be able to sense when a higher-tier individual was around, and somewhere in the back of his head, he knew that sneaking around would be way too much fun to never do it if he had the ability. The Seed would tell him eventually, but its timing was almost comical, and it never, not once, told him when the danger had actually passed.

Focus. He shook his head. *Is this thing fucking with me?* His stomach grumbled again. *Stupid question, of course it is. How much, though?*

"Twenty-two." Her voice rang in his ear once again.

A tight ball of nerves formed a pit in his stomach. Stretching his hands forward, he gingerly plucked the seed out of the air.

A rush of mana seeped into his fingers, and his mouth almost dropped to the floor as his Constitution suddenly went up a point.

Instinct possessed him.

Slowly, he brought the pomegranate seed to his mouth, rested it on his tongue, and sealed his lips around it. For a brief moment, he considered inventorying the pomegranate seed but discarded the idea nearly as soon as it came to him.

Whoever the woman was, she could see into storage rings. He had no reference for how easy, difficult, or common that feat was, but if she could find some random artifact in one, sneak past any protections the Rebel had put on it, and find what she was looking for, then it was safe to assume that she would notice something as obvious as the pomegranate seed she had given him vanishing into something that wasn't his stomach right after he put it in his mouth.

The last thing he wanted was her to find out about his greatest secret. Not when she had deduced basically every other one he had moments after she met him.

His shoulders sank in mouthwatering bliss. Even more mana gushed from the seed and sank into his tongue. This time, every single one of his stats surged over two points, and the rich taste of the fruit spread across every taste bud.

I could probably still put it in a storage ring . . . but I don't have one . . . What am I thinking? His thoughts were a jumbled mess that darted from biting into and not. Uncertain even as he placed it between his molars and prepared to crush it.

A burst of deliciousness, tastier than anything he had ever sensed before, bloomed in his mouth as one of his teeth accidentally made a small prick in its smooth shell.

Fuck it.

He closed the space between his teeth.

"That's a good lad. I'll be going now. Until next time," she said, and he felt a soft hand rub his back and the scent of buttery popcorn once again wafted through the air.

The seed dissolved into mana—something he hadn't even known was possible.

A veritable river of energy ran down his throat and into his heart. With his blood, it was carried into every cell in his body.

Every stat he had suddenly began to tick up. Eyes wide and head suddenly clear, he opened his status.

Status | Skills | Quests | Inventory

Name: Lukas King

Tier: Warrior

Bloodline: Eyes of Insight

Mana: 499,000.05 / 2,343 [178 seconds]

Rate: 17% per hour

> Strength: 21 > 36
> Agility: 15 > 41
> Constitution: 50 > 66
> Arcana: 50 > 71
> Stat Points: 19
> Charges: 7/10

He took one look at it, ripped the perforated tab off another protective talisman, and leaped into action.

While the improvements to his stats across the board were nothing short of astronomical, the most significant change was in his available mana. It was maxed out, and if the ticker meant what he thought it did, he didn't have much time to spare.

A cocky grin stretched across his face.

He knew just what to spend the mana on, too.

The First Stance sang its song in his head, and the First Truth of Death created ghostly apparitions of every single warrior in his sight—showing him exactly where each of them would be.

Like a pane of glass shattering, the illusion that kept everyone ignorant to the comings and goings of the suspected goddess fell apart.

The two warriors stationed beside him were the first to notice his move, and the first to face the effects of his technique. Both of them lashed out at the spot he had occupied moments before, one with his spear and another with his daggers.

Both missed him entirely, and Luke didn't even bother attacking them as he raced toward the Rebel, only vaguely aware of the guard with a spear accidentally impaling his compatriot.

Poor amateurs. They aren't even using talismans.

A pained yell had every eye inside the barrier and out immediately focused on him.

He grinned back at them.

They launched explosive talismans at him, but seeing them coming moments before they were even fired, he maneuvered himself so that each burst behind him and added to his momentum as he shot toward their leader. Who, for her part, seemed ambivalent toward his charge.

The man dressed in golden armor stared down at him imperiously, and blades of wind formed in the air around him.

Showing Luke, for the first time, the might of a god's bloodline.

Impressive, but . . . He grinned at the befuddled look on the warrior's face.

One blade of air after another shattered harmlessly off his shield and Luke soon realized that the man's attacks, while strong for his tier, were of no consequence to him. Warrior-tier attacks wouldn't break a Hero-tier barrier.

Realizing that Luke wouldn't be slowed down by his attacks, the man shot toward him. Luke's blade pierced through a thin gap in his armor and stabbed him right above his pelvis. Blood splattered onto him, and Luke casually activated a Warrior-tier explosive talisman right next to his head. The concussive force did no damage in and of itself, absorbed as it was by his armor, but it succeeded in breaking his opponent's concentration.

He tumbled toward the ground and in the process cleared Luke's path toward the would-be empress.

Ducking between three attacks, his gaze met her single eye.

She snarled at him.

Her ghost moved past her body and to his right.

He positioned his sword in her path.

Her blood once again sprayed into the air as her last remaining limb tumbled to the ground.

The whole world seemed to hold its breath, and a look of fear flashed across her face, vanishing as quickly as it came.

Her head blurred, and even with her apparition warning him of her attack, Luke didn't have enough time to react as her forehead slammed into his bubble. The force of her blow sent him rocketing back toward the barrier encircling her castle and nearly into Blinky's eye-covered tentacles.

Desperately, he gushed mana out from his body and latched onto the space around him. He barely managed to come to a stop before he was removed from the field of battle entirely.

She screamed incoherently.

A tornado swirling with blades of wind formed a shield around her. One after another, torrents of sharp wind freed themselves from her storm and lashed out in random directions.

He ripped the tab off the talismans Heracles had given him with increased urgency, while funneling tens of thousands of points of mana into the space around him. The effort kept him rooted in the air even as her allies who were unable to endure the wind were thrown out of their own castle and into the waiting tendrils of Rex's demon.

Her attacks, unlike her clan members', were actually capable of breaking through his defense. Not that it mattered.

He was undeterred by her onslaught, and, gritting his teeth, he inched toward her, ducking and weaving between each attack before it was unleashed at the direction of his technique.

Just a few more seconds, he thought, watching her carefully. *She's almost out of steam.*

He was so close to victory he could practically taste it. She was weak, her face was pale, her flight unsteady, and blood dripped from the wounds he had dealt her.

Suddenly, the moment came.

Her cyclone flagged, and blood spilled from her mouth. Even still, she charged toward his waiting blade.

Only this time it wasn't her arm or her ribs that his sword bit into but her heart.

"I hope someone eats your soul," Luke whispered as the light faded from her eyes and more mana than he knew what to do with flooded his body.

CHAPTER 16

Her Dying Breath

The instant Luke's blade pierced the Rebel's chest, a hush fell over the world, from those still aboard the *Argo* to every warrior flying in the sky within the barrier. All of them stood still and quietly witnessed the dying breath of a hero.

They listened with rapt ears to the wet *shluk* of his sword as it sank into her chest and slid out of her back.

Watched with unblinking eyes the way her limbless form slumped on a blood-stained golden blade and then fell lifeless to the ground. Like every other thing that had lived and died over the eons of Theos's existence, and no different than they themselves expected to die.

What they had seen was incomprehensible.

To most of them, a hero was an unattainable desire and an unbeatable foe.

A hero was a great power that ruled empires. A hero was someone who held others' lives in the palms of their hands.

It was something they needed to mind their words around. It was something that you tiptoed around lest you provoked its sleeping fury. It was something that they needed to fear. To obey and, perhaps, even worship.

A hero was not something that could be killed by the likes of them. Let alone by a man who had days ago been a mortal.

To Luke, however, killing a hero was nothing, but pure, undiluted suffering.

The Rebel's mana was countless tiny blades worming and wriggling in a space between the physical and spiritual. In the natural order of things, it was above him. It punished him for his disobedience. For reaching above his station and defying the laws that ruled the world of cultivators. After all, it wasn't an ant's place to trample an elephant, no matter how weakened it was.

He wasn't a stranger to pain. Far from it, in fact.

His ribs had been broken. His limbs shot with arrows. He had boiled himself alive more times that he cared to remember. He had endured the Mask of a Thousand Faces remaking his body into his current form.

Even so, nothing, not even the Warrior-tier mana of the sky serpent, had hurt this much.

Still, he held on. Tears of blood dripped from his eyes, and he waited.

Waited patiently for the God Seed to rouse from its slumber and collect the mana that was wreaking havoc on his body and tell him how many stat points he had earned for doing the impossible. Every moment that passed felt like hours, but he waited. Quietly, and expressionless. His mind absent of any thoughts, one excruciating breath escaped his lips after another.

His grip on the space around him slipped and unconsciously he funneled mana into the air-walking boots, preventing himself from falling to the ground. The drop by itself wouldn't harm him, but losing control of his mana was tantamount to admitting that he had been weakened.

Even with the agony that he was in and his mind empty of all thoughts, he was unwilling to show the toll killing the hero had taken on him.

Not when he was still surrounded by potential enemies, and not when he had spent so much time and energy making sure his secrets were kept. Even if the secret of his sword was exposed today, it wouldn't be because he didn't try his best.

His bubble flickered around him, signaling that it was about to burst. Something was off, but he was in too much pain to spare the mental capital that it would take to figure out what.

So, it was with twitching fingers that he reached into his pocket and pulled out a protective talisman. Blood oozed from his nail beds, staining the paper red, but, ignoring it, he moved it to his mouth and bit off the perforated tab.

A fresh barrier sprang into existence around him.

He waited, unaware of every Skyscar clan member watching him with bated breath and oblivious to the thoughts running through their heads.

It was in silence that one second ticked by after another, but the relief he was anticipating never came, and neither did the notification telling him how many stat points he had earned from his kill.

Eventually, after what felt like literal years, the Seed broke its silence.

Quest Alert: Name Your Blade

He stared unthinkingly and with gratitude at the prompt in front of him.

It looked both familiar and strange. Crisp and raw, compared to his blurred vision, and in the depths of his misery, he focused on it with every fiber of his being. Through the cloud of pain that was his world, it was all that let him keep his sanity.

It took him an embarrassing amount of time to decipher the letters, and longer still to learn the meaning of the words the characters formed.

He had known, of course, that he needed to name his sword at this moment. He had read and reread the quest countless times just on their journey here, the same way he did with every quest.

He even had a few names in mind. He'd known killing her would hurt, but nothing had prepared him for the pain that he was feeling now.

He also knew, in his heart, that each name he had thought about before, and the one he had tentatively decided on prior, was wrong. Each of them lacked a weight that was necessary for what was demanded from him, and even with all the pain, he knew that giving his sword the wrong name would not end well.

Blood dripped from his nose and eyes as he forcibly came up with one name after another. None of them were good enough. None of them *meant* enough.

Color washed away from the world. All-consuming fear reared its ugly head, and a cold epiphany rang like thunder in his mind as the will of the world itself focused his attention on him. He would die, right here, right now, if he didn't pick a name, and soon.

Not even the Seed would help him. Not against the will of eternity and the primordial energies of order.

What he was facing wasn't a foe he could kill. Or a challenge that needed to be overcome.

It was reflection and clarity. About who he was and whom he wanted to be.

Like the Paragon's Path all those months ago, it was a price baked into the fabric of reality itself, but unlike it, it wasn't something he could deny or shy away from. It wasn't a call for action; it was an ultimatum. A price for his transgression.

It was do or die. There would be no in between if he failed. Merely being trapped at a tier until his body withered away from age was nothing compared to what awaited him if he failed the tribulation.

A name, he realized, was heavy. It needed to encompass everything, and it needed to be able to grow as he grew.

His struggle to climb toward divinity. His majesty when he became a god. The acts, just and unjust, that he would commit with it. They were all elements that needed to be addressed and could not be ignored.

Naming it Ascalon, or Excelsior, Dawnbreaker, Reaper, Soul Eater, or a dozen other cool-sounding names wasn't what the quest had been about. Neither had it been about killing a hero. It was meant to lead him to this moment.

And as the blackness encroached on his vision, he realized that he didn't know what to do.

Rex's demon peeled herself free of the golden bubble, and a moment later the barrier fell. Nel's griffin, Lukeus's Pegasus, Heracles, Jason, and a dozen other Argonauts flew through the air and encircled him. Someone deployed a talisman that created a massive bubble around them, pushing away all the Skyscar clan members.

"Stay back!" Jason hissed, his voice barely above a whisper. Not to the bald warriors of the Rebel's clan who had begun to flee the second the barrier fell, but to the other Argonauts.

"What's happening to h—" Rex started to say, only for Maleager to shut him up with an angry stare.

Unaware of his surroundings, and with shaking hands, Luke lifted the sword into the air and stared at its razor edge.

The name, he realized, had to reflect not just him but the blade. It wasn't alive, but it also wasn't unfeeling. It would reject a name that it deemed unsuitable, and if it did, he would die.

As the object of his first quest, Bellerophon's Blade had become his companion moments after he had arrived on Theos. Even before he had picked it from the walls in the armory of the Luminous Sky Society it had become his, and its existence had guided his decisions since.

He suspected that the Seed had even chosen his body just for its proximity to the weapon.

Risking both Nefkha's greed and discovery by Arke to give him a blade belonging to a failed god. A sword the demigod had neglected in favor of other, perhaps better weapons. A blade that had wilted after his death and gathered dust for centuries before it ended up on a wall on a tiny, insignificant island, belonging to a tiny, insignificant society. Where it was constantly passed over by insignificant disciples and elders. None of whom were wise to its true potential.

They thought it a vain accessory. From the man he had bought it from to Arya and even Cyzicus. No one until Cybele had seen it for what it truly was.

No one could see the desire it held—to not only reclaim the heights it had fallen from, but to transcend them with its wielder.

It was its ability to effortlessly cut all his foes that had kept him alive. It was its ability to siphon the mana of those he killed that had allowed him to so rapidly climb through the ranks of the Mortal tier.

Even with the Seed, a Primordial-tier artifact, the sword was the greatest accelerant of his success thus far. It was the greatest weapon he could ask for.

The greatest, huh.

His lips stretched across his face, revealing a row of red-stained teeth. Blood dribbled from his mouth and dripped onto the ruined castle below. He smacked his lips, and, ignoring the taste of copper in his mouth and the waves of pain shooting through his body, he tightened his grip on the sword.

He was close.

I'm a paragon. A being that will stand greater than any other at the end of my path. My weapon can't be anything less.

Suddenly the answer seemed oh so obvious. There was only one name that felt right, and as destiny would have it, it was a name that was, in a way, already his.

In the past, it had belonged to a boy that a fisherman had found floating at sea. A boy who had died pathetically after being chased away by some debt collectors. One who hadn't even known of the existence of gods or of his own divine heritage. Nevertheless, he had died with a desire.

To hold his own destiny in his next life. Just as Luke would do with his new life on Theos. Just as his sword had desired after Zeus killed its last wielder.

"I . . . Lukas King, paragon, warrior, slayer of monsters and heroes—name you . . . Maximus," Luke said, the words, strong, loud, and clear, forming unbidden on his tongue and reverberating in the air with a mysterious importance.

Pain instantly gave way to numbness.

The blade flickered between azure and gold before shining a blinding white. A link snapped into existence between him and it, and mana, both his and the Rebel's, flooded from his body and into the sword.

"He's—" Heracles put his hand on Atalanta's mouth, preventing her from speaking as he looked at Luke with wide eyes.

"Oh, for fuck's sake! He's done it—just give the poor young lad a healing potion already!" A woman wrinkled her nose and slapped Heracles up the side of his head.

"Grandma?" the son of Zeus said in surprise. "What are you doing here?"

"What am I doing here? What are you doing tearing holes into the Aether?"

"Um . . . we had to get through the . . ."

"NO EXCUSES!"

"I'm sorry," he mumbled under his breath, seemingly cowed by her glare.

Luke, like the rest of them completely unaware of Cybele's continued presence and her short exchange with Heracles, fell from the air, only to be caught by Nel's griffin.

No stat points then, huh? he thought miserably as his vision faded to black, only vaguely aware of someone stuffing the end of a vial into his mouth.

762 Stat Points

Never mind, he thought, a grin stretching across his face.

CHAPTER 17

Spoils of War

When Luke came to, he was back in his room in Cyzicus's castle, wearing the same clothes he had fallen unconscious in.

Rubbing the sleep out of his eyes, he immediately shot to his feet a moment later, a protective talisman appearing in his hands and encasing him in a golden bubble. His heart thumped in his chest in panic as he reconciled the last thing he remembered to his current situation.

It was only upon seeing the familiar surroundings that he gradually began calming down. He took a deep breath, just taking a moment to bask in the magnitude of what had happened.

"Holy shit," he whispered.

A grin slowly formed on his face.

He had killed a hero, avenged Sophia, upgraded his sword, and, to top it all off, earned hundreds of stat points. In the span of a couple of days, he'd gone from the beginning of the Warrior tier to around a quarter of the way through.

Not bad at all, he thought approvingly. *Super dangerous, but when everything works out that well, I can't really complain. No risk, no reward and all that.* He clenched and unclenched his hand, taking a moment to just bask in his newfound strength.

A single stat point in the Warrior tier went much further than one in the Mortal tier. With a ratio of one to one hundred, he had known that intellectually, but feeling it only made that more real and left him eager to test his strength.

Soon, he affirmed to himself, already planning on challenging every warrior he could think of, from Clite to Nel and even Heracles. He wanted a true measure of his abilities.

The prospect made him both excited and nervous. He was impressed and satisfied with how much he had grown, but knowing the distance he had covered and what still remained . . . Well, it was hard not to feel insignificant in the face of powers so much greater than he.

Even so, he was happy with what he had. The gains he had made were nothing short of astronomical, and cultivation was a marathon, not a sprint—mostly.

Let's see . . . He felt for the Seed planted in his soul and went to open his status.

Instead, a glint of gold caught his eyes, and his gaze immediately locked onto his sword—*Maximus*—resting on a polished wooden rack on the other side of the room. Almost in a trance, he flew toward it.

It looked different.

Since he had bought it in the Luminous Sky Society, Luke had lost count of how many hours he had spent staring at the beautiful blade. He was intimately familiar with every nook, edge, and bend. Then, once he had killed his first sky serpent with Nel over a month ago, he had right away noticed the thin blue line that ran down the groove in the center of it.

The changes this time were much more significant.

The blade had gained a foot in length and looked both graceful and menacing—where that extra length had come from, he didn't know. Considering all the other ridiculousness he had borne witness to since he arrived on Theos, however, the added mass didn't concern him too much. Chalking it up to another mystery of mana to be looked into at a later date, he resumed his inspection of his upgraded blade while making a mental note to start keeping a journal of questions, lest he forget what he needed an answer to.

The gem encrusted in its pommel shimmered a little brighter than he remembered, and the blue line in its groove appeared to have deepened a little. As if the color had sunk a little farther into the blade.

It looks like an entirely different sword. He nodded to himself, feeling a tad relieved.

He didn't expect to run into anyone from Carim or maybe one of the handful of people from the society who might recognize the sword. Nor were gold blades uncommon among cultivators, but it was something he had been concerned about in the past. Not enough to never use his sword again, but enough to give him minor bursts of anxiety at night on the rare occasion when he didn't exhaust himself enough to fall asleep the second his head hit his pillow.

I probably should have changed my name when I got here, though. He sighed deeply. *It is what it is. Luke is a fairly common name, so it's not like anyone will be able to track me just based on that. Moreover, I look completely different, and now with my sword looking nothing like it used to . . . I'm even more in the clear.*

But did I really tell everyone my full name . . . and that I was a paragon? He slapped his forehead in irritation. He knew instinctively, especially after having almost died, that he had achieved more by naming his sword than met the eye, and that the words he had spoken had had to be said, but even still, doing so left him feeling more exposed than he would have liked.

Couldn't she have just died when I stabbed her in bed? Instead . . . He shook his head clear of the what-ifs while he ruminated over the rest of what happened.

Cybele's intervention, the pomegranate seed, suddenly maxed-out mana—it all felt so alien and bizarre to him now. As if the whole thing had been a fever dream, but the sword sitting before him was all the evidence he needed. It really had happened, and he would need to deal with the fallout. Whatever that looked like.

Not great . . . but not the end of the world, either. Luke or Lukas King, it doesn't really matter. It's also not like "king" means anything in this world's language . . . unless it does? I haven't heard the word used, but—hmm. Another thought sprang to his mind.

But then . . . don't a lot of English words have Greek origins? The language I'm speaking isn't actually Greek . . . but Zeus is as Greek a name as names gets. Maybe.

I never thought about it before, but were Arke and Aeolus speaking in English when he abducted my soul? Obviously not, but I could understand everything they said. I didn't get Max's memories of the language until I took over his body though. Hell, I didn't even have the Seed in my soul at that point, so I can't lean on that for an explanation. Could the other souls understand what they were saying, too, or was it just me?

It could be a property of the Aether, or is it something else? Neither Arke nor Aeolus seemed to think we wouldn't understand them. Arke even gloated after killing him . . . She wouldn't do that if we didn't understand her . . . Would she?

He shook his head and added it to another list of questions he should probably find the answers to. He suspected, though, that any questions that concerned the Aether would have to wait until he was much stronger. Heracles meddling with it had after all drawn to them someone much more powerful than he could even begin to fathom.

Training his eyes back on the sword, he realized that the connection that had snapped into place when he named it still existed. It wasn't obvious. Quiet, if he had to describe it, but noticeable when the blade was at the forefront of his mind.

Unconsciously he eased the hold he had on his mana, and, like water winding down a river, it drifted down the path that existed between him and the newly named weapon.

The second his mana touched the sword, it began to glow an iridescent azure. Awareness blossomed in his mind.

He could feel Maximus. The same way he felt his own hands, and on instinct, he let his mana surge out from within the bounds of his sword and commanded it to latch on to the space around the weapon.

A grin came over his face as it rose into the air and slowly began to glide toward his waiting palm. He had seen other warriors telekinetically move objects, and while he hadn't had the time to test it for himself, he had an inkling of how it was done.

Feeling his sword in the air, he realized that what he was doing, while similar in result, was much more impressive than the standard brand of Warrior-tier telekinesis.

His sword had become a conduit for his mana. He didn't know quite what that meant for him, but as the blade readily absorbed the resource and *held it*, and his own regeneration kicked in and began to fill his reserves, he couldn't help but grow excited. It was like a battery, and something told him he was just scratching the surface of what it was capable of. As his mana filled it, an inkling of what it was began to emerge in his mind . . . a hunger, a desire to consume and grow and—

Someone knocked on his door and broke him out of his musing. Before he could answer, the handle turned and a middle-aged woman dressed in white robes confidently strode in, lugging a cart behind her.

"Hi?" Luke cocked his head to the side.

She rapidly grew pale, and her mouth opened and closed, her eyes darting from the sword in his hand to where his feet hung a foot above the ground.

Clutching the side of her robes, she bowed until her spine was parallel to the ground.

"Forgive me, Elder. I thought you were asleep. I came to clean your r—"

"It's fine," Luke said, awkwardly scratching the back of his head. "Would you mind coming back later? I want to rest for a little while longer," he said evenly.

"Of course, Elder. I'll inform the emperor that you've awakened," she said hurriedly, and then before he could respond, she rapidly pulled the cart back and disappeared down the corridor.

Shaking his head in amusement, he found a sheath for his blade, and strapping it on, he slid the sword into it. He had plenty of time to learn of its new capabilities, especially with the tournament months away, but now wasn't it.

Taking another deep breath, he looked around his room again and touched down onto the ground. It was time to face the music. Striding toward the door, he rested his hand on the knob before suddenly stopping in his tracks.

A single thought rang in his mind: the final part of the quest.

The Rebel's storage ring.

Patting himself down, he reached into his pocket and sagged in relief when he pulled out two rings. One had belonged to the hero and the other to the warrior he had killed.

Thanking whoever it was that had moved him for not taking them, he turned them both over in his hands. It was obvious which one belonged to whom. Both were simple, unmarked bands of metal. One gold and one silver.

The silver one belonged to the bald teen he had killed, while the gold one belonged to the Rebel—that was the real prize. Whether they belonged to a warrior or a hero, though, both of them were dangerous. Booby-trapped if what he knew was right.

I guess I could just give them to Cyzicus and see if he can get into them. It's not like anything that's in there is going to implicate me in any way.

But . . .

An unwilling expression spread across his face before he shook it off.

I've been cautious so long that it's becoming a habit . . . That's not good. They left the rings with me, and I'm the one that killed her. I can't really speak for every Argonaut, but I don't think any of the people here would rob me.

Besides . . . Cybele probably took the one thing of value that was in the ring anyway . . . Maybe even what the Seed wanted me to get. I wonder what that circlet was? A crown of some sort? She mentioned Clan Skyscar being descendants of Ouranos . . . which is wow . . . and then said something about him imprisoning his wife here. If I remember my myths right, that would be Gaia.

Gaia, a crown, and the descendant of a hopefully dead god, trying to rule over where another hopefully dead goddess was imprisoned eons ago.

Considering that the island is attacked by earthborne . . . I doubt it's a coincidence.

Is that the curse? he wondered absently, lightly rubbing his thumb over the ring, careful to keep his mana fully contained. *Was the circlet something to do with the island? Is that why the Rebel was trying so hard and going so far to dethrone Cyzicus?*

Resolving to bring up the issue with the man himself, he put the two rings back into his pocket before stopping once again.

On a whim, he activated his inventory and attempted to send both objects inside. Fully expecting to fail like he had every other time.

Instead, they both went in.

Huh.

CHAPTER 18

Even More Spoils

'm guessing I can put them in now because the people they belonged to are dead. Hmm.

I've been reluctant to really test my inventory, mostly because I don't want my secrets getting out, but this is interesting—this kind of proves I need to spend some time on it. It should be easier now, though, Luke thought as he retraced his steps back to his bed. Opening up his inventory screen, he surrounded himself with mana and let himself fall slowly onto the bed.

Status | Skills | Quests | **Inventory**

Storage Ring (unbound) (armed)

Tier—Hero

A storage ring created by Emperor Cyzicus of Sylcra.

Items:

[Expand]

Storage Ring (unbound) (armed)

Tier—Saint

A storage ring created by Primarch Asius of Samos.

Items:

[Expand]

Reading through the descriptions, he had a hard time keeping a smile off his face, even as the details and the fact that they were armed gave him pause. Truthfully, he had already suspected that to be the case.

The warrior's ring having been made by Cyzicus wasn't a surprise, either, considering that the emperor ran a merit exchange. It wouldn't be strange if the warrior had traded for it prior to the Rebel returning, or perhaps even received it as a gift from an older warrior, considering his young age. Cyzicus had been ruling Sylcra for centuries, at the least, and there were probably an uncountable number of items he had crafted floating around the island.

What was a surprise was that the Seed had identified the creator at all.

Thinking back, Luke realized it hadn't done that before—but by itself, it wasn't a huge concern.

The descriptions it provided tended to be all over the place, and Luke had given up on trying to solve the mystery of what the Seed told him and didn't tell him. What it said was what it said, and up until now, at least, it hadn't withheld anything that Luke would have wanted to know—with a single notable exception.

Knowing that Cyzicus had crafted his boots and would be able to recognize him from them definitely would have changed how he interacted with the man. At the very least, he would have kept them stowed in his inventory in spite of the utility they provided.

After all, the way he thought about it, the whole point of leaving Carim was to get out from under Nefkha's thumb. If someone could discover that connection, then that just meant he was replacing one vulnerability with another.

As it was, his boots had allowed the emperor to not only know where he came from but instantly determine who had taught him his techniques. Which had prompted the man to invite him to compete for him in the tournament—an invitation that had since led him to rapidly advance through the Mortal tier and make substantial progress in the Warrior tier not long after.

It was far from a bad result. Cyzicus had proven to be a trustworthy ally, and the events had served the Seed's purpose of guiding him toward godhood, but a chill ran down Luke's spine regardless.

I already knew that the Seed was stacking the deck in more ways than one. Putting me on Carim in the first place is an example of that, but . . .

Frowning, he looked at the name, Primarch Asius of Samos, with renewed interest.

I should be paying more attention to this kind of thing going forward.

The situation with the shoes worked out in my favor, but if it's telling me about this person, then I have to assume it's significant. Considering that Clan Skyscar are descendants from one of Zeus's predecessors . . . Well, I don't really know enough to speculate. All I can really do is keep an ear out and avoid this Asius if I can. Just being aware of the connection, now that I know about it, is bound to be useful.

I'll also ask Cyzicus if it's even safe to use the ring—assuming there's a way to get into it, and if I even can with its tier being so high.

The last thing I want is this guy doing what Cyzicus did and recognizing me as the man who killed one of his buddies. I'll probably be fine considering I have the God Seed, but still, not really worth the hassle, and if it makes me use a charge?

Yeah, no, thanks.

I wonder what a primarch is, though? If nothing else, it sounds more distinguished than an emperor, and considering that Asius is creating and presumably handing out Saint-tier items, stronger than one, too.

The obvious answer would be a Saint-tier equivalent of an emperor but with bigger territory. If I'm being honest, though, I'm not even sure what an emperor really is.

Sure, they rule the land and the people, but didn't Cyzicus say he could teleport around the island because he was one? Called it a perk of the job, if I'm remembering right.

Shaking his head slightly, Luke discarded the train of thought for the moment, making a note to research it later, preferably in a library if he ever found one and had the time to peruse it.

Books, as far as he knew, wouldn't grow suspicious at the strange gaps in his knowledge.

The subjects themselves weren't likely to be taboo or anything of the sort, but any knowledge accrued from the Seed was knowledge that he couldn't explain having, and a single slip to the wrong person could have consequences that he didn't want to deal with. Things had turned out fine so far, but it best not to push his luck. As far as he was concerned, paranoia was a virtue. At least until he became strong enough to not care.

Now that I think about it, though, if I spend enough time with the Argonauts, people will think that one of them let something slip. If nothing else, it's a good excuse for any random bits of trivia I have bouncing around in my head, but it isn't an infallible excuse.

It's probably a good idea to ask them questions while they're here, too. As travelers I bet they're more likely to not question the quirks in what I know. Hopefully.

Taking a deep breath, he scratched the back of his head and stared nervously off into space before firmly putting his worries aside for the moment.

Rabbit holes of existential dread definitely put a damper on his mood, but the thought of all the loot he had waiting for him was more than enough to make up for it.

Best for last, so warrior first, he thought, and, prodding the Seed, he expanded the contents of the storage ring.

Scrolling through all the items, he couldn't help but be disappointed.

Whoever the teen had been, he was poor. Incredibly so.

Did this guy spend every dime he had on the ring? Luke thought miserably as he skimmed through one description after another. The most valuable items in his possession were three vials of Warrior-tier healing potions. Other than that, it was just small bunches of talismans, a Warrior-tier bow, a bunch of arrows, and some odds and ends, like camping equipment, preserved food, spare clothes, and a veritable armory of mortal weapons. Things like spears, swords, and shields. Not useless by any stretch, but they were of limited utility to the current Luke.

I guess the ring itself isn't a bad prize . . . but fuck. Am I spoiled? I would have to be, right? All this time, I never thought too much of it, but I've been chugging down fortunes in healing potions, and I don't even know how much all the talismans I have are worth.

Collapsing the list, he pulled the ring out of his inventory. Briefly, he considered putting his mana into it, in spite of the ring being armed, before shaking his head and immediately discarding the thought as stupid.

Besides, risking injuries for the trash this guy kept isn't really worth it.

Stuffing it into his pocket, he began to look through the Rebel's ring.

Status | Skills | Quests | **Inventory**

Storage Ring (unbound) (armed)

Tier—Saint

A storage ring created by Primarch Asius of Samos.

Items:

Limitless Thunder Bow

Tier—Hero

An artifact forged by Primarch Asius of Samos. Allows users to mold their mana into lightning darts.

Blastguard

Tier—Saint

An artifact forged by Primarch Asius of Samos. Reduces damage done by explosive talismans.

Sasis Amulet

Tier—Hero

Prevents injuries from worsening at the cost of mana.

A Guide to Sheep Husbandry

Tier—Warrior

A journal written by Cyclops Sophia of Ovesis, detailing the steps required to breed sheep with mana-rich milk.

Flame Blade

Tier—Hero

A sword, enchanted with both durability and sharpness, along with the ability to alternate between tangible steel and intangible flame.

Blood

Tier—Hero

A vial of blood belonging to a cyclops.

Headless Female Corpse (Cyclops) x1

Tier—Hero

Headless Male Corpse (Human) x 3

Tier—Warrior

Headless Female Corpse (Human) x 16

Tier—Warrior

Headless Female Corpse (Human) x 13

Tier—Mortal

Headless Male Corpse (Human) x 4

Tier—Mortal

Teleportation Plate x 9

Tier—Hero

A clay plate that, when broken and filled with sufficient mana, allows for teleportation to a preset location.

[...]

Talisman Paper x 5,000

Tier—Mortal

Luke skimmed through the entire list of hundreds of objects with disgust before backing out of his inventory and staring at the ceiling. In his excitement, he had forgotten exactly whom the ring belonged to.

In spite of her macabre liking for keeping the headless corpses of her victims and allies, it was a good haul. He just couldn't bring himself to be happy about it.

I should have expected it . . . but for fuck's sake. Did she really have to keep so many bodies in her ring? And why did the Seed want me to take it? he thought, his mind flashing back to the circlet.

This stuff is valuable, and there's no questioning that. Just the amulet and the blast-guard alone increase my survivability by tremendous amounts. Especially considering how well they'll synergize with my mana levels once I'm back at the top of my tier.

Except, as good as they are, they aren't game changers. My sword is going to be with me for my entire journey, and the mask will let me hide myself whenever I need to. These things, while useful, are all at the Hero and Saint tier . . . which is high, yes, but I'll outgrow them.

Shaking his head, he called the ring from his inventory before closing his fist around it.

Or I guess, this is just me being spoiled again. I already have the low-hanging fruits I needed, and now the rest of my journey is going to be staying alive long enough to make it to the end.

And, I suppose, I can't really blame the Seed for sending me off to kill the Rebel for this stuff. It offered me a charge, and I refused—maybe this is just it correcting for my risk assessment? Being harder to kill isn't a bad thing.

Whatever. I won big. He forced a smile onto his face and opened his status.

Time to see how big.

Status | Skills | Quests | Inventory

Name: Lukas King

Tier: Warrior

Bloodline: Eyes of Insight

Mana: 3,234 / 3,234

Rate: 17% per hour

Strength: 36 > 41

Agility: 41 > 43

Constitution: 66 > 77

Arcana: 71 > 84

Stat Points: 812

Charges: 7/10

I've been a warrior for, what, less than a week, and I'm already more than a quarter of the way through the tier.

That's . . . wow.

If I wasn't a paragon, I'd only be one hundred and four points away from becoming a hero.

A weak one, for sure, but this is . . . incredible.

Feeling his mouth go dry, he took a few moments just to stare blankly at the screen, deciding how he was going to spend all the points.

If I can get another manasink, then adding every free point to Arcana would be worth it. If it maxes out, then I'm just converting time to points. But I also have to factor in my other stats. Having a lot of mana is good, but raw attributes have their own place.

I'll be competing in the Olympics soon, and honestly, with these kinds of numbers, I should even have a chance at winning. Even if there are people comparable to Heracles, I should have the time.

That said, my growth has been much too fast.

Going from mortal to warrior is whatever. Lukeus is only a year older than me, and he's one, and I think Rex will reach the level in time for the Olympics as well, but if I show up in front of a bunch of gods as a sixteen-year-old kid and curb stomp their kids—kids that have grown up with a silver spoon in their mouths and basically every resource imaginable—then that might be a problem.

Potentially a big one. Not to mention that Prometheus is also now someone I need to worry about.

I'd assumed that because he told me not to tell anyone about him that there wasn't a way to find out. Which is out of the window now; Cybele knew I was a descendant of his, probably the moment she saw me. A dumb one, but one nonetheless. Then again, she didn't seem to care too much, either, so there is that.

She also said I look just like Poseidon . . . which is really fucking bad, Luke thought as he floated in front of the mirror. *The face I'm wearing was one that was preloaded into the mask.*

A mask belonging to a woman who got killed by the Atlantians. Atlantians who are very likely ruled by the god I happen to look like.

What the fuck was she doing, what does that mean for me, and was using the mask a mistake?

A knock on his door interrupted his thoughts.

"Luke, I was informed that you're awake," he heard Cyzicus say from outside.

CHAPTER 19

Emperor of Sylcra

am," Luke said after a second, his voice catching in his throat and his mouth dry. Suddenly he felt nervous, even though he didn't quite know why.

He wasn't going into battle. His life wasn't on the line. His secrets were safe . . . or, well, as safe as they could be.

No, this nervousness was caused by something much more mundane, and strangely, it caused him even more dread.

His life on Theos, thus far, had seen him quickly become used to high stakes, impossible odds, and the threat of impending death.

It hadn't prepared him for what might be a hard, emotional conversation with a man who had just lost his fiancée.

Battles and struggles for victory and life were easy. Luke gave it all he had because his soul was on the line. Which made the outcome simple and easy to accept. There was comfort in knowing what he needed to do and then knowing he had done all he could.

In a way, it absolved him from the consequences of failure. Because if he had done all he could and still failed at the end, then that was that. Some things simply weren't meant to be.

A conversation like this, though, was a minefield. There was no winning, just doubt and heaviness.

The door slid open, and Cyzicus strolled in. His back was straight, and the battle with the Rebel hadn't left any visible scars on him. His long hair was combed neatly under his crown, his golden robes were clean and crisp, and he didn't even have bags under his eyes or anything that visibly alluded to the fact that he was less than a hundred percent.

The vitality of Hero-tier beings was too high for such minor concerns. Even so, the stark emptiness in his eyes betrayed him. Especially when compared to his usual animated cheer.

"I'm glad to see that you're well. Come, let's go for a walk."

Feeling a hitch in his throat, Luke thumbed the Rebel's ring, stuffed it in his pocket, and nodded. Absently he noticed Cyzicus's gaze traveling to it before he averted his eyes, seemingly uninterested. Whether that would remain the case, Luke didn't know, but either way he didn't have any intention of hiding his spoils. There was no need to. He trusted the older cultivator, and if Cyzicus wanted to, there was little Luke could do to stop him anyhow.

They walked the deathly quiet halls of the castle at a sedate pace. The bright lights, the white marble, and the silver furnishings looked more sterile than grand with the weight of Sophia's death hanging over them. Even the servants scampered out of the way whenever the pair rounded a corner—a stark contrast to how they had been around the emperor the first and last time Luke had walked through the castle with him.

Looks like they heard the news, too, Luke thought nervously. *Still not a reason to be scared, though—it's not like he's going to do anything to them.*

After minutes of near-unbearable silence, they made it to their destination: a balcony overlooking the rear of the castle. Thousands of cultivators, a mix of both warriors and blue-robed mortals, were lined up around the same illusory map of Sylcra.

Unlike the last time he had seen it, the balance between the red dots signifying the attacking giants and the green dots representing safe locations had been skewed completely, with more than two-thirds of the island actively under attack from the Gegenees. Even so, it looked like they had enough bodies to stem the tide. Not that it was ever in question. There were more than enough cultivators on the island, likely by design, to keep the giants in check.

Clite was standing at the forefront with another warrior that Luke didn't recognize, directing teams onto the altar. At her direction, the platform would shine and flicker with rainbow-colored light and the teams would vanish. Once in a while, another team would return, most whole, but once in a while a team would flash back with a body in tow.

A grim reminder for all of them that while the Mortal-tier giants weren't particularly strong, they were dangerous and not to be underestimated.

"Who's powering it?" Luke asked. The last time he had been here, the tide had only just begun and Cyzicus was toiling away under the strain. Now the whole assembly seemingly ran itself.

"Contrary to popular belief, I don't have to be there full time. There is a reserve of power that I fill over the years, which keeps it serviceable. I activate it when I must kill a Hero-tier giant if one appears. Of course, it will exhaust itself in a few days, but that's all the time I typically need to dispose of one of them. A few hundred warriors gathered together can also power the system, but then there's not enough of us to combat the horde and recharge the wards around the castle."

"I see."

"Mmm-hmm. Right now, however, it's being run on a Saint-tier mana crystal. They are exceedingly rare—as far as I know, they only appear in the holy lands of the gods. I requested aid from one of my friends when your and Lukeus's actions led to the removal of Arke from the archipelago and Sophia was slain. This was her solution."

Shit . . . Luke thought, and his face turned pale at the implication.

"Did the Rebel call for help, too? Is that why . . ."

The emperor sighed. Reaching up, he pulled the crown off his head and held it in front of him.

"I . . . I don't know. The moment the borders opened, there were too many beings that entered the island, and I was too occupied to keep track. One of them may have been answering her call. Whoever it was, though, if there was anyone at all, they're gone now," he said quietly, only to smile slightly at Luke's rapidly paling face.

"It's not your fault. It was Heracles who broke the blockade, and he did not know the balance of power that had been established on this island. Probably too much of a muscle-bound meathead to even know what that means, and too full of conviction to care. The young often are." He grinned slightly. "Truthfully, I should have freed him myself, but doing so would have only invited reprisal from that wretched woman. I could not feign ignorance of her intent and rules, and the soft spot Lord Zeus carries for the youth would not apply to me, even if it was his own son I aided. Arke is an Olympian and as such privileged to the rights they have granted to themselves.

"Besides," he continued with forced cheerfulness, "when we get mandates from those stronger, what can we do but obey? I was bound to listen despite my concerns, and no doubt, whoever solicited you to action is suitably powerful to warrant an action from you as well. They would have to be if they could come here and give you a quest without my knowledge. So, even if Tyrisa had outside help, the fault does not fall to you. None of it does."

Cyzicus looked meaningfully at Luke. "I'm quite surprised she let you live. Lukeus garnered some level of protection, him being my grandson and all, but . . ." He trailed off.

"I almost didn't," he admitted, his voice heavy in guilt.

"Do not be sorry." Cyzicus sighed. "Your guilt is unnecessary—and, truthfully, annoying. I enlisted Sophia's aid, and I left her alone to combat my greatest foe. I've lived for millennia . . . in that time, I have learned not to blame children for the actions of those thousands of years older and immeasurably more powerful," he chided. "Could you imagine how petty I would need to be?" he said, cracking a small, half-hearted grin.

Luke didn't respond right away and for the moment continued to watch the cultivators line up and go off to battle in front of them. Even with the emperor's platitudes, his guilt ran rampant.

It wasn't a god that made me go and free Heracles; it was the God Seed. It gave me the quest . . . after I poked it.

It's obvious in retrospect that the Seed acts with my thoughts in mind. I am just as vital to becoming a god as the environment and the opportunities around me. It's childish to assume that it won't act to put my mind at ease or to motivate me, whether that manifests in ways that stroke my greed, or by putting me in a fire and letting me get strong enough to crawl my way out, or any other method it has to promote growth.

In a way, I guess it doesn't even matter if the situation I'm in is actually threatening or not. If I think it is, and it hampers my progress, then the Seed will direct me. Its purpose is to make me a god . . . whether I want to or not.

Huh.

I wonder what will happen if I suddenly stop and give up? Will it give up and just wait until I die? Will my death separate it from my soul, or will it remain attached and follow me to the afterlife?

Did Aeolus really detonate his soul, or was the Seed tearing itself free from a failed subject? Is that why it always lands me in situations where I'm constantly forced to advance?

Thinking back, even Nefkha's favor was meant to be repaid when I became a warrior.

His mouth went dry.

When I look at it like that, am I responsible for the Seed's actions, or am I stuck with them?

Cyzicus thinks some unknown god incited me to action, but it was a quest. I don't know what happens if I fail one, and how I would even begin to determine if a quest is legit, if my fears are legit, and if it's okay to fail or not.

Honestly, I can't.

As I am now, the Seed might as well be omnipotent. Mortal, Warrior, Hero, Saint, maybe—probably something in between—God, and then Primordial.

I'm getting cues from something higher than a god.

He frowned as the realization sank in.

The Seed is controlling me, and I've been more than happy to be controlled. After all, my desires and its purpose have always aligned. I want to be a god. I want to be free to decide my own fate. But the tool that will take me there might not be as benevolent as I thought.

And there's nothing I can do about it.

He looked at Cyzicus from the corner of his eyes.

But I can't let my advancement be at the cost of others, he thought. Then, with a heart full of anger, he prodded the Seed. *You hear that? I'll become a god. The strongest deity to ever live, even, but you're not going to drag anyone down to get me there, you understand? I won't climb higher by sacrificing others. That's not the god I want to be. I won't make this world hell to feed my own strength like some kind of sick vampire, not even unwittingly.*

"I guess . . ." Luke started to say, the words feeling heavy in his mouth. "I'm sorry for the part I did play. While higher powers were involved, I may not have had a good choice, but it was still me and my actions that led to . . . I don't think that the action of higher powers absolves me of all wrongdoing. Maybe most of it. I didn't know what my actions would lead to, and I didn't think them through enough to be sure. But it was a choice I made. I could have made a different one, but I didn't. I'm sorry for that."

Cyzicus turned away from him and laughed. Loudly, and for a long time.

"Don't be so serious. It's fine, you're forgiven, and don't beat yourself up. It's okay to act in the interest of your own safety. The gods know how often I do it." He grinned.

"Thank you," Luke said earnestly, feeling just a little lighter. Then, fishing the Rebel's and the Warrior's rings out of his pocket, he held them in his palms. "Um, while I have you here, I have these . . ."

"You're giving them to me?" Cyzicus grinned. His finger twitched, and both rings flew into his hand.

"No!" Luke said hurriedly. "I mean . . . I was hoping you could open them. I've heard of people putting protection on them, but . . ."

A disappointed expression appeared on the emperor's face, and for a tense moment the man just stared at him.

"Sixty percent," he said after a while. "I'll do it for sixty percent of what's in here."

Luke opened and closed his mouth, doing a great impersonation of a fish.

"Five. I did kill her."

"Fifty. I softened her up."

"Ten. I went into her castle and pulled it free while she was sleeping, and you're already rich."

"Forty. You can't get in here without me."

"Fifteen."

"Thirty-five. Who else is going to open it for you? And that's plenty of wealth for you. More and someone will rob you. Do you want to be robbed?"

"Twenty."

The rings floated from Cyzicus back to Luke.

"Thirty, or I walk and you can try and find someone else to open them. Let me tell you, kid, good luck with that."

"We meet in the middle—twenty-five."

Cyzicus began to inch away.

"Twenty-seven!" Luke called after him. He didn't stop moving. "Fine! Thirty!"

CHAPTER 20

Breaking Them Open

Cyzicus flashed Luke a half-hearted grin. "All right, follow me," he said, and with a parting look at the cultivators teleporting away, he retreated into the castle.

"Now, one of the rings I believe you got from a warrior. I recognize it as one I made, and the defenses in it are rather easy to break. Well, for me, since I made it, but you can give it a try if you want. It will be good practice."

"So they don't go away when the owner dies, then?" Luke asked.

Seems I made a good call after all.

"Of course not." Cyzicus turned back and flashed him an expression that bordered on offense.

"I don't know how any of this works." Luke shrugged. "I don't even have a storage ring yet."

"Humph. Allow me to educate you, then. Crafting items is much like creating talismans. You inscribe runes onto objects and fill them with mana. The patterns for talismans, however, have been perfected through countless millennia, improved and iterated by the gods themselves, and simplified to such an extent that any hoodlum with mana can copy one down, fill it with mana, and it will function consistently and reliably. They are perhaps the most refined works of runecraft known to cultivators. Attack, defense, preservation, communication . . . Those are the tools that allowed us to escape the caves of our ancestors and spread throughout the world and conquer it."

"That's . . . I can see how that would be useful." Luke nodded along as Cyzicus led him to a blank stretch of wall.

Cyzicus's ring flashed, and a large brass key appeared in his hands. He pressed it into the air, and Luke watched intently as it disappeared.

The emperor turned it over, and the world shuddered. A mechanical noise reverberated through the castle, and the wall in front of them receded into the ceiling like a cleverly designed garage door.

"Many overlook their usefulness. Fighting with basic armaments has its place, but such tactics expose you to risk and require skill that isn't easy to gain. Fighting with talismans requires that you have some spare time, paper, and a writing instrument, or friendship with someone who does. We can talk more about how they revolutionized the way sapient life thrived on Theos, but I can refer you to a few scholars and texts that will be able to educate you much more than I."

"That would be amazing, actually."

"I'm sure it would. The history of this world fascinates me more and more the longer I live," Cyzicus said, stretching his hand out in front of him. Taking the cue, Luke stared into the gaping darkness of the hidden room and back at the emperor himself before confidently striding in.

A moment later, he heard the same mechanical noise, and the wall slammed shut behind them. Torches lit up gentle white light all along the walls, revealing a wide stairway that descended deep into the earth.

"Come," Cyzicus said, walking past him and into the bowels of his castle. "Now, in principle, creating artifacts is the same as creating talismans, but in practice it is substantially more difficult. While the patterns that you draw contain all the necessary information to make a functional talisman, they require no understanding from you. It takes actual knowledge of the runes to create artifacts. You cannot draw them blindly and hope for the best. Doing so would have no effect beyond leaving markings on your material. Whereas using runes you do understand, and pairing them with ones you do not, will lead to a result that is much more destructive."

"What are runes, then? Is there like a dictionary or something that we can use?"

Cyzicus scoffed. "No, there isn't a dictionary. The meanings contained in the runic alphabet aren't something that can be verbalized with something so paltry as the squawking of animals. Learning one is like learning a technique—you connect with something that exists beyond the physical. Will you be able to teach someone the stances passed on to you by Alexia by saying some words?"

". . . No," he said eventually. He had tried once, after all, remembering the frazzled and gaunt eyes of the person they had tried to teach. Trixie hadn't learned in spite of his, Arya's, and Spiros's best efforts. He frowned, absently wondering whether the older cultivator was still there and how many others were still trapped with her.

"Correct. Even though the gist behind them can be verbalized, the depth behind those words, the realization, the *magic*, cannot. It's an effort of years to learn a single rune enough to etch it into an artifact and not have it be inert. It takes decades to learn enough of them to create something serviceable. Centuries to create something even worth making. Once you do, however, reproducing past results is rather easy."

The stairway opened up to a large chamber. Easily the size of a football stadium, it was filled with clutter. All manner of weapons, shields, pieces of armor, and other knickknacks were littered haphazardly through the room. Scattered between them were countless tools—anvils, hammers, lathes, crucibles, and a dozen other things that Luke didn't recognize.

Not breaking his stride, the emperor led Luke to an unassuming workbench right in the middle of the room and held his hands out. Fishing in his pockets, Luke pulled out the pair of rings.

The moment the rings touched air, they floated away from his hand and into the emperor's.

"For breaking into things, there's two things to remember. One, if the person they belong to is still alive, then getting into them is near impossible. Not unless you're many tiers higher than the tier of the ring."

"Yeah, about that . . . I'm not sure if anyone else saw this, but when I was— How much do you know about how we killed the Rebel?"

Cyzicus looked at him oddly. "I talked to Nel, Lukeus, and Rex and took all their accounts. The only thing I don't know is what happened inside the castle." His eyes drifted to Maximus resting on Luke's waist, and he smiled. "Sentimental, huh."

Luke blushed red. "It is."

"I believe you. It's quite the surprise that some random brat I found is a paragon. Or that you now carry a named weapon. Most people don't survive the tribulation."

"A tribulation. Is that what that was? I got the sense that I was pretty close to the end of my existence."

"A tribulation is a test. If you pass it, you get a reward. If you fail, you die."

"A test by who?"

Cyzicus shrugged. "That's not something I can answer. I'm not even sure that the gods know that answer. There are things about this world that, quite frankly, I don't know."

"I see," Luke said, his thoughts churning in his head.

Hmm. It felt kind of like my paragon quest—and that emerged from the primordial order alongside the creation of Theos according to the Seed. Not that I have a clue what that means. Is it some kind of mana, a group of gods, or something else entirely? It also said something about the creation of Theos . . . did someone make this world? A god? Or maybe something higher?

The vision of Prometheus trapped in the cave, sitting in a pool of his blood, with a crazed look on his face, flashed in Luke's head. A chill went down his back, and he forcibly shut down that train of thought.

Whatever had seized him when he was naming his sword was not a power he had any right questioning. Just thinking about it filled him with an ominous feeling, and he didn't know if that was just him being nervous or if it was the weight of something unfathomable resting on his back, threatening to break his mind.

Cyzicus cracked a grin at his nervous expression.

"I knew there was something odd about you when I picked you up from Sophia's forge, but I couldn't place it. You had more mana that day than I'd ever thought possible for a mortal. But a paragon . . . I've heard about them, but"—he shook his head—"most consider it a curse of the greedy. Unparalleled power, but the inability to advance. Perfection in everything is not easy to achieve—if it's possible. Those that know about it know not to take the choice when offered, and many shy away from the price. If they're lucky, or supremely talented, they'll break through one tier, maybe two, but as far as I know, no one who has accepted it has ascended past the Saint tier." He looked at Luke meaningfully.

"I think I can do it."

"Considering how far you've come in such a short time, I wouldn't underestimate you, but I do believe you underestimate the difficulty of advancing through the higher tiers. Regardless, I do wish you the best. Once you become a god, don't forget this old man on this little island on which you spent a few months of your youth." He grinned.

"I won't," Luke said, his face full of amusement, while he wondered what the emperor would think if he knew about the Seed and its ability to cheat the requirements. "Anyway, I wasn't alone in the castle. There was this woman . . . I think she was a god."

Cyzicus suddenly grew still, and his gaze locked onto Luke.

"Truly?"

"Yeah. Her name was C—"

He snarled.

"No need to say it. I'm aware of who it is that you speak of. What did she do?"

"She took something from the Rebel's ring."

"A crown?"

How does he— "Yeah, that was it. Do you know what it is?"

"I do. That crown is something that I've searched for over the millennia. Alas, it's not something you should concern yourself with," he said, his face carefully neutral. Only his hands, clenched in a white-knuckled grip, betrayed his carefully controlled anger. "Did she do anything else?"

"She knew stuff about me and about Rex. She knew who Heracles was. She also gave me a pomegranate seed. Once I ate it, my mana surged. For a few minutes my mana was limitless . . . that and my technique are what let me kill the Rebel."

"I see." Cyzicus nodded. "Well, there's no reason to be concerned. The pomegranate seed was a valuable treasure and not harmful. I won't pry into your secrets, but what did she know about Rex?"

"She called him a descendant of uh . . ." He scrambled for the name. "Ep—"

"Lord Epimetheus," he finished, slightly more at ease. "That name will mean little to you, but Lord Epimetheus is an Olympian. That is where Agnella, Lukeus, and now Rex's ability to control animals comes from—they carry his bloodline."

"What exactly is a bloodline? I've heard you say it before, but . . ."

"Ah, of course. A bloodline is essentially a technique that is passed down from a god to their offspring. They aren't particularly rare. The only condition to them being passed on is for the parent to have unlocked their mana, and when the child unlocks theirs, they will possess it as well."

Hmm. So the original Max was probably a descendant of someone who had Prometheus's bloodline, just not awakened, considering I needed all those stat points to unlock it.

"I see."

"Is there anything else you would like to share with me?"

"Not that I can think of."

Cyzicus nodded at that. "Very well, now, where were we? Right. Breaking into the ring is all but impossible unless the person it belongs to is dead. Even when they are, it isn't an easy thing to do. Storage rings, truthfully speaking, are more like talismans than other objects. The runes that enchant the metal are given to emperors by Olympus to be made and distributed and don't require too much learning. Any emperor worth their salt will pick up the skill relatively fast. Unlike talismans that even mortals can power, however, rings require the weight of Hero-tier mana. Now, as the maker of this ring, I know exactly the protection I put on it." He tossed it back at Luke and smiled. "Go ahead and channel your mana into it," he said, his earlier anger at the mention of Cybele seemingly gone.

"I thought it was protected."

"Oh, it is. Just be careful not to push too much."

Hesitantly, Luke looked between Cyzicus and the ring, and then, deciding to trust the man, he slid a small tendril of his mana into it. Immediately a jolt of lightning latched onto that connection and traveled through his body, leaving him paralyzed for a moment.

"Ghk," Luke wheezed.

"That was too much mana. Try a little less. So it can't do that," Cyzicus urged him, a consoling expression on his face.

Luke looked at him reluctantly.

"Well, if you don't want to learn how to break into storage rings, I suppose I can do it for you." He held out his hands once again. "Now that I think about it, this isn't a skill I should be teaching you about anyways."

Luke frowned and sent an even thinner amount of mana into the ring.

"Ghk." His arms shook, and the ring clattered as it hit the ground.

"A little less," Cyzicus said. "Agnella learned this in three tries, so I'm sure you're close," he said, and the ring flew up from the ground and landed in his hands again.

Why am I getting the sense that it was his idea to boil people for training? Luke thought with a sigh as he once again sent his mana into the ring.

CHAPTER 21

Breaking and Entering

Sitting cross-legged on the ground, Luke closed his eyes and focused entirely on the ring in his palm. Visualizing his mana, he thinned the strand as much as he could. It wasn't possible to see it with the naked eye, but he was confident that it was still too thick, and yet he also couldn't make it thinner.

He had tried dozens of times already, and after failing so many times, he was beginning to get used to the numb feeling of electricity latching onto his mana and the violent spasms that followed.

It wasn't something that he wanted to get used to, but he wouldn't give up.

As his Constitution and Agility both ticked up once again, he found that he didn't mind pain quite as much as he should have. He was safe, he was learning, and he was getting stronger at the same time.

It was painful, but strength often came at a cost. Whether that was freedom, risk, or pain, that had always been consistent, and something he had long become used to.

Even so, he had a limit to his patience. Pulling the mana back into his body, he raked his eyes across the cavernous workshop and the uncountable objects within it, looking for Cyzicus. The emperor had wandered off after a few minutes of watching him fail and begun to rummage through his stuff.

As if he was drawn by his gaze, the hero wandered back.

"It's not working," he said suddenly. "I don't even know what I'm doing wrong."

"You must use less mana—there is no other solution. If you're subtle, the ring will be unable to detect the presence of foreign mana and it will allow you access to the controls."

"How do I use less mana? . . . Is it possible that my Arcana is just too low?"

"I wouldn't assign you a task that's out of your ability," the emperor chided. "This is a question of control, not strength, quantity, or power. While improving your Arcana will no doubt aid you in this, it's not needed. More than that, even if you increase your Arcana to the limits of the Warrior tier, the process and the difficulty would remain roughly the same. Consider it this way . . ." He tilted his head to the side, carefully picking his words. "If I asked you to lift a glass, grab a jug, and pour water in it, being stronger, faster, and more nimble will aid you in the task. And yet, you are able to do so already with your current abilities."

Yeah, but pouring water into a jug doesn't hurt me, he grumbled internally. *Still, if Nel can do this, there isn't a reason I can't.*

Gritting his teeth, he once again took control of the energy within him and brought it close to the ring. Then, stretching it out as much as he could, he narrowed it down to the thinnest strand he could manage and brought it into contact with the ring.

Bracing himself, he made the plunge. Like every time before, electric shocks ran through his body, and every muscle he had seized and spasmed.

Gasping for breath, Luke dropped the ring and forcibly broke the connection.

I'm missing something, but what?

Taking a minute to let the jitters pass, he once again inspected the ring. Over the course of the next hour, he tried every idea that came to him, from trying to pour mana in at different points to putting in more than one strand in at a time.

None of them worked.

All the while Cyzicus milled about his workshop and slowly fashioned what could be best described as a contraption.

Luke beheld the finished product with curiosity. It had multiple hammers, arrayed in a circle around an anvil. Each had its shaft affixed to a hinge, which was in turn attached to the bench. A cable made of braided gold and silver wire was tied around their heads and joined into one thick cable that ran through a pulley, which spit out the other end of the cable a dozen feet from the workbench.

Frowning slightly, Cyzicus tugged at the end of the cable, and at once, all six of the hammers anchored to the table slammed into the anvil. A clunking noise reverberated through the room, so loud it made Luke's ears hurt—something he hadn't even known was possible.

Cyzicus grinned as Luke winced in pain.

The ring on his finger flashed, and three shields appeared in the air and surrounded the anvil-hammer-pulley assembly in a triangular formation.

"Okay, that should be everything I need," he said, crossing his hands over his chest and raking his eyes over Luke's miserable figure. "Any progress?"

"No."

"Are you just doing the same thing over and over again?"

"No."

"Well, keep at it. The Rebel's ring will take a while yet."

"How is all this going to help anyway?" Luke asked, rising to his feet and walking in a slow circle around the anvil.

"Unlike the ring you've been working with, this one is in the Saint tier, which means the defenses will incinerate me if I even make a small mistake once I send my own mana into it. Before I forget, I should mention that you shouldn't attempt what you're doing with that ring with any other one you find until you can do that one with ease. Since I'm the person that created it, I was able to reduce the potency of the defense to tolerable levels. Most people keep theirs at an intensity that would kill the average warrior. A single mistake with someone else's ring will have consequences that are not so forgiving."

". . . That's good to know."

"Right." He nodded. "Now, since the Rebel is dead and the ring is ownerless and unbound, it will slowly lose its mana, and the lethality of its defenses will decrease over time. Perhaps in a few millennia it would be safe enough to give it a try, but obviously, we don't have that much time."

"So you're going to hit it with hammers until it—"

"Until it loses most of its mana, yes." He walked forward and placed the golden ring in the middle of the anvil, then stepped back. Closing his eyes in concentration, he made a vague gesture, and immediately light emerged from each of the shields and solidified into a translucent red barrier around the anvil.

He tugged the cable, Luke shielded his eyes, the ground beneath his feet rattled, and a bright flash of light illuminated the workshop.

"A few thousand of those should do it," Cyzicus said out loud. His ring flashed, and a clay plate appeared in the air in front of Luke. "If you could channel some mana into that, I would appreciate it."

The second Luke did, a gray bubble appeared around him and the hero, silencing the majority of the sound and dimming nearly all the light coming from the anvil-hammer assembly.

Luke watched for a few minutes as the emperor beat away at the Rebel's ring before he turned his attention to his own.

So he dialed it down enough that this thing doesn't kill me, but he couldn't have done more?

He opened his mouth to raise the question, only to see the man with his hand extended and wearing a knowing look on his face.

"What?"

"You aren't going to ask me to weaken the defenses even more?"

This f—

"No." Luke turned on his heel and sat back down. It was stupid, and perhaps his ego had gotten the better of him, but he wasn't going to say that he was too weak willed to handle a little pain.

Besides, I'm improving two stats at once without having to go out and kill things. That's worth a little bit of pain. Right?

Mind made up, he closed his eyes and once again began his attempts to sneak mana into the rings.

Cyzicus watched him with clear—and perhaps sadistic—amusement dancing in his eyes before turning his own attention to the Saint-tier ring with uncharacteristic focus.

Thirty minutes later, Luke picked the ring up from the ground with shaking hands and just stared at it. He had lost count of how many times he had been electrocuted, and he was beginning to fear that if he went on, he might even do some permanent damage to himself.

Warrior tier with high Constitution or not, getting buzzed so often in a short amount of time could not be healthy.

All right, let's just think about this for a moment. I've made my mana as thin as I can, and I've tried putting it into the ring as many ways as I know how. Going in fast. Going in and out. Trying from different spots. Trying to move through the pain. None of that works. Clearly, I'm missing something.

All I need to do is put such a small amount of mana in here, that the ring doesn't even . . .

Fuck me.

The solution snapped into his mind with all the grace of a train hitting a bird. It was obvious in hindsight.

He had been going about it wrong the entire time.

Thinking back to the Cyzicus's analogy, if he was trying to pour water into the cup, the thickness or the thinness of the stream played a role in how much of the liquid went in, but the real determinator was the actual quantity of mana.

The energy, despite how he thought of it, wasn't a physical substance. Narrowing it into a thin line, while a useful tool for picturing what exactly he was doing with it, wasn't what the task was about.

Closing his eyes, he felt his mana rippling along with his heartbeat through his entire body. With an effort of will, he stilled it.

For a moment, his attention went to the two pebble-like anomalies in the backs of his eyes—filling mana into them would activate the Eyes of Insight. Of that he was sure, but this wasn't the time or the place. The first time he delved into the secrets of his ancestry, he wanted to be alone.

He trusted Cyzicus, but he wasn't ready to confess all his secrets to the man. He doubted he ever would.

Focusing on his breath, he pulled a small blob of mana free from the rest of his body and let it hang in the air in front of him, and then stretched it out as much as he could. It ballooned to the size of his head before he recalled the majority of it back into his body.

Watching the reduced orb, he inflated it once again to the size of his head and called the excess back into his body.

He repeated the process a few more times until only the smallest fetters of his mana existed in the air in front of him, and he grinned in satisfaction. Considering the minuscule amount of energy he had started with, what he was left with was a tiny fraction of a fraction of a single point.

This might actually be too little, but if it is too little, I won't get singed.

Mentally preparing himself to be shocked once again, in spite of the progress he had made, he physically moved the ring to where he kept his mana and then slowly inched it forward.

To his relief, it entered the ring without shocking him.

"I'm in. What do I do now?" he asked Cyzicus with urgency.

"Look around, but don't try to take anything out of the ring. You should find the runes quickly," he said, not turning away from where the hammers were relentlessly striking the Rebel's ring.

Nodding carefully, Luke did just that. The inside of the ring was a box, and not one that was particularly big—only the size of a closet. Big enough to hold a few changes of clothes, as many talismans someone could want, and an assortment of weapons.

Ignoring the objects currently in there, none of which were of particular interest to him, Luke used the perception granted by his mana to scout out the place.

Quickly, he found a smattering of runes seemingly floating around what looked like a tiny red gem.

"I found them. Now what?"

"Good. Now, without touching any of the runes, you need to remove the drop of blood that they are orbiting."

"How do I do that?"

"If you suffuse the blood with your mana, you will be able to control it the way you fly. The energy in the blood will try to rebuff you, but if you've been diligent with the manasink, it's well within your abilities."

Nodding carefully, Luke attempted to do just that. His mana spread evenly through the droplet without any trouble, but the second he tried to move it toward the walls of the ring and out, it suddenly became heavy.

Straining against the resistance, he slowly eased it out from within the encasement of the runes, but just when it was about to touch the walls, his hold on it slipped and it shot back toward the runes.

Luke blinked as his perception fizzled out. He had expended the mana he had within the ring.

Even so, he grinned. He was close.

CHAPTER 22

Thirty and Seventy

After a few more tries, and getting buzzed one more time, Luke managed to drag the drop of blood out of the ring. In the process, he disabled the protection on the ring.

At Cyzicus's direction, Luke withdrew Maximus from its sheath and made a shallow cut on one of his fingers. Holding his bleeding finger against the ring, he watched, fascinated, as blood dripped from his wound and seeped into the metal.

"Good. It's bound to you. The ring will preserve and compare the mana in the blood against your own every time it feels the touch of the energy," said Cyzicus.

Luke nodded at his words as he flooded the ring with his mana. Like the emperor said, it went in without him incurring any negative effects.

So there is a way for me to be found out by my mana, so long as they have my blood . . . That's not good, he thought nervously as he let it flow through every nook and cranny of the ring, feeling each and every object inside it.

Unfortunately, but not unexpectedly, the Seed had already indexed what was in there, and none of it was any more valuable on his second pass through than it had been on his first.

Still, some arrows, a cool bow, and a shit ton of Mortal-tier weapons aren't anything to sneeze at. Even the healing potions by themselves aren't a bad haul. I'm already running out of the ones that I found in Sophia's forge, although I should probably be able to buy more. Killing the Rebel has got to be worth some merits.

Leaving the items alone for the moment, he brushed his mana against the ring's controls. There was more going on there than he had anticipated.

Part of the mana he put into the ring was subtly being siphoned away by the drop of blood, making it glow red within its runed prison. Curious, he increased the amount of mana he was channeling into the ring by an entire point, and without missing a beat, the blood swallowed it up.

Interesting.

Resolving to ask Cyzicus about the ring being so thirsty, he moved his attention to what he presumed were the controls.

They were surprisingly basic. One governed the strength of the shock, and true to the emperor's words, the defenses were set at only a tenth of their full strength. Fiddling around with it, he discovered that he could manually disable them, allowing anyone access, or engage them to the maximum extent, which as Cyzicus claimed would likely kill even a warrior.

Dialing it up to the highest setting, he turned his attention to the remaining controls. One of them managed what he was pretty sure was a warning protocol, which slowly amped the intensity of the ring's retaliation from levels that would mildly inconvenience a mortal to instantly delivering a lethal dose of current.

I should probably enable that. Or should I? On one hand, I don't want to kill someone by mistake. On the other hand, I don't want people fucking with my stuff. Cyzicus did say that it's virtually impossible to get into an already-bound ring, so there's that, and I can always change it later . . . Besides, it's not like I'm going to be keeping anything truly valuable here anyhow. That's what the inventory is for, and speaking of—

He diverted his attention to the Seed, and on a whim, he sent a random vial of potion directly from his inventory into the ring and pulled it back out again, all without the ring even flashing.

Now that's pretty useful.

The last command just gave a read on how charged the ring was, which turned out to be not very. Either the warrior he had killed hadn't filled it, or it was designed to hold Hero-tier mana, but either way, the amount of energy currently in the ring was less than a percent of what it could hold. Unlike his sword, the energy the ring held wasn't available for his use, but to power the ring itself, but he resolved to fill it up nonetheless.

Guess Cyzicus wasn't joking when he said it would take centuries for it to drain if only a percent of the energy inside was able to shock me as much as it did.

Satisfied for the moment, Luke withdrew his attention from the ring and turned to the waiting emperor.

"So, how should we do this? Do you want me to dump everything here?" Luke asked.

"I'm afraid I don't follow."

"It's seventy-thirty right. Do you want to split it now, or . . ."

"Ha. You're truly amusing." Cyzicus shook his head and smiled. "You can keep all of what's in there. I'm afraid none of it is of any value to me. I won't even count it as part of your share."

"Well, I won't say no to it." Luke shrugged and, after some deliberation, slid the ring onto his finger, only mildly surprised when it resized itself to fit him perfectly.

Turning his attention back to the series of hammers repeatedly striking the anvil, he settled in for a wait and spent his time getting used to taking things out of and putting them back in the ring. Even though the ring offered an ability that he already possessed, he couldn't help but be excited. Having another dimensional space was just cool—doubly so because he was free to use this one publicly and it would let him use one of the Seed's greatest abilities openly. So long as there weren't any gods around.

And you know what, might as well . . . he thought as he wrapped his sword and its sheath in mana, placing them first in the ring and then into the Seed's inventory.

Contrary to Cyzicus's expectations, they ended up standing in front of the contraption for the rest of the day. It took hours longer than Cyzicus originally predicted for him to consider the ring's energies depleted enough that he felt breaking into it was worth the risk.

So, it was with bated breath that Luke watched the hero solemnly turn the Rebel's ring over in his fingers. The hero's nerves warred against his desire to open it and claim the wealth inside with the danger the task represented.

"It'll be fine," Cyzicus said to himself more than to Luke as he built up the courage to break into the ring. "I've done this hundreds of times."

"You have?"

"With Hero-tier rings, yes. I battled many warriors when I was young, and I wasn't shy about taking their wealth as my own. This is the first time I've tried this with something of the Saint tier, however."

"Well, maybe we should hammer it a little more—"

Cyzicus closed his eyes in concentration. Beads of sweat rolled down his temples and splashed off the floor.

A moment later, a drop of her blood appeared in the air.

Cyzicus grinned before every trace of joy was wiped from his features, and, knowing what was in the ring, Luke couldn't even begin to fathom how he was feeling right now.

He had wanted to warn him, tell him what was in there and perhaps prepare him for the eventuality, but without a way to explain his knowledge, there wasn't much he could do.

An oppressive aura blasted out from the hero and sent everything that wasn't bolted down slamming against the walls. Cyzicus's jaw clenched with poorly suppressed rage, his chest heaved, his eyes turned an electric blue, and arcs of lightning writhed like serpents over his frame.

"Cyz—"

The pressure faded as suddenly as it came. Both the Rebel's ring, and the one on Luke's finger shone a brilliant and blinding gold. The hero forced a neutral expression onto his face, and a ring flew from his fingers and landed in Luke's palm.

"Your seventy percent is in there," he said curtly. Then, before Luke could say anything else to him, he flashed forward faster than Luke could perceive and rested a hand on his shoulder.

The world flickered and turned black. When the light returned, Luke was back in his room with the emperor of Sylcra nowhere to be seen.

Sitting down heavily on the bed, he sighed. He felt bad for Cyzicus; he truly did.

I've been through some pretty fucked-up shit since I've been here, but that . . . that's on another level. At least with me, it's only ever been my life on the line. This world sucks. But I can't even imagine what it's like having it take what you love from you.

Surviving alone is hard, but having a family, protecting them, making sure they're safe and sound, and then failing because some greedy asshole with more power than sense comes along and ruins it all?

That's fucking bullshit.

Heracles is right, he decided. Those who acted as the Rebel had couldn't be allowed to live in peace, with the world ignoring their deeds. *What was the saying? All evil needs to spread is for good men to do nothing. It doesn't matter if it's dangerous—if I can help, then I should.*

Sighing, he turned his focus to the Saint-tier ring. It was gold, but as he turned it over in his hands, he found that it wasn't the same one Cyzicus had given him. It was fancier, studded with gems, and—

Did he give me his ring by mistake?

Calling the Seed into action, he attempted to send it to his inventory. Surprisingly, it went in.

Status | Skills | Quests | Inventory

Storage Ring (unbound)

Tier—Saint

A storage ring created by Chiron of Pelion and gifted to a pupil.

Items:

Limitless Thunder Bow

Tier—Hero

An artifact forged by Primarch Asius of Samos. Allows users to mold their mana into lightning darts.

Blastguard

Tier—Saint

An artifact forged by Primarch Asius of Samos. Reduces damage done by explosive talismans.

Stasis Amulet

Tier—Hero

Prevents injuries from worsening at the cost of mana.

Blood

Tier—Hero

A vial of blood belonging to a cyclops.

Teleportation Plate x 9

Tier—Hero

A clay plate that, when broken and filled with sufficient mana, allows for teleportation to a preset location.

[...]

Talisman Paper x 5,000

Tier—Mortal

So it is a different one. Chiron . . . that's the person Jason and Heracles were talking about, weren't they? Their teacher, if I remember right. I guess Cyzicus was trained by him, too, then. With how old people can get in this world, I guess it's not strange for the same person to be teaching now who was teaching back when Cyzicus was a kid.

With nothing else to do, he looked through the list and came to a startling conclusion. Cyzicus hadn't actually taken his thirty percent. All he had sought fit to remove were the headless corpses, the Flame Blade, and Sophia's book.

Even the sword was probably hers. Thinking back, it was the only good thing in the ring that wasn't made by Asius.

Removing the ring from his inventory, he sighed and, summoning his sword, pricked his finger once again.

The drop of blood went into the ring without any fuss. Emboldened by it, Luke sent his mana into it. The space inside was drastically larger than the Warrior-tier ring, at least by a factor of a hundred based on his own estimation.

Fishing through it, he pulled out the object that fascinated him the most.

The Limitless Thunder Bow was as tall as he was. Fashioned from an unmarked flat strip of gold, and lacking a drawstring, it was far from the elaborate weapon he'd anticipated. Grabbing its grip, he funneled mana into it, and immediately a tendril of mana snapped into place between the two tips.

Huh. He went to pull it back, but before he could, a blur passed through the ceiling of his room and hovered in the air in front of him. A beam of light shot out from it and blasted his new bow across the room—disarming him.

Is that a drone? he thought incredulously. It looked nearly identical to the ones he remembered from Earth, but even more advanced and different from nearly everything he had seen on Theos thus far.

Its body was a perfect orb made out of seamless silver metal. Four arms stretched out from each corner parallel to the ground, and on each one of them was a rapidly spinning propeller that made a nearly inaudible buzzing noise.

He stepped back nervously, and the drone moved a foot forward, filling the space, but for the moment doing little else.

Not sure what was happening, Luke summoned his sword from the ring and held it out in front of him.

"What are you?" he asked, preemptively activating the First Stance. The technique didn't work. Forcibly stopping himself from panicking, he activated the First Truth of Death.

It didn't work.

Another beam of light shot out from it, but this time, it reflected harmlessly off the flat of his blade and struck his bed. It caught fire instantly.

All right, fight first, questions later. Lunging forward, he swung his blade down, aiming to split the thing in two.

He missed. The drone twitched at the last second, and his blade slashed through empty air. Frowning, he tried attacking it again and again, but with his techniques not working, no matter what he did, he wasn't able to land a hit.

Not seeing any other options, and with the room rapidly catching fire, he did the only thing that came to mind.

"HELP!" he yelled at the top of his lungs while activating a Hero-tier protective talisman before dashing toward the door—only for the drone to position itself right in front of it and block his path.

Another beam of light shot out and popped the talisman like a bubble.

What the fuck is this?

CHAPTER 23

A Bad Invitation

Please remain within the confines of this room for the remainder of your assessment," an androgynous voice rang out from the drone while it shot scorching beams of red light toward Luke's feet. It was pushing him back deeper into the room, toward where it had lit his bed and the other furniture on fire.

Luke blinked slowly as the thing finally decided to say something. Even if what it said only served to make him more confused and raised a million more questions.

Rising into the air so as to not get clipped by the attacks, he muttered curses under his breath at whoever or whatever was behind this.

"What assessment?" he yelled at the flying machine while deflecting another beam of light with the flat of his blade. It scattered beautifully in every direction, leaving a charred, circular scar along the floor, walls, and ceiling. Any other time, he would have been impressed with the movie-like effect, but as it was, the only emotions he held were fear for his life and anger at the unwarranted attack.

An attack in a place he had considered safe.

"Listen, I don't want to be assessed, so can we stop?!"

The drone suddenly came to a halt, seemingly considering his words it moved back a few feet. Silently it hung in the air. Blinking in surprise, he inched back himself, his gaze moving between the drone and the door behind it.

Is that it?

It wasn't.

"Forfeiting the assessment will result in immediate disqualification. Do you wish to proceed?"

". . . What? I don't know what you're talking about." The drone tilted over to its side in mock confusion.

"Please confirm that you are the entity known colloquially as Luke of Sylcra."

That . . . unless it's talking about Lukeus, it should be me, right?

"I . . . I think so," he said, looking nervously behind him. The fire was beginning to stick to everything in the room, and it was only due to his Warrior-tier Constitution that he hadn't become a coughing wreck from the smoke invading his lungs. Even so, feeling the waves of heat licking his back, he knew he didn't have long if he wanted a shot of surviving whatever *this* was. If the thing didn't kill him, the blistering heat of the fire would. It burned much hotter than it had any right to, and even with a healing potion or two, he didn't like his odds of surviving prolonged exposure.

"Acknowledged. Do you intend to compete in the five thousand, three hundred, and fifty-eighth tournament of Olympus under the banner of Emperor Cyzicus of Sylcra?" the drone asked.

His eyes widened in realization.

So that's what this is.

"I—"

"Please be advised that if you forfeit now, you will be disqualified from the games and will not be able to reregister," it interrupted him. "You have three seconds to make your determination. Three."

Isn't the tournament supposed to be a few months from now? he thought while opening his status. He began to steadily add his stat points into Constitution and Agility in intervals of three and four. It was potentially not the best choice in the long run and not at all what he had initially planned, but without his techniques, he would only have his strength and speed to rely on.

A small part of him was disappointed at having made a suboptimal choice, but he was fast becoming used to the idea that his techniques, while potent tools against most foes, had weaknesses that he couldn't afford to ignore. Not anymore.

Whether it was the sky serpent's invisibility or the Rebel's insane speed, both were able to compensate for his battle sense and future sight. With that in mind, there was only one thing that he could be sure he would always have—raw attributes.

There had been and would continue to be times when only his strength, speed, and heartiness would make the difference between life and death.

"Two."

Luke waited patiently as it counted down. He already knew he would accept; it wasn't even a question to him at this point. If this was truly a part of the tournament, then the decision had been made long ago, back when they were flying to Sophia's forge.

Taking the few seconds that it offered to think of a plan, though, was only wise. Even if nothing actually came to mind.

"O—"

"Yes. I want to compete. Can you tell me what this is meant to be, though? How do I pass?"

"Acknowledged. Proceeding with assessment."

"Wai—" he protested half-heartedly, his sword already in hand and ready to deflect the incoming attacks. Immediately beams of red light once again began to rain down on him. Dodging them with every ounce of skill that he could muster, he carefully observed the drone and picked apart its every action in case it revealed any clue. None came.

All right. So this is some kind of preliminary qualifier. Which, hopefully, means that I'm not in any true danger. What I am in danger of, though, is failing. Which means I need to pass. Somehow.

So what's the win condition? Is there one?

My techniques don't work, which makes sense. They all involve killing, and that thing isn't alive, and if there is someone piloting it, I can't see them . . . which means I have to do this the hard way.

Whatever this is.

Frowning in determination, he sent a strand of his consciousness into the ring and retrieved a shield. He hadn't fought with one in a long time, but if there was ever a moment that warranted it, this was it.

Neither the Rebel nor the guard he had killed had one in the Hero tier, but there were a handful of Warrior-tier ones in the Rebel's ring. All of them were fairly basic, but they were better than the unenchanted Mortal-tier ones he had taken from the Hero's Tomb.

Each of them was enchanted with durability, self-repair, and a grab bag of tertiary abilities.

The one he withdrew was a rectangular hunk of brass that had the ability to stay in the air a fixed distance from wherever he anchored it relative to his body, which would provide some measure of kinetic resistance independent of his own control. It may not have been the best shield among the bunch, but against a foe that stayed in front of him and fired in straight lines, it would do.

He would have preferred something that shielded him from heat or fire, but with the exception of Hero-tier talismans, he didn't have anything that fit the bill, and the talismans had already proven ineffectual.

The fact that his sword held up to the barrage, however, gave him some hope that maybe its ability to pop talismans was limited to those items.

Only for it to crash and burn when the center of the shield began to glow an ominous red before the beam cut through entirely and burst out the other side. Ducking out of the way, he watched the shield clatter to the ground with a sense of dissatisfaction.

Come on.

"Hey! If this is a test, then why are you breaking my shit!"

"The acceptable use of talismans and artifacts is defined under section three, paragraph four of the tournament rules. Further violations will be deemed as grounds for forfeiture," the drone answered while still firing its attacks.

Slapping a beam away, Luke groaned in frustration. "So, tell me that before, jackass! How am I supposed to know all this?"

"A copy of the rules was sent to all Olympian sponsors two weeks ago, along with pamphlets containing frequently asked questions, which were to be shared with all contestants."

"Of course they were." Luke frowned as he narrowly batted away another beam. *Just when I stumble onto a literal fortune of artifacts, too, there's a rule saying I can't use them . . . Which, in hindsight, is probably for the best. If there's someone like Heracles competing, then fighting them at all is gonna be painful, but fighting them and their parent's wallet would be impossible, no matter how many heroes I kill.*

Whatever . . . that's a problem for me in the future. For now, I need to focus on getting past this farce of an assessment.

Which, destroying property and lighting supernatural fires aside, is pushing me to my limits, but overall pretty tame. It could have killed me if it wanted to. Easily at that. No way something that has enough juice to casually destroy the things it has would struggle with a warrior with a sword. And if Hephaestus is actually the one behind the tournament, and this thing was made by him . . . Well, I don't need a reminder of how ridiculously powerful gods are.

Still, what in the actual hell is this thing testing? My endurance? Is it scanning me and determining how far along I am in the Warrior tier? Some mixture of both?

Not knowing what else to do, he continued to dodge and deflect the drone's attacks over the next handful of minutes while it completely wrecked his room. With every second that passed, though, it seemed to become harder. Funnily, it reminded him of Tetris and how the blocks would fall quicker the higher his score.

He made a handful of attempts to destroy the thing before giving up on the idea entirely. Whenever he tried, the drone would dodge with a speed greater than what was possible in the Warrior tier, making the attempt itself a fruitless waste of energy. Whatever the goal of the assessment was, he figured that breaking the drone wasn't it.

After roughly five minutes of enduring the onslaught, however, the intensity of the laser beams superseded what he could react to and he slipped. A beam of red energy hit him square in the chest and sent him hurtling into the flames.

Surprisingly, it failed to actually hurt him, and a moment later a cool, refreshing mist wafted through the room. It put out the flames and healed the small burns that had accumulated on his body. Rubbing slow circles on his chest where the beam had struck him, Luke sat up. The drone had stopped its attacks the instant it had landed a strike and moved to the center of the room, where it put out the last licks of flame.

"Is that it? Did I fail?" Luke asked worriedly.

"Based on our models and the data assembled from other aspirants, your current rank is three hundred and eleven, with a combined total time of five minutes and three seconds. Congratulations, your application to participate has been tentatively approved. Please note: in the unlikely event that your rank falls below ten thousand, you will be reevaluated, and if found insufficient, your acceptance will be revoked," the drone said, then, flying above his still form, it dropped a token on top of his head before blurring away. Out of his room, and out of his sight. Hopefully forever, but something told him that it wasn't the last time he would be seeing the machines or others like it.

"What the fuck was that?" he said to no one in particular before shaking his head at the absurdity of it all.

Picking up the token, he turned it over in his palm. On one side there was a symbol of a hammer striking an anvil, and on the other was the number three hundred and eleven.

As he watched, it ticked up twice and landed on three hundred and thirteen.

Huh.

Someone knocked on the door and, before he could respond, slammed it open. Immediately Heracles and Rex tumbled through.

"We missed it." Heracles sighed.

"That's fine—what was your score?" Rex yelled impatiently. Completely unbothered by the wet and charred remains of Luke's room, Rex's eyes stared intently at the token on his hands.

"Hi." Luke waved at him. "How are you doing today, Rex?"

"I'm good. Now, can you please just tell me your score already?" he pleaded desperately.

"Three hun—"

"Shit," Rex hissed, and, reaching into his pocket, he slammed a slip of paper into Heracles's waiting palm and marched away while yelling, "Don't tell Nel I gave you that."

The son of Zeus grinned triumphantly, his ring glowed, and the paper disappeared.

"I believe congratulations are in order," he said, leaning against the door frame. "Five minutes isn't bad for your first time."

"You know what that was?"

"It's something one of my brothers made. My teacher had a few that we would spar against when we were children."

Of course.

"I see. So, what was all that about?"

The grin on his face stretched even wider.

"One of the biggest draws for the tournament, aside from the actual prizes for the contestants, is the gambling. The official bets won't open until the tournament begins in earnest and only on the final round, but a few minutes before you, the adjudicator tested Lukeus. Rex said that you would score lower than him, and I disagreed."

"Well, thanks for giving me a warning. That was appreciated," Luke snarked before flying over to where he had dropped the Limitless Thunder Bow.

Heracles laughed out loud. "I would have told you if I could find you, but we were told you were with Cyzicus. It didn't seem right to disturb you, and before that, you were unconscious for a week." His eyes raked across the bow and to the two rings on Luke's fingers. "You managed to unlock her ring?"

"Cyzicus did," he said, returning the bow to the Saint-tier ring. "What was Lukeus's score, by the way?"

"Come, let's go eat. I'll let him tell you himself."

CHAPTER 24

The Games Begin

<table><tr><td>+ 4 Stat Points</td></tr></table>

Luke grinned at the notification and ripped his sword free from the Warrior-tier giant's corpse. His chest heaved in exertion from the long battle. It never failed to surprise him just how much punishment the creatures could withstand, and not even the First Truth of Death had an easy solution for defeating them. Instead, it served to help him avoid hits and land the most damaging attacks while the monster's mana ebbed away and it was forced to heal itself over and over again. Death by a thousand cuts.

He could kill one relatively easily if he relied on his higher-tier weaponry, but watching the giant fall from the sky, hit the ground, and send a plume of dust into the air was a reward of its own. It also made for good training on top of it all.

After all, in mere hours, he would be leaving Sylcra to participate in the tournament. There, he wouldn't have access to any tools, bar his trusty blade and whatever the game master saw fit to provide them during the course of the tournament.

Taking a moment to make sure none of his Mortal-tier charges were in any danger, he opened his status and split the points evenly between all his stats.

Status	Skills	Quests	Inventory

Name: Lukas King

Tier: Warrior

Bloodline: Eyes of Insight

Mana: 117,001 / 128,018

Rate: 17% per hour

Strength: 41 > 254

Agility: 43 > 256

Constitution: 77 > 506

Arcana: 84 > 506

> Stat Points: 0
>
> Charges: 7/10

Four points wasn't a lot in the grand scheme of things, but considering how rare Warrior-tier giants and monsters turned out to be outside the Northern Marshes, it might as well have been a windfall. One of convenience more than anything else.

Killing hundreds of mortal giants was cathartic, on the rare occasions he was able to actually let loose on them, but also inefficient considering the time it took to go into battle and kill each of them one by one with his blade. Sparring with other warriors, on the other hand, tended to both net more stat points and actually improve his skills.

Flying back toward the town's walls, he sent his sword back into his storage ring and watched, bored, as the mortals he was babysitting finished off the last of the giants assaulting the barrier. Briefly, he entertained joining them before deciding against it. There weren't enough of them left to even give him a single point, and the last time he had done so, Clite had given him a talking-to. A tenth of a point wasn't worth another one.

Something dumb about "stealing experience from juniors," whatever that meant. Technically he was younger than all of them, but it wasn't considered proper for an Elder—or rather, warrior—to overtly interfere in battles of the lower tier. Unless, of course, their lives were in danger.

So, he just withdrew the Limitless Thunder Bow from his ring and observed while waiting for Clite to emerge from the city, where she was recharging the wardstone, letting his thoughts wander as he did.

Like they often had over the past month, they drifted to his new quest.

Status | Skills | **Quests** | Inventory
First and Second Place:
Ensure Spiros of House Paris wins the tournament of Olympus.
Place second in the tournament.

It was by far the weirdest and vaguest mission he had ever received, and the one that made him most nervous.

He didn't know what it was about, and the more he thought about it, the more uncomfortable he got.

Whether it was getting his sword, escaping Carim, kicking Arke off the island, or killing the Rebel, every quest so far had benefited him in an obvious way. They had made him safer, or they had made him stronger, sometimes both, and it had always been obvious how they did that. This was anything but.

If it was just finishing second place, I would understand. Maybe the prize is more suited to me or whatever. But where the hell does Spiros fit into all this?

Obviously if he's fighting in the tournament, he made it out of the tomb. It's not even a stretch for him to make it to the Warrior tier, if I'm being honest. If he cultivated manually, he could have done it pretty quick, too. And joining the tournament itself isn't a massive deal.

Emperors have a real and tangible reason for sponsoring us, and I'm not shy enough to admit that both me and him have quite literally a killer technique. Even with its limitations, it still stands head and shoulders above the others I've seen.

Hell, it let me kill a hero—granted, I had unlimited mana at the time, but still. Emperors would drool at a guy like Spiros with that kind of potential.

But . . . Why does he have to be first? More importantly, how does that benefit me? I doubt the Seed is doing this out of the goodness of its heart, so it has to tie into my chances of becoming a god in some way . . . but, how?

A cry of pain from below pulled him out of his thoughts, and instantly he slipped into the First Truth of Death. His mana sank into his ring, and the Limitless Thunder Bow appeared in his hands. Funneling a good fraction of his mana into the artifact, he pulled back the drawstring the second it manifested and let it go.

A blinding bolt of lightning flashed forward and, with perfect aim, turned to dust a single Mortal-tier giant.

"You good?" he asked, firing the bow a dozen more times in quick succession at all the remaining giants, clearing the field instantly. His earlier concerns about allowing the mortal cultivators to have their own challenges were gone the second he felt he had a just cause.

"Umm . . . Yes, Elder Luke. Thank you for your assistance." A blonde woman in her midtwenties bowed down to him.

Keeping his expression neutral in spite of his discomfort at being addressed so formally, he raked his eyes over her form. His gaze landed on her arm, where she had been clipped by one of the boulders the giants were so fond of throwing.

His ring flashed, and a vial of Mortal-tier healing potion appeared in the air in front of her.

"Drink it."

"Elder, I'm okay—"

He dropped the vial in her hand and flew away, not at all interested in her denial. It came from a good place, but saving potions wasn't worth an injury to someone actively fighting the tide, and he knew for a fact that the emperor himself would agree with him.

Sure, supplies were limited this deep into the tide, but being stingy would likely lead to her accruing even more injuries, which would in turn reduce her role to printing out talismans for the rest of the tide—assuming that her next injury wouldn't be fatal. It still amazed him how thin the island was stretched this late in the relentless war with the Earth itself.

Still, just another three weeks and it'll be all over, and they'll have ten years to recover, replenish, and whatever they need to do.

Quickly checking up on all the others that had come with them, he nodded in satisfaction and flew back into the town.

He found Clite exactly where he had left her, with her hands held over an altar in the middle of the city and her eyes closed in concentration as she pumped it full of mana. Stepping forward, he rested his own hand on it and immediately dumped three-quarters of his remaining mana, instantly bringing it to full.

Her eyes fluttered open, and she looked at him with exasperation. "You killed them all again, didn't you?"

"There were only twelve left, and the disciples were getting tired . . . One even got hurt."

" . . . "

"Look, it's a dumb rule, and I waited until one of them was injured. I still don't get why I have to sit around and wait for them to kill all the giants when we can end an attack instantly. Isn't that a better use of our time?"

"Because we don't have enough warriors to both power the wards *and* fight the giants. Coddling the Inner Disciples weakens them, and letting them battle strengthens them. We can't always be there, and if they come to rely on our presence, then that results in more deaths, not less. I understand that sitting back and allowing them to do the work is uncomfortable, but experience matters."

"How well have you researched that?"

She didn't dignify him with a response and brushed past him.

"You know I'm kidding, right?" Luke called out as he walked after her. "Mostly."

"You've been insufferable ever since you became a warrior."

"I think I've always been this way. We just didn't know each other that well before," Luke said, a smile playing across his lips.

"I remember you listening more than you talked and not arrogantly dismissing knowledge accumulated over millennia of battle with these creatures."

"Are you sure about that? I think I've always been like this." He smiled and nodded to the nervous-looking townsfolk as they made their way toward the teleportation platform.

"Perhaps. You were very fond of running off, so I didn't have much time to get to know you," Clite said.

"In my defense, I had pretty good reasons both of the times I left. And, if anything, I got stronger faster because of it. You remember I kil—"

"Yes. All of Sylcra remembers how you alone valiantly charged into battle against the Rebel and all her forces and struck her down in the seat of her own power days after rising to the Warrior tier. Children sing songs, women look at you longingly, and men wish they could do as you did."

He blushed red.

"I don't think any children know of me, do they? All this cultivator stuff is—" He stopped in his tracks as a loud noise rang out from his storage ring. Retrieving the token the drone had left him, he sent a small pulse of mana into it, silencing it.

"How much time is left?" Clite asked.

Luke glanced at the countdown displayed under his current rank of five hundred and ninety-eight. It had steadily ticked down the first few weeks after his assessment before plateauing in the late five hundreds as the final entries were finalized. It was significantly higher than Lukeus's, Nikitas's, and Rose's rankings—they had all placed in the thousands—and embarrassingly lower than Rex's, who had scored in the top one hundred. How he was allowed to use Blinky to tank all those hits, Luke didn't know, but he didn't look forward to facing the creature in the actual games, that was for certain.

"Just under seven hours."

She frowned at him disapprovingly. "Yet you still came here and wasted your mana. Is that truly wise? The tournament is not something to be trifled with, and entering it at anything less than your best is not wise."

"You're forgetting I'm a paragon. I recover mana a lot faster than you. And it's not like the tournament is going to start the moment we arrive." *That's not even mentioning my other advantages. Maximus can store the same amount of mana I can, which, combined with my already insane reserves, is a considerable advantage, and that's only half of what the sword does. On top of that, the Eyes of Insight should give me an advantage as well. Granted, all they let me do is see my mana with my eyes, and the only use I've found for that so far is making talismans faster, but I might figure something else out. Maybe.*

"Besides," Luke continued, "I was hoping I could make some last-minute improvements with my technique, so you can't call it a complete waste of time." *Even though that's exactly what it turned out to be,* he thought miserably, having failed to make any improvements to the First Truth of Death even with all the effort he had dedicated to the task over the months.

Clite flashed him a look that perfectly conveyed how unimpressed she was. "Your dedication is admirable, but I'd advise you not to grow arrogant." Her lips twitched upward. "At least not until you have defeated me in a spar."

"You turn invisible—that's practically cheating!"

"You have never defeated Heracles, either."

"He glows so bright I can't see anything. Most of the people there won't know how to get around my technique the way you two can."

"Rex."

"Excuse me, that's a low ball and you know it. Blinky is ugly and fighting her is disgusting, but she's weirdly cute and I don't want to hurt her. If he ever fought me one on one, he wouldn't last a minute, and everyone knows it . . . including you."

"Truly, your ability to make excuses for your shortcomings is formidable."

"No, it's not. I'll be able to take Heracles eventually—" Clite snorted. "Look, he's just had a longer time to figure his stuff out, and he's practically in the Hero tier. Honestly, with how strong he hits, he might be."

"He's not."

"Why are you so mean today?"

She rolled her eyes. "I'm not mean. You're overconfident. Yes, you are very strong for your tier and age, and have accomplished much, but it will not do you any good to underestimate those you are competing against. You will face the best Theos has to offer. Do not forget that."

"It's not like I have to win, though. Cyzicus will get his potion if I rank in the top ten. Which you know as well as I do is well within my abilities." *Besides, if the quest is anything to go off, then I have what it takes to make it to second place.*

Luke shook his head and looked over his shoulder where the Inner Disciples were trudging their way back. Despite his bravado, he was just as unsure about his odds of winning—or even doing what the Seed wanted, for that matter.

He had managed to complete his last two quests by the skin of his teeth; he had nearly been killed and had been forced to use a charge by Arke, and he'd nearly died when it came time to name his blade. Just because he had a quest didn't mean things couldn't go sour.

CHAPTER 25

The Holy Land

In Cyzicus's throne room, Luke, along with all the hopefuls and the emperor himself, stared at the back of his token.

Out of the dozen or so trainees that the hero had originally recruited to participate, only four, Luke, Rex, Rose, and Nikitas, had succeeded in both advancing to the Warrior tier and passing the assessment. Of them, only Rex and Luke were truly optimistic about their chances.

"Two minutes." Lukeus sighed from his spot atop Nutbutter. His eyes were locked on his own token.

"Why did you decide to compete, anyway? I thought you were against the whole idea," Luke asked idly. Lukeus's sudden shift in opinion had caught him off guard, especially with how vitriolic he had been about not participating before. Even now, months later, he hadn't been able to figure out what had changed. Not with Lukeus's habit of running away whenever the subject was brought up.

The emperor's grandson shrugged. "I'm allowed to change my mind."

Rex snickered, and Blinky, shrunken down to cape form and draped over his back, gazed at everyone in the room. "You know, I was talking to Maleager earlier." Instantly, Lukeus shifted in his saddle. Undeterred, Rex pressed on. "I bet it has nothing to do with the fact that Atalanta beat you up and called you a weak, unfilial coward when we were—"

Lukeus pulled a fist-size rock from his storage ring. His arm moved like lightning, and the object cut through the air with a whoosh. Rex, wearing a face-splitting grin, stepped forward and caught it with surprising ease.

"You're throwing rocks now?" he teased, tossing it up and down. "I wonder what she'll say about that. Hitting your own little brother. How shame—"

Cyzicus cleared his throat, and instantly the smiles slipped from everyone's faces and the mood sank into an awkward silence.

Luke glanced at the Hero-tier cultivator before looking away. Even now, months later, Cyzicus was still affected by the death of his lover. More even than by the death of his grandson.

So much so that Luke wasn't even sure if Cyzicus even wanted to break through to the next tier anymore.

A day or so after they had broken open the rings, he had glued himself to the teleportation altar and, as far as Luke knew, hadn't spoken a word to anyone since. He had actively ignored attempts to the contrary from both Clite and Nel.

It made Luke consider what Cyzicus had actually lost. The emperor had no wife, and all his kids and grandkids were in the Warrior tier. Where warriors lived for centuries, heroes measured their life span in millennia, and advancing to the Hero tier was a bottleneck that most cultivators lacked the ability to cross. Meaning he had lost someone he'd thought he would be spending the rest of his life with.

Luke felt sympathetic, but it made him think about his own reasons for doing what he had been. All this time, he had been rushing through the ranks and had happily celebrated every single stat point he had earned. After all, it meant he was doing the right thing. That he was getting stronger.

He hadn't ever stopped to consider if that power had a price. He had been appalled by killing at first, but increasingly, he felt numb at the act. Since then, he had just assumed that killing others, and living with that guilt, was a part of being a cultivator. He had assumed that a guilty conscience was the only price for his power.

He hadn't even considered the idea that any friends he made would die before him. Assuming he did it and became a god. What then? What would happen to the friends he made along the way?

Deep down, he knew the answer—they would die.

After all, when weighed against eternity, let alone a thousand years, even hundreds of thousands would be but a fraction of his life. The only ones he knew for sure would always be at his side were other gods, and he didn't know how to feel about that.

Living a life where the only people he could count on to always be there were jaded, callous, and nearly universally despised immortals didn't sound like a good time.

Or maybe I'm just being harsh. Zeus seemed all right. Cybele was chaotic . . . and I'm pretty sure that she robbed the shit out of me when she took the circlet—whatever that was—but she also paid for it. Sort of? I'll have to see what one of those pomegranate seeds goes for, but even then, I still don't know what the circlet was worth. Considering that she took it at all, though, I doubt it was a low-tier item. Saint at least, but probably higher. Possibly even divine.

Before his thoughts could spiral even more, the token rose from his hands and into the air, where it rapidly began to spin.

Cyzicus cleared his throat. "The time has finally come! I wish you all the best of luck. Do your utmost, and do not be disheartened if you do not do well or fall short of your expectations. I have seen the effort you have put into your training these past few months, and I want to thank all of you for working hard at my behest. Whatever the outcome, know that I am grateful."

The second he spoke the last word, the tokens slammed into each competitor's chest. The world flickered red and blue around them, and when they opened their eyes, they were standing in a large open field among thousands of others with the nine suns of Theos beating straight down on them from the highest point in the sky.

Luke took his first breath in the new land, and his eyes widened in wonder the moment the crisp air made its way to his lungs. Just the mere act of existing in the world seemed to make his cells sing. He felt his own mana come alive in a way that he had never felt before and devour the energy in the air.

He didn't need to open his status to know that his Arcana stat had gained some points just by the sheer virtue of him existing in this place.

Beside him, Blinky's jaws clattered around her eyeballs in rabid excitement, and he had to avert his gaze as her form writhed and undulated in excitement.

"This is insane," Rose muttered. Her hand flexed, and a moment later, it was enshrouded in a bright-blue flame. It, Nutbutter, and Blinky drew the eyes of everyone in their immediate vicinity for a scant few seconds before more interesting things stole their attention.

Nodding slightly to her, Luke attempted to rise a few feet in the air, only to find that his mana was completely unable to grip the space around him. After trying a few more times, he gave up and, spinning on his heels like everyone else, he surveyed the crowd.

Like the crew of the *Argo*, the people assembled in the field were diverse beyond what Luke had anticipated.

A few miles away from him, there was a group of cyclopes dressed in orange leather, each one of them dozens of feet tall and looming over the crowd. Their lone eyes stared at the rest of the contestants with a mixture of nervousness and mistrust.

A ways behind him was a herd of minotaurs. They too were giant, the shortest among them fifteen feet tall. They possessed massive horns decorated in ribbons, large floppy ears pierced in a dozen places with golden rings, and flattened snouts in place of their noses.

Behind them, a collection of white-winged and white-haired women immediately put him on guard. None of them, however, were Arke, despite the uncanny resemblance.

More members of her species, I guess.

The winged women, like the cyclopes, looked nervous. Their oval-shaped heads were on a constant swivel as they examined the assembled warriors with caution.

None of them, however, shocked Luke more than the familiar forms of two people fewer than a dozen feet away from him. His thoughts ground down to a screeching halt as he burned their images in his head and turned away before Rex or Lukeus noticed him staring at their backs.

Both Arya and Spiros looked just like he remembered them. Both were dressed in the red robes traditional of warriors who called the Dolion archipelago home. Spiros was even leaning on a spear—the same gold one that Luke had spent hours trying to steal while he was in the tomb and waiting for the altar to charge.

It's fine. They don't know it's me. Can't, really. I look completely different, I've gained like six inches in height, and my sword gained a foot in length and looks different on top of that. Even my voice is deeper now, so, really, I have nothing to worry about, he thought, unable to help the feelings of disappointment or the nervous lump forming in the back of his throat. He had known that Spiros at least would be here, but his own feelings caught him off guard.

The realization of his safety wasn't the comfort Luke thought it would be either. There was so much he wanted to talk to them about, share where he had gone and what he had done, but none of it was stuff that he could say.

Before he could dwell on it further, though, a hush fell over all ten thousand of those assembled.

A fire swirled to life in the sky above them. It started small, but as the seconds passed, it became increasingly larger and hotter. A tenth sun in the sky, but unlike the nine orbiting the world, this one was *close.*

He felt the blistering heat on his skin, and the air itself began to ripple and distort. Sweat escaped his pores and evaporated instantly, leaving him parched and dehydrated in a few short seconds.

Struggling to stay standing, he resisted with every fiber of being the urge to reach into his inventory and swallow all the water he had stored inside it. It was here, above anywhere else, that he needed to be careful not to let anything slip.

He knew enough about cultivation and the abilities of warriors and even heroes to know what would and wouldn't stand out to them. What could be explained by talent and what couldn't. Gods, however, were a drastically different problem.

As ageless beings that had lived on and watched Theos for ages, ones that knew the intricacies of mana better than anyone else alive . . . he couldn't take even the slightest risk. So while he was confident that not even Cyzicus could sense when the Seed raised his stats, he knew instinctively that deities wouldn't fall under the same umbrella.

Danger Detected.

The warning flashed before his eyes, and Luke dismissed it instantly, but unlike every other time, it didn't go.

A red icon, an eye, appeared and floated at the very corner of his vision.

It was the first time he had seen the symbol, but the message couldn't be more clear. He was being observed.

Don't use it. Don't pull anything out of the inventory. Don't mess with stats . . . nothing. Just appear normal, Luke. He repeated the mantra over and over in his head.

In the sky, the heat coming from the flames gradually began to wane. The flames began to congeal and thicken, forming sinuous strings that combined to form a vague, humanlike shape.

It brought its hands together and clapped.

Water began to rain from a cloudless sky, and, like balm seeped into their skin, giving them sweet relief from the blistering and all-encompassing heat from moments before.

The figure clapped again, and as soon as it had come, the water vanished, leaving them once again standing on a field of green grass under a cloudless blue sky.

What did he just do? Luke thought, his mind an anxious mess and his mana palpitating nervously.

Hephaestus looked down at them from his spot in the sky. He looked young, in his early thirties, and was dressed simply in white trousers and a shirt that hung loosely over his muscled frame. He lacked shoes. His hair was bloodred, and steel-gray eyes bored into Luke and everyone else with an intensity that betrayed his power.

CHAPTER 26

A God's Might

Hephaestus smiled.

Each and every person standing in the field found themselves unable to tear their eyes away from the benevolent god in the sky. Unable to look away from him. How could they, when their lord was smiling upon them with such mercy? With such beauty? They needed to be grateful. They had to be.

His place above them was *proper*, and suddenly not being able to fly only made sense to Luke in a way it hadn't before. It wasn't right, after all, for someone like him to share space with a being that was perfect in every way. A being that had seen more, done more, was *more*.

He felt silly for even trying. For even daring to think that what he did was okay. He should be punished for even thinking of tainting the air with his presence. How dare he possess such hubris? How could he even allow himself to attempt becoming a being that great? Him? A petty mortal. Some guy who had lived and died on earth without doing anything of note could become a god? There wasn't anything more ridiculous in the universe.

I can't believe I even wanted to fly when I should be worshi—

No. Something solidified within him, within his soul and within his mana. A seed of resolve. Its very essence hated what he had just been about to think. It was angry. Angry that he had even considered it. Worship was not the path of a cultivator. It couldn't be.

NO, his thoughts screamed at him. Louder than they had ever been, they demanded he not give in.

The veins on his forehead and temples bulged while nervous sweat formed beads on his brow and slid down his face. He felt hot, and his robes stuck to the moist skin of his back, but this time it had nothing to do with heat.

He bit down on his tongue, hard enough to draw blood, and then harder still. He reveled in the pain and used it to find clarity, not letting up even as his mouth filled with blood. He was unwilling to let it spill down, so he swallowed it. He would not show that thing in the sky the price he had paid for his own thoughts.

One smile and he had been ready to prostrate himself before the Olympian. It terrified him as much as it filled him with rage. It was one thing to have his back forcibly bent under the weight of someone else's power. Arke could dominate him because she was stronger than he was. She could kill him as easily as she could breathe. But his mind was his own, free to rebel, curse, and revile her existence for as long as his soul was his.

Luke may have respected a god's strength and ability, but he decided then and there that he would never worship one. Not after what he had seen. Those that wielded power deserved caution, much like a rabid animal—not adoration. Anything more than that had to be earned with action and deeds. No matter how strong they were. Aeolus, Arke, and even the Rebel were proof of that.

Tearing his eyes away from the deity, he, without turning his head, looked at the other competitors. Like he had been moments ago, they were staring at Hephaestus with wide, adoring eyes. Like puppies waiting patiently for their owner to hand them a treat.

Luke bit his own tongue harder in response, but try as he might, his gaze was once again drawn back to the god. Whether it was some strange force or his own morbid curiosity, he didn't know.

His eyes found the god's, which were staring back at him. Taking a deep breath, he hardened his gaze and widened his stance. Reaching into his storage ring, he retrieved Maximus and pointed the blade at him in challenge. It was a dumb decision, entirely driven by ego, but he needed the god to know that he would not be bullied. Even if he had to die for it. His pride as a cultivator would accept nothing less, and not doing so would mean admitting defeat, admitting that he would never be as good as him.

Deep in his heart, he knew he would be better. Not today, not soon, but he would.

Hephaestus continued to stare at him, and his smile stretched into an approving grin. Like an excited child's, his hand crept up, and he rested a single finger vertically across his lips. Immediately, the action doused the rage burning inside Luke.

The god's meaning was clear.

Swallowing the mixture of saliva and blood in his mouth, he nodded. The god winked and turned away. Suddenly feeling awkward, Luke lowered his sword.

Was that a test?

In front of him, Spiros lifted the butt of his spear off the ground and, in a single smooth movement, twirled the golden shaft in a half circle and silently slammed the sharpened head into his sandal-clad foot, impaling himself. Having broken free of the divine thrall, he stared defiantly into the sky, completely oblivious to the blood oozing from his foot, staining the grass red, and the spear still lodged in it.

Hephaestus nodded once again and made the same gesture, asking Spiros to stay quiet. Not that the rest of those on the field noticed, and if they had, they were too far into the trance to care.

A moment later, Lukeus, still atop Nutbutter, punched himself so hard he fell face first off his Pegasus. Rose's hand once again caught flame, but this time she brought it to her neck and gritted her teeth.

Rex balled his fist and punched himself between his legs as hard as he could. He dropped to his knees, and Luke cracked an uneasy grin at the sight.

That's one way to do that, I guess.

A flash of light attracted his attention, and he grinned slightly as a dagger appeared in Arya's hand. She slammed it into her palm.

Similar scenes played out all across the field as, one after another, the contestants inflicted some level of damage onto themselves and broke free of the god's divine thrall.

In the sky, Hephaestus silently watched the scene unfold and then, without warning, clapped his hands. Those who were still caught in the trance shook their heads clear and looked around, confused. A few even rubbed their eyes, like they had just awoken from a long sleep.

"You fail, go home," the god said, his voice barely above a whisper but heard clearly by all of them.

Luke watched as Nikitas suddenly erupted with an orange and red light and, wearing a miserable expression, vanished. The same scene played out all across the grassy field.

Nearly nine thousand warriors, each of them prodigies who had achieved their rank at an extremely young age, had been eliminated mere minutes after arriving, leaving those who remained blinking in surprise.

Well, that was fast, Luke thought nervously.

"The rest of you I welcome to Vulcan. My home," the god said, stretching his hands out to the side and spinning in a slow circle. Coming to a stop, he closed his eyes, inhaled deeply, and exhaled slowly. Having taken a moment to smell the grass, he smiled down on them.

In front of each of them appeared a vial filled with glimmering blue fluid. Luke recognized it as a Warrior-tier healing potion but obviously of higher quality than any he had ever seen before. The vial itself looked like it was made from diamond, while the cork was a diamond as far as Luke could tell, and the fluid itself was so rich in color that it made the rest he had seen seem like trash.

"Drink and be healed," the god commanded, and immediately Spiros ripped his spear from his foot and stabbed it into the ground. Uncorking the vial, he downed it in a single gulp.

Smiling at his fast action, Luke did the same. Waves of cool healing energy traveled through every inch of his body, stitched his tongue back together and replaced the coppery taste of blood with something that was distinctly fruity, and the remaining energy settled lightly into his gut, waiting to heal his next injury.

That's . . . that's not a Warrior-tier potion, is it? Luke thought numbly, observing the energy within him. Normal potions didn't linger. Their effects washed through the person who drank them and faded in a few seconds to a few minutes, depending on how fast they were swallowed.

Sharing a confused glance with Lukeus, who was staring at his now-empty vial with wonder, they shrugged before turning back to the god in the sky. He waited patiently as the rest of the contestants drank their potions.

"Your friends that failed will never be gods. They will never ascend past the Warrior tier. Their will is too weak. Those of you that remain, those of you who hated me, might go further. So long, of course, as your spirits aren't broken and you continue to live. Each of you who stands here has the one quality essential to rise through the tiers—pride. What you felt was neither technique nor artifact but my presence. The mere weight of my existence. Nearly all mortals, most all warriors, and even some heroes, when exposed to a being such as I, cannot help but surrender. Give up and serve. It is not a choice that they make, but the core of who they are. And those who are gone are those that will bend their knees rather than die. You, who are still present, when faced with a choice between servitude and defiance, would rather die than kneel."

He seemed delighted at that.

"Many wonder why we gods hold this tournament. Why we prevent mortals from cultivating. Why we make them live in ignorance. You will hear a different answer with every person or even every god you ask, and that is only right. There are many answers and many reasons. Among them, however, is one that *I* believe to be paramount: cultivators are those that struggle. If a mortal is so satisfied with his existence that he never seeks the world thinly veiled behind shallow walls begging to be looked beyond, questioned, and conquered, then he should not cultivate. Cultivating is the privilege of the curious and the brave. Of those that will grasp opportunity, no matter the risk. It is why those that seek answers are never turned away. It is why each of your sects, kingdoms, and families have institutions in place for accepting all mortals who try their hands at finding answers, and to welcome into the fold and not punish those that learn the truth after having sought it. Those who are curious, however, are all greeted with the same test. It is why those that know the secret are exiled if they do not progress. That which you call the midstage of the Mortal tier is the first, and perhaps greatest, barrier to shedding the mortal coil. After all, curiosity without determination and resolve is useless." He took another deep breath and solemnly regarded the assembled warriors.

Luke's mind flashed back to the day he died, and he found perhaps the answer to that single question that had bothered him since he had been chosen by the Seed.

It picked me because it knew I would say yes. I was the only soul there that was stupid enough to watch a demented god eat the souls of the dead and then take it from the woman who killed him.

"With that, we shall let the games begin."

Luke and all the remaining warriors were engulfed in a red and orange glow. The world flickered away, and when they emerged, it was at the foot of a silver pyramid that stretched so far into the sky it pierced the clouds and so thick it encompassed the horizon.

Stairs cut through the middle and climbed in a straight line to its peak.

"You have proven to me that you are not weak of will. Now, you will show me how strong your will is when tested against others who do not falter when pitted against even the divine. Climb until there are only a hundred of you left," Hephaestus said, his voice echoing down from the peak of the pyramid, where he sat on his throne—waiting.

The thousand contestants gathered at the bottom immediately broke into murmurs.

"Nutbutter's gone!" Lukeus said suddenly.

"So is Blinky!"

"The competition is for us, not your mounts," Rose muttered under her breath, brushing past them and onto the steps.

Luke shook his head and joined her, patting the brothers on the back as he walked past them. His gaze darted between all the contestants before landing on Spiros and Arya, only a few feet in front of him.

"I have this test in the bag," Spiros said excitedly.

"Just don't poop your pants in front of a god," she replied.

". . . I'll do what I need to."

Luke burst into laughter.

CHAPTER 27

An Old Friend

His laughter contrasted sharply with the nervous milling of the rest of the contestants, and a few of those around him flashed him an annoyed expression. He couldn't bring himself to care.

This guy, he hasn't changed a bit, has he?

As Spiros's eyes met his, the teenager's face blushed an angry red, and Luke realized that he might have come across in a way that he didn't want to.

"I had a good reason, okay," Spiros hissed at him and then turning toward Arya, leveling an angry glare toward her. Her own lips stretched into a small smile at his expense.

"I—I'm sure you did." Luke smiled and ignored the nervous ball of tension in his chest. Then, glancing at his companions, he walked forward, quickly closing the distance between them, and held his hand out. "I'm Luke, by the way," he said, looking Spiros straight in the eye.

Nothing strange here, nope. Nothing at all. I'm just some guy who heard that you shat your pants and came over to introduce himself. That's totally not weird. Just be cool, be collected, and don't let anything slip. Yep.

Spiros watched his hand and, after a brief moment of hesitation, took it. Luke's smile stretched even farther, and he considered briefly feeling the other warrior out with his mana. He wanted to see how well Spiros had progressed since they'd last met but decided against it. The warning Clite had given him back when she was teaching him the lesson rang in his head.

"It's considered immensely rude, shy of assault, but many will consider it an act of aggression nonetheless. Like yelling or grabbing someone's nose without cause. There are of course times and situations when it is acceptable, and I'll leave them for you to determine. I will warn you, however, especially now that you are a warrior, to be cautious with who you do it to and when."

The way Luke thought about it, it was getting caught that was the rude part. The actual act of sensing other people's mana was pretty simple and, if done subtly enough, imperceptible. He just needed to send a wave of mana into his target, and he would get some feel for the potency of their mana compared to his own. The sense was more limited than he had initially thought, and the resolution, for a lack of a better term, wasn't great, but it did give him a very rough idea of how strong someone was.

Both Heracles's and Jason's mana felt like an insurmountable and sturdy wall. While that of someone like Rose, who had broken through a month after him, felt like a shoddy picket fence. Mortals ranged from having mana that felt like air to pushing his hand against a shirt hanging to dry on a line.

Still, betting on Spiros being incompetent wasn't the way to go. The kid was oblivious, but he was far from dumb, and if he had any training in the Warrior tier, he would be on the lookout for exactly that. Especially when he was in contact with a stranger.

Yeah, let's not, he thought, observing the pair's reaction to his name.

Both Spiros and Arya went slightly stiff, and they shared a tiny, almost imperceptible, glance before looking at him oddly.

It warmed his heart just a little to know that he hadn't been forgotten.

Turning around, he ignored the oddity and began to introduce his new friends to his old. It felt awkward in a way that he didn't quite expect, but he smothered the feeling and pressed on. "That's Lukeus. Sometimes he goes by Luke. Beside him is Rex, his brother. The angry blonde is Rose."

The three of them waved uncertainly, no doubt wondering why he was talking to the competition.

I probably could have handled this better, but the poop joke . . .

"I'm Spiros!" the son of House Paris introduced himself, unwittingly coming to the rescue.

"Arya," she said, her eyes lingered on the three, darting between their robes and their faces before raking across Luke's body, clearly searching for something but unsure what it was.

For a moment, he feared he had been discovered, but he dismissed that thought as soon as it entered his mind and reminded himself that they had no reason to suspect him.

"I have a friend named Luke," Spiros suddenly chimed in, and it took everything Luke had to portray what he hoped was just the right amount of interest. "The asshole just kind of up and disappeared, though."

"Did he?"

"Yeah." He turned to face the stairs and began walking up them. "I was hoping he'd show up for the games. It would have been nice seeing him again."

"Maybe he did? We did just lose a few thousand people."

"No." Spiros shook his head. "If he was here, he wouldn't have lost so quickly. He's . . . he's better than that. A prodigy. A *smile* wouldn't have fazed him."

What the hell did I do to make him so confident in me? Luke thought curiously, beginning to make his own way up the steps. *Other than going from never cultivating a day in my life to a pretty solid level in a few weeks, but still. This seems like a bit much,* he thought, feeling a small amount of pride. Not that he would let it show.

"Well, being smart doesn't always translate to whatever *that* was. One look and Hephaestus had us—" Luke shivered, the mere memory of the experience bringing forth a sense of disgust.

Spiros shrugged. "Maybe, but I doubt it."

Luke heard a rhythmic thumping noise coming from behind him and, glancing over his shoulder, he immediately pressed himself flat against the warm metallic wall. It wasn't a second too soon, as half a dozen thirty-foot-tall cyclopes bolted past them at a speed that felt unnatural even when considering their cultivation.

"Should we be running?" Rex asked, scratching the back of his head.

"I . . . don't . . . think so," Lukeus said.

"Me neither," said Luke. "The winners are going to be the last one hundred people still on the pyramid, not the ones who get to the top first. Let's just keep climbing until something happens. With how tall this pyramid is, we'll be climbing for days anyways, that's plenty of time to make up the distance if we need to, and longer than any of us can sprint. Besides . . . I don't think Hephaestus cares how quickly we can run up a flight of stairs. I bet there's something more to this, that we haven't—"

"They stopped," Rose interrupted him as, her eyes narrowing to slits, she watched the cyclopes leading the way up the metallic stairs.

Even from where he was, Luke could clearly make out their surprised expressions. Whatever it was they encountered, it didn't hold them back for long, because a moment later, they began climbing again. This time, though, they didn't bother running and instead resumed at a sedate pace. Considering their height, though, they were still clearing a dozen steps at a time.

Huh.

Spiros and Arya shared a brief glance with each other and, nodding politely to Luke, began climbing.

He watched them go with a sense of unease. On one hand, he knew that it was a normal reaction. They didn't know him, Rex, and Lukeus, and he had intruded on a random conversation the two of them were having. A mere eavesdropping stranger, that's all he was to them now. It hurt a little, thinking like that, but it wasn't enough reason to divulge his identity.

Following a step or two behind them, he felt a surge of anger toward the Seed before he ruthlessly crushed the emotion.

Completing its quests had made him kill strangers and run from his first—and, at the time, only—friends on Theos, and it didn't even have the courtesy of leaving them alone after that. Instead, it tasked him to help one of them win the tournament for a purpose he couldn't even begin to fathom.

Another, smaller, part of Luke, though, couldn't help but be a little thankful for it, too. Because in spite of everything, it felt good to know that they weren't trapped in the Hero's Tomb. He had never wavered in his belief that they would make it out, but the confirmation was nice.

And at least now I won't be tempted to go back in a few years when I'm Hero tier or higher to break them out. Small victories . . . But going back might not be a terrible idea, now that I think about it. Maybe check up on the tomb and take everything that's inside, free the people still trapped if they're alive . . . Hell, it may even be worth it seeing what Nefkha is up to. It wouldn't hurt to tie up that particular loose end.

. . . All right, let's not get too dark in here, Luke. He shook his head silently and just focused on putting one foot in front of the other, concentrating on the tournament and what he needed to do to complete his quest. Watching Spiros practically march forward, though, he felt that he didn't have to worry too much, if at all, about him at this stage. Not when he had willingly shat his pants to massively outperform others on a test like this in the past. Spiros would be the last person to ever give up here. Of that he was confident.

Besides, if this round ends with a hundred people still in the running, this is probably just the first real challenge. Hephaestus is still thinning the herd. The real stuff will be after. That's when I'll probably need to step in.

A few minutes later, when Luke and the rest had made their way to the thousandth step, they found out exactly what had convinced the cyclopes that this wasn't a race.

The one thousand and first step felt like they were wading through water, but without the feeling of buoyancy that came with it. The space in Vulcan was already weird, in that it actively rebuffed their mana and prevented them from flying. Now it seemed to push against and resist the mana within them, too. It felt like it was opposed to the mere idea of them traversing through it and had decided to be obstinate and challenge them for every inch they took.

Even so, it still wasn't *hard*.

All those competing were in the Warrior tier, and their bodies were stronger and full of more vitality than they had any right to be. When combined with the nourishing and energizing mana soaking the air and filtering into them, the stairs actually felt kind of pleasant. It brought Luke back to what it was like when he was a mere mortal. When moving his limbs hadn't always been so easy or effortless.

A thousand steps later, the difficulty rose again, making the nature of the test clear to all of them: the higher they climbed, the more strenuous it would get. Which worked just fine for Luke. He suspected that he had a significant advantage over most of the others when it came to cultivation. He knew firsthand just how hard it was to raise attributes for those in their level, and he was confident that when it came to raw stats, there was no one here that would be able to beat him. Not when manasinks for warriors seemingly didn't exist and he had Maximus to rely on.

On top of that, not only was he a paragon, with a perfect foundation, but he was also a quarter of the way through the tier itself. He doubted others could boast the same.

But I can't be too arrogant. I'll bet anything that there's at least a few people here who have backgrounds and training that's as good as it gets. Not to say my own techniques and advantages are lacking, but I can't assume that no one here has better.

A commotion broke him out of his musings.

It happened suddenly, within the time it took to blink, but the moment the cyclopes at the very top crossed over to the fifth layer, the whole pyramid shook and came to life.

The silvery walls of the pyramid that lined the steps undulated in a way unbefitting of a metal. Moments later, large, featureless humanoid things walked out.

Each one looked exactly like the last, with smooth, androgynous bodies made of what looked like mercury.

Luke paused in his step and stared at the indents where one's eyes would be. The thing looked down at him and, in a single, robotic motion, lifted three fingers in the air.

One dropped down.

Luke withdrew his sword.

The second finger dropped down, and its other arm burst into liquid metal and reformed as a blade. Its sharp edge glinting in the light.

Luke cursed internally as the First Truth of Death failed to activate for a thing that wasn't alive.

The final finger dropped.

CHAPTER 28

A New Rule

Luke stared nervously at his foe, dimly aware of the others facing their own robots but unwilling to tear his eyes away from the one pointing its sword-shaped limb at *him*. Its lifeless stare, large size, metallic luster, and complete lack of cultivation made it a more menacing foe than most he had faced before. Those, he knew, could be killed, but this, he wasn't sure. Seeing as it was made by a god, though, he didn't have high hopes of being able to defeat it.

Even discounting the First Truth of Death not working, the way its body turned to liquid and then back to solid gave Luke the impression that not even a clean blow to its heart or severing its head would do any damage to it.

Which means that if it's not there for us to beat, it should just be an obstacle, and hopefully one that won't try and kill me.

The Olympics weren't lethal, of that he'd been assured time and time again. The gods' own children competed, after all.

But, as he raked his eyes over the mercurial body of the machine marching toward him, each of its footsteps ringing with the sound of a dull bell, he knew that losing the tournament didn't just mean going home with a bruised ego.

The Seed's intent may not have been easily decipherable, but he doubted that it was planning something that wasn't important to his path. Each quest was a building block on top of the last, balancing risk, reward, and safety in an endless churn toward the ultimate peak.

Any hiccups might well lead him to needing to use his charges, and that was unacceptable. They were his biggest guarantees for continued safety, but just like losing lives in any game, they acted as a sign that he was slipping—losing. That he wasn't good enough. That he would succumb to the same fate as Aeolus.

And that's not going to be me. I'm not going to just be a god. I'll be the greatest.

He felt Maximus stir in reaction to his thoughts, his will inadvertently prompting it to action. The store of his mana within, always equal to his own, began to rush through the bond that connected them and into him. Activating what was perhaps becoming Luke's favorite ability.

Enhancement. It did one of three things—made him twice as strong, twice as fast, or twice as durable.

It wasn't quite as domineering as his technique, and not as practical as his blade's ability to give him stat points, but the heady *rush* that came with using it was like nothing else, and the cost was more than affordable. Unlike the ever-hungry First Truth of Death, it applied a negative modifier to his mana regeneration. Instead of gaining seventeen percent of his total mana pool every hour, he would lose twenty percent. His reserves, combined with the blade's, meant he could sustain it for ten hours if he didn't spend mana on anything else.

This won't take that long.

The robot lunged forward and slammed its bladed arm clean against Luke's sword. With his strength doubled, he caught it with ease that surprised even him. Pushing it back, he changed the focus of his ability from Strength to Agility and watched it tumble back. Instinctively, he made to pursue it forward before deciding against it entirely and backpedaling, retreating as quickly as he could to the next step. If he was right, then he didn't need to fight at all.

The robot squatted down, its feet turned to springs, and its bladed arm morphed into a giant claw. It leaped forward, its claw stretched out, and grabbed a fistful of his robes. Undeterred, Luke swung down and cut himself free. With a gaping hole in his robes, he landed on the next step.

His sword raised, he was ready to defend himself if it continued its attack.

The robot stopped in its tracks and, after staring at him for a moment, strode back to the wall, where it stood still.

Immediately after, another robot, identical to the one before, walked in front of him and lifted three fingers.

Luke deactivated the blade's ability, returned it to its sheath, and, ignoring it, walked to the next step.

Should I? he thought, watching the rest of them desperately catching the robots' well-telegraphed blows on their weapons. They were driving the other competitors back toward the bottom, where he suspected they would be eliminated. It was a competition, and regardless of the fact that they had come here together, there would only be one winner. Practically, it didn't matter if they lost now or in a few rounds. So long as he did well, Cyzicus would get what he wanted.

His eyes landed on Spiros. The brown-haired teen was holding up better than he expected, but like the rest of them, he was steadily being driven back. Arya was already eyeing the stairs, and for the briefest of moments, her eyes met his.

He nodded.

"Climb and they ignore you," Luke called out and, not waiting for them, he advanced to the next step. A few seconds later, they caught up to him.

"Thanks!" Spiros slapped him on his shoulder and glanced meaningfully at Arya. She nodded at him.

"No need, you all would have figured it out without me," he said, tracing his eyes over them and his own companions.

With the current level of their attributes, the climb was beginning to take its toll. Sweat soaked their brows and drenched their robes, making the garments cling to their skin. Even for Luke, every step forward was like wading through molasses, and he couldn't imagine it being any easier for the rest of them.

Climbing to the next step, he deliberately let the machine of liquid metal count to two before he rose to the next step. "The test is pretty clear. He's setting a pace. Three seconds a step isn't bad, but I think the timer is going to decrease the more we climb. If it follows the same pattern, we can expect a decrease every time we get to the next thousand steps."

"That's not great," Rex said, his chest rapidly rising and falling.

"Well, he needs to eliminate us somehow."

"Yeah, but what's he testing?"

Luke opened and closed his mouth. "Our determination?" he said eventually. It was the best he could come up with, but even to him, it didn't fit. Not anymore.

Hephaestus had compared this trial to what mortals typically had to do to join a sect, but even that didn't make much sense anymore.

It would have if the robots had appeared behind them and attacked the stragglers, but even then, the test wouldn't be about determination but endurance.

They were all warriors, and none of them were strangers to training or ones to give up. If they lost, it would be because their cultivation was lacking. Not because they didn't try their best.

So what's he really looking for? Or is resistance a mental thing, and different for all of us, but equalized in difficulty? Maybe a mix of both?

No easy answer was forthcoming, and with a frown, Luke continued his climb, keeping an eye on his companions.

Already they were beginning to struggle, and as he looked at both those above them and below them, he realized that they weren't the only ones. Most everyone was, making the ones that were moving more easily stand out like sore thumbs.

There weren't many of them, maybe a dozen or so including Luke, but their demeanor was different. They were composed.

Most, like him, were being efficient and using the three-second timer as an opportunity to recuperate some small measure of their stamina before advancing to the next step. They were distinguished from their peers by their straight backs and light steps—a stark contrast to most of the others, who already had their shoulders hunched, were panting for breath, and looked more like they were crawling than walking.

There was one, however, who looked entirely unconcerned by the mounting resistance against his mana. He walked quickly and methodically, lifting and planting his legs with such symmetry that he seemed more like the robot sentinels observing their climb than a cultivator competing against them.

For a second, Luke found himself entranced by his presence and, somehow sensing his gaze, the other teen looked back at him.

His eyebrows lifted in surprise, and he waved while Luke's heart nearly stopped beating. He nodded to the other teen and trained his own gaze forward, his mind reeling in well-disguised shock. They looked so similar they could pass for brothers, maybe even twins, from the color of their hair to the structure of their faces, and he only had a dead hero to blame.

When he had gotten the chance, he had looked into the Mask of a Thousand Faces once again. His Warrior-tier mana had revealed a lot about it.

Mainly it had confirmed his suspicion that all three of the faces that he had found in the mask, from his current one to the female version of the current one and the supremely ugly one, were all specifically crafted by its last owner. With his denser mana, he could now adjust his features with much more precision, to look like anything that he desired—not that he would, of course. He had too much riding on his current identity to throw it away, and he had to live with the consequences. Whatever they may be.

He didn't know what ham-fisted scheme the dead empress of Carim had been cooking up before she'd been executed by the Atlantians, but it very clearly involved impersonating a god or one of their children.

So she fucked around and found out. Then I fucked around, and now I might find out, he thought miserably.

I can't believe I'm stuck impersonating a child of a god while being in a body descended from a titan. I should have just picked the ugly-looking form, but no, I had to get greedy and pick being handsome.

At the very back of the procession of warriors, Hephaestus walked with them, observing and thinking.

His form was unassuming, and fake sweat poured down his brow. His face was the mask of a man struggling with each step, while internally, he delighted in his acting skills.

None of the mortals suspected him of secretly being among them. It pleased him, and he resolved to do it more often. Maybe even live as a mortal in the territory of a young hero? It had been a while since he had done it last, and the more he thought about it, the more the prospect appealed to him.

Alas, time often slipped while he was in his workshop.

He would still be there if Zeus hadn't come knocking, insisting that he host the silly little tournament and preaching about the pact the twelve of them had sworn ages past and then banded together and forced the others to do the same.

How they had agreed to not be like the fat, cruel, and lazy titans they had overthrown. Promised to tend to the world and the people on it. To make Theos into a place where the mortals could live long and healthy lives while nurturing the next generation of cultivators to be their protectors, guardians, and, for the few worthy, maybe even gods.

But hosting a tournament was a boring task. You could watch an infant take its first steps only so often before growing sick of it. Still, he consoled himself, it was something that needed to be done. So he would see it completed. It had been a long time since he had, after all, and maybe some time away from his forge would be entertaining. He doubted it.

Moreover, something about how Zeus had come to him didn't feel right, and it had taken him all of a single second to suspect his king's intentions, and another two to confirm them. His drones acted as eyes and ears all across the realm, and the news he was looking for was not hard to unearth. Zeus had sired a son named Heracles and was overjoyed, for he believed the child possessed the potential to reach divinity. An emotion Hephaestus could understand. It was hard watching kids die, and those of a kind nature were even harder to come by. Which was why he hadn't sired any since the last passed on to the Aether millennia ago, failing to climb past the Saint tier, even with all the resources at his disposal.

Heartache from the past, however, did not dull his thinking today.

It wasn't hard to predict why it was that Zeus was calling on him specifically to host the games. The king of gods was rich, as all gods were, but not all gods shared the same specialties.

While the others had waged wars, killed mighty beasts, built empires and holy lands, explored Theos and the worlds beyond—he had chosen to learn.

The true tongue was mysterious, even to him. It was old. Older than them, the titans, and the ancients before them. If Thoth was right, as he suspected he was, the true tongue had come into existence alongside the Aether itself during the dawn of time.

His own mastery of it—though he would never claim to be a master—had allowed him to become the greatest craftsman.

An artifact made by him was unquestionably the best, because only he could craft something that could invoke the eternal will and demand a name to be given. It wasn't a surprise, then, that Zeus wanted such an artifact for his son.

Which was fine, but Hephaestus didn't like being lied to, so he had changed the rules to make Zeus's son ineligible.

If the brat wanted a weapon, he could come barter for one himself. It was only fair. Zeus, it seemed, had forgotten or was too blinded by love to remember that coddled children did not make for good people, let alone good cultivators. Once the king of gods remembered, he would thank him.

But as Hephaestus spread his senses through the pyramid and locked on to one he was sure was a child of Poseidon, he couldn't help but think that the world was truly unfair. Most gods couldn't even evoke the eternal will, but some child, not even eighteen, had done it and named his sword.

CHAPTER 29

Ridding the Chaff

Rex is going to fail, Luke thought as Cyzicus's youngest grandchild desperately clawed his way to the next step.

Counter to his expectations, even three thousand steps later, the robotic sentinels still gave them three seconds to catch their breath before beginning to attack. Neither did that pattern seem like it was going to change.

In hindsight, it was easy to see why. If a contestant couldn't keep up the pace, they would be punished, and if they couldn't withstand the punishment they would be attacked, and if the androgynous humanoids succeeded in pushing them down a step, they would vanish in a burst of red-yellow light.

Luke had already seen it happen hundreds of times, and he expected to see it hundreds more. Even so, a small part of him was unwilling to see it happen to Rex. He would be the first to admit that he wasn't looking forward to facing Blinky in any future rounds, but seeing him lose so early was disheartening.

But it was also an opportunity. A few steps ahead of him, both Arya and Spiros were also showing signs of fatigue, Arya more than Spiros, who seemed remarkably steady even now, which made Luke wonder what exactly was so special about him. His uncanny level of strength even at the Mortal tier was hard to forget, but even after all this time, he didn't know what exactly was responsible for it. Not that it mattered much; after analyzing the competition, Luke couldn't be sure he wouldn't lose despite his own advantages. Everyone still in the game had something going for them, it seemed.

So, as a robot sprang to life, and nipped at Rex's heels while he desperately scrambled forward, Luke grabbed the other teen's robes and yanked him forward, forcibly dragging him to the next step.

All right, so that's allowed. We can help each other, he thought, making sure not to let the relief he was feeling show on his face. He hadn't known if doing that would sic the robots on himself or not.

"What . . . are you . . . doing?" Rex asked, his voice escaping in short bursts.

Eyeing the robot that stepped up to him and began its countdown, Luke attempted to frame his actions in a way that would make sense and not destroy the other teen's ego, before giving up. He was tired, mentally more than physically, but tired nonetheless. There was something soul crushing about walking up boring metal steps with absolutely nothing around for miles.

"Helping you."

"Why?" Rex asked, looking confused.

Because I'm not an asshole, Luke grumbled internally while he mulled what to say out loud. He watched another bot step up to him, and before the machine ended its countdown, he yanked Rex to the next step, where another robot immediately took the place of the last.

"Really, what are you doing? I don't want your he—"

Luke cut him off. "I'll pull you for a little while until you gather your energy, and then when I start to get tired, you do the same to me. Some of the people here are absolute monsters—that guy up there looks like he can do this forever," he said, pointing toward his look-alike. "It's better if we work together for any advantage we can, otherwise we might both lose. Deal?"

"Deal," Lukeus answered for Rex while he waited out his own timer. He was faring better than his younger brother, but Luke suspected that he would fail sooner rather than later if his hunched back was any indication. Considering the number of participants still in the tournament, the more cynical part of Luke's brain realized it wasn't enough, and Lukeus wouldn't make it to the top hundred at his current rate, either. Maybe top two hundred and fifty, if he was lucky. A respectable placement, considering the caliber of their competition, but ultimately not good enough.

Maybe another fifty or sixty ranks if pulling them along with me works out as well as I think it will. I'll have to rotate partners and tug them all at some point, but my stats are high enough that the next few levels should still be doable, especially with the boost I can get from my sword, but I should hold off on that as long as possible. This is a marathon, not a sprint, and who knows how much time, if any, we'll have to recover between this round and the next? Double the points in Constitution or Strength are really going to go a long way, though.

"Count me in, too," Rose chimed in, a miserable expression on her face.

Ignoring them for the moment, Luke dragged Rex to the next step. "Well? Are you in?"

"Fine," Rex said begrudgingly.

Nodding slightly, Luke indicated for Lukeus to help pull Rose forward and let himself relax slightly when he did. If they couldn't make it all the way, staying longer would still be a better outcome, even if their only gain was improving their cultivation by exerting themselves in a god's holy land. Luke himself had already gained more attributes the short few hours he had been here than he had in the past two weeks, and with the Seed, his rate of improvement was already head and shoulders above the others'. To most of the people here, this place was a cultivator's paradise.

Pulling someone along was only a little harder than just climbing by himself, and letting Rex and Rose catch their breath for even ten to fifteen minutes would let them recover a significant amount of their stamina. A favor that, when repaid, would work well for all of them.

We're competing, but it's not so restrictive yet that we have to turn on each other.

All that, however, was only his secondary aim. Considering the fact that they were effectively strangers, if Luke wanted to help Spiros take first place in the tournament, he needed to do it in a way that didn't come off as suspicious or expose his identity.

I can't help him directly or even too obviously, but if both Arya and Spiros happen to hear our strategy and decide to use it for themselves, well, that's fair play. It doesn't even matter if other people hear it, too. Most of them probably don't trust each other enough for this or are struggling too much by themselves to offer help. Spiros won't give up, but if Arya passes, too, he'll have someone he can trust more than me to watch his back. Hopefully . . .

Even to him, his plan was far from the best, but no matter how he sliced it, there wasn't a way to cheat under the watchful gaze of a god.

The rules had been clear enough on what they were allowed to use and what they weren't; everyone was permitted a single artifact at the Warrior tier, which they had to register prior to the start of the tournament. No potions or talismans were permitted, with the exception of those provided during the tournament itself. The god hadn't seen fit to take them, but Luke had no doubt in his mind that the second he took one from his storage ring with the intent to drink it, he would find himself back in Cyzicus's throne room.

Bloodlines and techniques were considered inherent powers and weren't restricted. Even tamed beasts were allowed, so long as you could prove they were part of your skill set—meaning they had to be controlled by an ability—and were registered before coming. Or they would be eventually, seeing as they weren't yet.

Seeing that most of those present were likely descendants of gods, some probably even sharing Rex and Lukeus's ancestor, it made sense, but it also felt a little unfair to Luke, considering that it effectively made any battles two against one.

His own bloodline, while useful, didn't have many combat applications when it came down to it. At least none that he had discovered over the past few months. The Eyes of Insight didn't let him punch harder, move faster, or even see all that better. Considering all his other advantages, and his inability to negotiate the rules, though, he decided not to dwell on it.

And it's not like I don't have my own shit going for me, too. My sword is busted, my mana is plentiful, my technique solid, and I have enough raw stats that were I not a paragon I might be pushing the Hero tier.

But I'm not the one who needs to win this.

Shaking his head, he and the others continued onward for longer and longer. He never actually needed Rex's help, but with every level they climbed, Luke needed to pull more and more, and as he did, even he began to feel the burn.

"Two hundred and three people left."

Rose groaned out loud and then, in a surprise move, stepped back and stood still. They had already been on the step for two seconds, and before any of them could even process what she was doing, a sentinel leaped in front of her and kicked her down the stairs. Luke scrambled forward and watched numbly as she disappeared in a flash of orange-red light.

"Shit," Lukeus cursed under his breath.

"Guys . . . I think . . . I think I'm done, too," Rex said a moment later, ripping himself free from Luke's grip as he did. "You've been carrying me long enough. I don't want you to lose because of me . . . and Gramps only needs one of us to—"

"Shut up." Lukeus sighed and, in a move that surprised both Rex and Luke, bent his knees and heaved his younger brother onto his shoulders. His face flushed red with exertion, he hobbled forward. "I'll carry you as long as I can and then forfeit. Blinky is strong, so whatever the next challenge is, if you can use her, you'll have a shot of getting into the top ten."

"Let me carry him," Luke said. "I still have plenty left—"

"He's my brother. I've got him for now. You should conserve your energy as much as you can in the meantime. I'll carry him for as long as I can, and after that it's all on you," Lukeus said.

"No, really—I can."

"Listen, Luke. I have no shot here. Nutbutter is a good steed, but I can see I'm not going to win this. Hanging on any longer will just be me being stubborn. You and Rex both have a good shot of going further if you make it, though, so that's what you should focus on. I don't even know if Gramps wants the potion anymore, but if he gets it, he becomes a Saint. That's why we're here, remember?" Lukeus looked pointedly between Rex and Luke.

Staring into his eyes, Luke nodded. It was a shame, but he had known for a while that it would come down to something like this.

"Fine. Carry Rex as long as you can, and I'll make sure to bring him with me to the next round."

"Good. If you make it to the finals, Gramps will get an invitation to come and watch. We better get one too." He grinned.

Luke grinned back, and, free of his burden, he continued onward, keeping track of both Spiros and Arya in front of them and patiently watching as one after another people were attacked by the sentries, only to vanish in golden light.

Half an hour later, Lukeus collapsed onto his knees. Rex climbed to the next step by himself, and three seconds later, they watched as Lukeus was sent back home with a stern kick from the robot—eliminated.

"Come on," Luke said to Rex, pulling him up. The emperor's grandson nodded and, a little refreshed from his break, continued what would be the last stretch of their journey with him.

He walked under his own power for an entire layer before he lost the ability to keep pressing on. Focusing his mana into his sword, Luke activated its ability and cycled through doubling each of his attributes before settling on an increase to his Strength. Doubling his Constitution and Agility helped, but not nearly as much as raw power did.

Then, with his enhanced attributes, he let Rex climb onto his back. Things went as well as they could for a while, and it was when there were only a hundred and twenty-five people left that Arya collapsed.

Shit.

CHAPTER 30

The Next Challenge

Luke's eyes darted to Arya's crumpled form, and the robot beside her counting the seconds on its fingers, and then toward Spiros. Much to Luke's frustration, he was so focused on climbing to the next step that he hadn't even seen Arya stumble and fall, leaving Luke in a conundrum. Did he help or not?

Unfortunately for him, and fortunately for Arya, he didn't have much time to think about it. The smart thing to do would be to leave her and allow her to be eliminated, but of all the stupid things he had done so far, this didn't rank all that high.

Luke's reasoning rang hollow even to himself, but he knew deep down he would regret it if he didn't help her, and for more than one reason. And he had been keeping close track of the number of people still in the game—only one more person needed to fall behind for the rest of them to advance to the next stage of the tournament. Rex had even rested for long enough that he would be able to continue under his own power for the remaining duration, and even now Luke had enough in his tank to go for hours longer if needed. It wouldn't take too much added effort to swap between carrying Arya and Rex if it really came down to it. None of them were great reasons to help Arya, who was supposed to be a stranger in a tournament, but he decided that he didn't care much, as they weren't *actually* strangers. Even if he was the only one to know that.

Was it reckless? Yes. Would it make sense if he tried to explain it? Not really. He shrugged Rex off his shoulders anyway.

"I'll be right back," he said quietly and, not bothering to wait for a response, he kicked off the ground toward Arya.

His ring flashed and his sword appeared in his hand, cutting loose for the first time since the tournament started and, empowered by his sword's abilities, he *moved*.

Having spent most of the trial traveling at a rather sedate pace to conserve his stamina, letting loose felt better than he thought it would. He found a primal satisfaction in pushing himself as hard as he physically could—something he had developed an appetite for since his first moments on Theos and something he was just now realizing he craved. Sometimes he wondered if that was an effect of the Seed, subtly pushing him to cultivate more, but deep down, he knew—or at least hoped—it wasn't. Cultivation simply felt good. Combining that with the fact that working himself to exhaustion put his mind at ease, it wasn't a surprise that he had developed what he thought might be an addiction to it.

"Where are you going?" Rex shouted after him. A grin stretched across Luke's face, and he ignored him. There was no time to explain.

Fractions of a second before the robot of liquid metal pushed Arya down the step and eliminated her, he swiped at its neck with his sword. Like an acrobat, it bent backward horizontally at its waist, dodging Luke's attack.

Scooping Arya off the ground, Luke didn't wait for the robot to correct itself before he pressed on toward the next step.

The second he made it, regret instantly filled his entire being. Swallowing the spit in his mouth, he looked down at Arya in his arms, only to find her looking up to him with wide and familiar brown eyes.

Holy fuck, this was such a bad idea.

"Hi," Luke said, suddenly aware of his own lungs, how often he blinked, and the fact that he was drenched in sweat and probably smelled like it, too. Sweat that wasn't even all his. He had never regretted carrying Rex more.

She blushed red and broke eye contact. "Hi?"

"I'm Luke."

"I know . . . you told me your name earlier. I'm Arya."

"I remember."

Another robot started counting down next to him, and not in the mood to optimize his step to conserve energy, he brute forced his movements to the next step and then the next.

"So this is a little weird. Do you want me to put you down?"

"I . . . Why are you carrying me?"

"Well, we were only a single person away from the next stage and I, uh . . . I didn't want you to lose?" Luke said truthfully, feeling heat rising in his own face. He had never really thought about it before, but Arya was beautiful, and now he was holding her. In his arms. Him.

Fuck. Fuck. Fuck, Luke thought as his heart hammered away in his chest and he hoped beyond hope that she couldn't feel it. Considering the fact that he could hear it thumping, though, he doubted that she couldn't.

Moving onto the next step, he felt someone step beside him. Looking to his right, he found Spiros staring at him. His expression was blank, and his arms were crossed over his chest.

Swallowing the spit that had somehow accumulated in his mouth, Luke looked behind him, only to find Rex struggling up the stairs with a shit-eating grin plastered across his face. Their eyes briefly locked, and then the emperor's grandson nodded and gave him an encouraging thumbs-up while he patted himself on the chest.

Why's he patting his chest . . .

He looked back at Arya, only to find her looking at Rex as well.

The blood drained from his face, and it was only the fact that a robot stepped in front of him and began counting that broke him out of his shock, and he gained enough mental capacity to remember to take the next step.

Fuck. Fuck. Fuck.

"I, uh . . . It's not what it looks like. Rex isn't the brightest guy I know—one time he even tried drinking milk. Never mind. Um, do you want me to put you down?" he asked her again.

Arya took a deep breath in his arms and closed her eyes before opening them and looking at Spiros. Something unsaid passed between the two, and Spiros shook his head.

"Sorry, Arya, I'm in love with Helen, and you know I promised her never to touch another woman. She thought I was joking, but I'm a man of my word. I can't carry you, but if this guy does anything, say the word and I'll take care of him." His ring flashed, and a golden spear appeared in hand, its butt planted onto the ground. Grinning challengingly, he lifted it in the air and pointed the business end at Luke.

"What . . . I wouldn't do . . . what?" Luke stammered while he glanced between the gleaming tip of the spear inches from his nose and the woman in his arms.

Rex's ring flashed, and a bow appeared in his hands. He drew it back and leveled an arrow at Spiros's head. "Put that away, or I'll shoot, and don't think I'm bluffing. I promise I'm not. I'll do it. I shot Zeus himself, so I'm sure as hell not afraid of you."

"Says the guy who needed to be carried by two different people to even get this far. Please. And there's no killing here. I wouldn't test a god's patience if I were you," Spiros scoffed.

Rex grinned and angled his bow so it was pointing between Spiros's legs. "You make a good point."

Luke's mind ground down to a halt.

I fucking give up.

"All right, that's enough. Let's put the weapons away," Arya said, squirming in Luke's grip. "Can you let me down? And let's all move up a step. No need to get violent here, all right?"

"Oh . . . right." Luke nodded and dropped her to the floor, shaking his head slightly in annoyance as he moved up a step. He turned around and saw her struggle forward, and after a moment's hesitation, he held out his own hand. She stared at it, and then back at him, before accepting it, and Luke pulled her forward.

"Thank you—for saving me. Now, why are you helping me?" she asked.

"Why am I helping you?" Luke parroted blankly.

Spiros scoffed. "The same reason he was laughing at your dumb joke earlier—he thinks you're pretty."

It took Luke a moment to remember that Arya had joked about Spiros pooping his pants.

"I . . . that's not . . ." Luke scrambled for something to say that would neither make this awkward nor give him away, before he stopped himself. What Spiros said certainly wasn't the truth, at least not entirely. Arya was pretty, but that wasn't why he had helped her.

She was his friend, even though she didn't know it, and it truly would have been a shame to see her eliminated so close to the next round and miss out on what were bound to be truly astronomical prizes.

Opportunities like these, Luke recognized, didn't come often in the lives of cultivators, and he wanted her to continue advancing.

He wanted all of them to.

It was something he hadn't thought about extensively in the past, but cultivation wasn't just getting stronger. It was a longer life, better health, and more freedom. If a few seconds of effort and awkwardness on his part could give Arya any of those, then he would gladly pay that price. After all, if she won something from the tournament that let her advance to the Hero tier or even higher, where she otherwise might not— well, that was the difference between living centuries and millennia. Numbers that still blew Luke's mind.

Besides, even though she didn't know who he was right now, that didn't mean he couldn't tell her, either. Nor did it mean he, as his true self, couldn't rekindle his friendship with the pair at a later time and come clean about his deception once he was more comfortable in his position in the world—and once he tied up some loose ends more thoroughly.

And I don't know. I didn't know them for that long, but I sincerely doubt that either of them will hand me over to Arke even if they knew my true identity and what I possess— not that I ever will tell them. It's not like knowing I have something that tells me how to be a god will do them any favors. No, that's one secret I'll keep until I'm confident that no one will be able to hurt me with it. Which will probably be never, he realized.

Even if he himself became strong enough to fight off whoever lusted after the prize bonded to his soul, there were more ways to get to it than by attacking him. He didn't know what decision he would make in the future if some nefarious entity held someone he loved hostage, but just thinking about it served to deeply unnerve him and made him angry.

Reining his thoughts in, he shook his head and climbed to the next step, extending his hand out to pull Arya along with him as he climbed.

"I helped because I could, and because I wanted to," Luke said eventually. "There's not much more to it, and I don't need to be paid back or anything."

Spiros looked at him before shrugging his shoulders. "If Arya's fine with it, it's none of my business. But do anything weird, and you won't get the chance to regret it."

"Why do you keep saying that?" Luke asked, unable to mask his annoyance at the suspicion.

"Please," Spiros scoffed. "I recognize your type. Pretty-boy sons of Poseidon, Daddy's a god, so you'll get away with everything. Tch."

"What?" Rex yelled suddenly. "You're a son of a god, too? That . . . that explains—"

"I've already told you. I don't know who my parents are, Rex," Luke said, annoyed and more than a little paranoid. "Don't go calling me a son of a god when I'm probably not. I don't want to get into any trouble or anything."

Spiros scratched his chin. "Well, you could be a bastard of one of his sons or grandsons, or great-grandsons? They're pretty common in Troy. You're not from Troy, are you?"

"I'm from Sylcra," Luke answered tiredly.

"I—" Spiros started to say, but before he could finish, all their visions were obstructed by flickers of red and orange light.

They had passed the trial.

CHAPTER 31

Eyes of Insight

When Luke blinked next, he was standing between Rex and Arya along with all those who had passed the trial in four long rows on what he recognized as the top of the pyramid they had just been climbing. It lacked any sort of roof or walls, leaving them free to survey the holy land of Vulcan for as far as their eyes could see. Not that there was much to look at.

All that existed was fields of endless green grass and blue skies. The pyramid alone broke the monotony of the otherwise desolate environment.

Is this the divine kingdom of a god? Just some grass, denser mana, and, while impressively big, a single structure? Saskatchewan might have more going on than this place. For a place called Vulcan, I was expecting at least a volcano or something, Luke thought, unimpressed, before he focused his attention to the only thing of interest for thousands of miles.

Hephaestus was seated on a throne, a massive thing but simple in style and fashioned from the same silvery metal that everything else here was made of. With big armrests and a straight back, it lacked any sort of embellishments. Nor did it look comfortable to sit on, but nonetheless, the god looked right at home on top of it. And despite every surface being spotless, shiny metal, the flattened tip of the pyramid somehow managed to seem warm and inviting. Luke felt like he had stepped back into his childhood home.

For a moment, paranoia clawed at him, and he wondered if he was under some strange mind-altering effect again, but that didn't seem to be the case, and he was inclined to trust his instincts.

Not that there was anything to be done if the ancient being before them decided he wanted to bring them harm. The difference in power between Luke and the god was ridiculous. Even entertaining the thought of fighting back would do him no good. Not that physical opposition was the only form of resistance one could achieve.

But something tells me I'll get smited if I mouth off to him and that there won't be any signs that I ever existed once he's done.

Before Luke could delve deeper into his thoughts, Hephaestus cleared his throat.

"Congratulations to all of you for making it this far. Each of you has shown me your grit and determination, and for that I applaud you. Your feats today prove that you are among the brightest stars of your generation. Not all of you, however, have come here as equals." He clapped his hands together, and a cylindrical slab of metal rose out of the floor in front of each of them. "As such, your rewards for coming this far are also unequal."

The podiums hissed as the tops split apart, and a scroll rose into the air in front of him, stopping its ascent once it was at the level of Luke's eyes.

He didn't need to open it to know that whatever knowledge was contained inside was precious. Its mere presence seemed more *real* than anything he owned, with only his sword, Maximus, and the God Seed comparing.

Not daring to touch it just yet, he looked toward his left and right and was unsurprised to see a small assortment of objects floating in front of each of the contestants.

A few more had scrolls just like his, some had vials containing all sorts of things, and others had weapons and even articles of clothing. He saw that Spiros had been given a scroll, too, which, like his, glowed with the weight of power of the knowledge it contained, but both Arya and Rex had gotten something else.

In front of Arya was a bottle that seemed to hold flickering blue fire that Luke had no idea the purpose of. Rex had gotten a bow. Considering who had given it to him, it was bound to be both powerful and useful, but compared to the esoteric nature of the other rewards, it was by far one of the more mundane prizes. Which, to Luke, at least, made sense. Rex had quite literally been carried for a significant portion of the trial by both him and Lukeus.

It's probably just a Warrior-tier bow, too. Well made, no doubt, but nothing too crazy. Then again, this isn't the end of the tournament, either. The real prizes will come later.

Seeing some of the others reach toward their own rewards, Luke did so as well.

The scroll unfurled the second it touched his hands, a beam of red light shot out of it, and instantly, he felt *knowledge* and *understanding* knock at his consciousness and request entry.

His instincts practically screamed for him to do so, much like they had when he was confronted with Cybele's pomegranate seed.

Might as well, he thought with some amusement; it wasn't like he wasn't going to take it. The draw of a gift from a god was much too high, so, both excited and apprehensive, he allowed it in.

Before he could regret his decision, the scroll disintegrated and a spike of pain shot through his head, leaving him dazed even as whatever it had imparted to him vanished except for a rudimentary knowledge of what it was and how to use it.

It took a few moments for his mind to clear, but when it did, he couldn't help but stare at the god with wonder in his eyes.

Hephaestus had given Luke a *spell*. A part of Luke was tempted to compare it to a technique, but that would be wrong.

Whereas the First Stances and the First Truth of Death were the realization of a fundamental truth of reality, spells were simpler, and not a permanent ability, but no less amazing for it. What the deity had given him was akin to a button lodged in the same metaphysical space where his mana was. One that, when pressed, would execute its purpose. The major difference between it and techniques was that the spell didn't require any understanding or commitment from him, and, as such, it wouldn't interfere with his status as a paragon.

So long as the spell was charged with mana, it would work. The only thing he could compare it to were talismans, and in a way, that's exactly what it was. Except better in every way. For one, since it was planted in his mana, he could use it instantly, whenever he needed it. Second, if the knowledge that came with it was correct, he could use it roughly a dozen times before it dissolved, making the talismans he had been using feel like cheap trash in comparison.

Closing his eyes, Luke meditated on his mana, and immediately, he found the spell, ready to be used. It appeared as an icon and was moving in an orbit around where he knew his heart was.

Its form was indescribable and constantly shifting. Like an optical illusion, and just focusing on it made his head ache, even as suspicion and hope rose unbidden and in tandem in his head.

The reward was too good.

Does he know what my bloodline is? He discarded the thought as soon as it came. If the god knew about Luke's ability, then he was unexpectedly generous. Not that Luke thought that was the case. Something told him, had Hephaestus known whose blood flowed through Luke's veins, he would have gotten a bow instead. Not because the spell was that amazing of a prize or that he held a grudge against the titan, but because of what Luke could learn from it.

The Eyes of Insight was an ability he had inherited from Prometheus.

After he had killed the Rebel hero and settled into routine in the capital, he had wasted no time in taking the plunge and sending his mana into the two pebble-like beads in his eyes.

At first the ability seemed underwhelming, but Prometheus wasn't a god—or a titan, for that matter—who was famous for his destructive nature or as a great warrior. All successful cultivators knew their way around a battlefield, but it didn't mean all of them enjoyed it or put more thought into it than was required. As such, it wasn't a surprise that what Luke had inherited from Max's ancestor didn't have readily apparent combat applications. Until now, perhaps.

What he remembered from the myths of his world, combined with the name of the ability and what Prometheus had told him when they had met, had given Luke a good inkling of what he could expect from the power. Prometheus was a teacher, a crafter, and a scholar.

And his eyes were tools that facilitated that role, but to Luke, they hadn't been of major use. At least not when compared to a bloodline ability like Rose's, which gave her the ability to control fire, or Clan Skyscar's talent for controlling wind. The emperor's grandchildren, too, had the remarkable ability to bond with and command animals. His ability, in his own opinion, was much less interesting, and that had inspired some amount of envy in him—an opinion that the spell and the potential it represented were threatening to overturn.

In simple terms, the Eyes of Insight let Luke see mana, or, more precisely, they let him see his *own* mana—and how it interacted with the world—in great detail. Both aethereal mana and that which others cultivated inside themselves were no more apparent to him than they had been before. But it was useful, even if only for a single task—creating talismans.

Without activating his eyes, making talismans was a long and boring process. He would draw the runes from the book Nel had given him on a sheet of paper and then fill them.

The rate at which they would absorb his energy, though, was exceedingly slow, and that speed was the main bottleneck to their creation in the first place. Supposedly, the more you filled a specific talisman, the quicker the process would become as your mana learned the pattern, but it took months and, in some cases, years of effort to get the time down to something reasonable. One that couldn't even be sped up, as it was entirely a subconscious process.

As a consequence, most warriors would cultivate until their bodies could no longer absorb mana from the environment and then spend their remaining centuries dedicating their time to other pursuits, like enchanting weapons or creating talismans, which his bloodline seemed purpose-built for.

Clite, being centuries old, could create most common Warrior-tier talismans in minutes. Nel had practiced creating protective talismans and could create Mortal-tier ones basically on demand, but it still took her a few hours to make a Warrior-tier one.

The initial process, and even the runes for them, were the same, but to get a talisman to the Warrior tier, you kept pouring your mana in until it flashed a second time.

Luke, because of his eyes, could create basically every talisman he knew the runes for, both at the Mortal and Warrior tiers, in minutes. Something he had spent much of his spare time doing, and he had no small number of the things stored in his inventory, and he had sold even more for a tidy number of merit points.

His bloodline showed him how his mana was interacting with the drawn runes, and as such, he could tweak it so that it fell within the lines of the glyphs better. Whereas others were limited to pouring their energy into the paper blindly and repeatedly until they learned the path by instinct, he could see it, plain as day.

The actual structure of the runes was much more complicated than the shapes of the lines they drew suggested, and it wasn't two-dimensional, either. Like the Aether had so long ago sucked his soul *in*, the mana funneled into the runes of a talisman built into itself in an inward direction. It didn't fit with Luke's understanding of space-time as he knew it, but with his ability, he could perceive it anyway.

The result was the difference between a blind man trying to trace his finger over the lines of a drawing and someone who could see the drawing doing the same task.

And, feeling the spell in his mana, he activated his bloodline and instantly had to tamp down his excitement as its previously shifting and incomprehensible form turned to something he could look at without trouble.

Something, he suspected, he could replicate, and maybe, just maybe use to extrapolate the knowledge that was held within to create his own spells based on the runes for talismans he already had. Even if he couldn't, though, he knew he could recreate the same spell and would now, forever, have the ability to fire jets of scorching flame from his fist.

Prometheus stole fire from the sun and gifted it to mankind. Now I've done something similar. Less impressive, but taking the ability to make fire from a god, when he thought you could only do it a dozen times, is kind of like it. Right?

He grinned.

CHAPTER 32

World of Monsters

Taking a deep breath, Luke reluctantly tore his attention away from the icon floating within his mana and deactivated his bloodline. The potential the spell held was extraordinary, and if he could accomplish with it what he thought he could, then he'd succeed in having a powerful and versatile tool in his arsenal. Something he sorely needed, considering the fact that, twice now, his only technique had been subverted—once by the invisible snakes, and repeatedly by the machinery Hephaestus was so fond of.

It was a problem that had been weighing on him with increased urgency, and until now, one he didn't have a good solution for.

Being a paragon meant that he had to be extremely picky about what techniques he could learn, because regardless of what he chose, he had to see it through to the very end—until he became a god. It was one of the few, but also one of the most glaring, weaknesses of his path. Others could pick up techniques with wild abandon and zero concern for how they were going to advance them beyond the effort required to make them useful in battle. If even that. As far as Luke knew, there were no consequences to beginning to learn a technique and then never advancing it again.

Moreover, he didn't really know what to do with the technique he already had.

There was no procedure he had followed, or even steps that he could take, to reproduce the moments of epiphany that had progressed it to the Warrior tier in the first place, and the path forward was just as clouded in uncertainty as the one behind it.

I really need to figure something out for the First Truth, and soon. I still have time until it becomes the bottleneck, but it would be better . . . much better to get it done with now rather than later.

I shook Arke's trail, for now, but in this world there's no such thing as relaxing. Not for anyone. Personal power is the greatest insurance I have, and not having the strength to defend myself and the things I care about . . . It's a sin.

But . . . a few years shoring up my foundations on Sylcra or even with the Argonauts on the ship doesn't seem terrible. The idea rose, not for the first time, to allow himself to take it easy, but like every other time, he dismissed it.

On one hand, he did in fact have the opportunity to lie low and slowly work his way to the Hero tier under the emperor's shelter, or even as one warrior among many onboard the *Argo*, but deep in his gut, he could feel that the Seed wouldn't allow it, or something would blindside him and change everything. Especially considering his most recent quest. Despite its relatively simple goal, it would be stupid to forget the fact that Spiros was from Troy, a son of House Paris, and in love with Helen . . . Taking it all under consideration, he didn't know what to think, but every time he dwelled on the subject, a nervous pit would form in his stomach.

Shit, he thought, *is going to hit the fan when Spiros wins, and I doubt none of it's going to splash on me.*

Or I could be wrong, and whatever the second-place prize turns out to be will be more useful to my cultivation. That would be good. Really good. Still doesn't explain why Spiros needs to be first place, though. Realizing the futility of his thoughts, he resolved to do his best, no matter what happened, and focused on Hephaestus instead.

The god was drumming his fingers idly on the armrest of his metal throne as his eyes danced impassively over the assembled forms of the warriors. Occasionally his gaze would linger on someone, and flickers of emotions would travel through his eyes, from recognition and interest to derision, and at some, even anger, but the moments went by so quickly that Luke wasn't sure if it was actually happening or if it was entirely his imagination.

Minutes passed in uncomfortable silence as the god allowed them to indulge their curiosity and familiarize themselves with their rewards before he decided he had had enough. His finger stopped bouncing on his knee, and immediately the crowd stilled. The innocuous movement instantly had all one hundred of them on edge and focused.

"Now that we have rid ourselves of most of the chaff, it's time for the tournament to begin," Hephaestus said. Standing, he paced in front of the throne with his muscled arms behind his back.

An image from an old movie flashed through Luke's mind, of a strict army commander pacing in front of his troops. Except Hephaestus, with his baggy white clothes that hung loose on his frame, muscled build, and scarlet hair and beard, looked more like a hippie than a military man.

Unaware of Luke's thoughts, the god continued to talk. "I've tested your pride, and now I've tested your resolve. This next test will be unlike the previous. It will test your competence, for the pride to envision yourself a deity and the determination to seek it are useless without intellect to navigate the challenges achieving such lofty goals demands you overcome.

"My presence before you should tell you of one critical truth. You share this world, not just with your equals and lessers, but those infinitely greater than you can even imagine. Behold."

The world flickered red and orange. Luke blinked as the scenery in front of them changed once again. The god had moved them in front of a forest. Startled, people yelped and rapidly backed away from Luke. Their rings flashed, and an assortment of weapons was suddenly pointed in Luke's direction even as roars and growls of beasts echoed from deep within the forest.

What— Oh. Luke grinned in realization when the familiar sound of gnashing teeth reached his ears. Staring nervously at the tip of a spear pointed at him, held by none other than Spiros, he withdrew Maximus from his storage ring and lifted both of his hands up. He didn't think he would need the sword, but it was a good precaution in case someone attacked. Not that he could blame them if they did.

The other contestants weren't stepping away from him, but from Rex, who was standing right behind him—or, more accurately, they were avoiding the eldritch demon that had draped herself over his shoulder.

With her large mass of uncountable hair-like tentacles, drooling and snapping teeth, and indeterminate number of eyes, Blinky made for an extremely menacing sight.

That wasn't even counting the fact that just looking at her inspired feelings of fright and revulsion, ones that weren't entirely natural.

Now that I think about it, she feels like Hephaestus did when we got here . . . but lesser, and instead of worship, you just want to get the fuck away. At least to begin with.

Luke had, over the months, gotten somewhat used to her presence. He wasn't sure if it was the dreadglare intentionally doing so, after she'd learned who her allies were, or if repeated exposure had inoculated him from the worst of the symptoms she caused, but he was grateful, nonetheless. Looking at Blinky too long would still make anyone uncomfortable, but it had gotten a lot better now than it was a few months ago.

"It's fine. Put your weapons away, please," Rex said, stepping past Luke with his arms outstretched. "She's harmless. I've got full control," he assured them.

Spiros snorted and opened his mouth to say something, only to be interrupted by a burst of aura.

The source was Hephaestus, who, with his arms crossed over his chest, didn't look the least bit amused that he had been interrupted. Nonetheless, once everyone was facing him, he nodded and continued with his speech.

"In front of you is a forest I have created and stocked with all manner of ferocious beasts." He twitched his finger, and in front of him appeared thirty-two different scrolls. Half of them were black and the others white. "These scrolls are your objective."

The second the words escaped his mouth, the scrolls flew from his hands to a destination deep within the forest. On cue, the leaves on the trees ruffled and another series of strange noises and loud roars rang out from the forest.

"To pass this trial, you must collect one of each scroll. Collecting a white one will reveal the location of the nearest black one, and vice versa. Once you possess both scrolls, you must hold on to them for one entire week, surviving both the creatures that prowl the forest, and each other. If you lose your scroll and later collect another complete pair, the time you held on to your original scroll will be counted toward your total time. Meaning, you can hold one pair for six days, and another for one, and you will have completed the objective." He paused, letting them consider his words.

Well, that seems simple enough, Luke thought, sharing a nervous glance with Rex. *It's not going to be easy, though. Getting one scroll will mean that you're automatically pointed toward someone else and vice versa, so that's not too bad. But having both scrolls means that someone with a single scroll will know where you are, and considering that you have to hold on to a pair for seven whole days . . . while someone is gunning for you, and you need to survive whatever fucked shit is in the forest to begin with . . . Damn.*

A moment later, Hephaestus twitched again, and this time drones, the same ones that had tested them initially, appeared in droves. At least two hundred of them, and each one zipped around silently before rising into the sky and disappearing, becoming invisible in the process. A proud smile stretched across Hephaestus's face.

"The potion you drank earlier is still in your system, as you no doubt are aware. It will heal any minor and most major wounds. If you lose a limb or suffer damage that the potion cannot heal, I will restore it or treat you to the best of my ability before sending you home. You have my word that none of you will leave here any worse for wear. Be warned, however, that along with the continued presence of the scrolls within the forest, the potion will act as your timer. The moment its efficacy is expended, you will be disqualified. The drones will act as my eyes and ears. While I will not personally oversee every action, do note that nothing you do from now until the end of the games will escape attention." He looked at them meaningfully, letting his words sink in before continuing.

"That in mind, and considering your young age, I urge you not to commit any acts that you don't want witnessed and heard by me and those in my employ. This includes anything from acts of intimacy to violence that borders on or is sadistic. Especially if it is deemed to be against the spirit of these games. I'll let your own judgment govern what is and is not an acceptable level of force."

The god scratched his chin, seeming to think of other things to say, and Luke watched with nervous amusement as a series of emotions flickered across the deity's face. Whatever he was thinking was making him uncomfortable, but eventually, his expression straightened and he looked down at them with suddenly glowing eyes.

"In the interest of honesty, I have no desire to behold youthful passions, and I will expel you immediately if I have to. If I find your conduct particularly gruesome, you will be punished until I'm personally assured that you have learned from the error of your ways, even if it means not returning to your home for the foreseeable future. Are there any questions?" Hephaestus asked, looking at them. An aura, heavy and full of authority, proliferated from him and over the rest of the remaining competitors.

It wasn't full of anger or demanding obedience, and it didn't press them face first into the ground like Arke's had on the multiple occasions when either Luke himself or Cyzicus had provoked her anger, but it was no less menacing. More, even.

Whereas Arke felt like someone desperately clinging to power and hiding insecurity even as she lashed out, Hephaestus didn't. He felt powerful, unafraid, and confident. Neither his tone nor his demands brooked disobedience. He was just stating facts, not blustering about demanding his voice be heard and his wishes be realized, but stating what felt like the obvious.

At least what he's asking is reasonable, Luke thought with amusement, even as his body involuntarily stiffened. *I wouldn't want to watch any of that, either.*

"Good." The god nodded. "You may begin." Then, in an explosion of red and yellow light, he was gone. And as if detecting that the god was no longer present, monsters spilled out of the forest.

CHAPTER 33

Into the Wild

Calling forth his mana, Luke rose a few feet into the air, glad that whatever had been preventing him from flying had released its hold. He hadn't had the ability for long, but losing it sucked—a lot. It reminded him of the time his car had broken down in the middle of winter, and he'd had to go back to taking public transportation. Standing at bus stops when it was below freezing wasn't fun. Not to mention how annoying it was to buy groceries and carry them back home with him.

Of course, considering how driving ended up sending me here, maybe trains were the way to go . . . nah. He shook his head, amused by his own thoughts.

Then, drawing his sword, he inspected the monsters, although perhaps that was an unfair word. Compared to the Gegenees and the winged serpents Luke had seen on Sylcra, these were just juiced-up animals. None that he recognized from Earth, but similar to what he was used to. There were a few different varieties he could see, but the vast majority belonged to the same species: muscle-bound four-legged creatures the size of horses, with black-and-white-spotted fur, giant unicorn-esque horns that promised to skewer him clear through if he let his guard down, and rabbitlike faces that looked a little too cute for something he suspected he would be killing a lot of. It didn't quite sit right with him, but when it came down to it, he knew he would do what he needed to, and he would sleep like a baby after. He remembered vividly his disgust at killing the snake so long ago, and, taking a moment to mourn the loss of his own innocence, he activated the First Stance with his fingers crossed.

Thankfully, they were actual living creatures capable of death. As such, for the first time in the tournament, the ability he had sacrificed so much for actually seemed to be worth a damn. The knowledge that he had the skill set to actually kill the damned things felt surprisingly liberating. Like it was with flight, after going so long knowing that he could pinpoint a way to kill practically anything, suddenly losing the means to do so made him feel naked.

All right, how do I play this? Luke thought, even as the more hot-blooded contestants withdrew their own weapons from their respective storage rings and charged into the forest, eager to get their hands on the scrolls.

He was tempted to join them, but this wasn't something that could be rushed into. Finding the scrolls wouldn't be hard. There were a hundred of them, and thirty-two of the scrolls, and the way Hephaestus had thrown them into the woods, all of them knew roughly where they were. A thirty-two-percent chance wasn't incredibly high, but he was confident that he was at least better than half the people here.

No, finding the scrolls wouldn't be hard, not even if someone else found them first. The commotion that would ensue when the fighting began, and the fact that whoever had them wouldn't be going anywhere for a long time, was both comforting and removed most of the stress in the situation. The scrolls, though, were only a single aspect of the trial.

Compared to the last two—three, if he counted the drone that had attacked him months ago—this was the most cerebral of the Olympian Games. He liked it.

The trick is in not getting injured. Fuck the scrolls—once the energy from the potion runs out, that's going to be an automatic elimination. Which means not only do we have to hold on to the scrolls, but we need to avoid getting blasted when we have them. And considering the other rules—

No wonder he was talking about not being sadistic—being an asshole and wounding people more than necessary is a way to get them out of the game.

"This is going to be fun," Luke said, grinning slightly. It was going to be hard; the slightest mistake on either his part or Spiros's would see him fail his quest, but even so, he found himself looking forward to the challenge.

"It is . . . Good luck," Rex said as Blinky doubled, then tripled in size in the span of moments. The teen made to fly away, but Luke grabbed his sleeve and yanked him back.

"Wait—where are you going? We should work together," Luke said to Rex, flying toward Spiros and Arya as he did before either of them ran off, too. "You two as well—all of us should stick together. Going at it alone won't work. Defending the scrolls for seven whole days, day and night, in a forest full of monsters, while everyone who needs a scroll relentlessly attacks you, is going to be impossible. We don't even know how much damage we can take before the potion runs out. That's if you manage to get a scroll in the first place. I doubt I'm the only person here who sees the value in teaming up."

Arya and Spiros shared a silent glance.

"I think I'll be fine with Blinky," Rex said arrogantly, and as if the universe conspired to prove him right, one of the rabicorns, a stupid one unafraid of the demon's anxiety-inducing aura like most of its friends were, approached too close. A mistake it wouldn't have long to regret.

Luke averted his gaze in disgust as Blinky sent forth her tendrils and pulled the helpless Mortal-tier creature deep within her mass and started biting. It screamed and thrashed as the eye monster ate it alive, one tiny bite at a time—literally. The dreadglare's countless mouths were barely big enough to contain her eyes, and as such each bite only tore away a thin slice of flesh. Even so, within seconds, the entire creature was gone. The only thing that remained of its existence was the blood that had spilled. It stained Blinky's eyes and the grassy ground red.

Luke resisted the urge to empty his stomach, even as Spiros staggered away and didn't.

The chattering of countless jaws snapping shut and the heaving of a cultivator quickly put a damper on any and all enthusiasm Luke had felt moments before.

Sorely tempted to tell Rex to go off and do his own thing, Luke closed his eyes and took a deep breath, forcing himself to think rationally. Despite how gross the way she fed was, Luke knew firsthand how strong the demon was, too. He knew how useful she would be. He just needed to convince her master of that.

"Blinky is strong, but she's not fast, Rex. Anyone or anything here worth their salt isn't going to do what that unicorn-rabbit-horse-cow thing just did and walk into her. You remember her mom, right?" Luke said and promptly turned away while Rex opened and closed his mouth, likely thinking of a rebuttal. Not that it would matter—he would agree. Rex could be obstinate, but Luke had developed a good measure of the teen. Rex liked to act tough and pretend to be cool, but there was never any way that he would go into the forest by himself when Luke offered a better alternative. That in mind, he focused on the two he really needed to worry about.

Seeing the looks on their faces, though, he knew he had already gotten through. They just needed a push. "Spiros, Arya, right now, we all have a choice not to compete against Rex and his pet demon and have her on our side instead. That and my previous point . . . I don't know what else would convince you. So what do you say?"

"How do we split the scrolls?" Arya hedged.

Got 'em.

"Simple. First we find a complete pair. There's four of us, so we each hold it for eight hours a day before passing it onto the next person. Once we get two sets, we each hold the scrolls for sixteen hours each. That way, we're all banking the same hours." Luke looked between them, hoping that they were following it. Seeing as none of them looked too confused, he continued. "And we don't stop hunting for scrolls until we have four sets, one for each of us. We'll keep holding them for equal amounts of time and trading them between us. If everything works out, we all get out of here at the exact same time."

"What about who gets the first pair of scrolls?" Rex asked.

"We'll draw straws or something, I don't know. It's something we can figure out later. Are you three in or not?" Luke looked each of them in the eye.

"Yeah, why not." Spiros shrugged and looked toward Arya.

She eyed Luke with a hint of suspicion before nodding.

Leaving only Rex. He made a show of looking between them and Blinky. In the meantime, another rabicorn charged into the demon's mass and was shredded to pieces. "Yeah, let's do it," he said after a moment.

"SCREEEEEEEE!"

"SCREEEEEEEE!" One rabicorn after another started screaming. They ignored them.

"Great. Let's get started." Luke clapped his hands together and turned his attention back to the divinely constructed forest and began charting a path.

Their entire conversation hadn't taken long, but already most of the other contestants had burst into action, some in groups of four or five, others in pairs, and a few alone. All but a brave few were visible over the tree line, flying being by far the fastest and, for now, safest mode of transportation.

"So, that thing won't eat us, right?" Spiros asked.

"No," Rex replied, having the gall to look offended at what Luke thought was a perfectly reasonable question—one he had asked himself more often than he would like to admit. Luckily, the demon was well-fed, and Rex's bloodline and the fact that he had possessed her since birth meant that she was remarkably well-behaved.

"All right, we can get to know each other better later. Let's get going," Luke urged.

Blinky suddenly began to shrink into herself before assuming the vague shape of a cape that draped itself over Rex's shoulders. Luke spared a final nervous glance at Blinky, and they all took off.

Luke scanned their competition once again before steering everyone toward one of the scrolls that had been thrown toward the west side of the forest.

His decision, however, wasn't random. He had purposely chosen to go in that direction to avoid those he thought of as the stronger contestants. The fact that one of them happened to look just like him—and that any meeting with him might spawn a conversation he was in no way ready for—had everything to do with it.

Not that it mattered too much at this point. Everyone with eyes could see the resemblance between Luke and the king of Atlantis and his offspring.

The only thing he could hope for under the circumstances was that his presumed situation as an unknown and unclaimed descendant wasn't uncommon, or at least not entirely unheard of.

Poseidon was a god, and based on that alone, there should be plenty of people with his genes running around Theos. Depending, of course, on how . . . promiscuous he and his children were.

If you have thousands of kids, who themselves may live millennia, and each of them has their own kids, and so on and so forth, then there's a good chance that not all of them would be responsible. Avoiding them altogether is the best course of action, but when we do inevitably meet, just deny, deny, deny.

I don't know why I look like you. Promise. I don't know who my parents are—it's very sad, let's not talk about it.

Despite the seriousness of the situation, a grin came over his face. The more time he spent thinking about the whole looking-just-like-a-god thing, the less severe it seemed.

After all, it hadn't gotten him into any trouble yet, so what were the odds of that changing anytime soon?

CHAPTER 34

The First Scroll

A little to Luke's annoyance, the four of them blasted through the forest without too much trouble. Blinky made what should have been an arduous slog through an unending number of enemies and stat points a breeze. He tried not to let his disappointment show too much, even as the demon soaked his robes with her slobber.

It was true when Luke had said that she was slow. What he hadn't accounted for, however, was that they could carry her. Even though *carry* wasn't the best word.

It was more accurate to say that all four of them wore her like some sort of tent and used her mesh-like body as a mobile spiderweb-type thing, trapping any and every monster they came across in her writhing mass as they went. Each of them acted as a pole in a vaguely diamond-shaped formation and held one of her surprisingly slimy tendrils above their heads. From a distance, it just looked like the four of them were trapped under a net—a net that would, in moments, dissolve into blood and mist any mortal creature unfortunate enough to get caught.

Blinky, they all realized, was insatiable.

Alas, she was still in the Mortal tier, and the three Warrior-tier monsters had been indigestible and too tough for Blinky to chew through in a reasonable time frame. Even then, if they hadn't run away from them at Rex's insistence, Luke was sure Blinky would have eaten them, too. It would have taken longer, and it wouldn't have been a quick death, either, but the Warrior tiers would have died all the same. Slowly, over the course of hours, she would nibble away at the poor creatures while they thrashed in her grasp.

No one really has a good answer for what a demon is, but they're fucking broken, Luke thought, impressed in spite of the mana—and, in turn, attributes—slipping through his proverbial fingers. Even so, he pressed on without complaint. While regrettable, it wasn't the end of the world, and he consoled himself with the knowledge that by the time the tournament was over, the giant tide would be done as well. After that, he might be able to secure an expedition to the Northern Marshes of Sylcra and really grind.

In the meantime, I wonder what we need to do to get Blinky to become a warrior. Maybe she follows the same rule as my sword and needs to eat a hundred warriors? Or will eating enough mortals do the trick, too . . . Or it could be something completely different, but animals that cultivate do so automatically anyway, so I guess there's not much we can do about it. If she does advance, though, that would be a big help.

. . . Or get us all eliminated if she turns on us.

From the corner of his eye, Rex shot him a haughty smirk, no doubt taking satisfaction in the fact that Luke wouldn't be harvesting points. After the events at the Rebel's castle, many of his secrets had been spilled, the most important of which were the fact that Maximus wasn't all it seemed to be and that he was a paragon.

The latter had more than one person wishing him good luck and offering their sympathies. Embarking on the Paragon's Path was a rare but not unheard-of way for people to permanently handicap their progress. No one really knew what triggered the interference of the heavens, only that it was typically a choice offered to those at the Hero tier and higher. It wasn't unheard of for mortals to be offered the choice, but very, very rare, and rarer still for them to actually advance to the Warrior tier if they accepted it.

Not that any such handicaps would apply to Luke . . . So long as he had the God Seed, the path forward would never be shrouded for him. And he would have the God Seed until the day some greedy god or goddess ripped it from his soul. Assuming, of course, he could keep up with its quests and keep his nose clean while he was at it.

He took the sympathy in stride, though, not even bothering to argue his qualifications. Ultimately, it didn't matter if others thought he had a cap to his progress or not, and arguing his case would only serve to expose his secrets and make him vulnerable. No matter how pitiful the looks he had received were, he grinned and took them in stride.

The reveal of some of his sword's abilities, though, had been met with greater fanfare.

Suffice to say, weapons that could siphon mana and feed it to their users were both exceedingly rare and astronomically valuable. Not even Heracles had one, but for some reason, Luke didn't think it was because he couldn't afford it, and when asked, the son of Zeus just shrugged his shoulders. All he had to say on the matter was "Cultivating naturally is better anyway." Luke got the sense he was hiding something but decided not to press it. Heracles was entitled to his secrets.

Even so, more than one Argonaut's eyes had alighted with greed, but another boon of a named weapon was the bond formed between the person who named it and the artifact itself. Something that, fortunately, rendered the sword's multitude of abilities unusable by anyone but him. Which would hold true when, or if, he died.

In that circumstance, the sword would just become an inert chunk of gold, useful only as a paperweight. Too weak and malleable of a metal to even swing around.

Five hours and countless dead monsters later, they finally found a scroll. White and unassuming, it floated above a podium, bobbing slightly in the wind.

Hephaestus, however, hadn't left it unguarded.

The entire time they had been in the forest, the rabicorns had been spilling out in massive droves. Seeing the *thing* staring back at them from behind the scroll, Luke finally thought he knew why that was.

They were escaping a *hydra*. Or, if the other scrolls were guarded similarly, hydras.

It was a big beast, comparable to the Warrior-tier giants they had fought on Sylcra, but where those were humanoids, albeit with six arms, six eyes, and lacking a mouth or a nose, the hydra was pure *beast*.

Covered in gleaming golden scales, it had four catlike legs, each one with wicked claws that excreted noxious green venom. Its torso was similarly covered in golden scales, but its faces were what made Luke tense in nervousness.

If I remember right, Heracles was supposed to fight one as a part of his twelve labors. Every time he would cut off one of its heads, two would grow in its place. He solved it by cauterizing each head after he cut it off so others wouldn't grow.

But . . . didn't his hydra only have nine heads or something?

Why the fuck does this one have a hundred? Luke cursed under his breath, even as he urged the other three to retreat for a few seconds.

Even though they had managed to get to the scroll quickly with the help of Blinky, the other contestants wouldn't be far behind. Battling the hydra would be hard enough without the interference of outside parties, but if they were going to fight it, they needed to be on the same page.

"Anyone know what that is?" Luke asked, hoping they would. Not a single bestiary he had read on Sylcra, or even the one he had read on Carim, had the creature listed on it. Not that it was a surprise—Theos was gigantic. A world so big the islands were the size of Earth's continents. Not every animal was present in every ecosystem, and as such, the locals only kept indexes of monsters that were present where they lived.

Luke resisted the urge to curse as both Arya and Rex shook their heads in the negative. Turning to Spiros, he saw the teen with his hands cupped under his chin, staring thoughtfully at the hydra as its many heads hissed and snapped in their direction. Unwilling to leave the scroll, that was all the creature could do.

"I think that's Ladon?" Spiros said eventually.

"Ladon?" Luke asked, his thoughts churning in his head.

Ladon sounds familiar, really familiar . . . but what the fuck was it again? More importantly, how do we kill it?

Rex scoffed. "It's not Ladon. He's a divine beast that guards Lady Hera's garden—a god. Why would it be here? This creature bears a resemblance, but it's not the same. It can't be," he asserted.

"You know Lady Hera?" Spiros asked, and both Luke and Arya shared surprised glances before looking back at Rex.

It shouldn't have been a surprise that Rex did know more about beasts than he did. Rex and his siblings made sure they did, considering how relevant the information was to their bloodline ability, but it still caught Luke off guard. The number of times the youngest grandson of Cyzicus had said anything useful was pitifully low.

Rex shook his head. "Of course I don't know her. I'm from Sylcra, not Olympus. But I have a friend, Heracles . . . He mentioned it."

"You know Heracles, too?" Spiros blinked rapidly, and this time both Luke and Rex looked back at him with surprise.

"We both do," Luke said slowly. "You said you're from Troy, right? Did he visit you there?"

"Well, I saw him once, but he's going to be my brother-in-law. So . . ." He shrugged. "I guess I do know him."

Rex burst into laughter. "You do know that he's the son of Zeus, yeah? Are you saying that you're going to marry Zeus's daughter?" He cocked his head to the side, the amusement drained from his face, and then he stared at him like he was just seeing Spiros for the first time. "Who are you again?"

"Spiros."

Rex made a face and, gesturing with his hands, prompted the other teen to continue.

Spiros sighed and twirled the golden shaft of his spear, an unwilling expression coming across his face before he sighed again. "I'm Spiros, heir to House Paris of Troy."

Rex scratched the back of his head. "Am I supposed to know what that means?"

"Maybe if you were important enough . . . Troy is Lady Aphrodite's holy land. She's a god, if you didn't know already," Spiros said.

"Oh." Rex nodded nonchalantly. "Well, when you have your wedding, please be sure to invite me. Actually, I'm sure Heracles will—me and him go way ba—"

"All right, can we focus, please?" Luke cut the two off. "We should try and get the scroll before someone else shows up and the situation gets complicated."

"Do you really think anyone followed us to this specific scroll? Not only are there four of us, but Blinky ate an army on the way here. There are easier targets," Arya said. "I think we have time."

That's . . . probably not wrong.

"You have a point, but I still don't think we should waste time. We'll have seven days to talk to our hearts' content when we each get a pair of scrolls. So . . . how do we do this? I don't think anyone has any great ideas about how to go about it, so let's think. It's venomous for sure, if the green stuff dripping from its gajillion heads is anything to go by, so I'd rather not get too close. Rex, you got a bow as your prize, right?" Luke asked.

"I did." The other teen nodded, and his ring flashed. Rex wasted no time in drawing back the string, an arrow made of fiery energy manifesting into existence, and he let it loose.

The bolt of fire shot through the air, leaving a smoke-filled trail behind it, and collided with one of the hydra's heads, where it exploded with a bang. The creature flinched back, and its snakelike golden head hissed at them in anger.

Which turned out to be the least of their concerns. A drone appeared in front of them.

"Would participants Arya, Luke, Rex, and Spiros like to challenge creature [HYDRA] for the scroll?" it asked.

"Yes," Rex responded right away.

Instantly, Luke activated the First Truth of Death.

"Acknowledged," the drone said in its typical androgynous voice, and before any of them could have any second thoughts, a red light bubbled out from within the body of the drone and rapidly bloomed into a barrier that passed over them harmlessly, trapping them in a bubble with the vicious beast.

Blinky chattered and exploded into activity as her eyes and tendrils flattened against the walls of red light . . . outside.

Rex made to protest, but before he could get a single word out of his mouth, Luke activated his sword's ability, momentarily doubling his Agility and with it his speed, and tackled him.

The two narrowly managed to dodge as the hydra roared and poison-green flames erupted from its heads.

"Careful," Luke chided, even as they dodged another gout of flame. The hydra, it seemed, had taken offense to Rex.

Luke was just glad that it wasn't him that it was gunning for and that it actually was a hydra like he thought it was. At least he knew how to kill it—kind of. Now he just needed to tell the others, without telling them, actually kill it, and take the scroll.

Pretty easy. He grinned.

CHAPTER 35

Too Many Heads

This isn't easy, Luke thought, tempted to smack his previous self over the head. Feelings of dawning horror and a hint of panic permeated his thoughts as he narrowly avoided another jet of flame. This one condensed into a thin, laser-like stream that followed him around, missing him by the narrowest of margins, but missing him nonetheless.

Ruthlessly stomping on his emotions, he shifted his technique from the First Stance to the First Truth. He used the opportunity to dodge and commit to memory where the great golden beast and its hundred fire-breathing and venom-fanged heads would be, and then fractions of a second later, he shifted back to the First Stance to conserve mana. He didn't have the time or the mental capacity to let anything cloud his judgment, so he wouldn't. The fight, even with the four of them attacking together, was brutal. None of them had taken a single scratch yet, but that was part of the reason why it was so hard. There was no room for error. They had to dominate, and do it completely, because if they didn't, they would lose. Killing the creature alone wasn't enough.

Oddly, it reminded Luke of playing Mario Kart and being in first place, except dialed up to eleven and with stakes much greater than the celebration of his friends. He remembered when he would be winning, everything going well, but the anxiousness he felt stemming from the player behind him inching closer and closer, knowing that he if messed up or crashed a single time, he would be overtaken—or, well, in this case, his non-regenerating health bar would deplete, and he'd be removed from the tournament entirely.

Not the worst outcome—he'd already won big in his own mind with the spell and the secrets it held, but failing the quests was something he very much dreaded—even with the reservations he had about this particular one. It was, after all, one thing to be opportunistic and entirely another to potentially kick off and be responsible for one of the most famous wars in history. If that's what the Seed was trying to do.

"Ready!" Luke yelled, and then, trusting that Rex would have his back, he acted on his brief insight to the future. Flying left, he lowered himself in the air, ducking under the fiery beam even as it whizzed past where he had just been, and then, with a single smooth movement, he sliced horizontally, not even bothering to watch as a snakelike head that had been sneaking up from underneath him flopped to the ground.

Instead he was already ducking under a cloud of flame spewing from a few heads the monster kept close to its body. The hydra, he found, liked to do that. It was constantly shifting its breath attack from a wide area to a focused laser, but with their techniques, he, Spiros, and Arya could predict its intentions well enough.

Briefly he activated his sword's abilities and doubled his Constitution stat to better withstand the heat before letting that ability fade the second the monster switched back to attacking him with a more focused attack.

Mana needed to be conserved at all costs, even if going all out was looking better and better at the moment. Except this fight would be a marathon, not a sprint, and carefully coordinated on top of that, so the creature didn't grow even more heads if Rex missed a shot.

"To your right!" Rex called back at him, and instantly, Luke flew to the left.

Moments later, a fiery bolt of energy streaked through the air and lodged itself into its bubbling neck—were it left alone, another two heads would have sprouted in exactly three seconds. Instead, the flesh of the creature sizzled and charred.

The neck, losing its animus, fell limp around the monster's body, joining the odd dozen others they had destroyed. The way the early stages of the battle had gone, though, the creature had more heads now than it had when the battle first started.

Not for a lack of trying, though. Luke had suggested cauterizing the stumps the moment the first head had grown back, but reality wasn't so simple. Knowing what to do didn't make the how of it any easier, and being locked in a force field with an angry hydra wasn't conducive to clear thinking or good communication. Still, Luke was glad they had managed to work out a rhythm, and he reactivated the First Truth.

The moment the vision of the hydra's ghost played out in front of him, he cursed under his breath. Three of its heads were about to attack Arya simultaneously, and while he couldn't see Arya's actions that would happen in the future since she wasn't attacking him, he had gained enough experience over the months and had become familiar enough with both her and Spiros's limits that he was confident she didn't see it coming. To top it all off, her nervous expression and startled yelp were all the confirmation he needed.

"Ready one at Arya!" Luke yelled at Rex again. Heaving Maximus over his head, he channeled mana into the blade and flung it with every ounce of strength he could muster, even as he willed his mana to spill out of it and push off space itself, propelling it forward so fast his sword appeared more like a beam of light than a single object.

At the same time, he rapidly backpedaled as another one of the hydra's heads snapped at his heels, only to slam into the red barrier maintained by the drone with a loud crash and an angry hiss when Luke once again ducked out of its way. For maybe the hundredth time, he cursed at the fact that they weren't allowed to use more than one artifact. He loved Maximus, he really did, but being able to use the sword Cyzicus had given him when he first arrived at the castle would have made this battle so much easier.

Shaking the thoughts of another sword out of his head, he reactivated the First Truth and, using his mana, adjusted the trajectory of the blade slightly so that it sliced cleanly through one of the heads while Arya severed the other two coming her way with a single swing of her dagger.

Rex, fast on the uptake, already had his bow focused, and a bolt of fire cauterized the stump moments later.

"Thanks!" Arya yelled, already weaving away as the two heads she had severed rotted away into nothing, and the stumps blackened from *something*, and the necks fell limp.

God, that's fucking creepy. Luke winced, telekinetically maneuvered his blade back toward him, and continued to fend off the hydra's attacks as best as he could without a weapon in hand or a shield to hold the flames at bay.

Then, seeing an opportunity, he diverted his sword just a tad and cut two more heads off. It was a risk, as he could only use a fraction of his strength when controlling his sword with mana alone, and he ran the chance of the hydra batting it away and stepping on it or something. In this case, though, it only made sense to punish the creature for having its neck overextended.

Rex, like a well-oiled machine, fired two more arrows with perfect precision and burned shut two more stumps.

After shooting Zeus, the emperor's grandson had developed an obsession with the bow that bordered on fanatical, and it had paid off. He'd taken the feat as a sign of his immense talent in archery. Luke personally thought the king of gods had purposefully allowed himself to be hit, likely for comedic purposes, as there was no way in hell he didn't see the arrow coming, but he wasn't going to ruin that for Rex.

Whether he was joking or not, Zeus had been hit by an arrow fired from the unskilled hands of a mortal.

While Rex's skill with the bow was admirable, it was Arya and the way she fought that really interested Luke.

The way she ducked and wove between the golden heads and the sprays of flame was known to him. After all, he possessed the same Stances of the Sword, Shield, and Spear she did; even though the ways hers were expressed were different, the foundation they were built on was the same.

Where Luke would find opportunity in the movements and see a path forward, weaving between his opponent's offense and into their guard to deliver the final blow, Arya had a different, more passive approach.

She would let the hydra attack—only, instead of finding flesh, it would always without error find the edge of her blade instead. Where he pressed forward, she repositioned herself. A slight difference that Luke suspected was born from the fact that while he had leaned heavily on the First Stance of the Sword to learn the truth embedded in the empress's teachings, Arya had made her initial breakthrough with the First Stance of the Shield. All that, however, he could understand.

It was the way the hydra's flesh rotted from where she cut that he didn't.

It seemed eerily familiar, and if he had to put a name to the feeling, it would be déjà vu.

Luke was certain it was something she was doing, too, and not an ability of her dagger. Even so, now wasn't the time for questions, especially if his suspicion was right. If what he was witnessing was Arya's own evolution of the First Stances, comparable to his own First Truth of Death, then focusing on it in the midst of battle definitely wasn't the way to go. No matter how much he wanted to.

Any breakthroughs in his own technique would rapidly drain him of his mana, and while that had been fine when he was fighting the Mortal-tier giants, it was unthinkable now. The six-armed giants could only dream of hurting him, even when he was drained of mana. They were too dumb, and when he fought them in earnest, he had already been at the peak of the Mortal tier. Even the boulders they threw just broke on his skin.

The hydra wouldn't be as forgiving, and its attacks were relentless. He didn't need to test its poison to know that it would kill him, and he could feel the blistering heat of the fire. It would cook him alive were he to be caught.

So when Maximus slammed back into his grip, Luke instantly reactivated the First Truth for the umpteenth time since the battle had begun. Then, finding the next vulnerable head, he went to slice it off, only to stop abruptly when three heads thunked to the ground at Spiros's feet.

"Here!" Spiros yelled, and on cue, Rex once again fired off three arrows, impaling each of the heads the heir to House Paris had severed.

"Call it before you decapitate it," Luke yelled at Spiros, a hint of irritation seeping into his voice even as he tried to keep it out, making sure to meet the other teen's eyes through the long, ropy, snakelike necks of the hydra. Spiros, like Luke, needed Rex to burn the hydra every time he severed one of its heads or it would just set them back. Unlike Arya, and a little to Luke's surprise, Spiros's attacks didn't rot the creature. Luke wasn't sure if he just hadn't progressed his stances into the Warrior tier at all or if he was limiting himself to the Mortal-tier technique to conserve mana. He suspected it was the latter.

"Sorry," Spiros shouted back apologetically.

"Just make sure it doesn't happen again. If Rex isn't ready or expecting it, then us cutting off a head just makes this harder."

"I will. I will." Spiros nodded, leaping out of the way of a jet of flame.

"Good. Three here, Rex!" Luke yelled again and cut off two enterprising heads with one swing of his blade, and another a moment later.

The rest of the battle continued in a similar vein—the three of them cutting off one or two heads at a time, and Rex darting around the red dome with his bow providing them cover. Contrary to Luke's own expectations, it wasn't them that tired first, but the hydra. He had been so used to fighting the Gegenees and their virtually limitless endurance that he had assumed all monsters were like that. The winged serpents hadn't done much to dissuade him of that notion, either—those things were durable as all hell.

He should have expected it, though. The hydra would obviously lose mana with every jet of flame it sent their way, and combine that with the trauma of losing as many heads as it had, and then having those wounds sealed with fire . . . Luke was surprised it was still on its feet.

Before they knew it, it was just the four of them facing off against its last head.

With a heaving chest, Luke eyed the podium and dodged as the hydra half-heartedly spewed fire at them. He had almost forgotten why they were fighting it in the first place, but clearly the hydra hadn't. Even now, it stood protectively over the podium.

The monster's once-golden scales were dyed red by its own blood. Its long, limp necks draped over its muscle-bound legs, and it trampled over its own dead flesh without care.

"Let me finish it off," Luke said, grinning slightly even as Rex shot him a strange look. Before any of them could protest, his sword shot out of his hand and cut off its last head. Rex pulled back the string of his bow and, like he had the last hundred times, burned the stump shut.

Before the giant, many-necked, and now headless beast hit the ground, though, Luke, with a flex of his will, buried his sword where he thought its heart would be.

Stat Point Accumulation Currently Paused.

He read over the message before dismissing it entirely.

Oh, right, Hephaestus is watching, he thought and grinned in delight as the creature's mana soaked directly into his muscles. It was inefficient, and a lot of it escaped back into the environment, but it felt good, and his stats still ticked up a little. He was happy.

Rex whisked past him and picked up the scroll. "Now what?" he said.

CHAPTER 36

Meeting the Competition

A shadowy figure writhed around them, and Blinky draped herself around Rex in her cape form, jittering in what Luke presumed was happiness from finally being reunited with her human. He knew it was probably wrong to presume that about a creature of eyes and teeth that had only hours ago rendered countless rabicorns into mists of blood.

I wonder where she puts all that meat, he thought, and then, in an effort of will, ripped his eyes away from the dreadglare and focused on Rex, just now remembering he had posed a question.

"What do you mean?" Luke asked, walking up to him with Spiros and Arya in tow. The three watched as the other teen fiddled with the scroll, each of them raking their eyes over it, as if doing so would reveal all its secrets, only to feel disappointed that it didn't have any—or at least none that were apparent from a few feet apart.

"Should I open it or something?" Rex asked.

Spiros shrugged. "I mean . . . it's a scroll, so it would make sense."

One vote of confidence turned out to be all the confirmation he needed, because the second the words left Spiros's mouth, Rex unfurled the scroll without an iota of hesitation.

The result was anticlimactic, to say the least. A small part of Luke had still been holding out for something, maybe a surprise or perhaps another caveat to the challenge, but that turned out to be nothing more than wishful thinking.

The scroll was a mostly blank white surface, with a fancy arrow drawn in black ink pointing to the east, deeper into the forest and toward their next objective. Rex rotated the scroll, and sure enough, the arrow, like a compass, didn't stray from its chosen direction.

"So I guess that's where we need to go to get the black scroll," Luke said. "We could go after it now, but . . ." His ring flashed, and his sword returned to the space inside it. "I say we rest up for a bit. I don't know about you three, but I spent a lot of mana. If the next fight is anything like this one, then I'll run out for sure," he lied. With Maximus essentially doubling his reserves, and how stingy he had been with the use of his abilities, he felt he could go another round with the hydra if it weren't dead. Especially considering that out of the four of them, he'd probably had the most mana to start with.

Just because he wasn't at his limits, though, didn't mean they weren't at theirs. Even if he didn't know exactly where their limits were.

And it's better to be the voice of reason than not. Not that I really need to—Rex isn't the brightest bulb, but he understands the need for caution, and neither Spiros nor Arya is especially gung ho. That said, Spiros is trying to impress his lady friend, so he might be. Which isn't the worst—this isn't the pyramid anymore, so caution to the point of being lethargic won't do us any favors.

Spiros and Arya exchanged a glance before nodding in agreement.

"Yeah, that's fine with us. It's getting dark, too—maybe we should find a defensible space and get some rest. Depending on who has the scroll nearest to us, they may already be on their way, so we'll need to keep that in mind," said Spiros.

"As long as we're not sticking around here, I'm good with anything," said Rex, turning his nose up at the corpse.

"We can go somewhere a little less messy," Luke said, and then on a whim, he walked up to the hydra's corpse and kicked it. "Is it fine with you three if I take it?"

"If you want," Arya said, looking at him oddly. "There's no point, though. We're not allowed to use talismans, including preservation ones, so all the mana in it will dissipate by the time you can do anything with it. The venom might be valuable, though, but that would be in the fangs."

Oh, right. Time passes normally in my ring, and putting it in the Seed's inventory is probably a bad idea . . . My rings are a Saint-tier artifact, though, so it's not like I'm hurting for room, but there's not much point carrying around a rotting carcass, either.

"Well, you never know when some poison might come in handy," Luke joked with a smile. He didn't actually plan on poisoning anyone, but he hadn't planned on poisoning Yjarn when he had collected the scorpion's venom, either, and that had proven very useful. "But I don't see the point in lugging around the whole thing, either—Rex, do you think Blinky will be able to eat it? If she grows a little stronger, or even breaks through, things will get a lot easier . . . as for the heads, we can split them four ways."

Rex shifted uncomfortably. "I . . . I'm not so sure," he hedged.

"Why not?" Spiros asked, poking around through the decapitated heads. Picking one up, he brought it to his face and looked into its eyes. Nodding in satisfaction, he tossed it around in his hand, and a moment later his ring flashed and it disappeared.

Rex watched him for a moment before beginning to pick out his own severed heads, not answering right away.

"She's easy to control because she's still in the Mortal tier. I'm not sure our bond will hold if she advances." Rex sighed, and reaching over his shoulder, he rubbed a hand over one of Blinky's glassy eyes, only to flinch back and dry his hand on his robe a second later when her jaw-lid suddenly snapped shut.

"Nel and Lukeus don't have any problems, though," Luke pointed out, regretting the words as soon as they slipped out—realizing too late that he was encouraging Rex to make his monster stronger. No matter how cute she acted, she was still a demon, and one belonging to Rex. He was a perfectly nice guy, if a little slow and antagonistic at times, but not someone Luke, or most people who knew him, felt should be responsible for a creature as dangerous as Blinky.

Or maybe I'm being too harsh. Nothing bad has happened in a few months; things could stay that way, Luke rationalized.

Rex looked like he had swallowed a particularly bitter pill. "Their bloodline is stronger than mine, and their familiars are with them willingly. So is Blinky, but I bonded with her while she was still in her egg. She's never really tried resisting the bond, probably because she doesn't know what it's like not having it, but I was a lot stronger than her when she hatched, and now I'm a whole tier higher. If we're on even footing . . . Well, it's hard to say if she'll . . ." He trailed off, choosing his next words carefully. "I don't know if she'll respect me enough to stay with me once she has the option to break free, or even respect me enough not to kill me or any of you if she does get free."

Luke, Arya, and Spiros all took a step back from Rex and the demon he was wearing as a cape.

Rex scoffed and rolled his eyes. "Look, she's not a normal animal. She may not seem like it, but she's hungry all the time, and she doesn't care who or what she eats. If it weren't for my bloodline dominating and pacifying her wilder instincts and making her more agreeable, then she would have eaten me when we freed Heracles."

"Freed Heracles?" Spiros perked up.

"I'll tell you another time," Luke chimed in. The last thing he wanted was Rex blabbing about Zeus asking him for favors or something. Not with Hephaestus listening to every word they said. It was one thing lying to the likes of Lukeus and even Cyzicus, but none of them had given any indication that they had a direct line to actual gods or even enough significance to get them to pay attention to them. Hephaestus very well might bring it up in casual conversation the next time he saw the king of gods, though. Which was unacceptable.

"Fine," Spiros grumbled before shaking his head. "I'm assuming the power of your bloodline is dependent on the relative difference between your and your bonded animal's power?"

"It is, kinda. There's more than one thing that goes into it, though," Rex said.

"But she's already stronger than you," Luke said, crossing his arms over his chest.

"Maybe, bu—"

"Come on. You're saying you and Blinky, one on one, is a conversation?" Luke scoffed.

Rex deflated, even as he picked up another severed hydra head. "Okay, she might win were we to fight, but my mana is heavier than hers and my willpower more focused. Which is what matters."

"Oh." Luke nodded. "So I guess the plan is, we don't give Blinky any good food until you're at the Hero tier, or she might advance to the Warrior tier and kill us all. Got it. Out of curiosity, how far is she from the Warrior tier?"

"Very," Rex said confidently. "I talked to Gramps a little before . . . you know, but he said demons cultivate differently than humans. They get really strong for their tier, stronger than most cultivators and regular beasts, actually, but it's very hard for them to advance. Unless I start feeding her higher-tier blood, she'll be mortal for decades at the least, if not centuries."

"And let's say you fed her the Rebel's corpse?" Luke asked.

"Oh, we'd die so fast." Rex shivered, even as he patted one of Blinky's eyeballs again.

"What happened to her corpse, anyway?" Luke asked.

"You don't know? We fed it to Aura."

"Really? What if I wanted it?"

"You should have said something."

"I was—never mind. Let's get these heads and get out of here." Luke sighed and kicked one of the hydra's heads. Arya had decapitated that one, and it was in such poor shape that just prodding it made the jaw fall off. Not wanting to touch it due to its diseased appearance, Luke moved on to the next, taking the chance to open his status as he did.

Status | Skills | Quests | Inventory
Name: Lukas King
Tier: Warrior
Bloodline: Eyes of Insight
Mana: 86,321 / 132,834
Rate: 17% per hour
Strength: 254 > 276
Agility: 256 > 281
Constitution: 506 > 524
Arcana: 506 > 507
Stat Points: 0
Charges: 7/10

Hephaestus, Luke realized, really must have been keeping an eye on everyone, because the Seed hadn't once deigned to touch any of the excess mana that had accumulated in his body. Normally it would whisk away every drop that wasn't absorbed immediately and store it as stat points, but the god watching them must cross the Seed's threshold for acceptable risk.

It was good knowledge to have. He had always been worried about the fact that someone would be able to detect him suddenly growing stronger in bursts, but mortals, warriors, and even heroes were unable to detect mana that precisely.

It's nice to know, though, that the Seed cares just as much about hiding itself as I do about keeping it hidden. So long as I don't have the icon of an eye watching me, I'm good, but if I do . . . best keep things on the up and up. Which, hopefully, shouldn't be too often.

Gods really ought to have better things to do than to Big Brother the citizens of Theos and obsess over mortal and other low-ranked cultivators. Hopefully.

Still, this isn't bad progress. The mana is so thick here that even with all the excess mana evaporating and being wasted, I'm still up, what—sixty-six points. That's bonkers for less than a day's worth of effort. That said, it's not that much of an advantage, either, because everyone here will have grown this much.

If Spiros grew up in a place with mana even remotely like this, then no wonder he was kicking so much ass at the society, even when he had barely started cultivating.

If I'm remembering right, though, his family kicks everyone out until they become warriors. That's . . . brutal as fuck. This kind of mana density, he could have become a warrior at ten if he really worked at it. Which begs the question, why isn't he? Actually, why aren't all the gods' children already at the Hero tier?

Even Heracles is bumming around on Sylcra instead of hanging around Zeus's palace. What, to gain experience or something?

The conclusion seemed as likely as any other, Luke decided, dismissing his status and collecting the last head. This one, too, had been severed by Arya, unlike the rest she had cut, he decided to keep it. Not for the poison, but for the rot still spreading through it.

He doubted he would learn anything from it, especially when compared to watching Arya in action, but it was better than nothing.

Just as he was about to send it to his ring, though, he noticed a shadow move through the woods. Fast as he could, he chucked the severed hydra head at it. His ring flashed, his blade appeared in his hand, and he activated the First Truth of Death.

"Whoa, take a deep breath, brother!" a voice echoed through the woods. Luke lifted his sword in response as someone came out of the tree line, his hands raised over his head. He relaxed slightly when he realized that no ghostly apparition was moving from the figure—which meant that, for the moment at least, whoever it was wasn't hostile.

Only to tense again when a face exactly like his own smiled at him. "I'm Theseus . . . It's nice to meet you!" He grinned.

Fuck me.

CHAPTER 37

Son of Poseidon

Luke stared silently into the eyes of his look-alike, while his look-alike grinned at him and waved. The same look-alike that had been climbing the pyramid steps, even to the very end, without any signs of struggle.

Luke had been hoping that he would never have to interact with him, but that very hope felt like it had been taken to a scenic cliff in the middle of nowhere and shot in the back of its metaphorical head by someone it had trusted.

For a second, his mind flashed back to the time he had met Lukeus, and he had the horrible superstition that this meeting with Theseus might have consequences as far-reaching as the ones from that fateful day. Considering that meeting had brought him here in the first place, Luke wasn't stoked.

Maybe not now, or even in a century if he lived that long, but eventually he knew that this moment was going to cause him a significant headache. Considering he hadn't had a headache since he broke through to the Warrior tier, well—

Saying that he didn't look forward to it would be putting it lightly.

All right, I planned for this . . . just gotta stick with it.

Just deny everything, and I'll be fine. Theseus was pretty famous back home—had a boat named after him if I remember right. I think he killed the Minotaur, too, which doesn't bode too well for the other minotaur still participating. That said, he's just another child of a god.

Like Heracles, who, other than being unnaturally strong, is pretty chill. Nothing to be weird about . . . nothing at all.

Besides, there's probably a fuckton of Poseidon's descendants running around. So, as long as I don't come off as interesting, he'll forget all about me.

Rex walked up behind Luke and poked him on the shoulder; then, leaning into his ear, began to whisper. But it was so quiet that even with his advanced hearing, all he heard was the sound of his breathing.

"What?" Luke asked, irritation from having his ear blown into clear in his voice.

Rex cleared his throat and stepped back. "You've just been standing there. Is everything—"

"I've never been better, Rex, and sorry, did you say brother?" Luke asked, his eyes boring into Theseus's, making sure to keep his face carefully blank. A benefit of being a warrior was that he had excellent control of his muscles—including those on his face. Which he hoped would make the heaps of bullshit that were about to spew from his mouth more believable. And rather than try and feign an emotion, he figured that it would be better to come across as someone unusually stoic.

Theseus scratched the back of his head. "I mean, yeah. You've seen what you look like, right?" he said, gesturing to his face, then to Luke's.

"I do own a mirror, and I can see that we're both pretty handsome," Luke agreed easily, not seeing a point in denying the resemblance. Instead, he tried to remember what he had told Rex, Arya, and Spiros about his past.

Assuming that they hadn't already connected the dots and figured out who he was. Which, now that he thought about it, wasn't a possibility he could dismiss out of hand. He had been able to recognize aspects of their movements as belonging to the First Stances, so there was no reason they couldn't have done the same. Except for the fact that Luke had known what to look for, and unless his cover had already been blown or they suspected already, they wouldn't have picked up on it.

But that wasn't even his biggest concern, or at least not one he could do anything about. He wasn't toothless without the techniques, but not using them at all was like trying to fight with an arm tied behind his back—which he might have to resort to in order to keep his identity hidden.

What worried him more immediately was getting his story, or rather *stories*, straight.

People might excuse one or two superficial similarities, like his name and the fact that he used a gold sword, especially when everything else didn't match up. What were the chances, however, that there were multiple Lukes running around, all of whom had been found at sea by fishermen? And, to make it all worse, he didn't remember exactly what lies he had told to whom. He realized, not for the first time, that living in a web of untruths was just asking to get caught in it.

Wait . . . I don't think I told Lukeus about who raised me. I just gave some bull about being raised by my father and then admitted that it was a lie . . . I've only told the fisherman story to Al, Arya, and Spiros.

Rex, then, shouldn't have the slightest clue who I am, because no one really asked after the first few days, and Cyzicus didn't care. Cyzicus also knows that I'm from Carim, but he swore himself to secrecy, so that's one person I don't need to worry about.

But holy shit, keeping lies straight is a pain in the ass. Why the hell do people have to ask questions when you randomly show up in their lives out of the blue?

"I know, right! Our family is the best-looking in the world." Theseus grinned, blissfully unaware of the tumultuous state of Luke's mind. Then with a smile still on his face, his storage ring flashed, putting all four of them on guard. To their confusion, though, what he took out was a comb, which he promptly began to run through his already perfectly combed hair. "So, have you met Pops recently?"

Here we go.

"Sorry, I—you have me at a loss. I don't know who my dad is." Luke shrugged.

"Really? I thought Dad visited all of us at least once a year. Does he know you're alive?"

"I—I don't even know what to say to that, if I'm being honest." Luke sighed. "Who is your dad?"

Not only Theseus, but even Spiros looked at him oddly at that.

Okay, maybe laying it on too thick . . . Spiros did just say that I look like Poseidon, but Theseus doesn't know that, so it's fine.

"Poseidon. Our father is Poseidon," Theseus said, his eyes beginning to roll before he caught himself and adopted a more serious expression.

"Yeah, I think I would know if my father was a god."

"Are you sure?" Theseus frowned. Once again, he pointed to his face, then back at Luke's. "I think the evidence is pretty clear. Orion said he didn't know until he was Dad's son, either, not until he became a Saint and went to Atlantis. So, maybe Dad just forgot about you, too?" he offered, his face becoming more and more sympathetic by the second.

Luke didn't know what to say to that, and he felt a little bad for Orion, but he liked what he was hearing. The more promiscuous Poseidon was, the better.

"I'm pretty sure Mom would have mentioned it . . . Is there any way to test it?" Luke asked instead, knowing what the result would be.

"Uhhh, yeah." Theseus nodded. "There is." Then, looking around, his eyes landed on the headless corpse of the hydra. A look of concentration came over Theseus's face, and suddenly, Luke felt his robes get wet against his frame.

What the . . . Luke's eyes widened as the son of Poseidon's arm turned transparent while the rest of him was covered in a wet sheen. Glimmering in the light of Theos's nine moons, the teen pointed a single finger at the carcass.

A loud torrent of white water shot out of his forefinger, and mist sprayed everywhere, drenching each and every one of them to the bone and making rainbows in the beams of moonlight. When the thunderous noise of pressurized water faded away and the mist settled, it revealed a hole big enough to crawl through on the giant monster's body. Cut so clean, it looked like someone had taken a giant hole punch to the thing.

Holy shit, Luke thought, eyeing the teen with wide eyes. He had known that a son of Poseidon wouldn't be weak . . . but this was far outside what he had expected.

"That's it?" Spiros chimed in for the first time. Walking up to the corpse, he poked his head in the hole and started inspecting it. "I've seen better."

"Who are you?" Theseus lifted an eyebrow at the son of House Paris.

"That's Spiros," Luke answered for him, "and no . . . I'm positive that I can't do that."

Theseus and Spiros continued to stare at each other until Theseus turned away. "You have to have it, though—that's our bloodline."

"I don't know what to tell you, but I know I can't do that." *Even though it would be awesome if I could. Killing the hydra would have been cake.*

"Can you check?" Theseus insisted. "Even if you're not my brother, you should be a nephew . . . or related in some way."

"Look . . . uh, Theseus. Don't take this the wrong way, but I really can't do that. If I was related to a god, believe me, that would be amazing. Maybe Poseidon is my great-great-great-grandfather or something. Besides, I'd only have the bloodline if my parents were cultivators and awakened their mana. Mine didn't." Luke shrugged.

Theseus, looking dejected, nodded, and Luke had to hold back a sigh of relief. Just when he thought it was all over, though, the son of Poseidon opened his mouth again. "Even if you don't have the bloodline, it's not too late to awaken it. Considering how alike we look, you can't be too many generations away from Dad. Why don't you come to Atlantis once this is all over, and I'll ask Dad if he can do it for you?"

Okay, this is getting weird, Luke decided. *It's one thing for him to be curious about some guy who looks just like him, but another to keep pressing. So what does he want? Our scroll? That would explain how he found us, at least.*

But . . . I've never heard about bloodlines being awakened, either.

"How would that even work?" Luke asked, partly because he was curious and partly because saying no outright would be strange. No cultivator in his right mind would turn down what he had just seen Theseus do, barring some very serious costs, and definitely not without hearing more about it.

"It's pretty simple. You just need to drink a drop of his blood, and if you're descended from him, you'll have it! It won't even hurt that much, honest."

"All right, that's not happening. I'm not going to Atlantis to drink a god's blood for a fraction of his power . . . I've come this far on my own without relying on any handouts. I don't need to beg favors from distant family, who I've never met before, to increase my power," Luke said, injecting a little heat into his voice but knowing full well that had he actually been related to Poseidon and didn't already possess a bloodline, he would be jumping on the opportunity to mooch off a god.

As it was, he couldn't ignore the fact that he didn't naturally look like this, and the last owner of the mask he'd used very likely had been killed by Theseus's family. Even though the Seed's description said that the disguise was undetectable, it didn't mean he'd be passing any DNA tests. Which he wasn't even sure didn't exist. Considering Hephaestus had drones and rip-off T-1000s, it would be weirder if they didn't.

"Are you sure?" Rex said, his eyes darting between the hole carved in the hydra and Theseus. "As a friend, I think you should go for it."

"Yes, Rex. I'm sure." Luke sighed. "Anyways, it was really nice meeting you. I appreciate the offer, but I'll have to decline."

"Well." Theseus shrugged, disappointment clearly written on his face. "If there's nothing I can do to convince you, I'll just take that scroll and be on my way."

Luke reached into the sword with his mana, used it to double his Agility instantly, and reactivated the First Truth of Death.

CHAPTER 38

Breaking the Unbreakable

The First Truth of Death gave him just enough warning to leap out of the way so that when another torrent of water blasted toward Luke, it dug deep trenches only in the ground and not him.

A cursory inspection revealed that the force of that attack was significantly less than the one Theseus had used on the hydra's carcass. Which honestly annoyed Luke more than anything. A fact not helped by the teasing glint in Theseus's eyes, or the fact that he had brought his hand to his face—faking a yawn.

It *was* good to know that Theseus wasn't attacking with enough power to kill, but even so, it grated on both Luke's nerves and his pride that he wasn't being taken seriously.

It stung, and more than he would like to admit.

Luke was good—really good when compared to the average warriors of Sylcra, nigh unbeatable, in fact. He was better even than most of those who had competed in the tournament—after all, he was able to overcome Hephaestus's divine presence, and where most others had struggled on the steps, not even carrying Rex had slowed him down.

That single attack, however, had revealed something that he had suspected since they had locked eyes on the pyramid and that had been all but confirmed when Theseus gouged a hole in the hydra.

Luke wasn't a match for him.

His technique was geared toward finding openings to attack, but to attack, he needed to get close enough to hit him. Which, if the future he was seeing was correct, wasn't going to happen. There was no way to get close to Theseus without being hit.

Perhaps if the son of Poseidon fought with an actual weapon, he and Luke would be able to compete on more even grounds. Maybe if Luke were allowed to use all his weapons and his rapidly growing collection of talismans, he could put up a better fight against Theseus. Assuming, of course, that Theseus wouldn't be able to use his own substantial wealth and resources against Luke.

Seeing how the tournament disallowed all that, the smart thing then was to give up and hope that once Theseus had both scrolls, he would leave them alone.

And Luke was reasonably sure he would, too—once he had both scrolls, not only was continuing to fight pointless, but Luke couldn't shake the thought that Theseus wanted something. Whatever that was, he wouldn't get it if he eliminated Luke.

But fuck that—there's no way I'm giving up our scroll. It's still four, no, five of us against one of him. We have the advantage. I just need to get in close—and son of Poseidon or not, he only has so much mana before his bloodline drains him dry.

Hell, if he's smart, he'll give up before he comes close to running out, or risk someone coming after him when he's vulnerable.

Which means we just need to force him to spend enough of it that going after a weaker target would be more worthwhile.

"This will go faster for all of us if you just give me your scroll," Theseus chided, pointing another finger at Luke. He held off on attacking, as if he fully expected Luke to take him up on the offer.

"For a guy as outnumbered as you are, you sure are cocky," Luke spat back, keeping a close eye on him and his specter, preparing to dodge at a moment's notice.

Theseus sighed audibly, his ghost slashed its finger twice, and apparitions of two lines of lethally fast water cut through the air toward him. They covered an area wide enough to not only pin him but Rex as well, with a third wave trailing fractions of a second behind—it would hit Luke if he dodged the attack by flying up.

Luke's sword immediately left his hand and positioned itself, seemingly of its own will, in front of Rex, while he leaned so far that his back was nearly pressed against the ground.

Most of the water sailed harmlessly over his head, grazing and cutting a few strands of his hair that lingered in the air, while the rest turned to mist against his sword. In the process, it knocked Maximus over thirty feet away. While Luke was confident the blade itself was fine, the grip his mana had on space was weaker when channeled through the sword—which was why he already hadn't chucked it at Theseus. If the other contestant managed to catch it, then Luke would be completely unarmed for the rest of the battle, and when dealing with reflexes as good as those belonging to warriors, that wasn't a possibility he could ignore. It was a lesson Heracles had beaten into him often enough.

"Hmm. You're good at dodging." Theseus grinned at him. "What about your friends?" he said, and this time he aimed past Luke and toward Arya. Just as easily as Luke had, she dodged as well. Suddenly, Theseus's smile looked a little more strained than it had a second ago. It told Luke all he needed to know.

Theseus wasn't used to people being able to avoid his attacks.

Yeah, that's right. You won't have any luck with Spiros, either, jackass, Luke thought, calling his blade back to his arm and completely unable to stop smiling as Theseus took aim toward the lovestruck spear wielder.

Unfortunately for the son of Poseidon, that's when Rex decided to join the battle. With Blinky expanding behind him menacingly, he fired one bolt of blistering flame at Theseus after another, only to have him erect a wall of water in front of him, stopping each fiery projectile in an explosion of steam.

Theseus clicked his tongue and sighed. Holding his palm out, he rose a foot into the air, and a cloud of thick mist settled around him, obscuring him from sight.

Shit. Luke cursed internally the moment his technique cut out. *And not just mine, either . . . Spiros and Arya are probably down for the count, too, unless they learned other techniques, but even then . . . we can't attack if we can't see him.*

Wrapping his body in mana, Luke shot into the sky, intent on giving himself some space now that he couldn't foresee the trajectory of Theseus's attacks.

Below him, he saw a horrifying sight.

Blinky had left her cape form and filled the entire clearing where they had slain the hydra with her writhing mass. Most of her form was obscured by the mist, though, showing only the vague flashes of writhing eyeballs and tendrils.

Moments later, Arya, Spiros, and Rex all escaped from the misted area, no doubt having the same idea as him.

"What is this—thing?" Theseus's voice rang out from within the mist. His tone, unexpectedly, didn't reveal any signs of nervousness or even fright, but instead radiated with pure and utter glee. "How novel." He laughed, and immediately, Rex fired an arrow at the direction of the noise. The hiss of evaporating water was the only proof that he had both struck true and ultimately failed.

Luke watched, at a loss for how to proceed. It didn't make sense to him—he thought Theseus would be in a rush to escape the foggy hell that the clearing had become. Even if he could defeat Blinky, that didn't mean it was a good idea to fight her.

It never was.

She wasn't particularly strong, or even fast, but the amount of damage she could withstand was obscene. The only way to kill her was by destroying every eye, and Luke didn't think anyone knew how many of those she had. The number constantly shifted from moment to moment, from hundreds to tens of thousands in the time it took to blink. Even cutting her tendrils was more akin to cutting through a human hair than it was flesh, with her consciousness distributed throughout. Just severing the tendrils wasn't enough; so long as the eyes on the appendage were intact, and the flesh remained alive, Blinky would just reattach it. It was why Lukeus had resorted to killing Blinky's mother with a Hero-tier talisman in the first place.

Simply put, dreadglares were aberrant. Their biology, if it could even be called that, defied conventional sense. Unfortunately, neither Spiros nor Arya was aware of the fact, and in the heat of the moment, Luke didn't remember to tell them.

"This is going to suck," Spiros cursed, his spear twirling in his hands as he, like Luke, watched the fog helplessly, waiting for the inevitable moment, he thought, when Theseus would kill the demon and turn his attention toward them.

"Any ideas?" Luke asked him, not realizing they were on completely different pages.

"Yeah." Spiros scratched his chin and closed his eyes in concentration.

Immediately, Luke realized what he was about to do, but before he could stop him, it was already too late.

Spiros's ring flashed, and his spear disappeared from his hands. Seconds later, both his fists erupted into brilliant gold flames, the heat of which Luke could feel even dozens of feet away from him. "Rex!" Spiros yelled. "Call back your familiar."

"Wait—" Rex yelled, but without heeding his warning, Spiros dived back toward the ground. Massive balls of fire shot out of his fists one after another toward where they had last heard the son of Poseidon.

In the fog, Blinky screeched when a stray fireball caught a few dozen of her eyes. Then, moments later, her shape congealed into eldritch wings, and a mass of eyeballs pushed against the air and rose in the sky.

Luke cursed under his breath at the wasted opportunity and blamed himself for it. Had he communicated better, then perhaps Theseus would continue to waste his mana on a foe that was insidiously difficult to damage, let alone kill.

Completely opposite to his expectations, though, Theseus left the cover of his mist, and chased after the dreadglare, letting both Spiros's and Rex's continued attacks peter out on his watery shield.

Okay, what the fuck, Luke thought, his eyes narrowed in thought as Theseus recklessly pressed on.

His actions failed to make any sense, but then Luke realized why he was doing what he was doing.

The guy's fucking trophy hunting. Does he think we're jokes? Luke wondered incredulously, holding his sword in a white-knuckled grip. Theseus's dismissive attitude was getting under his skin.

The fact was that Theseus didn't think of them as threats. He would rather hunt an interesting creature than finish them off and take their scroll.

Luke resolved to not let his arrogance go unchallenged.

Activating the First Stance of the Sword, and careful to keep the prince of Atlantis in his sights, he dropped low to the ground.

They weren't allowed to use any artifact other than their storage rings and a single preapproved artifact. That didn't mean he couldn't find something that wasn't a weapon and use that instead. Anything gained within the trial was free game, after all.

Shifting his blade's secondary ability from boosting his Agility to Strength, he threw Maximus straight into the sky. Concentrating, he poured his mana into it and propelled it faster and higher.

Then, gathering a fistful of the hydra's necks in each hand, he spun on his heels. Once, twice, three times, then four, and with the aid of his technique aimed the hydra at Theseus before letting go.

Theseus, in the sky, sent one scythe of water after another toward Blinky, strategically cutting away one tendril after another, slowly but surely wearing her down.

It wasn't even working. Her eyes were intact, and she would just reattach the parts he cut off before they even touched the ground. He'd falsely assumed that the demon would run out of mana sooner rather than later, and clearly he thought this was a battle of attrition.

He might have even been right.

Unfortunately for him, though, before he could find out, the carcass Luke had thrown collided with his watery shield and, unlike the intangible flame projectiles fired at him by Rex and Spiros, punched clean through. Water, after all, was water.

The hydra itself didn't do much damage, but the gap created by its forceful ingress was enough for both Rex and Spiros to land an attack each.

Snarling in fury and steaming from the heat of the flames, both Theseus's arms turned to water as he launched simultaneous attacks on both Rex and Spiros.

Spiros, with the aid of his technique, dodged. Rex got hit straight in his chest. Faster than any of them could react, he flickered orange and disappeared.

Fuck.

CHAPTER 39

Can't Be Beaten

At the edge of the clearing, a white scroll bounced off the ground, and it was then that Luke remembered that Rex had been holding it.

Out of the corner of his eye, he saw Arya slowly make her way toward it. Luke would have thought the action brave were it not for the fact that Theseus was very distracted.

"FUCK. FUCK. FUCK," the son of Poseidon roared, his face set in a vicious scowl and his fists clenched. His eyes burned with anger and he stared as every inch of Blinky, and her many eyes, were engulfed in flickering orange light.

Blinky the demon had been eliminated from the trial along with Rex.

It made sense to Luke, considering that she was only participating because she was Rex's familiar, and secretly he thought it best. There weren't any indications that she would rampage or anything, but some part of him had never been able to let his guard down around her.

It was a shame, however, that everyone from Sylcra, save him, had been defeated, which left Luke's shoulders feeling heavy. If the quest panned out—and there wasn't any guarantee it would—he'd finish in second place.

High enough to get Cyzicus what he wanted and push the emperor to the Saint tier, in the process repaying him for all the favors he had done for Luke and the goodwill he had shown him. It might even cheer the hero up a little, help him get out of the spiral Sophia's death and finding her corpse in the Rebel's ring had put him in.

But first, he needed to get Theseus off their backs.

It's not going to be easy, though.

The son of Poseidon was glaring at Luke through his reformed water shield even as Spiros relentlessly assaulted him with the spell. The liquid defense rippled, hissed, and steamed but otherwise held up without any strain.

The two hits Spiros and Rex had managed to land, with Luke's help, had burned away the upper half of his robes, revealing two distinct patches of raw, pink skin that were already shrinking.

So that did hurt him, but not enough to deplete the potion we drank earlier. He really hit Rex hard, huh. Which means I won't have to feel too bad about stabbing him, Luke thought, grinning at the teen in challenge.

"This is your fault," Theseus yelled, his voice hoarse and cracking under strain.

Why he was so upset, Luke couldn't even begin to fathom, and so he didn't even bother responding.

He must be on something.

Wanting me to come with him to Atlantis because we might be related is one thing, and I can kinda get where he's coming from. If I met some stranger who looked like me, knowing that my dad was out there having kids, who I thought might be my half brother, I'd want to get to know them, too. Even wanting to extract opportunistic favors from family I get. But where the fuck does he get off eliminating my friend and then blaming it on me?

Why did he want to fight Blinky so bad, anyway?

All questions I'll never get the answer to, because he's going home, and hopefully, I'll never see him again.

Letting his mana flow freely, uncaring of how much he was spending, Luke accelerated his blade to the very limits of his ability. Then, watching Theseus's apparition, he preemptively dodged a torrent of water blasted his way.

"How are you dodg—" Theseus began to say, but the words caught in his mouth. Alerted by a strange whistling noise coming from above, he looked up and immediately dived out of the way.

Unfortunately for him, Luke had already known what he was going to do.

A single exertion of his will was all Luke needed to adjust the course of his sword to where he would be at the end of his movement.

But even that didn't turn out to be enough when Theseus's ghost suddenly changed its posture as if he was holding a spear. Before Luke could make sense of it, Theseus's ring flashed and a glimmering trident, seemingly made of diamond, appeared in his hand—threatening to bat his weapon away.

Humph. Looks like he's finally taking this somewhat seriously, but he couldn't have picked a worse time.

Summons from a storage ring were another weakness in his technique, but this particular weakness was something Luke could overcome with time.

Luke could see what someone would do in the future, but the apparitions he saw were based on what he could actually *see* and in part based on his own experiences. The First Truth of Death was a higher form of the deductive reasoning granted by the First Stances—one that showed the future as his opponent intended it. What it couldn't do, however, was peer into their storage rings, or even act on information that Luke didn't have or couldn't know. People did have tells, however, so even if the future he saw was incomplete, there was usually enough information to act on.

Someone moving as if a shield was about to pop into existence was typically a good enough indicator that a shield would pop into existence. That ran the risk of uncertainty, however, because people could act like they were about to summon a shield and instead summon something *like* a shield, or, much more commonly, a shield that was a shape Luke wouldn't be able to guess. Exactly like Theseus had just done by summoning a trident. As such, the act of summoning something, while a minor inconvenience, wasn't the end of the world. What tended to be more annoying, however, was that Luke wouldn't know what an artifact did until it was actually used.

Even that wasn't an insurmountable problem.

The technique worked better the longer he battled someone or knew them, allowing him to see more clearly the more he understood their abilities. Give him long enough, and the gaps in the predictive ability would shrink until they vanished entirely.

He hadn't known it then, but Luke suspected it was part of the reason the First Truth had worked so well against the Rebel. He had, after all, spent hours harassing her and seeing her deal with not only his attacks but Heracles's, too. Well, that, and the fact that when he had fought her, she was half-dead and his own mana was unlimited.

Considering all that, Luke tamped down on the unease that surfaced and decided to trust in his abilities. He might have overplayed his hand, and the trident Theseus summoned could be a game changer, but he wasn't without tricks or allies, either.

Spiros was still striking the bubble the son of Poseidon had surrounded himself in with dogged determination, unleashing blistering balls of flame one after another, over and over again.

Even for Theseus, something like that would take its toll eventually. And the strikes that had already landed on him, while not enough to send him home yet, were taking a toll on his mana.

Another good hit and he'll probably run. Even if he is stronger than us, we can dodge most of what he can do . . . All three of us. We aren't the only ones he has to worry about, either . . . he was by far the person with the best performance on the pyramid, but he needs to hold the pair of scrolls for seven days, and no one who's made it this far is weak. No one will go without some sort of fight.

So one more . . .

Readjusting the course of the blade by a few feet, he watched as it whizzed by Theseus, barely out of his range. Then, with every ounce of willpower he had, Luke stopped its downward momentum and attacked Theseus from beneath. It was a risk. He had drained a lot of the inertia and energy Maximus was carrying—if Theseus was smart, he would focus on trapping the blade in his bubble. It was an action that would take Luke out of the fight.

But he wasn't fighting alone.

His sword cut upward, at the very edge of his barrier. For a split second, it carved a line through the water as Luke had anticipated. Despite his best efforts, Theseus managed to catch his blade with the forks of his trident.

It was all the opportunity Spiros needed. His own ring flashed, and in the blink of an eye, a golden spear blurred through the air, clean through the barrier, and impaled the son of Poseidon through his shoulders.

Theseus winced in pain and tore it free. Blood sprayed from the open wound, but it wasn't enough to eliminate him.

Luke grinned and, using the fact that he was distracted, maneuvered his blade free from the trident and out of Theseus's range.

No sooner had Luke's sword left Theseus's range than Arya lunged forth and threw her dagger with perfect aim. Unlike Luke, she wasn't able to use her weapon as a conduit for her own mana, and strength was never her primary focus—which was why she had thrown it to Spiros, who was only feet away from their common foe.

He caught it in midair and held it tauntingly, dodging another jet of deadly water with an arrogant grin plastered over his face.

"Theseus, right? Why don't you give me back my spear, and your scroll, and we'll let you leave?" Spiros said with a grin.

"Why would I do that?" Theseus asked, seemingly unfazed even as he wiped blood from his mouth.

Luke took to the sky and joined the pair, a grin on his face. "Because you can't beat us, and you'll never get our scroll. While we've hit you, what, three times now. How much more before the potion runs out and you're eliminated?" he said, having a fairly good idea how much efficacy the potion had left. If there was one thing to be said of Cyzicus's methods, they had taught Luke how much healing he'd get from a single drop of the stuff. Hephaestus's may have been better than what he was used to, but he was confident in his guess nonetheless. One more solid hit and that would be the end of the road for Theseus.

"There's no one here who can defeat me. All three of you are too afraid to even come close, and none of you has anything that can break through my defenses. This one"—he pointed at Spiros—"probably has just enough mana to stay in the air."

"Your point? You think I can't land a hit on you, or that she can't?" Luke raised an eyebrow and nodded briefly toward Arya before glancing at Spiros.

He realized suddenly that Theseus had Spiros's measure. Luke didn't know exactly how much mana the spells Hephaestus had given them cost nor how much mana Spiros had, but it was clear that there was a cost and it was high.

It didn't take great observational skills to notice that Spiros was having trouble maintaining his flight, which was a *very* bad sign, and a bigger problem. With Spiros out of mana, Theseus would have an easy time hitting him and eliminating him entirely.

For the sake of Luke's quest, this needed to end.

Tilting his head to the side, Luke considered his next words carefully.

"Look. You're a stiff breeze away from being booted, and he's tired. I think we can both agree that continuing to fight isn't in either of our best interests. You say he's not great on mana, but I know you aren't, either. The number of attacks you let loose, there's no way. Besides, there's a reason you're talking this out now instead of blasting me with water. So, let's cut the posturing. You're strong enough that getting two more scrolls won't be a big deal. Give us yours and we'll have a rematch in the next round . . . and if you tell me the real reason you want me to come to Atlantis, I'll think it over." Luke added the last part on a whim. He had no intention of ever setting foot in the place, but Theseus still probably thought—and for good reason—that Luke was in fact related to his father, and Luke wasn't above manipulating that desire.

Theseus clicked his tongue, an unwilling expression on his face.

The three of them hovered in the air in silence, Luke with his Agility boosted and the First Truth activated, ready to leap into action if Theseus decided to attack. Eventually, though, the son of Poseidon nodded and, reaching behind him, he pulled the scroll from a pocket and held it out, his watery shield evaporating into nothing as he did.

Carefully, in case he pulled a trick, Luke reached out to grab it and pulled. Theseus didn't let go.

"Let me hang with you three," he demanded.

CHAPTER 40

Making Good Points

No," Luke said immediately and tugged the scroll again.

Theseus's obstinate eyes met his, and he tugged it back—still unwilling to let it go.

Fuck this, Luke thought, and, focusing on his sword, he doubled his Strength and snatched the scroll out of Theseus's hands. Doubling the attribute didn't max it out yet, but it did put him well past the midway point of the tier. Theseus was likely stronger even then, considering how dense the mana was in Atlantis, but the sudden leap in power would catch anyone off guard.

"Wai—!" Theseus yelled, his eyes widened in shock.

"No." Luke shut him down and flew back as he lunged forward, lifting his sword and putting the pointy end in between the two of them.

Fully cognizant of the fact that at any second the other teen could change his mind and attack, Luke sent a portion of his awareness to the spell hovering in his mana, ready to activate it at the smallest sign of aggression. It wouldn't do much against him—Spiros had demonstrated that point already—but Luke was aware, firsthand, how distracting blinding flashes of light could be when they burst inches in front of the eyes—warrior or not.

That's right, I have cards up my sleeve, too, asshole. I can't fire jets of water powerful enough to carve holes through hydras, but when it comes to attributes, I'm King, Luke thought, taking a visceral amount of satisfaction in the fact that he had *something* that was a surprise to the other teen. Being on the back foot the entire time had not been comfortable for him.

I'm still not a true match for combat-focused bloodlines yet, or probably anyone that comes from a powerful background . . .

If what I'm hoping for with spells doesn't work out, I'll pick up another technique, he decided. *Maybe the lightning one Cyzicus and Nel use, if they let me learn it—but after I become a hero. Or . . . maybe Sophia left something behind? I don't really know what happened to her storage ring, but considering that the Rebel's ring only—now isn't the time.*

Focus, Luke chided himself, and just in time, as Theseus made a half-hearted swipe at the scroll.

Without a shred of hesitation, he flung the scroll to Arya and immediately redoubled his Agility stat, flying back dozens of feet. His technique hadn't indicated that Theseus would try anything, but dodging if he needed to was paramount, and it was always better dodging from a distance.

Especially when Luke couldn't discount the possibility that Theseus's pride wouldn't let him walk away after all.

"Come on—why can't I join you?" Theseus protested, his mouth slightly agape as if no one had ever told him the word *no* in his entire life. Considering he was the child of a god, that may well have been the case.

The nerve of this guy. Is he for real? After all that, he wants to team up, and he's curious why I don't?

"You just eliminated my friend, and I'm mad at you."

"So, what does that have to do with anything! He'll be fine—Hephaestus will heal him up better than he was when he came here, and the whole point of this round is to eliminate people. Don't take it personally," Theseus said, crossing his arms over his chest.

Okay, he might have a point, but—

Spiros snorted. "The answer is still no. Deal with it, and give me back my spear before I take it from you. I still have plenty of uses on my spell."

"And I have one of those, too—what's your point? I was just stopping in order to give you a chance to continue on, but if you want to keep fighting, I will, too. I don't even care if I get eliminated, but I promise I'll take you with me when I go," Theseus said, and on cue a watery barrier appeared, separating Theseus from Luke and Spiros.

The First Truth of Death, however, remained silent.

He's bluffing. Or at least not willing to restart the fight just yet.

"Calm down, both of you." Luke sighed. "Theseus, you're right, this is a competition—and I'm competing against you and I want to keep it that way."

"What—you'll team up with them, but not me? Is that it? We're family!"

"What do you mean, I—we just met you!"

"Why's that matter? Everyone needs to meet people sometime."

"Why is it so hard to say no to you?" Luke asked.

"It's not!" Theseus denied.

"Dude, I've been saying no for how long now?"

"Well, you don't have to be mean about it."

Luke wanted to tear his hair out in frustration. Instead he closed his eyes and took a deep breath. When all this had started, the last thing he'd thought was that he would need to be considerate of Theseus's feelings. Well, more than normal, at least.

How did we even get here? He thinks I'm his brother and asks me to come to Atlantis. I say no, we fight, Rex and Blinky get eliminated, we whittle him down to a point that fighting isn't worth it anymore, and now he wants to join us?

If Spiros wasn't running on fumes, I would have just sent him home. He's the son of a god and someone who had myths written about him back on Earth. I'm sure he would have been fine even without the rewards from here.

"I'm sorry for being curt, but I think there's too much tension between us for all three of us to work together effectively," Luke said, and it wasn't even a lie. Spiros was so angry Luke could practically see steam coming from his ears.

Actually, having him with us is practically a guarantee of getting to the next round. A few hours of rest to recover some mana, and we can probably start going after the other groups with confidence. If nothing else, it would take us to the next round . . .

"Luke," Spiros said slowly. "What are you thinking?"

"I mean, think about it—it wouldn't be the worst thing to let him join us . . ."

"Yeah, let's do that." Theseus grinned, and then, realizing he was still holding Spiros's spear, he smiled sheepishly and held it out. His watery barrier gave way and dissolved in a spray of mist at the same time.

Spiros eyed the offered weapon with caution before slowly moving forward and grabbing it. The moment Theseus took his hand off the spear's shaft, his ring flashed, and it disappeared.

"I'm not opposed to letting you join us, but why do you want to?" Spiros asked.

"I just realized how boring it's going to be spending seven days alone, hiding with some scrolls."

"Arya, wha—" Luke started to say, but a flicker of movement at the very edges of his vision caught his attention.

Sword at the ready, Luke barely had a moment to dodge as an arrow tore through the forest and over his shoulder.

A moment later, Arya started thrashing. A thin green vine had caught her ankle and was threatening to drag her, and their scrolls, into the forest.

Surprisingly, it was Theseus who acted first. A thin arc of water flew from his finger and severed it cleanly, and the three of them rushed to join Arya while she rose higher into the air.

The moment they were close enough, water expanded to encircle all four of them, Theseus offering them what little protection he could.

Which turned out to be not very much at all, Luke realized as he batted away an arrow with his sword when it punched through the barrier.

While he, Rex, Arya, and Spiros had been a terrible matchup for the son of Poseidon, whoever was attacking them now was the complete opposite.

For one, their arrows were actually made of tangible material, and not energy that was wholly ineffective against his weight. Second, the attacker, or attackers, both had ranged options.

Desperately raking his eyes over the tree line, Luke tried his best to find the source of the arrows. But each one came from a completely different direction, and whoever was controlling the vines was so deep in the foliage that he doubted he would ever see them.

"Any idea who's attacking?" Luke asked instead. "Or where they're hiding, for that matter?"

No one answered, but their silence was all the confirmation Luke needed.

"All right . . . Arya, you stay with these two—neither of them has much mana, so look after them as much as you can."

"I can still fight!" Theseus protested. Spiros opened his mouth, likely to say something similar, before he stopped himself, and, flying closer to Theseus, he put a hand on one of his shoulders. Whether to hold him back from leaving, or to steady his wobbly flight, Luke wasn't sure. It did both those things regardless.

"What are you going to do?" Spiros asked.

"Fight, obviously. I haven't used that much mana yet, so it shouldn't be a problem."

"And the scrolls?"

"I'm not going to take them and run, if that's what you're worried about, Spiros." Luke sighed.

A glimmer of understanding flashed through Arya's eyes, and, reaching into her robes, she handed them to him.

"Don't lose them," she said.

Grabbing them, Luke attempted to put them both in his storage ring, only mildly disappointed when they refused to go in, so he stuffed them into his own robes and held them against his skin with his mana. His pockets had long since been destroyed.

"If I do lose them, it's going to be because they eliminated me, and that's not going to happen." Luke grinned.

Then, turning slowly in the air, he took a deep breath and flew out of the bubble, taking off in the direction the latest arrow had come from as fast as he could.

The fight had come at an inopportune time, but out of the four of them, he was in the best position to attack, and with both of their scrolls with him acting as both prize and lure, he was confident it would be him they came for.

Meaning they would leave Spiros alone.

Picking a fight with Theseus, even a tired Theseus, wasn't worth it. Luke was sure that even a minor display of his power would convince anyone looking to thin the herd of that.

And if worse came to worst, he trusted Arya and her power enough to know that while she might not be the strongest of those competing, she would be able to hold her own. The First Stance had made all three of them formidable opponents to the vast majority of people, and the chances of her running into someone that could counter her was near zero.

Of that Luke was confident.

They had chosen to attack from a distance and harass them instead of moving in. He didn't know how long the attackers had been watching them, but the timing alone suggested that they had waited until they were worn out.

Another vine rose out of the air and, quick as a whip, lashed out at him. Its movements were so easy to spot, though, that even without his techniques, he was able to act on it.

Cutting it down with a single swipe of his sword, Luke stood still in the air and turned a slow circle.

"Are you going to fight or just poke at me like cowards?" he yelled.

All he got for his trouble was a volley of arrows flying at him from all directions. They were fast, but he was better. Waiting until the last second, he dodged as many as he could by climbing higher in the air. Most of them whizzed past his feet.

A second later, another volley of arrows followed the last, one after another, each from different directions, sometimes from above him, sometimes from below, and often at one angle or another. He wove between them as long as he could, but the longer he stayed in the air, the more arrows took flight. The number of them increased by the dozens every second.

Cursing under his breath, Luke shot toward the forest, already covered in writhing vines. He realized something was very wrong.

It was only when Luke spotted an arrow that he had already dodged looping around and coming back at him that he realized what it was.

CHAPTER 41

Heaven and Earth

The arrows were being controlled, and not in the typical point-and-shoot way, but by either a technique, a bloodline, or perhaps even an artifact.

Or maybe some combination of all three.

Something to see or target me from a long distance. Another thing to control the arrows' flight, because there's no way whoever's doing this has their mana spread this thin and is controlling them with basic telekinesis. Last but not least, they're using something to control the vines—if that's the same person, and not two or more people working together.

Probably more than one person, which would explain both the arrows and the vines, but . . . considering the average level of the people still competing, it wouldn't be that strange if it is one person. It would explain the surprising level of coordination, if nothing else, Luke thought with a snarl as he cut away one green tendril after another.

Behind him, the arrows that had followed him into the foliage rammed one after another into the trunks of trees as he wove between them with skill honed under the careful and painful tutelage of Clite. The thrumming sound they made as they embedded into the ground and wood was like music to his ears, both revealing the limit of his enemy's control over them and reducing their number.

Unfortunately for Luke, his unseen foe wised up to that within minutes, and at once the majority of the arrows suddenly shot toward the sky, where they tracked him like angry vultures—waiting to punish him for the slightest mistake. That left only a few dozen to harass him as he maneuvered past the obstacles in his way—a task that proved to be challenging but doable.

At the same time, thorn-covered vines sprouted indiscriminately from the shrubs, the trees, the floor, and the carcasses of long-dead and half-devoured rabicorns, along with the corpses of woodland creatures whose bones Luke couldn't recognize. If there was a pattern to be found in how they emerged, though, it eluded him for the moment.

Even so, every tendril of plant flesh that came close fell dead to the ground before measured swings of his sword. They were alive, and so his technique told him all he needed to do to see them dead.

Even so, continuing to run like this left him with a bad taste in his mouth. He didn't need to be a genius to know what his attacker had planned.

They're trying to trap me by crowding the skies with arrows and hoping to catch me with the vines, or vice versa. Doesn't matter if it's the arrows that get me or the plants—the result is the same.

Rex did the same thing when he fought with Blinky—except he would hide behind her and shoot arrows while she would try to surround me. Of course, when I fought them I could use arrows of my own, but that's not necessarily a disadvantage for me. Not when my opponent is under the same restrictions I am.

The arrows are just basic Mortal-tier shafts, likely enchanted with durability, but if I double my Constitution they'll sting, maybe break skin, but not much more, which means that the bow is the actual weapon.

The arrows aren't enough to punch holes in me or anything, but the potion will drain even if it's healing wounds that only amount to bruises. Which means I can't let that happen.

But that's exactly what's going to happen if this drags out too long . . . so how do I end this?

I'll need to get in close, but how?

A vague idea, one too raw to even be called a plan, brewing in his mind, Luke charted a path through the forest. Right now his attacker had all the momentum, and frankly, that couldn't be allowed.

Playing someone else's game was just asking to lose, which meant that he needed to do something to upset them.

The easiest solution, then, was to drag them out of hiding and into the open. Which, if his attacker was worth their salt, would be difficult. Being exposed was the last thing they would want, so Luke would need to make them do it. Not give them an option but to do it.

Reaching into his robes with his free hand as he flew, he unfurled a scroll. It was a long shot, but Hephaestus had said that they would point to the nearest one of opposite color. In his case, that would be the other scroll on his person. He looked anyway, on the admittedly small chance that the god had meant the scroll nearest him that didn't already belong to him.

Unfortunately for Luke, his initial instinct was right.

A brief look at both scrolls revealed that the arrows were locked on each other.

That's definitely going to be a problem when we go for the next pair, Luke realized before stuffing them away again. It was something they would need to discuss when they went hunting for their next scroll, but that was a problem for the future.

For now, he still needed a way to actually find the person or people hunting him.

If things continued as they were, he would eventually slip up. Or worse, the person who was hunting him would get low on mana and retreat.

It wouldn't be the worst thing in the world, but Luke wanted their scroll. Even more than they wanted the pair of his. It was only fair for the trouble he was being put through.

Pressing forward, he continued to hack, slash, and weave his way through the trees, keeping an eye on the arrows trailing behind him and relying on the First Stance to cut any vines that came close.

Eventually the terrain itself began to change. Trees became sparser and were slowly replaced by formations of giant rocks jutting haphazardly out of the ground. The air became cooler, and in some nooks and crannies, snow and ice had formed.

And at the foot of one of those rocks, Luke saw the solution to all his problems: a cave.

Going into it was a risk, a big one, but it was obvious to Luke that whoever was attacking him was also following him. From a safe distance, and concealed, but they *were* nearby. They would have to be, or else they were so powerful that he might as well give up his scroll now and go home.

Unfortunately, even after all this time, neither the vines nor the countless arrows constantly pursuing him had revealed a clue to his foe's exact whereabouts.

Whoever they were, they were really good at hiding, and now he saw an opportunity to force them into the open.

If Luke went into the cave, and it was a dead end, he would be trapped and at the mercy of his pursuer.

If it was big and cavernous enough inside, though . . . Well, that changed things.

Not only would his foe lose the space needed to make good use of their arrows, which would leave him with only the vines to deal with, but it also had the right conditions to employ one of the uses he had found for his own bloodline and finally see exactly who was after him.

None of that would matter, though, if the cave turned out to be too small.

Realistically, he'd need it to be narrow and full of twists and turns, but also big enough that he didn't risk being caught in a dead end.

For that, he needed to find out exactly what was in there.

Changing course to the cave's general direction, he funneled mana into his sword and let it fly out of his hands.

With another exertion of his will, he activated his bloodline, and immediately, his mana came into focus.

All of it.

From the deep pools of the energy inside him to the mana that clung tightly to his skin flexing against the world, propelling him through the air, and most importantly, the mana in his sword.

At the moment, it was tightly constrained within the bounds of the named artifact, but the moment it flew toward the cave, it exploded outward.

He didn't like doing this; the mental strain of keeping his mana intact out in the environment drained him pretty fast. The rate it drained depended on how much attention he gave it—anywhere from minutes if he was dedicating his full attention to it to mere seconds when he was trying to do more than a single thing at a time. Which he was right now.

The quality of the image he saw wasn't great, either. Not yet good enough for either the First Truth or the First Stances to work, but it was enough to get a very rough feel of the cave. It was promising, but it wasn't enough to go off, so with a heavy heart he poured a tenth of his remaining reserves into and out of his blade.

Like a cloud of gas, his mana expanded into every nook and cranny of the cave. He saw, transposed over his natural light-based eyesight, a fraction of the inside.

What he did see brought a smile to his face.

The entry was narrow, barely big enough to fit a single person through, but just inside, it expanded in a small chamber not even large enough to stand straight, but opening up to three paths. One was a dead end, while the other two tunneled deep underground in opposite directions, farther than he could currently see.

Mind made up, he wasted no time flying toward it.

Recognizing what he was about to do, the arrows and the vines both tried to obstruct his path, and without his sword to defend with, he momentarily doubled his Constitution and tanked the attacks. The boost from his sword made his effective Constitution pass what normal warriors would have, even at the peak of the Warrior tier, but it didn't make him a hero or even at all comparable, really.

The enhancement of the sword didn't condense his mana the same way actually breaking through would, and he didn't get the qualitative and exponential improvement that came with Hero-tier mana, either.

Even so, he had become durable enough that the arrows felt more like heavy hail against his skin, leaving only shallow cuts and bruises. The thorny vines were even less effective—they succeeded only in shredding his clothes and leaving shallow white marks on his body. What they did do, though, was tie him down long enough for more arrows he was comfortable with to finally strike him.

To his dissatisfaction, the cool energy of the healing potion diminished when they did. Not a lot, only a fraction of a single percent, but it confirmed his fear.

If he allowed himself to be cornered, he would be eliminated, and every blow he took would leave him more vulnerable to future conflict. Much in the same way Theseus was, but his situation was nowhere near that dire yet.

The second he was inside, though, he decided that even that little amount was unacceptable. Picking up a large boulder near the mouth of the cave, he blocked the small opening where he had come in.

It wouldn't be an obstacle to whoever was attacking him for long, but the second he blocked the way in, he was given a short reprieve from both the arrows and the vines.

Not willing to waste even a second, he put into action the plan that had been brewing in the recesses of his mind. Pulling both scrolls free from his robes, he attached them to his blade, holding them to it with his mana.

Then, after a moment of hesitation, he shook his head clear of his doubts and sent Maximus shooting down one of the two paths while he followed the other. Once again, he used clouds of mana and the Eyes of Insight to map the pitch-blackness.

Once he was deep enough that a cursory inspection wouldn't reveal his existence, he focused entirely on his sword.

With it hidden and carrying the scrolls, the attacker's own scroll would follow it down the second path and past him.

Once they did . . .

I'll be the hunter.

CHAPTER 42

Predator to Prey

Navigating his sword through the mazelike underbelly of the trial grounds was difficult, especially since he was looking at and mapping the passageway through layers of dense rock with his manasight, and since his eyes transposed his mana overtop regular sight, the image he was seeing was pretty small at this point. Only visible at all due to the fact that raising Agility and Constitution had the effect of improving eyesight and the processing of the information from it. Were he still a mortal, he figured he wouldn't be able to see anything but a vague smudge. Honestly, he was surprised it was working as well as it was.

Luke knew that by using the Eyes of Insight he could see his own mana through barriers, and that he could use Maximus as a conduit for his mana, but until he sent it through to investigate the inside of the cave, he'd never realized how practical the two abilities could be when used in tandem. Now that he had, the possibilities seemed endless, growing larger every second he thought about them, and his ideas more viable whenever he imagined having more mana to work with.

Scouting was the most obvious of the possibilities, but if he could refine his control over his mana even more and make his mana cloud more efficient and the feedback it gave his eyes more detailed, then he suspected that one day, he would be able to use his techniques from a distance.

And if I can figure out this spell business, I might even be able to put them in the sword's mana pool instead of mine and give it more abilities that way.

Hmm.

Using his sword, his technique, and his bloodline together, he imagined himself having something not unlike Hephaestus's drones, except he'd only one sword-shaped remote-controlled hit weapon instead of countless millions.

Clunky, but cool nevertheless. I guess I really underestimated my bloodline, Luke mused and moved farther into his own tunnel.

It was pitch-black, and with the entrance blocked, the whole place was entirely devoid of light, so he was finding his way by touch to save mana. At the same time, in case of any surprises, he carefully kept his mana primed and ready to activate the spell resting in the metaphysical space within him at a moment's notice.

The hydra and the rabicorns weren't the only monsters lurking in the trial grounds and definitely not the last they would encounter. With the consequence of being caught unprepared and failing the quest so uncertain, he couldn't even dream of taking it lightly. So he wouldn't.

The day might come that he would fail a quest or get one that he was simply opposed to completing and finally learn what happened as a result. Whether the Seed would just move on or if he ended up needing to use a charge or something remained to be seen.

In this case, however, no matter the consequences of Spiros winning, Luke had decided to put his qualms to rest and help him do it anyway.

If Spiros finishing first in the tournament and me placing second is all it takes to start a war, then it probably would have started without my involvement anyway.

If I remember the movie right, though, the Trojan War happened because that one king, Agamenmo or something, used the fact that Helen left his brother to marry Paris as an excuse to rally the Greeks. In reality, he was already planning a war anyway. The Paris-Helen affair was just a way to instigate a fight that a lot of people already wanted rather than the actual cause.

Granted, that was just a movie, and I doubt they adapted the most correct version of the myth, but I don't think it's entirely wrong. Sure feels more realistic than people actually going to war over one girl, no matter how beautiful. But then again, it's not like I've ever been in love, so what would I know?

More than that . . . Zeus doesn't seem like the kind of guy who would let a true war, one with all the senseless mass death and evilness, take place. Not for love, at least. None of the gods do, actually . . . well maybe not Ares, but he's the god of war—but even that might just be bull.

From what I understand, most of the Olympians seem to have a vested interest in keeping the status quo. Most cultivators do, actually.

Then again, all the Olympians were okay with the Rebel.

At the same time, and I hate to admit it, but the Rebel wasn't exactly fighting a war in the traditional sense . . . her plan was better defined as a coup than a rebellion.

Whatever happens when Spiros wins the tournament, it's not on me. Not entirely. It won't even be on Spiros. If someone freaks out and starts a war because the girl he liked or even loved left him to be with a guy who willingly poops his pants and spends an inordinate amount of time justifying it, then that's on him. I can't go around walking on eggshells because people in power might throw a tantrum.

Dismissing the thoughts, Luke pressed farther into the cave.

It surprised him that whoever was tracking him hadn't already busted in after him, not that it was a major problem. They would come eventually.

Waiting wasn't what he would do, but he could understand the logic behind it. The idea that Luke might be laying a trap for them was all but certain, making the other person's hesitancy valid. On the other hand, though, the longer they waited before triggering said trap—and they *would* trigger it—the longer Luke had to prepare and rest, even though the latter was true for the attacker as much as it was for Luke.

His attacker was probably just taking time to make sure they didn't get ambushed immediately upon entering. Luke knew that would be hard to achieve without protective talismans, but considering he was in a cave, he had time.

So he focused on sending his sword deeper and deeper into the cavern. As long as the person had a scroll of their own, which he was confident they did, they would be able to use the arrow to figure out if he was moving or not. Meaning, until they actually triggered the trap, he would have to keep up the ruse.

The fight that was about to happen wouldn't just be a battle of swords and spells, but a mind game. Information was key, and if the person or persons chasing him thought he was continuing to run, they would be less cautious in their pursuit and, hopefully, less likely to notice Luke sneaking up from behind them.

After a few more minutes, Lue turned a bend and, deciding it was good enough, settled in for a wait. He sat cross-legged against the cave's jagged wall with his ears strained and his breath as quiet as he could make it, ready to leap into action at the slightest sound—whether that sound came from deeper into the cave or, as he preferred it, from the entrance he had used.

He only had to wait ten minutes before he heard the rumbling sound of the boulder he had used to block the entrance being shoved aside.

Immediately after, the sound of hundreds of arrows bashing against hard stone echoed throughout the network of tunnels.

He stilled and held his breath.

"Relax, he went down that one already," said a woman, her voice low and melodic, but proliferating through the tunnels with surprising clarity.

All right, let's call her Woman A. She's falling for it. Yay.

"Are you sure? What if that tunnel turns left and the other right? The direction our scrolls are pointing in is irrelevant," another woman refuted.

Shit. Lady B seems to be a little smarter than her friend. Even though she's completely wrong.

"Do you want to split up? I go left and you go right?" Woman A suggested.

I can work with that. Luke nodded to himself.

"Obviously not. What if you find him, take the scrolls, and run?" said Lady B.

Just—don't both of you come here, Luke thought, crossing his fingers. It wouldn't be the worst thing, but now that he knew there were two of them, he really wanted to separate the pair and take at least one of them out by surprise.

"That would make no sense. There isn't a single instance I can think of where betraying you would end in my favor," Woman A argued.

"Well, we just met; forgive me for not trusting you." Lady B sighed.

"Can't we be more like this guy? His friend just gave him both of their scrolls and he ran," Woman A argued.

"Well, obviously they knew each other," said Lady B.

"Why would you assume that?"

"They were all dressed the same, for one."

"Fair. It's a lot harder to be an asshole to someone when they know where to find you and give you a good smack in the face," Woman A agreed. "All right, we need to focus," she said, and then the pair went silent.

"Any ideas yet?"

"Yeah, we, by which I mean you, are overthinking it. Both of our scrolls are pointing that way, so we'll go that way."

"Fine," Lady B agreed.

They must not have waited too long after coming to a decision, because their voices went quiet for a moment, and when Luke heard them next, they were much fainter than before.

Which was all the confirmation he needed.

Rising silently into the air with his mana, Luke worked his way back out of the tunnel he had crawled in, making sure to keep as quiet as possible while he attempted to sneak up on the pair of women and hopefully catch at least one of them by surprise.

Hopefully it's the one who's good at hiding if it comes to that, but if I can get both at the same time, that would be ideal, Luke thought as he slowly turned a corner and peeked into the chamber he had come from.

A part of him expected to be greeted by arrogant looks and scores of arrows and vines, but it was empty. They *had* gone down a tunnel and weren't just waiting in an ambush of their own. It was always a possibility, but Luke was glad it hadn't come true.

Then, taking a deep breath, he followed them, ready to activate his spell and rain fire onto the pair at a moment's notice. Or, more specifically, the moment he saw their backs.

After some brief hesitation, he also began to bring his sword closer to him. If everything went well, he wouldn't need it, but he figured he could use it to make some noise in front of his two would-be hunters and, with them focused on the wrong thing, ambush them. Or if the timing worked out, he could attack from both the front and the back at the same time.

Which was exactly what he did.

Because he already knew the tunnel's layout, having sent his sword down it, he caught up to the pair of warriors relatively quickly, and backtracking the sword wasn't much harder, either.

He couldn't see them in the dark, and he didn't want to flood the tunnel with his mana on the off chance that they would sense it, but the noise they made was indication enough when he was close.

He didn't attack right away and instead waited for his sword to catch up to them.

When it was a single corner away, he enacted his plan and activated the spell.

It was like nothing he had experienced before. Knowledge of his new capabilities flooded his mind, waiting to be unleashed and used.

He waited.

Perhaps because they were truly off guard, or maybe because they didn't have a way to navigate the dark, but his sword turned the corner and, faster than either of them could even process what was happening, stabbed one of the women in her shoulder.

Before she could so much as scream, fire, hot, bright, and lethal, flooded past his hands and into the tunnel, burning both of them badly.

That was when they screamed, and Luke winced in discomfort. Unfortunately, he was rather used to the unpleasantness that came with combat, and he wouldn't be deterred.

A moment later vines shot out of every surface of the wall and wrapped around him. Some gripped his neck, but most surrounded his arms, chest, and neck.

In response, he poured even more of his mana into the icon floating in his mana pool, not daring to be stingy, and the plant matter sizzled and burned away from him.

Meanwhile, his sword, seemingly of its own will, pulled itself free from the first woman and stabbed her again in the shoulder. He was careful not to hit her face or anything that would result in truly permanent damage.

A second or two later, orange light not coming from the flames he had generated illuminated the cave walls, and the screams of the women were replaced by the sound of two scrolls clanking against the floor.

Well . . . that was more brutal than I anticipated.

CHAPTER 43

The Return Trip

With both Woman A and Lady B eliminated, Luke found himself at a crossroads. Picking up their scrolls, both of which were black—and explained why they had teamed up in the first place—Luke crawled out of the cave. He was in a hurry before he tempted fate and a monster *did* appear and chased him out of it.

Should I make a run back to the others or recover some mana? he mused, staring idly at his status screen.

Status | Skills | Quests | Inventory
Name: Lukas King
Tier: Warrior
Bloodline: Eyes of Insight
Mana: 7 / 133,341
Rate: 17% per hour
Strength: 276 > 277
Agility: 281 > 289
Constitution: 524 > 526
Arcana: 507
Stat Points: 0
Charges: 7/10

His stats had mostly stayed the same, but they were improving rapidly when compared to the world outside the holy land of Vulcan. Even without the Seed storing the excess mana as stat points, he had made very decent progress.

He was beginning to attribute that to his high Arcana as much as to the ambient level of aethereal mana.

He still wasn't exactly sure what the relationship between the stat and a person's natural saturation point was, nor did he think he ever would. Not unless he took on a mortal disciple with no natural talent for the field and watched them train while constantly and intrusively monitoring their progress day by day.

Or unless he asked someone more learned in the act of cultivating, because, now that he thought about it, there was no way something like that hadn't been researched, and researched well at that. Just the fact that Cyzicus knew and had created manasinks was proof of that. Even if the results of any such research weren't in any library he had access to.

Luke shook the stray thoughts out of his head and looked at the horizon. Despite the fact that he had been chased all the way to the cave, he had paid attention to where he was going.

He had to, really. Otherwise, leading his two pursuers away from the others would have been pointless. But he only had seven mana points in his body and about a quarter of his reserves in the sword. A significant chunk had gone to the activation of the spell, and even more had been spent fighting Theseus, dodging vines, and mapping out the cave.

Resting somewhere seems like a good idea on the surface, but I have four scrolls now, one white and three black. There are only thirty-two scrolls altogether, which means I have a solid fraction of them. The white one isn't that big of a deal, but the fact that I have three black ones so close to each other . . .

Luke frowned. He didn't know the exact odds, or even if his fears were founded, but he knew that having so many scrolls of a single color would mean higher chances that more people with white scrolls would be gunning after him.

Chances were, he was the closest black scroll for *more* than one person. Not to mention that there were plenty of people without scrolls that would be just as, if not more, eager to fight him.

Except they don't have a way to track me, while anyone with a scroll does. Which makes them a smaller threat. Not to mention that the people with scrolls will be stronger than those without.

I doubt that will make people less inclined to attack me, though.

Scratching his chin, he looked between the entrance of the cave he had just crawled out of and toward where he had left the others. Briefly, he considered somehow obscuring the entrance of the cave and hiding until he recovered more of his mana, but—

I'll go back, he decided eventually. Not only would he be safer with the others if he was attacked, but staying in a single spot seemed like the worst idea. Even if someone couldn't find him right away, it wouldn't stop them from camping in the area until he had to leave. Which he would, because leaving Spiros unguarded seemed like a bad idea.

Moreover, if he was flying, at least whoever attacked would have to put in the work to catch him first, and not to toot his own horn, but Luke was a fast flyer.

Slower than the likes of Clite and Heracles. A snail compared to Lukeus's Pegasus and Nel's griffin, but compared to the average steedless cultivator in his tier . . . very fast.

Not many focused on Agility to begin with, and it wasn't an easy attribute to increase. Especially not in the Warrior tier, when it took on greater meaning than just having better reflexes, reaction times, and speed. It still did all that, but it also had a relationship with how responsive his mana was, whether that was because his mind was just faster, or Agility was making the energy flow quicker, or even some combination of both those things—which was likely the case.

I guess it doesn't help that a lot of people don't really bother with it anyway. Or maybe that's just Sylcra not having a great foundation when it comes to nurturing speed.

With the giants attacking every ten years, most people just focus on getting good at killing them. Which is more a marathon than it is a sprint, and being able to take a hit is better than dodging one. No matter what you do, you always get hit when there's that many of them, and moving fast burns more mana. Especially if you're not good at it.

Either way, I can't—or rather, shouldn't—assume that just because I'm faster than the average Sylcran, that there won't be Agility-focused cultivators here.

Joining up with the others is still my best bet, then.

With that final thought, he took to the air and headed back, flying just high enough to clear the tree line, but not so high that others might spot him in the sky and come after him.

It was a tricky balance.

Between Woman A's arrows and Lady B's vines, nothing had really bothered him on his way here, and that also explained the vast numbers of dead corpses he had seen along the way.

Unfortunately, the way back wasn't quite so smooth, but nearly every monster that attacked him was of the Mortal tier. Not exactly a threat, but definitely a nuisance.

"SCREEEEEEEEE!" a rabicorn squealed while Luke tore his sword free of an entirely different rabicorn that had attempted to skewer him out of the sky.

Up until now, he had never really understood the purpose of them in the trial. Blinky had killed them much too fast for that to be the case. It was obvious now, though, that they were meant to attract attention. To prevent people from sneaking around silently.

But I'm the only one, it seems, who doesn't have a good solution for making them shut up, Luke grumbled internally before slicing another one clean in half.

The things traveled in herds of a dozen, and whenever he was spotted, they would leap into the sky in an attempt to skewer him. Which in itself wasn't a problem.

Using the First Stance on Mortal-tier creatures was practically free, and the cost was so low that he didn't even notice the dent in his regeneration.

The problem was that whenever one died, either by sword or falling headfirst into the ground after failing to hit him—

"SCREEEEEEEEE!"

They did that.

Which, in turn, acted like a call to attract more.

Sooner than he would have liked, the phenomenon turned into a vicious cycle and he was forced to escape by flying higher into the sky. Something that risked exposing him to the greatest threats in the trial—other cultivators—and made it so that he couldn't linger in the air for long.

Except coming back down would inevitably lead to the same screamfest that he had escaped in the first place.

Holy fucking hell, this is annoying, Luke thought, wanting to scream and overcome with a desire to sock Hephaestus in the face for coming up with something so aggravating.

It was on the fifth such cycle that his worst fears came true. He rose into the sky to get away from the incessantly exasperating rabicorns, but not a minute had gone by before someone rose out of the forest with their sword drawn and what looked like a cape fluttering behind them, making a beeline straight toward him.

The worst thing about them was that Luke was confident they didn't even have a scroll. If they did, they would have sneaked up on Luke from within the forest—ideally from behind. The fight that would follow had zero upside for him. Even if he beat them, he stood nothing to gain. *If* he won. There were no pushovers this far into the tournament, and his mana was dwindling as it was.

"Ugggh," Luke groaned, unable to withhold his annoyance. Now really was a bad time.

When the person got close enough that Luke could make out their features, he only got more irritated.

It was a girl with white hair, angel-esque white wings, and wearing a white dress.

With his mana levels still so low, and not at all interested in fighting anyone who might have a direct line to Arke, he shook his head and pressed on.

Theseus can deal with her, he thought vindictively. It was his fault that they were all as low on mana as they were. *Or Arya can fight her. She should still be pretty fresh.*

Unfortunately for Luke, his fantasies about pawning the upcoming battle off on his allies while he cheered from the sidelines and recovered his strength remained just that.

Maybe she was just faster, or maybe her wings did something more than trick unsuspecting souls into thinking one of her ancestors was an angel. Either way, she caught up with Luke in short order.

Contrary to what he suspected, though, she didn't immediately attack him. Keeping a respectful distance away, she instead cupped both her hands under her chin as if she was in prayer and just asked—

"Can I have a scroll, please?"

Looking over his shoulder, Luke came face-to-face with puppy-dog eyes. He blinked, then he blinked again, and just to be sure, he stuck one of his fingers in his ear and rolled it around to remove any wax that might be making him hear wrong.

All while the angel lady stared at him with wide silver eyes.

"Excuse me?" he asked, making sure the First Stances were activated. Only the technique didn't react, meaning she was either a robot or not intending on attacking him. Which couldn't be the case, could it?

This has got to be a trap, right? No, it's definitely a trap.

Determined that her request was indeed some kind of ruse, he raked his eyes over the tree line, waiting for the other shoe to drop, and for her friends to come bursting out.

None came.

"Can I have a scroll please?" she begged again. "All my friends are out, and some mean girl with vines took my scroll while I was eating. Without it, I can't find anyone else. I've been looking all over the place, and it's impossible. And . . . and you have four!" she said, her eyes tracing over the bulges concealed in Luke's tattered red robes.

You know what, I just realized that there isn't a rule about changing clothes. So I've been flying around looking like a hobo that got mauled for no fucking reason.

More importantly, did she say vines? *Huh. Small world.*

"Look . . . Sorry, what was your name?"

"Ella!" she responded with a little too much cheer. "I'm fourteen, and I'm from Iliad. So can I please have a scroll?"

"Hi, Ella, I'm Luke," he said, mulling over her words and deliberately not mentioning Sylcra, just in case she did know Arke and happened to know something that risked souring what was so far a peaceful interaction. No matter how unlikely that was.

Even as he slowly came to the conclusion that he *didn't* want to fight her. Not when she was so . . . earnest.

Who the fuck just comes and asks you so politely in a competition, man? I didn't even like fighting Blinky, and she's an eye monster that I'm confident will eat me the second Rex looks away. I don't want to stab a fourteen-year-old girl. What the fuck, Hephaestus, couldn't you make this capture the flag or something less gruesome?

"So . . . what do you say?" she asked again.

Dragging his palm over his face, Luke sighed. This was a bad idea. It was going to bite him in the ass. He knew he should just shank her here and now when she wasn't expecting it and be the cold-blooded killer that he knew was inside him.

"These scrolls aren't all mine. I'll have to ask my friends. Just follow me, and they can decide."

She smiled triumphantly.

CHAPTER 44

Doing the Explaining

When Luke finally returned, with Ella in tow, to where he had left the others, the sight that greeted him wasn't what he expected.

Battle scars littered the ground and his companions were nowhere in the vicinity. Just charred and smoking trees and puddles of water scattered on the ground.

"I think your friends went home," Ella said flatly.

Well, the Seed probably would have told me if the quest had failed, so . . . They should still be around, Luke thought, trying to keep himself optimistic. *Or at least Spiros made it through whatever this was.*

The evidence didn't support that theory, however.

Considering that both Spiros and Theseus had been drained of mana when he left them, and that they would have only recovered fractions of their reserves in the two hours he was gone, them putting up and winning a fight seemed unlikely.

Arya may have had a chance, since she was still relatively fresh. That didn't explain why they had left. Or why they hadn't left a message.

Or did they? Perking up at the possibility, he raked his eyes across the clearing in search of clues.

I did take the scrolls when I left, which means they would have wanted me to find them. If they thought that far ahead.

"Does this mean I can have a scroll, then?" Ella asked, pulling him out of his thoughts.

Luke closed his eyes, took a deep breath, and reached for his white scroll. Ella's eyes lit up in joy, and eagerly, like the child she was, she raced toward him with outstretched hands.

"Wait. I have one condition," Luke said, pulling it away.

She pouted.

"If you see a guy who looks like me, or a guy and a girl dressed like me—"

"We're splitting up?" she interrupted him.

". . . yeah." Luke blinked.

"Why? I thought we made a good team."

"We can still be a team, but I need to look for my friends."

"Why?"

"Why do you ask so many questions?" Luke asked tiredly.

"Well, this is a competition, and it's pretty obvious they got eliminated. Just find another white scroll and we can move on to the next stage together. I can even help you fight if someone comes for one of ours."

"And give you another black one?" Luke grinned at her.

"Well . . . you do have three," she said, her eyes greedily drinking in his three remaining black scrolls.

"I gave you the white one so that when we separate, my scrolls will show me the nearest white one. That's how I intend on finding other people."

"I thought you gave it to me to avoid a fight."

"No," Luke denied immediately. It wasn't entirely a lie, either. The truth was that he was pretty close to empty, but if push came to shove, he was confident he could win. That said, he wasn't sure he would survive whoever came after Ella, and he wasn't going to delude himself by thinking that someone wouldn't.

"But you don't need to give me a scroll for that. People would have come for you regardless. Why go looking?"

"You have a point," Luke admitted. "People will come for me, but that doesn't make being a sitting duck a good position to be in. Anyone can pinpoint where you are and attack you in all sorts of ways. They have all the leverage, while I'll just constantly be looking over my shoulder. I would rather be the hunter than the hunted."

"If you say so." She shrugged.

"I do." Luke sighed, running his hands through his hair. "Can you do me a favor and see if you can find any clues about my friends?"

"Fine, but I doubt we will," she muttered.

The two split up, with Luke looking east and his newly made friend searching the other way.

He didn't expect to find anything, but he couldn't shake the sense that there was more going on here than he realized.

Luke had taken both scrolls when he left, and both attackers had chased after him like he had anticipated.

Unless there were three people hiding out, but then why attack them at all? Without any scrolls, picking a fight isn't worth the hassle. This place is big enough that finding people without a scroll is a pain, too, and there aren't many rabicorns in the area. Probably because of the hydra, but . . . still.

If it wasn't a cultivator, then what? Some kind of monster? He frowned.

That was a possibility. Other cultivators were only a part of the challenge. Except there weren't any signs of a creature. No footsteps in the ground, no scales or severed claws, not even splatters of blood.

Did Theseus betray them? He didn't seem the type, but it's not like I knew him all that well, either.

Frowning, he stepped back into the clearing. He wasn't a detective, but he had been in enough fights that he could piece together the major beats of one based on the evidence that was left.

The whole clearing was destroyed. But everywhere there was a puddle were also the telltale scorch marks of flame, and vice versa.

If they fought, then the battle scars would have been separated more. Both Spiros and Theseus have long-range options. And now that I think about it, Arya would have had her dagger planted in Theseus the moment he showed any signs of aggression.

I know our techniques. Even without it constantly active, the truth underlying it is so ingrained that I can see someone gearing up for battle. Both Spiros and Arya should be able to pick up the signs pretty quick.

Not to mention that Theseus was one good hit away from being sent home. He wouldn't risk it.

"Luke, over here!" Ella yelled from the forest.

Racing toward her, Luke found her hunched over a message written in ice, reading, "We'll be back. T."

"Looks like you were right. Your friends are still in the tournament."

"Yeah, but why would they leave?" Luke frowned.

"I don't know—they're your friends."

I don't like this, but I guess there isn't much I can do about it, either.

"All right, I guess I'm staying, then." Luke sighed, even as he thought about his next steps.

Being forced to stay in one place was practically a death sentence when he was carrying something that could be tracked by the exact people who wanted it most, but maybe he was just looking at this the wrong way.

There wasn't a rule saying that he actually had to hold on to the scrolls.

Walking back to the clearing, he looked around. His ambush in the cave had been remarkably successful, and while this particular location wasn't suited to the same tactic, it didn't mean that he couldn't do something like it.

The scrolls he was carrying were, after all, not only a great target but amazing bait. If used right.

He walked around the clearing until he found a spot in the branches of a particularly leafy tree that was both protected and overlooked the clearing.

Then, about fifty feet away from it, in a puddle of water right next to a particularly scorched bit of ground, he buried his sword in a thin layer of dirt and dropped his scrolls on top.

A little clumsy, but whoever sees this will think two people fought, and both eliminated each other. Hopefully.

"All right, we have two options here. One, you can take the scroll I gave you and leave. Preferably, you go far away. Two, you put the scroll on the ground with mine and find a spot to hide with me. With this many scrolls, we'll have people coming after them in no time, and we can ambush them."

"Why not just give me a black scroll, too, and I'll be on my way?" she said, eyeing the black scrolls on the ground with greed. Her hand gripped her platinum blade with a white-knuckled grip.

All right.

With a flex of his will, Luke's sword ripped out of the ground and slapped into his hand.

"Listen, I didn't want to fight you. I just killed a hydra, fought a child of Poseidon, and then sent two people home. One of which was the lady with the vines that stole a scroll from you in the first place. There are people in this tournament that can give me a challenge, but, frankly speaking, I don't think you're one of them. Please don't mistake me rationing my remaining mana for an admission of weakness. It's only the fact that you asked nicely and didn't attack me that has stopped me from fighting you. I think it would be in both of our best interests if you didn't push me. I've already given you a scroll, because with this many black ones, I'll be attracting white scrolls all day long. It's only a temporary loss. I won't have you taking advantage of me, though."

Ella's wings extended out from her body and fluttered nervously, even as her face settled into a mask of neutrality.

The two of them stared at each other for a few moments before she nodded and, with a graceful flick of her wrist, tossed the scroll Luke had given her into the bunch.

"Glad to have you on board." Luke grinned. Then, using his sword as a shovel, he once again set the trap.

Once it was done, the two of them perched on the preselected tree and waited.

"So, tell me about yourself," he said after a while.

"Mmm. There's not much to know. I grew up in Iliad. It's Mom's holy kingdom, so it's pretty boring. I just spend most of my time with tutors trying to learn different techniques and stuff."

"You're mom . . . is she a god?" Luke asked.

Please don't be Arke. Please don't be Arke. Please don't be Arke.

"Mmm-hmm."

"Is her name Arke?"

Ella's eyebrows suddenly shot up and she frowned at Luke. "No. Arke is my mom's sister . . . and she's not a god, either. Have you met her?"

Well, she's hunting for a treasure bonded to my soul, and one time she tried to crush me to death until Zeus himself intervened. But there's no real need to tell you that.

"She's not a god?"

"She's close, but no. I'm surprised you know about her but not what she's most famous for."

"Well, I know some stuff. And she was kind of terrorizing the place where I'm from for a bit, until Lord Zeus came and took her away. Not a lot of people like her, do they?"

"No." She shook her head. "They do not."

"So what's she famous for?"

"She's something called a paragon. It's this thing where you have to ascend past each level perfectly, but—"

"She's stuck," Luke finished.

Ella nodded. "For a long time."

Well, I guess that explains some stuff. I always thought she was a god since she managed to beat Aeolus, but then if she was, she wouldn't need the God Seed, would she?

Not that something like that isn't valuable on its own merits.

"Have you seen her lately?"

"I've never seen her."

"Oh. So who's your mom, then?"

"Iris."

"Oh," he said, carefully keeping the relief out of his voice.

That sounds familiar. Goddess of rainbows . . . I think?

"What's it like? Having a god as a parent?"

She shrugged. "I don't really know. She's so busy that I haven't seen her since I was three."

"Oh." Luke stayed silent for a moment. Talking to people had never been one of his strong points. Talking about heavy subjects with kids he didn't know that well, even more so.

What do I even say to a girl who hasn't seen her mother since she was three?

"I'm . . . I'm sorry to hear that . . . I didn't know gods *could* be busy. I just kind of assumed that most of them would do what they want."

"My tutors said it's her turn to fight in the abyss. She'll be free for a few thousand years after that and able to spend her time with me. Assuming I don't die of old age before that happens. Honestly, even if I am alive . . . It's been so long since I've seen her, and it will be even longer until I do, that I don't even think that matters to me anymore . . . Does that make me a bad person?" she asked, her voice barely above a whisper.

"No." Luke shook his head. He wanted to ask about the abyss and ask her a thousand more questions about Arke. It was part of the reason he had let her tag along with him in the first place. Instead, he awkwardly patted her on the back between her wings. "It doesn't."

Ella curled into herself.

"Have you ever had circular doughy bread with tomato sauce and cheese on it?" Luke asked, and his storage ring flashed and a box of pizza appeared in his hands. One made by the best chefs in Cyzicus's castles. He grinned slightly when she shook her head no.

"Oh, you're going to love it," he said, ripping a preservation charm off the food and taking a deep breath of its distinctive and delicious smell. It wasn't quite as fresh as some of the pizza he had squirreled away in his inventory, but it would do for now.

Before either of them could take a single bite, though, a figure flew into the clearing.

CHAPTER 45

A Troublesome Ambush

Ella drew her sword, but before she could make a move, Luke stopped her by extending his hand in front of her face while simultaneously covering his lips with his index finger—a symbol that even on Theos meant *be quiet*.

Granted, Luke didn't know the full extent of her powers or abilities other than the fact that she was faster than him. What he did know was that if she attacked, or gave away that they were here, she'd ruin his ambush.

Thankfully, she didn't fight him and stayed put while the figure looked around the clearing from a vantage point above the tree line.

It wasn't anyone Luke recognized at first glance from the previous stage of the tournament, but that was because the newcomer was dressed in black robes and had covered their face with a robe.

Based on the build, it *could* be Spiros or Theseus, if either had changed his robes, but that wasn't saying much—outside of the occasional exceptions, most human cultivators gravitated toward similar builds and body types: lean with muscles that were prominent but not outrageous. The type that just looked fit, like runners or swimmers instead of the bulging muscles favored by bodybuilders.

He kind of looks like the grim reaper now that I think about it, Luke mused even as he slowly brought the slice of pizza to his face and took a bite. He took great pains to chew quietly lest he give away their spot. Then, turning to Ella, he urged her to do the same.

She looked at him like he was an idiot for suggesting they eat while a potential attacker was so close, and perhaps he was, but pizza time was pizza time.

So, pointing at her pizza and then her mouth, Luke took another bite of his own slice. She gave him another look, but eventually a hint of mirth found its way to her eyes. Unable to resist, she took a bite of her own.

It warmed Luke's heart to watch her face light up in delight the moment the taste hit her tongue and she eagerly went back for a second and third.

He couldn't say he had spent a lot of time with the castle chefs at the capital trying to teach them how to make his favorite food. Mostly because the head chef had caught onto Luke's meaning almost immediately and had a very close approximation of Earth pizza ready in under an hour with hardly any input from him.

But still, he was proud of the fact that he had introduced the dish to Theos.

Earth would always hold Luke's fondest memories, but pizza made the whole planet a little more tolerable. And some guy looking for a scroll wouldn't ruin pizza time, especially not when he was introducing the food to a sad little girl. Not on Luke's watch.

Whoever the guy inspecting the clearing was, though, he was cautious to the point of being annoying.

He lingered at the very end of the tree line for one agonizing minute after another, looking for signs of traps or an ambush. At one point he even disappeared and came back with a bunch of stones and dropped them into the clearing, hoping to set off a trap or something.

Which all but confirmed that he wasn't an ally. Theseus, who seemed the reckless sort, would have reached in and grabbed the scrolls with a tendril of water. Spiros . . . actually, Luke didn't know what Spiros would do in this circumstance.

Probably just charge in, though. He's not an idiot, but he's not a worrier, either.

It made for a rather boring show, but Luke kept a tight grip on his sword the entire time and activated the First Stance, too, on the off chance that their near-silent chewing exposed their hiding spot.

Luke didn't think that was likely.

The forest wasn't loud, but it was full of the singing birds, whistling wind, the shrieking of distant rabicorns, and a million other sounds of life. The canopy was too thick to see them from up above, and he had chosen their spot wisely. The only place they could be seen from was where he had left the scrolls, and the moment the guy went anywhere near them, he would find the trap he was looking for.

Hopefully.

As long as I don't listen to whatever sad story or good points he has for us to not fight and join up, I can send him home guilt-free.

Yeah.

Whoever said ignorance is bliss was really onto something.

Ten minutes and eight slices of cold pizza later, Luke was thoroughly irked.

Watching the newcomer investigate the clearing had been fun for a bit. Like a reality show. The longer it dragged on, though, the more Luke felt like activating another instance of his spell and just start raining fire on the guy.

Not that he would. He wanted to keep the spell intact long enough that he could replicate it. Which meant not using it unless he absolutely needed to.

Is my trap that obvious? There're obvious signs of battle. It's not crazy to assume two people went at it and mutually eliminated each other. Just go in for the scrolls, get stabbed, and clear the queue for the next guy!

At this rate he's going to stay here until someone else comes and starts fighting him for it.

Ella tapped him on the shoulder and then pointed at her sword and the intruder. They couldn't talk, but her eyes, full of judgment and impatience, bored into his with clear intention.

Luke shook his head and offered her another slice of pizza instead. They had already waited this long, and if the guy had gotten to this round of the tournament and already possessed a scroll, Luke reasoned he'd decide to go in eventually. Every second that something didn't spook him, he would be more and more tempted to take the scrolls and run. Especially since there were both colors of scroll in the pile.

Honestly, his caution is kind of admirable, Luke thought begrudgingly. Mostly because he felt that he would have fallen for the trap he set. *Or maybe I'm just being too harsh on myself. That many scrolls sitting unguarded is suspicious, but he's gonna bite . . . any second now.*

It took another five torturous minutes of the intruder flying around and looking for traps before his ring flashed under the sleeve of his robe and a wooden staff appeared in his hand.

Well, it's not a golden spear, a dagger, or a trident, so I guess it really isn't the others. Where did they go, then? After some other scroll, maybe? Obviously they fought someone or something, but . . .

Shaking the thoughts away, Luke refocused his attention on his sword. His mana spilled out of it and wrapped tightly around the blade in greater quantity, and just for fun he activated his bloodline. The blade lit up in his eyesight under the shallow layer of soil, ready to break free from the ground and eliminate yet another trial taker.

The guy, even after deciding to make a move, moved exceedingly slowly, inching through the air at a rate of some feet per minute, but eventually his feet touched the ground.

He walked gingerly with light footsteps toward the scrolls, his head on a constant swivel, and, with his staff extended all the way from his body, he poked one, then cringed back like he expected it to blow up at any second.

Luke waited.

The guy sagged with relief when nothing happened. Luke could feel the tension draining from his body.

Luke waited.

The intruder, with his staff pressed against one of the black scrolls, began to roll it toward himself.

Luke waited.

The scroll at his feet, he slammed the butt of his staff onto the edge of the scroll. One end slammed into the ground while the other lifted into the air, rotating all the way. The guy inclined his head and stretched out his hands to grab it.

Luke struck.

Maximus shot out of the ground and in a split second stabbed straight into the guy's stomach. Luke intentionally avoided hitting any major organs, but having a sharp hunk of gold severing your tissue was never going to be a pleasant experience.

To Luke's surprise, the guy didn't immediately glow with the red-and-orange light and flicker his way back home.

With how cautious he is, I guess it makes sense that he hasn't been hit yet, Luke mused even as he telekinetically pulled his sword from his foe's belly.

To the guy's credit, he immediately slapped the golden blade away and, in a move that bought him a few more seconds, pinned Luke's blade to the ground with the butt of his staff.

Were this any other person or time, doing so would have deprived Luke of his greatest weapon.

Instead, he hadn't even bothered activating the First Truth of Death. Mostly to save on mana, but also because the guy had trapped himself.

Luke was eager to see what he would do next. Perhaps extending the fight after it had started wasn't the wisest move, but he was curious to see what other warriors were capable of. He had a good measure of Spiros and Arya, but their skills and techniques were so close to his own that he didn't learn much. Theseus drew much of his rather significant power from his bloodline. Whether he had a technique on top of that remained to be seen. If Luke had to guess, though, he would have at least one.

Woman A and Lady B had been interesting foes, but Luke knew if he took that fight the slightest bit lightly, he would be the one going home. There was too much unknown about them and the way they'd pursued him to risk indulging his curiosity.

This guy, though . . . well, he was as good as defeated. For one, he couldn't move from his spot without freeing Luke's sword, and for another Luke wasn't alone.

The guy clutched his stomach and stumbled to his knees. His eyes scrambled over the tree line until they eventually found Luke and Ella.

Luke waved. Then, concentrating on his sword, he tried to slide it out from under his foe's staff. It didn't budge in the slightest.

Undeterred, Luke kept pulling on it, trying to slide it forward and back, even as the potion they all had consumed slowly stitched the overly cautious thief back together.

"Do you want me to finish him?" Ella asked, her wings stretching out behind her.

Luke was about to say yes, ready to activate both his spell and the First Truth of Death in an attempt to direct her attack, but a flicker of red and gold high in the sky caught his attention at the last moment. He smiled.

"Nah, give it a moment. We'll be fine no matter what," Luke said loudly, making sure his voice would carry to their newly arrived audience.

"Are you sure? He looks like he wants to take his time again."

Luckily for both of them, Ella was proven wrong a moment later.

The unknown trial taker stumbled to his feet, firmly planted his foot on the flat of Luke's blade, and lifted his staff.

They watched as he pulled his hood off and revealed himself. His nostrils were flared in pain, his chest heaving as he took one labored breath after another, and a mixture of blood and saliva spilled from his lips.

Instantly, Luke recognized him as one of the few people who was still going strong near the end of the last trial. His tan skin rapidly began to take on a pink hue, while his blond hair started to rise from his head.

Seconds later the veins on his forehead and neck began to swell, and his robes rapidly filled out.

Some kind of berserker? Luke thought, unconcerned, and took another bite of his pizza. Beside him, Ella shifted and flew off the branch in anticipation.

The guy kicked Luke's sword out from under his feet behind him while he shot toward them blindingly fast, using the hard ground and clearly augmented strength to propel himself and achieve a speed much faster than normal, kicking up a cloud of dirt and other debris from the forest floor.

Unfortunately for him, his attempt was doomed from the start.

Maximus turned in midair, and when the thief was a mere dozen feet away stabbed into his shoulder. Ella, unable to hold herself back, shot toward him, meeting his staff with her blade.

The guy grunted, and with a roar, he pressed against her blade and batted her away, sending her tumbling into the sky and surprising Luke. The guy seemed unconcerned and unbothered by the fact that Luke had his own weapon buried in his flesh.

Hmm. Stronger than I thought.

Not that any of it mattered. Because a moment later, a golden spear fell like thunder from the sky, and in a burst of red-orange light, he was gone and a white scroll fell to the ground.

"He hung around longer than I thought," Luke said, biting into the crust of his slice.

"He's a Spartan. Their constitutions are something else," Spiros said, flying into the clearing, Arya and Theseus close behind him. "What are you eating?"

"Bread with tomato sauce and cheese, want some?"

CHAPTER 46

Waiting It Out

Spiros scratched the side of his neck, shrugged, and said, "Yeah. I'll try it. Me and Arya kind of forgot to bring food, and this is definitely better than cooking some monster or scrounging for berries."

"I'll take some, too," Theseus eagerly butted into the conversation.

"Well, I have more food than I can eat, so I guess it's dinnertime." Luke shrugged, and with a flex of his will, entire boxes of the stuff came pouring out of his storage ring, enough to feed a dozen mortals, and each box covered in stasis talismans to keep the pizza fresh.

Cultivators actually required less sustenance than the average person; as they advanced, their need for sleep, food, and water would lessen until they all but disappeared when they reached the Saint tier.

But, because they *were* cultivators, they could eat far, far more than the average mortal. Luke wasn't even sure where the calories went. No cultivator he had seen was in anything but glorious physical shape, and more than a few practically inhaled one buttery and doughy delicacy after another.

Honestly, it seemed a little unhealthy, but seeing as it meant that he could literally eat to his heart's content without getting sick, he wouldn't be complaining—ever. It was one of the better perks of their occupation as far as he was concerned.

It almost made up for all the danger and stress that came with the act of shedding his mortal limits and ascending to divinity—almost. Only actually becoming a god, and finally being free from the rat race he had found himself in, would make the struggle worth it. Anything less than the ultimate prize was just consolation.

"We need to find a better spot to eat. There's too much cover for any attackers, and we have a lot of scrolls," Arya interrupted them before they could dig in.

"I can take care of that." Theseus grinned and shot toward the ground. A ring of water appeared at his feet and rapidly expanded with him at the epicenter.

Luke watched, stunned, as one after another every tree in a kilometer radius fell to the ground. If that wasn't enough, Theseus activated the spell he had won in the earlier stage and burned everything he had cut to ash. The Warrior-tier flames were far more effective at incinerating the Mortal-tier wood than any regular fire could even dream of being.

Then, before the smoke could even begin to irritate their lungs or eyes, a dome of water surrounded them and ballooned its way over smoldering ash that had once been a forest, soaking the soot and coal and filtering all the pollutants out of the air.

"No more cover for anyone to hide in," Theseus proclaimed when he was done with his grand work. His arms spread to his sides, a wide smile splitting his face in two and his chest heaving with exertion.

I can do that, too, kinda . . . but holy fuck, Luke thought, impressed in spite of himself. The whole affair had taken less than five minutes from start to finish and had completely changed the environment on a very impressive scale.

"That was a waste of mana and a spell," Spiros said, looking at the son of Poseidon with narrowed eyes.

Obviously. He's just showing off how much stronger he is than us . . . Which might be more than I thought. If I end up fighting him in the next round, it's going to be seriously hard.

Fuck . . . I need to advance my technique and fast.

Or I can just eliminate him now . . . No. Luke shut the thought down as fast as it came. Theseus had proven himself thickheaded at times, but he wasn't dumb. He wouldn't expend all his mana on something stupid like burning trees and not leave anything in the tank for one—or even all—of them trying something in his weakened state.

They were allies in theory, but in the backs of their heads they were all thinking the same thing: that they were in a competition and there could only be so many winners.

The glimmer of moving metal to his right caught Luke's eye, and he saw Ella not-so-subtly flex her wings and straighten her sword. Not enough to indicate a desire to attack, but a sly warning, letting all of them know that she was ready to fight back if need be.

She had been so silent since the others had come that Luke had almost forgotten she was there at all, and truth be told, he would be nervous, too, if he were suddenly surrounded by strangers. Still, her actions instantly changed the atmosphere, with both Theseus and Spiros suddenly on guard.

More surprisingly, he found Arya looking right at him, a knowing glint in her eyes, even as she averted her gaze to Theseus and began to subtly rub the hilt of her dagger with her thumb.

Whether she was signaling that she would have Luke's back if he did try something, or warning him away from trying it, he wasn't sure. If he had to guess, though, he would pick the former rather than the latter.

Theseus hadn't exactly made the best first impression, and among all of them Luke had the greatest reason to want him gone. The son of Poseidon had eliminated

Rex, and on top of that, they'd never really had the chance to finish discussing if they wanted him with them in the first place. So he could understand where Arya was coming from.

But Arya and Spiros had also spent a couple hours alone with Theseus. Which was its own can of worms as far as loyalty went.

This is such a clusterfuck.

Either way, if we do attack him, he'll take out at least one of us. Which is a no-go. Me and Spiros need to make it to the next round, and I'd prefer Arya make it as well.

It's already bad enough that Rex got eliminated—it's not worth risking the rest of us to get rid of him or even bothering to start something about it now. Like him or not, it's just safer to have him with us than against us. Besides . . . he isn't terrible.

"All right, let's eat!" Luke said, clapping his hands and donning the most charming smile he could in an effort to get everyone to relax.

Thankfully, it worked. The moment of tension passed, noticed but unremarked upon, and they all settled into a loose formation in the newly expanded clearing.

In lieu of tables and chairs, all of them propped themselves up with their mana and began to scarf down the food. It was a novel way to dine—not quite as comfortable as sitting down on a cozy chair in front of a table, but acceptable.

As they ate, Luke's mind wandered to what had been troubling him since he had returned from his side quest.

He was beyond curious about where the three of them had come from, but his questions could wait.

Especially since the rather distinctive scroll-shaped bulges the three of them had in their robes were very telling of their activities. Luke didn't know why or how, but each of them had come back with scrolls of their own. Four of them in total, unless one of them had hidden a scroll somewhere creative.

Considering the looks Arya and Spiros were giving Ella, though, he wasn't the only one waiting to ask questions, either.

I bet every cultivator from the archipelago has seen Arke, and Ella looks like a younger version of her. They're definitely going to have questions, even if she hadn't just appeared. Which, honestly, works pretty well for me. I can learn the answers to all my questions without having to ask them. Underrated ability, that.

"So . . . what's the story with you?" Spiros asked in between bites.

"Uhhh." Then, like a deer caught in headlights, Ella turned to Luke to do the explaining.

"Oh, right. Her name is Ella. I ran into her on the way here. She even helped us get another scroll. So, I was hoping she could join us. What do you think?" Luke said, phrasing it like a request while meeting each of their eyes with what he hoped was a deadpan stare that brooked no argument. Technically they were all a team, and if the others said no, he would try to convince them otherwise, but he wasn't willing to escalate the issue further than that.

What he would do was give Ella the scroll they had taken from the Spartan, both as an offering for not eliminating him when he was running on fumes and for being good company. He figured he owed her that much.

Luckily for all of them, it didn't come to that.

"We could use another girl," Arya said with a smile.

Immediately after, Spiros shrugged in acceptance and, seeing that he was outnumbered, Theseus nodded as well. Even if he didn't seem thrilled about it.

"So, where did you guys go?" Luke asked.

"Oh, you wouldn't believe it." Spiros grinned. "An hour after you left, this monster came running right after us. Some kind of lion, but its skin was impenetrable. Anyway, it had two scrolls strapped to its collar, one of each color, and there were a bunch of people chasing it. Apparently the person who challenged it initially failed and got eliminated, so now it's just running toward people who don't have any scrolls, while the people with scrolls find it and run after it. We didn't have a lot of mana, but it didn't seem right that you were out alone while we were just sitting here, so we went after it, too."

That sounds like the Nemean lion. Didn't Heracles fight one of those in the myths, too? And I guess it isn't too weird that there would be one of those in the trial. But hydras and now the lion—seems like there's some kind of theme. Huh.

"Sounds hard to beat. How'd you guys do it? Did you make it choke on something, did you strangle it, drown it?" Luke asked.

"Oh, we didn't beat it. That would be crazy," Theseus scoffed. "The thing was way too fast. But we took the scrolls from everyone who was flying after it and came back here."

"Huh. I guess that works. What scrolls did you get?"

Wearing matching grins, the three of them reached into their robes and pulled out the loot—one black scroll and three white.

Luke whistled in appreciation.

"Okay. Combining that with what I managed to get, we have nine scrolls total. Four complete pairs, and we're missing a white one. That's . . . pretty good," Luke said.

"No, it's really good," Theseus corrected him. "We'd be all done if it weren't for your new friend, and we could focus on resting up and defending our prize."

"That's not a big deal, though. With nine scrolls here, we should draw one or two more people. So it's not a problem," Luke said.

Arya shook her head. "There aren't many people in the trial who'll attack five people by themselves. Not when there are lower-risk options."

"I disagree. We can put the scrolls somewhere and ambush people from a hidden spot. Me and Ella already baited that one guy, and I can guarantee others will bite, too. It hasn't even been a full day since this round started, so there's plenty of time left until the first winners are teleported out. We can do it," Luke argued.

"I'm good with whatever," Spiros said with a yawn. "For now . . . I barely have any mana left, and I'm tired. Let's just figure out how we're dividing the shifts for the scrolls so we're all holding on to them for an equal amount of time. We also need to decide on a sleep schedule so that some of us can get some rest while the rest of us keep watch. To be safe, let's have three people awake and two asleep at any given time. Yeah? Also, is this the spot we're going to stick to?"

"Well, Theseus did clear it out, and there are a bunch of monsters everywhere else I've been. We can move tomorrow if we want, but for now let's just stay here. But you're right, we should rest up a bit, too," Luke said, realizing just how eager to sleep he was.

It was hard to keep time with multiple teleports, but it had been more than thirty hours since he had left Sylcra, and a good chunk of that time had been spent physically exerting himself. Had he still been a mortal, he would have long ago been laid out in exhaustion. As it was, he *could* keep pushing for a little longer if the need arose. At the same time, however, he really didn't want to.

That in mind, Luke reached into his ring and removed a sleeping bag. "I'll sleep first. Please don't stab me while I'm unconscious."

CHAPTER 47

Gods Give Lemons

They were in quite the dilemma.

Six days had passed faster than Luke thought they would, and their impromptu group still didn't have their tenth and last scroll. With the countdown ticking, well, they would have some things to think about soon.

Contrary to their expectations, no one had challenged them. No one fell into any of the traps they had laid out. Hell, they didn't even *see* a person outside their group from the moment they had reunited.

Instead, after their single day of rest, they had been constantly besieged by an endless stream of monsters, a horde that only relented for five or six hours when the nine suns went down and started right back up in the wee hours of the morning.

It wasn't just the rabicorns anymore, either. Hydras, all sorts of jungle cats, wolves, and even a few toothy black worms that had tunneled out from underneath them wherever the ground was damp.

The worms especially had been a close call. The first time the group had met them was after it rained on the fourth day. Silent and unseen until the last moment, one of them had burst out of the ground and swallowed Spiros straight out of the sky and dived back in. Kind of like one of the Gegenees but minus the minor earthquakes.

Earthquakes that at the time seemed menacing, but now Luke was grateful for them. A warning was a warning, no matter how intimidating.

Luckily, the son of House Paris had made enough of a commotion after being swallowed that they were able to cut him out of the worm's belly before it dived back into the ground and digested him enough to send him home.

A second later and it would have been curtains for Luke's quest, which still gave him chills. Since then, they had made especially sure to keep close watch on the ground for any signs of shifting earth, something that was as tiresome as it was necessary.

It wasn't all bad, though. The mana was, admittedly, quite nice, and so were the gains he was making in his attributes.

His progress was quicker than it had been for months due to a mix of factors. His high Arcana stat was paying dividends now that he didn't have access to stat points. With his saturation point so high, the rate he was absorbing the aethereal mana hadn't slowed even a little. Combined with the naturally high levels of the mysterious energy in the air, and the fact that a good number of the beasts he had killed were of the Warrior tier . . . well, things were looking very good on that front. Better than he ever could have hoped.

But the way things were going also made him nervous. A single day without an encounter with another contestant could be chalked up to bad luck. Maybe their ambush was seen through and their numbers scared away prospective targets like Arya thought they would.

Except, even when they took precautions to prevent that sort of thing, it didn't make any difference.

No matter how far away they set the trap, or how tempting they made the scrolls, they never drew anyone to them. At one point, they had even left a pair of scrolls completely unguarded hoping that someone would show their face. It didn't work. Instead, Luke started having flashbacks to his life back on Earth and all his unsuccessful fishing trips. The hours of waiting with a line in the water and no fish willing to bite while the cold wind nipped at his fingers and ears . . . not fun.

After exhausting every strategy they could come up with, they had even tried splitting up into two groups, three of them with a single black scroll and the rest with the full pairs. Both groups had gone in opposite directions, hoping that the black scroll would latch onto a white that didn't belong to them. They went full speed for an entire day, and the direction on the arrow hadn't deviated once from the white scrolls already in their possession.

In order not to waste time or unduly risk the complete pairs, they had reunited shortly after. All of them had come to the same conclusion Luke had, even if no one had vocalized it just yet.

Either we're just very unlucky, or, more likely, Hephaestus is putting his finger on the scales. Pulling strings like some puppet master. Hiding us from other people or messing around with our scrolls so that we don't find anyone else and no one finds us. He prevented Blinky from participating when we were fighting the hydra at the start of the trial, so it's obvious that the test isn't exactly impartial. The gods are looking for a particular kind of winner, and it seems they'll bend the rules a little to make it happen.

It's a little ironic, but I think Hephaestus actually wants the trophy to go to someone who isn't connected. A random cultivator who doesn't have a godly parent in their corner. Which, with Theseus and Ella in our little cabal, doesn't help.

He probably, and rightly, assumes that anyone who comes to us wouldn't have a fair chance. So he wants four of us to advance while leaving one of us behind to fend for themselves. Which it will come down to. It's inevitable, really. Pretty soon, we'll be hitting the seven-day limit and be teleported to the next stage. Unless we bury the scrolls and no one touches them. Which isn't going to happen.

The question, then, is who's going to stay behind alone while the others take their scrolls and leave? Luke thought, looking between the four others, knowing already that he would be the one to take the bullet for the team.

It wasn't even him being altruistic. Not entirely. Spiros needed to go to the next level, and fast. The last thing Luke wanted was for him to stay behind alone.

More importantly, he could use the time. No, he needed the time to rack up even more attributes, to advance his technique, and to figure out what to do with his spell. The longer he stayed in the forest, the stronger he would be.

Watching Arya and Spiros fight had the First Truth of Death practically itching, and he could feel in his bones that he had made some progress. He could feel himself inching toward some realization, but like an almost-remembered word, it sat on the tip of his tongue, unable to be vocalized.

I'll go back to that tomorrow, when the monsters come back. For now—I have real progress to make.

Closing his eyes, Luke meditated on his mana pool, slowly finding the floating icon that gave him the ability to turn his energy to flame and command it. Without his bloodline activated, it was as indescribable as ever: a complicated shape that shifted, shimmered, and distorted. Just paying attention to it made Luke's mind ache.

An ache that fell away the instant he activated his bloodline and its form suddenly became observable. Not comprehensible, not yet, but it was a start. A little chink that, with some creative leveraging, would reveal its secrets.

Even after looking at it every spare second he had gotten in the last few days, it still threatened to take his breath away. The spell was truly magnificent to look at and equally difficult to copy. The closest thing he could compare it to was a sculpture, and not a simple one, but a masterpiece. Something made by a genius at the height of their skill.

Within that vein, his self-appointed task of copying it felt like he was aping someone's masterwork, with all the difficulty that it entailed.

He felt like he had a slab of marble that was big enough, a chisel that was sharp enough, and the literal statue of David on his lawn, and he was trying to remake it. Technically Luke had all the references he needed to copy the thing, but he wasn't Michelangelo. Luke wasn't seeing an angel trapped in stone that he was setting free.

Not even close.

But it wasn't impossible, and he had quite a few things going for him. Which was actually just the one thing: the Eyes of Insight.

He didn't know how the god had done it, but the spell was made of his own mana, which was why activating his bloodline let him see it in the first place.

The scroll the god had given him atop the pyramid, Luke reasoned, was akin to a stencil or a stamp that had been pressed onto his mana. One that used his own mana as ink. One that, when he passed his mana through, gave him the ability to throw fireballs.

Wherein lay his first hurdle and one that he had been agonizing over the past few days.

I'm basically trying to make a structure out of water . . . underwater. My mana is uniform, and I can bend and twist it all I want, but if it's surrounded by the rest of my mana . . . well, then it's all just homogenous.

I can't really separate my mana within my mana pool, and that's where the spell needs to be. It's like writing on a blank page with a white pencil. Nothing's gonna show.

A switch flipped, and it was like a light bulb had gone off in his head. Suddenly, he felt stupid for not immediately coming to the right solution.

If he couldn't draw out the spell inside his mana pool, then he would just have to give his mana the correct shape *outside* his mana pool.

Grinning, he extended his palm in front of him and watched as a thin tendril of mana emerged.

Severing his connection to it, Luke just watched the blob hang in the air. Months ago, he had done something similar in Cyzicus's workshop. Back then, he hadn't tested his bloodline and been able to see his mana. Instead, he had relied entirely on feel to reduce the quantity enough to sneak it into the ring. If feeling was all he had to rely on now, what he was about to do would be impossible.

Instead, he turned his attention toward a random branch of the spell—one of a hundred and three—and with an effort of his will twisted the mana in the air into a shape that was as close to the runes he was seeing as possible.

I'm lucky I'm working with my mana instead of something I can run out of, Luke thought as he inspected both his attempt and the original, making minor tunes to it as he went, thinning a line here, thickening it there. Making sure the bend was just the way it was in the original.

When he was satisfied, he moved on to the next branch. Then the next. Then the one after that.

At which point he became aware of another problem.

Just holding his mana outside his body was an effort of will, and one that got harder and harder the longer he did it, and soon a dull pain began to spread through his head even as his construct threatened to be washed away in the mana of the world. He could hold it together for a while longer, but soon he would need to let it go, let his headache recede, and try again fresh.

The only thing that relieved him was that his mana held the shape he assigned to it without active thought. He had been half-worried that it would be like multiplying big numbers in his head, where it would be a pain to remember which number was in what place, which ones he had carried, and how many zeros there were and where.

All right, come on, Luke, focus, he thought. Then, doing just that, he continued tracing the branches of the spell until he had ten and his head felt like someone had jabbed a spike through it.

The more complex the shape, the harder it is to hold, I guess. Even if maintaining the shape itself doesn't cause problems. Let's see how far I can take it, though.

At thirty branches he felt ready to puke. Thirty-one branches, he thought he was going to lose consciousness. Thirty-two branches, his vision began to swim. Thirty-thr—

The whole thing collapsed, and Luke sighed in relief as his headache instantly faded and his Arcana shot up a single point.

Huh. That's useful.

Then, taking a moment to collect himself, he looked at the others, who were still sitting in silence and staring at the fire with long faces, no doubt wondering how to broach the subject of who would be staying behind.

Shaking his head, he looked to the sky. It was still pitch-black and full of countless stars.

I still have a couple more hours, he thought and got back to work. He needed to get this. If not today, then tomorrow.

Then I need to get a grip on my technique. As it is, I'm not going to win.

CHAPTER 48

Hacking and Slashing

Three hours later, Luke was slowly but surely getting closer to successfully copying the spell.

If it worked at all.

He was pretty sure it would act something like a talisman did and flash or something before settling into his mana, where it would be usable. Just like the original was.

Luke would also be the first to admit that he wasn't an expert in what he was doing. Not by a long shot. Especially when it came to replicating what was likely the handiwork of a literal deity.

Cyzicus had mentioned that runes typically required some understanding, not unlike what was required to operate techniques. But talismans were living proof that anyone with mana and time could get runes to do something, and the emperor had said what he said in the context of artifacts, not spells.

So Luke remained hopeful even as he geared up for his last attempt of the night.

I'm not going to get it, but let's see how far I really am, he thought while removing another blob of mana from his body and reactivating the Eyes of Insight for the umpteenth time. He winced as a dull and nauseating ache behind his eyes sprang to life. His bloodline cost mana to use, and the amount was negligible with his current reserves, but after hours of use he found that there were limits beside mana that kept him from keeping his ability active.

The pain wouldn't stop him, though.

Slowly, branch by branch, he began to construct the shape. After many dozens of attempts, he was able to shape the first fifteen branches with ease and from memory, only consulting the structure in his manapool for reference once in a while to make sure it was perfect. The next fifteen branches also went fairly quickly and without too much trouble; he only had to slow down once to correct a single branch.

After that, things became increasingly tricky. He was getting better at tolerating the headache that came from maintaining the mana outside his body, but it was slow going at best, and worse now that the stress of keeping his bloodline active was also hampering him.

Still, his progress was quicker than he'd anticipated, and he managed to make sixty-two branches before the pain became unbearable and the whole thing vanished, collapsing like a house of cards into the ether.

From start to finish, the process only took five minutes.

Maybe another day or two, Luke thought, grinning slightly as he felt his Arcana stat tick up once again. In the absence of a manasink, his training with the spell was proving to be a good way to increase the stat, which he dearly wished he had realized earlier.

But then again, he'd had no way of knowing before now if this kind of practice even improved his Arcana. Simply holding mana outside his body had never yielded these kinds of results when he had tried it on Sylcra.

Moreover, Luke wasn't sure if it was the act of drawing the spell that was making the stat surge or if there was just so much mana in the holy land that even the slightest exertion caused it to improve at an outrageous rate.

Either way, it was worth doing, and Luke resolved to test the hypothesis soon.

I'll have to see how many stat points I get for recreating the spell, how many I get for creating a random but complicated pattern, and how much for just a blob. If my guess is right, then the blob and the random pattern shouldn't improve my Arcana . . . but we'll see.

If I can replicate something like what happened with the manasink again, that would be amazing. Kind of. What happened with Arke back then wasn't intentional. I didn't even know I could push that far. I mean, how could I? It was like the entire time, I'd been pressing forward at the edges of my ability, and then suddenly what I thought was my limit turned out to be a suggestion. Like . . . lifting a weight. I thought my limit was x and it turned out to be a thousand x instead.

Except Zeus healed me after, and I can't forget that.

I don't know how stupid what I did was, because whatever potion he gave us after was definitely of a high enough tier to resolve any issues. Speaking of, there's also a god watching over us right now, too . . . one that promised to heal everything . . . I'd probably be fi—

Bad, Luke.

He shook the thought out of his head before he convinced himself that it was a good idea and forcibly reminded himself that stat points weren't going to be an issue. Were never an issue, not really. Compared to the rest of the world, his growth was simply monstrous. Except most of the world would never be gods, either.

Even so, the empress of Carim became a hero at sixty, and Cyzicus thought she was a prodigy. This body isn't even seventeen years old, and I've been at this cultivation thing for less than a year. There's no need to be hasty and resort to something desperate. Not yet, and not when it isn't bottlenecking my progress.

Besides, without the Seed capturing the excess mana, I won't get stat points anyways. Having the mana in my body even without that is still a major plus, but not big enough to be worth the risk.

Not that I'll be under Hephaestus's watch forever, either. Once all this is over and I can use the Seed freely, I'll reconsider it. Maybe if I get my hands on a good healing potion, but even then I'll just be saving a few weeks to months of time. Is it worth it?

Shaking his head, he opened his status.

Status	Skills	Quests	Inventory

Name: Lukas King

Tier: Warrior

Bloodline: Eyes of Insight

Mana: 189,021 / 191,888

Rate: 17% per hour

Strength: 277 > 419

Agility: 289 > 432

Constitution: 526 > 716

Arcana: 507 > 536

Stat Points: 0

Charges: 7/10

Well, I'm past the halfway mark.

The progress was good, really good. If the Seed hadn't shut down stat points, though, it would have been even better. Much better.

I could have been at the peak of the Warrior tier, considering how many monsters I've killed.

He intentionally hadn't kept track of the exact number, because he knew if he had, he would have been sorely tempted to cuss at the god overseeing the trial for being a peeping tom and spooking the Seed. As it was, he tried his best to stay satisfied with how much he had gained. It was five months' worth of the progress he'd made on Sylcra done in *days.* Progress that, if he played his cards right, didn't have to slow down for a while.

I just need to stick around, and— He raked his eyes over his temporary teammates. Spiros and Ella were still sleeping while Theseus and Arya kept watch with him.

Considering that monsters didn't attack at night, and no one had challenged them for days, keeping a watch of three people felt superfluous, and yet, it was necessary. A single one of Hephaestus's whims could change their circumstances, and none of them was willing to test fate by being stupid and leaving themselves vulnerable. If that meant only sleeping for a few hours every two or three days, then so be it.

"We need to decide who's going to stay behind. I was thinking—" Luke started to say, only for Theseus to cut him off.

"Not me. I don't want to stay in this forest for a single second longer than I need to."

"I can stay," Arya offered. "I'm still fresh."

"Actually, I kind of wanted to stay," Luke said. Immediately, both of them looked at him with raised eyebrows.

Me being self-sacrificing isn't that crazy, is it? Luke thought and raised his own eyebrows in turn. *Why didn't Theseus do that when Arya offered to stay?*

A moment later, Arya answered his question.

"But you got most of the scrolls. It wouldn't be fair," she objected. "And I wouldn't have even passed the last trial if you didn't help. Leaving you alone after all that seems—icky."

"Right, I vote for Ella. She hasn't done much for the group," the prince of Atlantis chimed in.

"Theseus, if we leave this to a vote, you'll be the one who stays behind." Luke grinned at his look-alike. "And I want to stay. My cultivation has never been faster than it is right now, and I can feel my technique is ready to advance. It just needs a push . . ."

Arya stiffened for the slightest moment. Her eyes bored into Luke's searchingly before she turned away. "If you're sure about wanting to stay behind, it's fine with me."

Luke resisted the urge to wince. After days of fighting together, it was hard not to notice that there were remarkable similarities in the way the three of them fought. Similarities that couldn't be overlooked.

Luke had picked up hints of the First Stances in Arya and Spiros's movements the moment he had seen them fight. Then, while it had remained largely unremarked on, Theseus had caught on to the fact that all three of them could dodge his attacks with ease—an ability they all derived from their time in the empress's tomb.

Honestly, Luke was pretty sure his jig was up and had been for a while. Maybe since the moment he had introduced himself to the pair on the steps of the pyramid. In hindsight, it seemed obvious that he was the same Luke they knew from the Luminous Sky Society. Even if they hadn't seen fit to mention it just yet, he knew an interrogation was coming.

Or maybe the two of them were just waiting for him to bring up the issue first. In a way, Luke had Hephaestus to thank for that. The god's warning at the start of the trial had been awkward to listen to, but it also made for a great excuse not to discuss anything potentially incriminating or sensitive.

Like why one of the contestants had surgically altered his face to look like a god. Or what Luke had done to Yjarn.

Whatever feelings Luke's deceit may have inspired, at the very least the two of them weren't willing to expose him for it.

I'll have to thank them properly for that later . . . and check up on Nefkha after all. He's the only one who knows my real secret, and if he was smart, he would've kept his mouth shut. If I can go back and bully him into an oath or, failing that, just kill him, things will be fine. It wouldn't even be a stretch to say that my new face was just an accident.

They don't know that I know what the mask did, after all. Which, now that I think about it . . . if Len really stayed behind until one of them showed up . . . they probably knew about it already. He was in there for days—there's no way he didn't know what I took just based on what was missing.

Which isn't that big of a deal.

Outside of some random and baseless speculation in the tomb, no one really thinks I can be the thief Arke was looking for anyway. I'm alive and obviously not the kind of undead and tainted zombie the world thinks the thief is.

"Here." Arya tossed him a scroll, pulling him from his thoughts. "If you're going to stay behind, hold on to it until you only have a few seconds on the clock. That way you can leave the moment you touch the next scroll."

Snatching it out of the air, Luke nodded gratefully. Then, pulling a scroll from his robes, he unfurled both of them and laid them atop each other.

Instantly the arrows melted away and, in their place, showed a timer. A nifty feature Ella had discovered a few days ago.

For Luke, it read: 17H:42M:14S

"A little under a day left." Luke sighed. Then, rolling both of them up, he stuffed the pair into his robes. They had been passing around the scrolls so that they all had roughly the same amount of time left. It wasn't precise to the second, but close enough for their purposes.

"Don't worry about passing it around for today. We'll manage the other three pairs to make sure the rest of us stay on time. We'll stay until this time tomorrow so you get some sleep, too," Theseus said. Then, pointing to the still-sleeping Spiros and Ella, with a grin on his face, he soaked them to the bone with a deluge of freezing water.

A second later a veritable storm of monsters rushed into their campsite, and once again they began to fight. Hacking, slashing, and tearing to bits every monster that came close with practiced ease.

For the last time in the trial before they would truly be forced to compete.

CHAPTER 49

Cutting the Ghosts

All five of them were flying in the sky in a loose circle when Luke cut down his three hundred and sixty-eighth monster of the day.

It was a vulture-type thing, an ugly bird with a long neck, scruffy black feathers, and a handful of bald spots along its wings. Judging by the paltry amount of mana he felt Maximus feeding him at its death, it was a Mortal-tier monster, too. Which was par for the course, and the lack of the challenge was both disappointing and relieving but not surprising.

The attacks always started the same, with the first few waves being weak Mortal-tier creatures, but slowly over the course of the day, stronger, more dangerous things would emerge.

Which was why they were fighting in a fairly reserved manner—high enough off the ground that the land-bound creatures had some difficulty getting to them, but not so high that they were easily visible to opportunistic contestants. Each of them used only their weapons and their wits in an effort to conserve energy. Every once in a while Theseus would lash out with an arc of water that thinned the herd and gave them a few minutes of reprieve, or Ella would summon constructs of rainbow light and rain death, but such instances were few and far between.

But . . . Luke turned to Arya and, with a quick nod, retreated within their formation. Immediately after, the rest closed ranks and the circle tightened around him, insulating Luke from most of the monsters and allowing him to take a bit of a breather and think.

Seeing as how he planned to be by himself in the near future, Luke contemplated taking advantage of the fact that he had allies at the moment to do something a little reckless.

Investigate and, if possible, advance the First Truth of Death.

Watching both Arya and Spiros fight after so long had been enlightening. Every time he had witnessed his own technique used by the two in a way that he didn't think of, or that didn't fit with his own style, it resulted in small bursts of inspiration—which he had intentionally shelved lest it trigger a reaction that he wasn't ready for and put him in a precarious position.

If past experiences were anything to go by, progressing his understanding of reality's truths wasn't without cost. It would drain his mana. How much mana remained to be seen, but his gut told him that it would be a *lot*. Which, up until now, had been unacceptable to him.

So unacceptable that he had held off on exploring his newfound insights even when conserving his resources wasn't necessary anymore, convincing himself that doing so would reveal who he really was.

It *was* a good excuse, but that's all it was—an excuse.

The real reason he had resisted was because the stupid and stubborn part of him was stuck holding on to the delusion that his identity hadn't already been exposed. Because if Arya and Spiros found out that he was their Luke, then that would mean *explaining* things. Which, putting it lightly, was the bane of his existence. Nothing could ruin his life faster than answering the most innocent of questions, and the type they would ask . . . Well, they wouldn't be innocent.

So, he buckled down and went the opposite direction, doing his best not to use his technique unless he absolutely had to and keeping talking at a minimum. Especially now that he didn't have Rex and Blinky as lightning rods for attention.

Now, though, there's no real need to keep up appearances. Theseus couldn't care less, and Ella doesn't have a stake in my life, either. Well, not one that sees her digging into my past, at least. Arya, if I'm reading the cues right, and I'm pretty sure I am, already knows. Spiros may not, but if Arya knows, chances are he does as well. Even if he doesn't know yet, he will soon, so it's a moot point.

Both of them are probably curious as fuck, not that I can blame them. I kind of swaggered up to them while wearing a fake face and what is, in hindsight, a razor-thin attempt at a new identity. Not my best work, but I blame the Seed. What did it even expect to happen when it gave me the quest? We're already near the top sixteen, and Spiros hasn't needed my help once.

Which . . .

A figurative light bulb flickered to life inside Luke's head.

I was never meant to help him win, was I? When the time comes, I'm just supposed to lose. Then again, the quest said ensure *Spiros wins, but it also said take second place. If my gut is right, then the next round is going to be one-on-one matches.*

It has to be, right?

Why do top sixteen if not to set up some basic brackets? So, really, I just have to throw the last fight. Considering that the whole world and multiple gods are going to be watching, though, that's not going to be as simple as it seems. I doubt I'll be let off scot-free for disrespecting an event hosted by a god, so however I do it, I'll need to make it look real.

Assuming, of course, Spiros doesn't kick my ass organically. Minus the Seed, he has every advantage I have, if not more.

Either way, it's pretty cool of them not to bring my false face up in here.

Besides, stalling my progress wasn't a complete waste of time, Luke consoled himself, even as he slid a few feet to the left and cut in two an overenthusiastic snake that had launched itself like a spring right toward him.

He hadn't lost anything by shelving his insights, and he was free to pursue them whenever he wanted. It's not like they were a now-or-never deal. Moreover, it was a good opportunity to shore up his basics in actual life-and-death struggles and without the safety of knowing what his opponent was about to do before he did it.

Luke's technique removed the need for a lot of the technicalities of swordplay and combat in general. Things like proper positioning, feints, and even the best way to swing his blade were all small things that, when improved, meant his technique worked better. Being a better fighter straight up reduced the cost in mana, mostly by decreasing the steps it took him to land the killing blow, but faster was faster and less mana was less mana.

Not to mention that just the act of killing without any fancy tricks seemed to offer its own brand of inspiration. Not anything as concrete as observing a fellow user of the First Stances, but not dismissible. Not when the truth the techniques were built upon relied so heavily on death.

However, those small gains he had made were nothing when compared to what his technique *could* be. Luke was sure of that now.

Which brought him back to the advancements Spiros and Arya had made since their time in the tomb.

Spiros—Spiros had done *something*. Luke was confident in that. What that thing was, Luke didn't have the slightest clue.

At the very least, it didn't manifest visibly. Just like the apparitions of the future Luke saw were visible only to him, maybe Spiros, too, saw something only he could perceive.

But Luke couldn't dismiss the idea that Spiros just hadn't used whatever technique he had stumbled onto. Perhaps because it was too mana intensive, or maybe out of a desire to keep it up his sleeve. Or because the spear wielder just hadn't been pushed far enough that he felt he needed it. Which was fairly likely.

With the sole exception of their fight with Theseus, the current round of the games was cerebral in nature. Their wins had come with strategic thinking and plotting rather than pushing themselves to the limits of their physical abilities. What combat there was wasn't a challenge for them. Not when they were together, at least.

The nature of the technique shared by the three of them and the substantial power of Theseus and Ella, both the children of gods, meant that as a group, they could either kill something or they couldn't. The stuff they could kill tended to die quickly and easily, and thus far, their cabal hadn't come across anything that they couldn't unalive.

Setting aside Spiros, though, what fascinated Luke was Arya's progression of the technique.

In his own head, the First Truth of Death was the natural progression of the First Stances. Functionally speaking, the two techniques were pretty similar, and the difference between them was subtle. Outside of the whole seeing-ghosts-of-the-future thing, that was.

Instead of reacting to physical cues to find an opening, based on what his opponent was *doing*, Luke could act on what they *would do*. That small change propelled the technique from dead useful to something that Luke honestly thought was broken. That was true, at least until the situations in which it didn't work started piling up fast. Whether it was because his opponent was invisible, not alive, or simply *couldn't be killed* with Luke's current abilities, like Theseus had been, the technique he had thought was undefeatable became not enough. Still useful for dodging attacks in some cases, or telling him when to abort a fight and run, but not nearly as useful.

What was it again . . .

Death is inevitable, and killing is easy.

That's the core of the truth my technique is built on—and it's too narrow.

Killing is easy. That's true, but it's only easy when I have the ability to kill something. The second I don't, the technique is only good for dodging hits and waiting for my opponent to run out of mana.

Arya isn't limited by that, though. Her advancement of the First Stance kills. It infects, festers, and rots. Her precognitive abilities are limited to what's possible with the First Stance, but her killing ability isn't. She lands a blow, and that thing is dead. Maybe not right away, and if it's big enough, not anytime soon, but it's dead.

Where my advancement was linear, hers went sideways. The stances gave her the same ability I have, but her Warrior-tier version gave her the ability to make death final.

At the end of the day, I just react to the information, but my actual kill comes from damage that I do with my weapon. Nothing fancy about it.

. . . And that's what I need to change, Luke realized. *It still won't be exactly what I want, but—*

It'll be enough.

Mind resolute, Luke glanced once at his allies and then, forgoing any attempt to fight strategically, dropped into the forest below.

Immediately he was inundated by countless beasts. Rabicorns tried to spear him on their lone horns. Jungle cats pounced from high branches with claws spread. Wolves snapped at his heels.

Uncaring of the cost in mana, for he had plenty, and not caring about what he might reveal to the competition, Luke activated the First Truth of Death and started killing.

Luke ducked and wove in and out of the path of the attacking beasts with inhuman agility. His every move ended with a creature impaled on his blade. A mountain of corpses soon surrounded him.

It's not enough, though, Luke realized.

Killing things with the technique was what he already did, what he had been doing. If that alone was all it took to advance his understanding of the truth to higher levels, he would have advanced it when he killed the Rebel hero or cut down armies of giants.

There had to be a deeper secret. Some sort of revelation that he was missing. So he pressed on. Replaying in his mind every instance of Spiros and Arya using the technique. Trying desperately to hear the song, the rhythm that would carry him to the next step.

Soon he became so engrossed in the task that he didn't even notice the monsters becoming stronger and stronger, to the point he was surrounded by more Warrior-tier creatures than mortal.

He didn't even notice the monsters at all, only that they died at his blade.

He didn't notice that he was seeing apparitions of their future movements earlier and longer. Or that his mana was beginning to decrease faster and faster, in step with the percentage rising in the skills tab of his status page.

He did notice, however, when he seemingly stumbled into a mistake and accidentally stabbed Maximus into a monster's ghost. His mana, both what was in his body and what he had stored away in his sword, dwindled away to nothing. And even though he hadn't touched the creature, a gash appeared on its muscled throat where he had struck its ghost before the edges of his vision darkened.

The last things he saw before consciousness left him were a rainbow barrier separating him from the salivating jaws of countless monsters and their wicked claws and wave of water washing those same monsters away. A figure wielding a golden spear shot through the air toward him, catching him as he fell.

And, most importantly—a prompt from the God Seed.

Fuck yeah.

CHAPTER 50

The Last Night

When Luke came to, the first thing he did was open his status.

Perhaps checking his condition and seeing where he was would have been a wiser course of action. Except he was alive, not in pain, and warm. Which was good enough. Either that was because his allies had stashed him somewhere or because he had been eliminated while he slept and was sent back to Sylcra, he didn't know. What he did know was that it was quiet and he wanted a few moments to think before he opened his eyes.

So without moving a muscle and making sure his breathing was steady in case someone was watching him, he delved into the Seed's interface.

Status	Skills	Quests	Inventory

Name: Lukas King

Tier: Warrior

Bloodline: Eyes of Insight

Mana: 215,397 / 215,397

Rate: 18% per hour

Strength: 419 > 486

Agility: 432 > 501

Constitution: 716 > 789

Arcana: 536 > 546

Stat Points: 0

Charges: 7/10

Wow, that's a lot of stats. How many monsters did I even kill . . . holy. It would have been more if I could use stat points, but damn, those numbers are rising fast, he thought excitedly, forcing himself to look over the changes even as his heart thumped in excitement and anticipation for what the skills tab would reveal.

I'm going to miss this place when I leave. Unless where I go has more points for me to harvest . . . which isn't impossible . . . and—

Holy fuck.

My regen . . . it improved? Only by a percentage point, but still, how? Never mind— obviously it's from advancing my technique.

Amazing.

I didn't know that was even possible, but not many warriors in Sylcra even had techniques. Those that did kept everything about them pretty hush. Hell, other than Clite and Nel, the only warriors that had them were the Argonauts.

My mana regen has gone up before, both when I accepted the Paragon's Path and when I advanced to the Warrior tier. Five and two percentage points, respectively. Both of those were because of me being a paragon, though. Once for accepting the thing in the first place, and the second for completing the first stage of the quest successfully. Most people, mortals and warriors, at least, still take about ten hours to get to full, if Rex and the Seed are anything to go by. I think Heracles was faster, but I never really pushed him, and he's practically a hero anyway.

I really need to spend more time with the Argonauts once I get back. Things were so hectic with training and the tide I never really saw them, but there's so much I still need to learn.

Hmm. Focusing on his regen rate, he began to run the numbers in his head and tried to figure out what else had changed and what he needed to do to capitalize on that.

I'm getting my mana back nearly twice as fast as the average joe. It's not exactly a game changer, though. Most of the stuff that uses my mana blows my regen out of the water. Most fights also only last minutes, at least right now, so it doesn't make a massive difference. Stamina is stamina, though—having more never hurts. Even if I can put a little more into my attacks for longer than the other guy, that's an advantage.

Especially when I get more copies of that spell.

Then, once I'm in the Hero tier and start having fights that last for days and months, I'll practically have twice my opponents' mana. Maybe then those fights wouldn't last days or months.

Speaking of—

Luke concentrated on the bond between him and his sword and focused his attention on his secondary mana pool in Maximus, which, if Luke was feeling it correctly, someone had wrapped in cloth and placed under his head like a pillow.

Unsurprisingly, he had drained it dry—there wasn't a single drop of energy left in the four-foot-long blade of gold.

Gotta fix that.

With a flex of his will, he started pumping mana into the blade at a rate that matched his newly improved regeneration. It would be nearly six hours until he was back at full capacity.

But considering my own reserves are full, I've been out for at least six hours. Not sure how to feel about that—

Wait. Where did the—

Fuck.

A startling change caught his attention. For days now, the energy of the healing potion he had drunk at the start of the tournament had resided in his mana. Full and ready to heal him should he ever need it.

Fortunately, it was still there, but barely. Only a small sliver of it remained. Maybe enough to recover from a solid hit if he got lucky, but that was it. Anything more than that would see him dismissed from the trial.

Well, shit. This just got a lot harder, he realized, even as he tried to keep the frown off his face. *I guess that's what I get for losing consciousness for multiple hours in the middle of a combat situation. Still, the fact that I still have any of it left is good.*

And the gains I made . . .

Worth it. And speaking of . . .

What was it again? he thought as he switched to the skills tab of his status. Immediately the truth he had comprehended rose to the forefront of his thought.

Death is inevitable, killing is easy, and the echoes of fate foretell the end.

Heavy stuff . . . but accurate considering what I can do now.

Status | **Skills** | Quests | Inventory

Foresight of the End

Tier: Hero

Progress: 10%

An expression of a Hero-tier truth created by Lukas King, evolved from the First Truth of Death. Gives users a limited ability to levy attacks against those that intend him harm through the threads of fate and time.

First Truth of Death

Tier: Warrior

Progress: 100% [COMPLETED]

[. . .]

. . .

That's busted as fuck.

Very . . . and I mean very busted.

Luke's mind was awash with possibilities. Truthfully, he had already known what he could do. Had known even before he lost consciousness. More than that, he could *feel* the ability. It sat ready to be activated at a moment's notice with a single thought.

Even so, it was magical. More than that, though, it was frightening.

Just imagining fighting someone who could use a technique like that . . . it would mean instant death. What else could it mean?

How was anyone supposed to fight a person who could attack a future version of them? If there was a way at all, Luke couldn't think of it.

He knew intuitively that it wasn't that simple, though, not yet. He could already feel how crippling the mana cost promised to be. If his gut was right, and he didn't have a reason to think it wasn't, then that meant that even against warriors, it would instantly drain every last shred of mana from his body and would continue to do so for quite some time. Perhaps when he reached the very peak of the Warrior tier, he might be able to use it once and not go to sleep. Twice if he was lucky.

Using it against a hero, if it worked at all, would likely be suicide. He would wring his whole body dry in the attempt. Activating it wouldn't kill him, but being unconscious would.

Even so, as an ace . . . it was monstrous. An instant win button if he ever needed one. Even with the cost making it impractical.

But still. With this it doesn't even matter if someone has a protective talisman or something. If their future self is a few feet away from their true body, I fire an arrow, and they're dead. Just like that.

What scared the shit out of Luke, though, was what it said about Theos. According to the Seed, he alone was the person who had made this particular technique. How he'd made it, Luke didn't have the slightest clue, but the fact that he had suggested that no one else had it. It was a small comfort, but now that Luke knew something like *this* was possible, he couldn't help but be paranoid.

Theseus's ability to command water and his precision and power had just hours ago seemed like the pinnacle of power. Except, if something like the Foresight of the End was only a Hero-tier ability, what could someone with a Saint-tier ability do . . . no wonder gods were called *gods.*

Most of them seemed to have the power to squash mortals like a bug, but if Luke could attack through time, what could they do?

What were their limits?

Did they even have any?

Suddenly, he remembered something Arke had said the day he died about Aeolus having a demiplane.

Cultivating was magical, it truly was, but up until now Luke had never really comprehended the scale of the abilities he was reaching toward.

Aeolus had seemingly constructed a *world* in the space between Earth and the afterlife. With a sun, trees, brick roads . . . the whole package. It had exploded, but still, a world was a world. Thinking smaller, people had ways to put things in pocket dimensions and lock them behind keys that you plugged into random points in the air.

Meanwhile, Luke's own journey had essentially been collecting mana in his body so he could punch harder and, more recently, fly.

Granted, he had just started, but never before had the distance between the heights he needed to achieve and his current state seem so unimaginably vast. Nor had it ever seemed so *achievable*.

Honestly, the way he had gained the technique felt . . . easy.

Months of absolutely no progress and then suddenly he had moved beyond it all. He wasn't one to look a gift horse in the mouth, but it felt strange even to him.

Then again, my bloodline is called the Eyes of Insight. I'm related to Prometheus, the titan famed for his foresight. I've had the ability to predict the future in a limited sense for a while, but this is—

I don't know what this is, but it's not a coincidence. Is having the bloodline making me predisposed to advancing in a certain direction? Am I inadvertently following in the footsteps of my titan ancestor?

I never really thought about it before, mostly because I unlocked the First Truth of Death before I freed Heracles and awakened my bloodline, but what if even that evolution was influenced by my bloodline when it was still dormant? Obviously I couldn't use it, but I did have it.

Who the hell is Max?

It seems awfully strange that someone descended from an imprisoned titan just ended up floating in the ocean as a baby, within spitting distance of a tomb that contained an egg from the beast that's eating his ancestor's liver.

Unless . . . Prometheus is imprisoned somewhere near the archipelago. Maybe he had some conjugal visit or something . . . I don't know. Or maybe one of his kids is just wandering around knocking mortals up. Weird, but Lukeus literally does the same thing. Who knows how many illegitimate great-grandchildren Cyzicus has at this point?

Anyways . . . What did Prometheus do to drive himself insane? Is that going to happen to me, too? Am I going to push my technique past some invisible threshold and just have something break in my mind? Obviously the titan's blood is pushing my techniques in some direction—is it really so insane that it pushes me to madness, too?

Okay. Relax.

I'm getting paranoid, and I'm getting ahead of myself. Hopefully.

"When do you think he's going to wake up?" Spiros said suddenly, his voice coming from Luke's left.

It pulled Luke free from his thoughts. Something that he was more than grateful for.

"Soon, hopefully," Arya said.

Taking that as his cue, Luke stirred. Shuffling on the surface he was laid out on, he fluttered his eyes and faked a yawn. "Hi," he said, taking in his surroundings.

They were out in the open and gathered around a fire. Just the three of them. Seeing as no monsters were attacking and it was pitch-black save for the many stars in the sky, Luke correctly assumed it was night.

"Welcome back to the waking world," Spiros said, poking a log in the flames with the butt of his spear.

"Glad to be back. Where are Ella and Theseus?"

"Next round. We volunteered to watch you while they moved on. Ella took a big hit and wanted to leave, and then Theseus asked to go, too. We didn't want to make it a fight, so we agreed to watch you," Arya said.

"Oh." Luke didn't know what else to say. Rationally speaking, he would have preferred that Spiros and Arya moved to the next round, but he also felt better about the two of them watching him rather than the son of Poseidon.

"Mmm-hmm," Spiros grunted.

"How long was I out?"

"You fought like a maniac for like two hours, and then you suddenly dropped. You've slept for the better part of the day. Missed most of the fighting, too," Spiros said.

Luke nodded. "Well, thanks for keeping me safe."

"It wasn't easy. We got to you pretty fast, but keeping everything off you was a pain. At one point we thought you were a goner. But you're welcome. You helped plenty, too, so we weren't going to leave you behind," Spiros said.

"Did you advance your technique?" Arya suddenly asked.

". . . I did," Luke admitted.

Arya and Spiros shuffled and looked at each other, and then as one they turned to Luke.

"Hmm. I thought so. It seems familiar. Where did you learn it?" Arya asked, her eyes boring into his.

It felt like they were looking into his soul, and Luke realized that the jig was finally up. It must have shown on his face, because the next moment Spiros burst into laughter.

"So, are we going to talk about it or what?" Spiros grinned.

CHAPTER 51

The Talk Starts

W hen did you guys find out?" Luke asked nervously, his eyes deliberately wide and his tone low, which he hoped asked them not to discuss the subject too openly. This was bound to be a hard conversation at the best of times. This wasn't the best of times.

The symbol of an ominous red eye, generated by the Seed, floating at the edge of his vision was a stark and unforgettable reminder that nothing he did went unnoticed by the watchful and all-seeing gaze of the god judging the trial. Granted, the main object of the surveillance was to root out impropriety and excessive violence, but there was nothing stopping Hephaestus from taking a deeper interest.

Considering that Luke had exactly the kind of thing that a god would usually be interested in implanted in his soul, well, he was nervous.

Hephaestus wasn't likely to care, though, considering he was spying on warriors who might as well be ants to him. The chances of any of them having anything of interest to the deity were pretty low, and as such, maybe the god wouldn't care to pore over and dedicate resources based on anything that interested him. But if he did, it would be a simple matter for the god to work backward from what he knew of Luke and find out that he possessed the God Seed—if he knew about it.

His task would be much easier than Arke's. It would be a simple matter for Hephaestus to go to the society, ask about Luke, find Nefkha, and then come back and dig the artifact out of his soul. Or for him to have one of his drones do all that and report back to him.

I have a charge or two to spare if it comes down to it, but let's not go there.

So, excessive paranoia or not, I can't let this conversation spill anything too secret. Better be safe than sorry and all that. At the same time, I can't be too cagey, either. Mind reading seems to be off the table as an ability people possess, but as old as gods are, they can probably read me like an open book . . . So play it easy, Luke. Try, but don't try too hard. Try without even seeming like you're trying. And when you lie, keep it simple and easy. I can control my body pretty well, so there shouldn't be any physical tells, but my words can probably give me away just as well.

"I knew the moment you helped Arya on the stairs," Spiros said, crossing his arms over his chest and donning a particularly obnoxious lopsided grin.

Maybe he suspected, but he didn't know then. And of course he's still on that thing with me and Arya. Luke let out an annoyed sigh.

"Don't be thick—stop preening, and it wasn't like that. I just wanted all of us to succeed," Luke said, and it was true, too. Maybe in a few years he would reconsider the whole thing and his priorities would change, but he couldn't care less about involving himself romantically with someone. Now he just needed to convince the biggest simp he had ever met of that. Looking at Spiros's loony smile, it was bound to be a tall task. Thankfully, Spiros also knew not to push it too far—at least while Arya was around.

Seeing as she was leveling him with a glare of her own, the son of House Paris probably wouldn't make jokes like that for at least the rest of the day.

"I've been living with a hero for the past few months . . . It's changed my views a little bit. About what living a long life is actually like. If we're going to climb to higher and higher levels of cultivation, then I want to do it with friends. As much of the journey as I can. But what about you? How are things?" Luke asked, in turn hoping not to derail the conversation with philosophical talk.

"We've been good," Arya answered. "Spiros and I mastered the technique at about the same time, and we met Len. He told us your message. After that, I returned to the society—"

"And I went to Mysiath."

Luke perked up at the name. Next to Sylcra, it was the biggest island on the Dolion archipelago, with two-thirds of Sylcra's square footage. But while Sylcra was on the fringes of the island chain, Mysiath was surrounded by a host of tertiary islands that paid it tribute—one of which was Carim.

Supposedly, it acted as the de facto and unofficial capital of the archipelago. A title that used to be held by Sylcra until trouble with Sophia, the Rebel, and the decennial giant tide had shifted the geopolitical landscape and made the island more dangerous in the eyes of traders. According to the books in Cyzicus's library, Mysiath was also one of five islands that were ruled by Hero-tier cultivators—emperors.

Of the remaining islands, most were overrun by monsters not worth fighting and, as such, were too much work to tame and make habitable for humans, so they'd simply been declared forbidden territory. Others had been cleared by enterprising organizations of warriors and immigrants. It was a careful balancing act, though, between safe and unsafe.

Taking over islands and naming yourself emperor wasn't quite as simple as Lukeus had made it sound, and there were hoops that you had to jump through to even be allowed the honor of trying. It hadn't always been the case, but like all good things, a bad actor had ruined it for everyone a few millennia ago by being an unrepentant, evil asshole. His atrocities had forced the gods to intervene in the matter. Now there was a committee appointed by the Olympians that prospective emperors had to appeal to and get vetted, and you couldn't just take a piece of uninhabited land anymore, either. Chances were, if it was on a map, then it was managed by the council of gods, making it the collective territory of Olympus, and you had to play by their rules to rule it.

If it wasn't on a map—which was *intentionally* a thing, because the gods did value enterprising individuals—it was free game for pretty much anyone, with the exception of known evil people. But you had to go *far* and would likely die on the way there. It was easier just clearing out an already-discovered land mass and paying taxes.

Because even if you went the extra mile and tamed an unmapped parcel, Olympus still claimed ultimate dominion over a good chunk of the planet. A chunk that, unless you were a deity yourself, you wouldn't be able to escape. Meaning, it just made more sense to make a good impression with something like the tournament and petition a deity that way.

Still, it raised a rather interesting question as to why Spiros hadn't returned to Carim and had gone to Mysiath instead.

"Why did you go there?" Luke asked.

Spiros scratched the back of his head.

"I wanted to get in touch with the family in Troy. Tell them that I learned a technique and ask if I could come home earlier. The emperor there is friendly with House Paris, and he's the one who arranged for us to be on Carim, so . . ." He shrugged his shoulders. "Anyway, the family said no, so I just asked him for a ride back to Carim after that Arke woman left to talk to Myko and June. That's when he asked a few of us from the tomb to compete in the tournament for him. I said yes, and Arya and a few others joined as well . . . and here we are! Unfortunately, most of the people who were able to make it out were too old, so . . . yeah.

"What about you, why Sylcra?"

"Honestly, about the same as far as the tournament goes. I went to Sylcra. Cyzicus asked me to compete for him, and here we are." Luke grinned.

"Why not come back, though?" Arya asked.

"It was the biggest island on the archipelago, and I wanted to see the world a bit," Luke said honestly—well, sort of. He had picked the place based solely on the fact that it was the biggest island, and seeing some sights had factored into that decision as well. Mostly, though, he had figured that he would draw less attention in a larger population. Unfortunately, that plan had gone out the window the second he returned to civilization.

I really should have thought all that through better, but you know what? Lesson learned. Next time I do anything like that, I'll be ready. I already have a few different sets of clothes and even an entire set of bog-standard Warrior-tier artifacts. The kind of stuff that's decent but so generic that you can find it anywhere. Those and the mask, and no one will know a thing.

"So what's with the—" Spiros spun a circle around his face with his finger.

Luke frowned and then shrugged.

"It was an accident. The reward I picked changed my face to look like this. It was a little weird, but I didn't mind too much at first . . . but it turns out I look just like—you know. And we all know how the empress died, so it's given me a few headaches since then."

"Hmm. I'm guessing you can't change it back. Or won't?" Arya asked.

Can I?

Obviously, he had thought of doing so before, but then, how would he explain that he had a new face? Just admitting that he had the ability to perfectly disguise his looks removed a major card from his sleeve. Not to mention all the potential consequences and trust issues that might arise from doing so.

The only reason he was revealing the information to them in the first place was that they had talked to Len and had already pieced together that he was Luke. It wasn't like he could pretend he had always looked like this.

Could I?

No. I'm way too handsome now.

"No, I'm stuck like this," Luke lied without hesitation. An argument could be made that they deserved an explanation of what the last few days of awkwardness and secrecy had been about, but this went beyond that. Luke wasn't just going to tell them his secrets because they asked.

Thankfully, both Spiros and Arya just nodded and accepted, either because they had bought his lie, or because they knew now wasn't the time to pry. Either way, Luke was grateful.

Unfortunately, the conversation kind of just petered out after that. With none of them knowing what to do or say, they just sat in silence.

"So, what's the situation with the scrolls?" Luke asked, shuffling around. He reached behind him and with a flex of his will sent Maximus to his storage ring, realizing a moment later that one of the black scrolls had been wrapped around the blade.

"All three of us can go anytime we want . . . Well, two of us can. We didn't get the last white scroll. We separated you from the complete pair with exactly a second left on the clock, though, and me and Arya are the same. Figured it would be an advantage when we fought the next person. Leave early and all that. The only question is, do we actually follow through with your dumb plan to stay behind and leave you to fend for yourself, or if we stick together as a group until we get the last scroll, and advance together," Spiros said.

"Or . . ." Arya drawled. "We could send you to the next stage, and Spiros and I can stay behind."

Luke blinked in confusion. "Why would you do that? I'm oka—"

"Because you took a few hits while you were asleep, and if Theseus and Ella can leave early because they're"—she pinched her fingers together, leaving only a tiny gap—"this close to being sent home, so can you. Especially after all you've done."

"Look, I appreciate the offer, but I—"

Spiros tossed something to him, and entirely on instinct, Luke caught it, only realizing after the fact that it was a scroll.

"We'll see you in the next round, Luke. Thanks for all the hel—"

The world flickered orange and gold, and the next thing Luke knew he was standing back in Cyzicus's throne room.

CHAPTER 52

The Unseen Shoe

What the—

Luke barely had a second to orient himself before the large and ornate double doors leading into the room were blasted open with such force that he was surprised they stayed on their hinges.

"WHO GOES TH—" Cyzicus shouted as he flew into the room, a curtain of molten sparks trailing behind him, only to come to a complete halt when he saw who had intruded. "Oh. Luke?"

"Yep." Luke awkwardly waved at the emperor. "Nice to see you again."

"You as well," Cyzicus said slowly, a hint of disappointment slowly clouding his expression before he hid it entirely. "I take it you were eliminated as well?"

"Um—I don't think so?" Luke hedged, feeling rather confused about the situation himself. He had gotten two scrolls, and shuffling around, he found them nowhere on his person. Even though he had been in contact with both of them moments ago. "I should have passed—I don't know why I would—"

A light buzzing noise drew both their attention, and one of Hephaestus's drones came flying from *somewhere*.

"Congratulations, Luke of Sylcra. You have successfully completed the round. The next and final round shall begin in two weeks. You may invite up to one hundred individuals to join Olympus in the festivities." Then, before departing, it flew right over Luke's head, deposited an intricately crafted storage ring, and disappeared without a trace.

On instinct, Luke caught the ring as it fell, and at the same moment, the ever-present icon of the red eye, informing him that he was under the observation of a god, disappeared and left him alone with Cyzicus.

"Phew." Luke sighed in relief. "Looks like I really passed."

And more importantly, it looks like I'm not being watched anymore, either. Fuck yeah. He celebrated internally, already planning all the ways he could take advantage of the situation that hopefully wouldn't draw unwanted attention when the last round started.

Slim pickings, if I'm being honest, but I should be able to push a little. At the very least, making as many iterations of the fire spell as I can is a must.

"You weren't sure?" Cyzicus said, his voice chock-full of amusement and curiosity.

"I was pretty sure. I just didn't think I'd be back until it was all over, and it wasn't exactly my choice to advance, so—" He trailed off and turned the ring over in his hand. It was glowing.

Immediately, the emperor's eyes locked onto it, shimmering with excitement. Even to a hero and emperor, a gift given by a god was no small thing. "What's inside it?" Cyzicus asked, appearing next to Luke in a blur of motion and looking over his shoulder.

Luke hesitated; he knew full well what kind of defenses storage rings came with. Both of his were capable of bringing down even the strongest warrior with the right tuning, while his Saint-tier ring could potentially kill even a careless Hero tier. Of course, knowing what he knew, there were ways around those measures if you were patient, careful, and clever. Even if they were risky.

Luckily, there was an easy way to check if a ring was already bound or not.

Cutting his thumb on Maximus's edge, Luke let a drop of blood fall onto the intricately etched surface of the bronze ring. If the blood was absorbed, that meant the ring was unbound. If it wasn't . . . then it was better not to risk anything.

It sank in.

Grinning, Luke sent a surge of mana into the ring and eagerly began to explore inside. Immediately, he took note that the space within was much bigger than even his Saint-tier ring and that it was almost entirely empty, save for a hundred tokens similar to the one he had gained when he completed the qualification, vials of many-colored potions neatly arranged in rows of ten, what looked like some neatly folded clothes, a few different stacks of talismans, a book, and a letter.

The tokens are probably the invitations. The potions, I'm not sure what they do, exactly, but they should be good. Pulling them in and out of the Seed's inventory should tell me everything I need to know. Same with the talismans. The book I can read anytime. The clothes . . . they might be enchanted with something, which is—yeah. The letter, though—

Luke withdrew the envelope from the ring and tore it open, with Cyzicus still peering over his shoulder, and began to skim over it.

The contents weren't as exciting as either of them hoped, but they were informative nonetheless: the rules for the next round were listed, and they had changed slightly.

The biggest difference was that everyone competing was allowed to use a total of ten Warrior-tier talismans. Any combination of the explosive or protective variety was left up to the individual to decide on. The rules on artifact use were also laxed, allowing them to use up to three Warrior-tier artifacts instead of one, and as many Mortal-tier ones as they wanted, with a warning not to be excessive. Meaning Luke couldn't splurge on a thousand shields and put them between himself and his opponent. Where exactly that limit was wasn't strictly defined, but Luke decided not to push.

Standard regalia would have to do. A shield and something that gave him long-range options, combined with Maximus, would fill his three Warrior-tier slots. A full load out of Mortal-tier armor, from a helmet to boots, would fill the rest.

Beyond that, there was an itinerary of events. The next round wouldn't start right away; instead there would be some kind of mandatory event immediately before the tournament began and then a host of voluntary events after the winner was decided.

Luke didn't know what to make of it, but he knew he didn't like it.

Going to a highbrow social function with at least one god in attendance didn't seem like a good time. Considering that at least two gods had children competing, there was a good chance of them showing up. Zeus being there wouldn't be out of place, either, and with that many gods already there, others might just come for a reunion. Luke felt his mouth dry in nervousness at the thought alone, but he also knew a lot of the people there wouldn't see it that way.

Making the right impression on the right god could drastically change the entire course of a cultivator's life. Even a random handout from someone tiers higher could change a person's destiny. Luke didn't have to look higher than Cyzicus to realize that.

The manasinks he had given them, while not necessary for Luke, had been instrumental in raising most of the people he had selected to compete on his behalf to the Warrior tier by giving them a way to improve Arcana.

Something that was, while not impossible, exceedingly difficult to do. Without a high Arcana value, a cultivator's body would naturally stop cultivating mana, forcing them to manually knead it into an attribute of their choice.

Luke had tried it once for curiosity's sake after pestering Clite about the proper method. It wasn't easy. At all.

For starters mana that wasn't immediately absorbed eventually evaporated back into the air. It wasn't quick, but it wasn't a slow process, either. It was a race against time. The cultivator would desperately try to use as much of it as they could while it slowly but surely slipped from their grasp.

Then, even when the energy was successfully massaged into place, Luke had quickly discovered that the end result was only a shallow mimicry of the real thing. The human body was a complex masterpiece. Difficult to understand, and even harder to improve. The end result of manual cultivation was workable, because people could and did ascend to the Warrior tier and higher relying on it, but anyone who had cultivated naturally would be a magnitude stronger. At least in the short term. *If*—and it *was* an if—a cultivator succeeded in breaking through to the next tier, they would have the ability to smooth out the wrinkles caused by the improper method, but in the short term they would be drastically weaker than anyone who had cultivated the right way.

Perhaps someone supremely talented, after many years of study, trial, and error, could get better and better, maybe even capture ninety percent of the easy grace of natural cultivation. Luke was pretty sure that was what most saturated warriors did when they hit the wall.

That was beside the point, though. If even *Cyzicus* was sitting on something that could let nearly any mortal climb to the vaunted heights of the Warrior tier, then what could a *god* have? Any random trinket could be the difference between stalling at the Hero tier for millennia or rising to the Saint tier in decades.

The fact that they were once mortals who had faced the same problems begged even bigger questions. What did the gods know that let them break free of the mortal coil?

More importantly, would they *share* any such information?

Luke was inclined to think they would.

The tournament was clearly a way to raise those deserving to higher tiers, and it stood to reason that if a competitor managed to make a good impression, they might find some deity or another to nudge them along on their path.

It's probably the purpose of the meet and greet in the first place.

Before Luke could mull on the subject anymore, though, dozens of warriors, armed to the teeth, suddenly stormed into the throne room. All of them with pale faces and haunted eyes. If Luke didn't know better, he would have thought they had seen a ghost.

"Lord Cyzicus!" Clite said, breaking away from the crowd. "A Hero-tier giant has spawned!"

The Rebel's ring flashed on Cyzicus's finger, seamless silver armor encompassed him from head to toe, and a spear appeared in his hand the moment the words left her mouth.

The emperor blinked, and a look of absolute horror appeared on his face before he once again schooled his features.

"Evacuate the city," he barked.

Within the span of a single second, a tremor shook the earth. A monster bellowed in the distance. A golden glow emanated from the open doors as a barrier once again engulfed the city for the second time in a year.

Lightning crackled around him, and Cyzicus disappeared.

Heart racing, Luke shot out of the castle and beheld his first Hero-tier monster. It was big. Bigger than any creature Luke had ever seen before. It loomed over the city, and its shadow cast a large chunk of it in ominous darkness.

Like its lesser brethren, it had six arms, three on each side, all of them scraping the ground. Six eyes the size of houses looked on in malevolent glee as, one after another, boulders the size of hills smashed into the barrier. Each one broke free of the earth, seemingly of its own accord, while the giant looked to the sky. An invisible seam split its face, and it howled in laughter.

Then, as if the gods themselves were punishing it, thunder roared in the cloudless sky, and lightning rained down, striking it hundreds of times in the span of seconds. The vague figure of Cyzicus could just barely be seen flying a mile above it.

Waves of warriors flew out from the city and formed ranks. One after another, they let loose what must have been thousands upon thousands of talismans and arrows. Each one struck the monster without fail.

All of them were ineffective.

Luke raced to join them, flying past countless mortals on the way, only dimly aware of the blue- and black-robed cultivators pouring onto the streets and funneling denizens of the capital to different destinations in the city, where they would be teleported away to safety.

He was halfway there when the *Argo* took to the sky behind him and joined the battle. Beams of destructive red light fired from cannons along its stern, one after another. Each one aimed perfectly at the boulders the monster was lobbing at the city, destroying them before they could damage the barrier, ignoring the monster that Jason knew he couldn't harm.

Before he even got there, Luke knew this wasn't a battle he could affect.

Killing a wounded, fleeing hero was one thing. The Rebel was half-dead when Lukeus, Heracles, and he had set off after her. Unable to use mana, she had endured their attacks for as long as she could before expending the last of it in an effort to teleport away. An act that had been her ultimate undoing.

This was different. Absolutely nothing in Luke's arsenal was capable of doing that *thing* even the slightest bit of harm. His blade was too small. He had Hero-tier weapons, but his mana was too weak to power them. Even his newly advanced technique didn't know what to do. Just activating it alone had drained a quarter of Luke's mana before he forcibly shut it down, which reminded him, once again, that the price of using it against a being of a higher tier was much too steep.

Even so, it came as no surprise to him when the God Seed, freshly awakened, issued him a quest anyway.

Quest Alert: Giant Slayer

CHAPTER 53

An Impossible Task

The city scrambled beneath Luke as he flew closer and closer to the monster. Most of the inhabitants were panicking. Some of them watched in sheer awe as, one after another, bolts of lightning split the sky and struck the creature, sloughing off its flesh in molten waves.

They cheered every time the *Argo* or one of the countless warriors pestering the monster deflected an attack before it struck the golden barrier keeping them safe, and they cheered even louder when someone managed to extract a pound of flesh from the thing.

Luke hardly paid attention to the battle. He was too busy reading the quest.

Status | Skills | **Quests** | Inventory
Giant Slayer:
Aid in the slaying of the Hero-tier giant attacking the capital and harvest its mana with Maximus.

He read it once, and then again, before dismissing it and letting out a sigh of relief. The quest would still put him in conflict with his strongest opponent yet, but it was straightforward and nowhere near as bad as he'd imagined it might be. Knowing the Seed, it could have just as easily asked him to kill it single-handedly.

This . . . well, this was just a cash grab—or, more accurately, a stat-point grab. Considering the last quest the Seed had given him might be an impetus to start the Trojan War, killing a giant was a nice change of pace. He knew the target, and he knew what he'd get out of it—a metric ton of points and some serious pain, which he hoped wouldn't hit him quite so hard as it had the last time he had killed above his weight class.

He also needed to kill a hundred Hero-tier beings, or a single Saint-tier being, to upgrade his sword to the Hero tier, so that may have been a benefit as well. All of which he was perfectly content with, even with the amount of hurt he knew he would feel when all this was over.

No pain, no gain, as they say, but—

The actual act of harvesting its mana gave him pause, yet the more he thought about it, the more assured he became that he could do it.

It wouldn't be easy, but it would be simple.

When his sword advanced to the Warrior tier, some of the restrictions that came with absorbing mana had loosened. Not because the blade suddenly got better at sucking out mana from the dead, but because Luke could simply use it *better*.

The ability to maneuver the blade in midair and direct it with precision, combined with the nature of the bond that connected Luke and his sword, meant that making sure it was embedded in the monster at the moment of its death was a simple feat. Relatively speaking. Especially when the monster was a giant the size of a skyscraper.

If it worked, that is. This would be the first time Luke had used his sword in such a manner, and never before had someone else killed a monster when his sword was lodged in it, and that's what this would be. Luke held no illusions that he would be the one to actually fell the giant. The damage he could do with Maximus was proportionally less than a mosquito bite. Even so, he was optimistic.

For the most part.

He still didn't know how the blade judged when something was dead, but he did have a hypothesis that, if correct, meant his nascent plan would work. Simple biology and half-remembered memories from his past life dictated that cells would remain alive and functioning minutes or even hours after a creature had passed. On top of that, Luke had seen more than one video of a dead, skinned frog twitching after someone sprinkled salt on it.

The internet commentators had said it was because some of the nerve cells remained alive and reacted to the sodium or something, which he was inclined to believe. In Luke's experience, monsters and the like would still be a little alive even after he skewered them through and got the points. They twitched, blinked, and sometimes even made noises minutes after their supposed death.

Which led him to think about his own death.

My soul left my body instantly in the car crash, meaning I died on impact or moments after it, but was all of me dead? Did my heart still beat a few times? Did my brain activity instantly go from alive to zero?

Probably not, or at the very least, it's unlikely. It would take at least a few minutes for my cells to starve from the lack of blood flow and oxygen, even if my neck did snap in half.

Even the Rebel. Was she all the way dead when I got the points from her . . . He shook his head. That was a bad example; there had been so much going on when that happened that he barely even remembered any of it. From the moment he had stuck his sword in her, all he had known was pain. But he rather distinctly remembered her falling off his blade seconds after he stabbed her heart, and she probably *died* died minutes after she hit the ground. He had gotten the mana, though, when she was still hooked on his blade. Of that he was pretty certain.

Every kill he had made with his sword, and the experiences of his own death, led him to the only conclusion he could think of: the sword gave him a being's mana if it was impaling them the moment the soul left their body and relinquished its control over the energy. It was the only thing that really made sense to him, but it left him with even more questions.

When did the soul decide that it couldn't stay in a body anymore?

Moreover, cultivators of a great enough tier could seemingly control their souls after their death and possess someone else, and Luke knew firsthand that those people still had mana. Corrupted mana, but mana, nonetheless. The practice was forbidden, and all Cyzicus's library had on it was that any such person was eternally doomed to a state of half-life and it was better for them to move on than haunt the world, as it were.

Allegedly, those that stayed were in for a bad time.

Unable to cultivate and possessing a mere fraction of their true strength, they became shadows of themselves. Over the course of time, their minds would begin to fray and they would mutate into *something*, but they wouldn't remain themselves. Most, if left alone, were said to let themselves pass on to the Aether after realizing that there was nothing for them, and those that stubbornly held on would be killed the moment the world caught wind of them. From what Luke understood, it had been a bigger problem in ages past. Nowadays most people who had the means to possess a body after death knew better than to try. Of those that did, they were so weak that even a cultivator in the midstage of the Mortal tier could overpower them.

According to the books, at least.

Luke could tell there was more to it than just that, but knowledge of the subject beyond the basics was restricted. Even the cultivation level of the people able to stick around after death wasn't mentioned—likely to prevent people from actually doing it.

Maybe they're demons? Luke thought half-heartedly before shaking his head and perching on a tower just behind the barrier. He blinked in surprise at the sight that awaited him.

He had expected to find scores of the Gegenees rising out of the earth and marching on the city, but that wasn't the case at all.

There weren't even any dead monsters. At all.

Now, this doesn't make sense.

If the Hero tier is the prime, then there should be hundreds of the monsters by now, considering it's been attacking for a few minutes. Even if they were all killed already, some body parts should be left. If the Hero tier isn't the prime, then there should definitely be more. At least one if the big guy was the second to spawn.

I mean, I suppose Cyzicus could have just disintegrated them, prime and all, but something should remain. A stray limb at the very least.

Hmm. Something about all this felt *off*.

Whatever it is, I'll do my best, but at this scale?

Shaking his head, Luke turned his attention back to the sole giant and tried to think of any ways he could help before deciding that there wasn't really anything he *could* do.

Activating his technique would just see him drained in seconds, and he already knew the way to kill the higher-tier giants was by attrition. You just had to keep pummeling them until they fell apart.

That in mind, he withdrew the Limitless Thunder Bow from his storage ring and took aim at one of the smaller boulders hurtling toward the city.

The rock had no chance of actually breaking through the barrier, but every attack that hit it would drain a little energy until eventually the bubble popped. If that happened, it would mean the end of the capital.

Luckily, even though the boulders were attacks sent by a monster much stronger than Luke, at the end of the day they were just rocks. Big, dense, obsidian, and extremely hot to the point that a single attack from one would likely kill him, but just rocks.

Funneling mana into the bow, he drew the string back, and a thin line of electricity longer than Luke was tall fizzled to life. Then, just as the boulder was about to hit the city, Luke let it loose.

The moment it was clear of the bow, the lightning thickened and transformed, turning so bright that it was hard to look at and, traveling blisteringly fast, collided with the giant chunk of obsidian.

"Tsk." Luke frowned and shook his head when it only gouged out a medium-size hole in the rock.

Guess I underestimated it. A lot. This really isn't a battle I have any right participating in, but you know what—

He pulled the drawstring back again and loosed another six bolts into the boulder before it finally shattered. Small chunks of jagged rock erupted over the city's skyline and rained on the barrier.

Shaking his head, Luke returned the bow to his storage ring. Just destroying one of its attacks had depleted more than a third of his mana, and after watching the *Argo* blast apart three much larger boulders at the same time, Luke decided that expending all his mana to stop two more smaller boulders wasn't worth it. Not at all.

Not when just being close to a battle of such magnitude put him in some amount of danger. Not that he believed it would come to that, as he fully expected Cyzicus to win. The fact that the emperor was evacuating the city as a precaution, though, spoke volumes.

So Luke gripped Maximus and craned his head, struggling to even see the giant's head from his vantage point. He raked his eyes over its form, trying to determine the best place to put the blade in.

Its head seems like a good idea. The torso is probably a better target, though, since it's bigger. Still, I should probably—

Thunder boomed in the sky, and the thickest bolt of lightning Luke had ever seen crashed straight into the giant's head. Blinking the spots out of his eyes, Luke watched in awe as the Hero-tier monster regenerated the entire left side of its head. Then, with a flick of its fingers, it sent hundreds of hill-size boulders barreling into the sky.

High up in the clouds, a golden barrier shimmed into existence around Cyzicus, and all the rocks shattered on what Luke suspected was a Saint-tier protective talisman and turned to ashy dust that rained back down. The aftermath of that single attack rendered the air outside the city's barrier entirely unbreathable. There was too much obsidian dust and particulates polluting it, enough to severely damage even a warrior's lungs.

Feeling grateful that he was protected, Luke turned his attention to the *Argo*. The city was safe, but maybe the ship, with Saint-tier protections, would be safer?

Jason hadn't steered it out of the city's defenses yet, but Luke could imagine that if Heracles was by his side offering him advice, that would change soon. Maybe then he could actually get a better shot.

Before he could leave, though, a prompt from the Seed sent chills down Luke's spine. And it took every iota of will he had not to break into a nervous sweat.

Danger detected.

Fuck.

"Humph," a woman beside him grunted. "That emperor of yours will kill it soon," she said, disappointment clear in her voice.

Luke felt his mouth dry as he looked at the person next to him. She was young, with regal features, appearing no older than ten with long blond hair that stretched for meters behind her. He didn't recognize her, but—

"Cybele?" he asked, his mouth suddenly feeling *very* dry.

"Who else would it be?" she said dismissively, as if she didn't look like a completely different person compared to the last time Luke had seen her.

"What are you doing here?"

"Mmm-hmm. Just seeing how my pet is doing."

Pet? The giant? Me? What? How?

"Oh." She lifted her finger up and looked right at Luke. Something in her gaze made chills run down his spine. "It occurs to me that the trinket I gave you earlier isn't quite enough to pay for the prize I took."

"Wh—"

Her hair shimmered, and a circlet made of twine and roses appeared atop her head.

A pit formed in Luke's stomach.

I can't believe I thought this quest was simple.

CHAPTER 54

The Giant Farce

Luke looked at the goddess before his gaze wandered back to the Hero-tier giant. Just in time, too, as another bolt of lightning fell from the heavens and sheared off two of its arms. The upper and middle limbs on the left side of its body fell to the ground. Its flesh glowed orange and red from where the emperor's lightning had severed them.

Not that monster seemed to care; it still had four arms left. It brought two to its stomach and began rubbing it in slow circles. Another hand moved to cover half its eyes. Then it lifted one foot off the earth, and a seam opened up between its eyes.

What the—

"HA. HA. HA. HA. HA," it laughed, deeply and loudly. The bass in its voice was so strong, it made everything not secured to the ground vibrate.

Then, with two of its four remaining arms, it grabbed the limbs Cyzicus had blasted off its body and began using them to haphazardly beat on the barrier like it was a drum, even as its stumps wriggled and new limbs grew to replace what it had lost.

Golden ripples reverberated through the barrier, making it flicker and distort. For a moment, Luke thought the only line of defense between the city was going to shatter and kill everyone inside at the same time.

Instinctively, Luke pulled a Hero-tier protective talisman from his ring and prepared to rip the tab clean off. He didn't think it was anywhere near enough to actually protect him from the monster should its attention fall on him, but maybe it would be enough to make it to the *Argo* or, failing that, allow him to escape through one of the teleportation platforms seeded throughout the city.

His panic turned out to be unwarranted, though, as the shield surrounding the city suddenly solidified and hardened against the monster's attacks, its color shifting from a translucent gold to an electric blue as it drew on another power reserve.

What that was, Luke didn't know, but he was glad that Cyzicus had made arrangements in advance.

Beside him, Cybele cackled in amusement at his antics. As if he was silly for being scared of a skyscraper-size creature that could flatten him like a pancake with only the barest hint of effort.

Luke bit back a retort and silently returned the talisman to his ring, suddenly reminded of the much bigger threat that was only feet away from him. Unlike the giant, though, Luke knew there was nothing he could do against Cybele unless the Seed offered him the use of a charge. Something he didn't think was likely. He didn't know what she wanted, but Luke suspected that whatever it was, it wouldn't be quite as easy as a quick death.

And she definitely wants something. The question is from who, and what?

A wide grin stretched across Cybele's face, and she pulled a snack from somewhere. The smell of popcorn and butter hit Luke's nose as she unscrewed a metal container. Then, noticing him looking at it, she tilted it toward him, a mocking glint in her eyes.

It took everything Luke had not to slam it out of her hands. What about this was funny to her, he didn't know, but he did know that anyone willing to go to the lengths she was to make Cyzicus miserable was not a person he liked. Remembering the look of rage on the emperor's face when he had mentioned her, he had no doubt that's what this was. Or at the least a part of it.

"Are you controlling it?" he asked, ignoring the food and doing his best to keep his voice neutral. Controlling himself was of the utmost importance. Letting the anger, fear, and disgust he was feeling leak into his tone would neither endear him to the stronger cultivator nor would it make the conversation fruitful. Cussing her out might feel good, but making her angry would just put him on her bad side. He might already be on it, for all he knew, but being on it even harder wouldn't do him any good. Arke was more than enough in that department.

Still, just because being rude is a bad idea doesn't mean I gotta brownnose. Just keep it professional, Luke.

"Obviously." She reached into the container, scooped out a handful of kernels, and, tilting her head back, dropped them one by one into her mouth. "What do you think the crown did?"

I didn't get the chance to find out, Luke thought sarcastically.

"I put it out of my mind once you took it," he lied.

"Mmm-hmm. Smart boy. Most in your position would rage and seethe, thinking I stole from them." She shook her head. "I don't steal."

Sure you don't.

"The pomegranate seed did save my life, so as far as I'm concerned, we're square."

"Perhaps. Yet it was a paltry sum—nothing compared to the Earth Mother's Crown," she said.

The what? Luke thought incredulously. Unable to help himself, he found his gaze drawn back to the circlet of twine on her head. He had known it was something good, considering she had seen fit to take it from him and because the Seed wanted him to have it, but Gaia's crown? That was quite a lot more than he was expecting. He would have expected something belonging to one of the first gods to be more . . . fancy.

"It's not as impressive as it sounds," Cybele said, shaking her head even as she stuffed her face with another fistful of the popped kernels. "Much of its magic has faded over the ages. Now it's just good for controlling these things." She nodded to her pet.

"I— Why are you doing this? If you can control it, why att—"

"As I said before, I don't think I paid you what you were due. Don't worry, I'll feed you another few Hero tiers, maybe even a Saint tier later. This one should be enough to let you win the tournament, though. We'll see."

What the fuck?

No, seriously. What the fuck?

"The tournament?"

"Mmm-hmm. I placed a good bet on you, and this"—she pointed to the giant—"should let you harness enough mana to hold your own against some of your competitors. I looked at the roster; you're not in for an easy time. Watch out for the Aresson—his father has trained him well. The child of Poseidon is strong, too, I suppose, but he lacks determination."

"I—thanks?" Luke scratched the back of his head. "Helping me like this, though . . . It's not against the rules?"

"Don't be silly. Of course it isn't. Hephaestus shared his little recordings with all Olympus. The other gods will be doing the same with their children, so they can hardly complain about me aiding you here."

For the sake of his sanity, Luke decided to take that at face value.

"I still don't get why you're doing all this. I'm not—"

"Prometheus. He may have mentioned it when you awoke your bloodline, but his . . . *insight* is what allowed the gods of this age to topple those of mine and claim Theos as their domain."

Not new news but, still, mind blown, Luke thought as he wondered what she meant by her "age." Was she a titan?

What is a titan, anyway? Is it just another, older word for a god or something different altogether?

"So is that what you want, revenge for something?" he asked randomly. That's what the titans would want, right?

"Pshh. Of course not—good riddance to the old coots. The way they were going, reality itself may have shattered. No, I was one of the first to turn against the titan king, at great personal risk, and it is with my blessing that Zeus became the god king. Alas, it was also me who convinced Prometheus to aid them. So you can imagine I was disappointed when the reward he got was eternal imprisonment. Of course, he *did* go mad and rip a tear in reality, the exact sort of thing we were trying to stop, and the hole still floods this world with creatures from the beyond, but—"

She shrugged and tilted the metal canister over her lips, downing the rest of the popcorn in one go. Her entire head increased in size to accommodate the vast amount of food inside. Eerily, it reminded Luke of snakes eating prey that was much too large for them, and that she wasn't the little girl she was pretending to be, either.

Turning away, Luke took a deep breath and tried to sort out his thoughts. It was hard.

I knew she knew I had a bloodline inherited from Prometheus. Don't know how she knew, but she did. Now that I think about it, though, the Seed seemed pretty confident that the Mask of a Thousand Faces alone would be enough to protect me from identification. So either that was wrong, or Cybele knows and talked to Prometheus after he talked to me. He was half-crazed, but he did see me, and maybe he can feel where I am, too. I guess it's not a stretch that she actually knows him and he sent her my way. Except she said she was drawn by the fact that Heracles created a portal through the Aether.

That could be a lie, though. It's not like being immortal and insanely powerful stops you from lying.

And, even though she took the crown, which might be the key to stopping the giant tide—if it can spawn and control one giant, there's no saying it can't control all of them. Anyway, she took the crown, but she also gave me the tools to kill the Rebel.

I may have been able to do it without the pomegranate seed; Rex and Blinky were able to break down the barrier around her castle, after all, and the Argo was there, too, but her help sure did make it a lot easier. If nothing else, it let me instead of Heracles kill the Rebel.

I don't buy the stuff about the bet, though. She's making me stronger, but it's not for the tournament. Or, at least, not entirely for the tournament. That could just be a favor for Prometheus. What he might want from me, though, I don't have the slightest clue. Unless he wants me to break him out, but the guy's also insane, so that's definitely not a good idea. I think.

It might be worth having him around if Arke comes sniffing, but then he'd know that I'm a body snatcher . . . Yeah, I better hope those two don't compare notes anytime soon. Or ever.

Still, there's so much I don't know. I can't even tell if I'm thinking in the right direction.

Feeding me mana or not, though, she's definitely fucking with Cyzicus. He got angry when I mentioned her, so they have some sort of past, but where do I fit in with all of this?

"Send your sword to the center of its chest," she said urgently, pulling Luke out of his thoughts. Eyeing her with suspicion, he did as she asked anyway. His sword slipped out of its sheath with a satisfying *shink* and darted out of the barrier surrounding the city. Seconds later, it embedded itself deep into the monster's flesh. The effortless action proved once again that Maximus was more than it seemed. Even Luke's Hero-tier bow had struggled against one of the monster's random boulders, but his sword sank into it with barely any effort.

Not that the monster itself seemed bothered by the fact that there was a golden sword halfway through its flesh. So focused was it on whaling on the city's barrier, it didn't even care about the bolts of thunder relentlessly falling from the heavens and sloughing off chunks of its flesh. Compared to those, the sword impaling it was negligible.

I should have stuck a few explosive talismans onto Maximus; it would have dinged up my sword a little, but the mana from killing the giant would have repaired it anyway.

And Cybele did go out of her way to tell me that this is just her paying back what she owes me, so it's not like I'm taking some Faustian deal here. I did that—

Cyzicus dropped from the sky, and in his hands was a bolt of lightning, as thick and as tall as the giant itself.

The world went white.

Mana of the Hero tier once again burned through Luke's flesh.

CHAPTER 55

The Hero Tier

Luke gritted his teeth as torrents of violent mana ripped into him. Perhaps it was because he had already done this once—twice if he counted the time, as a mortal, he had killed the Warrior-tier monster. Or maybe it was because he was deeper into the Warrior tier, but through effort alone he was able to stave off the darkness creeping its way into his vision and hold steadfast against the pain. The excruciating, shocking, and frankly disgusting pain.

He wasn't sure if that was a good thing.

Not when he could hear Cybele cackle with amusement and feel her predatory gaze boring into him and his secrets. Somehow, the pain only served to make the entire situation even more stressful. Then, as the flow of mana raging into him began to slow over a few short moments that felt like eternity, a question rose in his head. One that terrified him and made him feel stupid in equal measure.

Will the Seed even siphon away the mana when a goddess is this close?

It will, right?

Luke clenched his jaw in agony and attempted to activate his bloodline. It didn't work, and the act of doing so sent currents of pain through his body, but he felt that it was worth it.

How often would he get the chance to see his mana like this? It wasn't like killing a Hero tier was a common occurrence, and he felt obligated to learn what he could now that he had the tools. Even though he knew he wasn't going to like what he was about to learn, he tried again anyway.

His manasight flickered to life, and suddenly he could *see* the damage the heavy energy of the Hero tier was doing to him.

His metaphysical self was stretched and distorted. Where its shape normally conformed to the contours of his body, it now bubbled outward at his head, his chest, and his right leg in ways that he could only describe as tumorous.

It'll be fine. Luke tried to console himself and think through the pain he patiently waited for the Seed to act, taking comfort in the fact that he had survived this exact thing already and he was fine. This shouldn't be any different. So long as the mana was siphoned away, that was. If it wasn't, Luke didn't know how much longer he could take this treatment before he *popped.*

I won't. It's going to be any second now. And even if it doesn't get converted to stat points, the mana will just leak out of me. I won't actually burst.

Besides—

The Seed didn't store stat points when Hephaestus was watching, but that doesn't mean all gods are built the same or have the same abilities. Maybe Hephaestus just had some way to keep track of mana. Maybe he could see it or something? Or maybe he has a way to measure attributes. If there's a god that has a way to gamify the world, it's going to be the one that has a bajillion drones and robots.

And I can't forget that Cybele was there the last time I killed a Hero tier—but now that I think about it, there was also a lot more going on then, wasn't there?

I gave Maximus its name because the world itself demanded it from me, not to mention Maximus had just risen to the Warrior tier, too. Maybe that was enough to hide what was happening with the Seed.

Or maybe it didn't, and that's why Cybele is doing this.

"There, there." He saw the goddess move from the corner of his vision and appear beside him, where she patted him calmly on the back, like she was burping him or something. If she was doing more than that, Luke didn't know. He was able to feel when others tested his mana once he had learned to do it himself, but who knew what a god could and couldn't do?

Honestly, Luke hurt so much he was having a hard time caring. He would worry about Cybele if or when the Seed told him to. Until then, there was nothing he could do about the divine being, anyway.

Embarrassingly, and he would never admit it, but her burping him did seem to help. Luke grunted in agony as the last of the mana settled into him and his metaphysical self ballooned even farther. His previously tumorous appearance smoothed out so that he just looked incredibly swollen. The Seed, tortuously, remained inert.

That's okay, though. It's taking a few seconds—so what? Luke reassured himself, trying his level best not to panic and simultaneously keeping a careful eye on his condition.

He could see the foreign mana integrating with his own and feel his stats ticking up one by one as he was forced to cope and grow under the internal pressure. Normally, the mana his blade fed him would convert to stat points in short order, but the Seed always gave his body the chance to absorb what it could naturally. From what Luke had observed, that usually just meant that it would leave what his body could absorb floating around and squirrel the rest away.

In this case, though, it seemed the Seed was playing it differently and letting him suffer in the name of growth. Or so he hoped. Either way, he didn't like it.

I really fucking need the Seed to get its shit together. Like, right the fuck now. Luke cursed while watching his mana. He was becoming increasingly worried that he might actually pop or something. Intellectually, he knew that wasn't possible, but the way he hurt and looked, he was having a hard time believing.

Luke hadn't seen the aftermath of absorbing mana of a higher tier before, but now that he could, he was regretting his decision. It was one thing to be in pain and another entirely to see all the ways he had messed himself up.

Come on . . .

The pain suddenly spiked, his bloodline deactivated, and a moment later a prompt from the Seed appeared before his vision.

1,236 Stat Points

Luke collapsed to his back in relief, barely even registering the number. Instead, he just closed his eyes and tried to get a grip on himself. Then, after a few seconds, he reactivated the Eyes of Insight.

His metaphysical self looked like it had been pumped full of air and then deflated, leaving him stretched out and hanging over himself like some loose skin. It wasn't exactly a surprise, considering that's exactly what had happened, but it was awful to look at, nonetheless.

That does not look pretty. But for over a thousand points . . .

He opened his status.

Status	Skills	Quests	Inventory
Name: Lukas King
Tier: Warrior
Bloodline: Eyes of Insight
Mana: 217,397 / 298,626
Rate: 18% per hour
Strength: 486 > 491
Agility: 501 > 509
Constitution: 789 > 852
Arcana: 546 > 701
Stat Points: 1,236
Charges: 7/10

So fucking worth it, Luke thought, in disbelief about the progress he had made in such a short time. *I swear, this world loves putting people in pain. That said, if pain is all it takes to get these kinda gains, I'm in.*

Actually . . .

He added up all the points in his head.

Just under four hundred points to go before I'm a hero. If I do that, then—I don't really know, but I'll be another step forward. A step closer to near-ultimate power, a step away from danger and discovery, and maybe even a step back to Earth.

Man, they're all going to freak the fuck out when I show up.

I definitely have to use the mask to look like a Martian or something and drop down over the White House in a flying boat—or maybe not. I mean, maybe. What's the worst that can happen?

I'll be strong enough to teleport anywhere I want. Strong enough to cause the destruction of entire worlds, and strong enough to defend myself. Honestly, I won't be surprised if I can tank a nuke or two by the time I'm done with all this.

A little mischief never hurt anybody.

Before he could dive deeper into his fantasy, Cybele leaned over him, cupped his cheeks, and spilled something down his throat. Instantly, waves of healing energy washed through his body, and he watched as his metaphysical form slowly began to shrink and restore itself.

It would take some time, maybe a day or two, for the process to fully complete, but Luke suspected that a good night's sleep would go a long way.

But—

Luke hesitated briefly before pressing on and adding a single point to his Arcana stat. Probably not the wisest thing to do, considering that Cybele was *right* there and on the lookout, but he felt it would be stranger if all the mana suddenly disappeared without a trace. The fact that the Seed let him do it at all was proof enough that it didn't feel threatened by her presence. Especially now that Luke knew for a fact that the Seed would turn its functions off without him doing anything if it felt it was necessary.

She probably just thinks that all this is a feature of my sword and maybe even the Eyes of Insight. It's sure as hell more believable than me having a Primordial-tier artifact in my soul.

Honestly, I wonder if she even knows about the God Seed, like, at all. Arke obviously does, and so does whoever made it, but who else is on that list, and how big is it, exactly?

Well, considering Arke is the only one looking for it as far as I know, it's got to be somewhat secret. Or maybe I'm just too low level to hear the kind of gossip that concerns Primordial-level artifacts. I'll have to sniff around a little at the tournament. Hang by the watercooler or something.

Smiling at his dumb joke, he added another two points to Arcana and perked up slightly when it boosted his recovery just a little bit. Emboldened, he added another two.

"How was it?" Cybele asked.

Luke slowly rose from his position on the floor and, ignoring her for the moment, focused on his connection with his sword. It seemed strained but still intact and, like himself, already on the mend. At his command, Maximus freed itself from the giant's corpse and flew back toward him.

"Painful, but I think you knew that," Luke said, catching his sword by its handle and sending it straight into his storage ring.

"Mmm. I guessed as much. Do you feel up to another one?" She smiled at him, and the circlet atop her head glowed with an earthy green light.

"I'll pass," Luke said immediately. As nice as being fed literal power was, he didn't think he'd survive another infusion so close to the last. Nor did he want to accidentally fall into debt. He still didn't know exactly why Cybele was taking such an interest in him, and while resistance might be futile, he didn't think just accepting whatever scheme she cooked up would be in his best interest.

Not when she thought bringing a giant to attack a city full of hundreds of thousands of people was an acceptable course of action.

"Your loss." She shrugged.

"What do you really want from me? This is the—"

"The impatience of youth. I truly don't miss it." She sighed. Luke wilted as she leveled him with an ancient and tired gaze, one that reminded him exactly whom and what he was talking to. "There will be a time for answers, but now isn't it. Grow stronger. Once you're of the Hero tier, we may be able to come to a proper accord. Until then—"

She disappeared from his sight just as soon as she'd come.

Shaking his head, Luke looked beyond the barrier. Cyzicus and his warriors were already cleaning up the aftermath of the battle, and at that moment, he didn't exactly feel like socializing or helping. The giant was dead, he was tired, and his mana was maimed. And although he had just woken up, he felt like sleeping.

He'd go talk to Rex and the others tomorrow and then get started on his training. He only had two weeks left until the tournament resumed, and he needed to do a lot of work to make sure he lasted long enough to finish in second place.

The least of which was learning the flame spell. Then, once he recovered, it would be a good idea to kill some monsters and bank the last points he needed for his ascension to the Hero tier.

Breaking through right now would get him disqualified, but having the ability to push himself to the next level whenever the need arose was tempting. Until then, he'd leave enough wiggle room that he wouldn't break through to the next stage by accident.

Maybe nine hundred or nine fifty in every attribute would be a good place to be, he thought, racing back to his room in the castle.

CHAPTER 56

The Flame Spell

When Luke woke up, he felt amazing. Until he remembered the reason he wasn't in agony was because of the potion Cybele had force-fed him. Which in turn reminded him of the fact that she could kill him just as easily as she had fixed him. Then he felt sick. He could feel in his bones that a bill would come due. Regardless of what the goddess claimed about owing him for what she had taken, he couldn't escape the sense that he was a mere pig she was fattening up for slaughter.

Power might not lead to absolute control and subversion of free will, but there could be no equal exchange between him and the goddess. Not when the difference between their current stations was night and day. It was just like his deal with Nefkha so long ago. Irrespective of what the older warrior had claimed, their bargain was shallow, and the Seed's quest to escape Carim was all the proof Luke needed that it was a deal struck in poor faith. The old man had lorded Luke's weakness over him, and while he'd been lucky enough to escape, Luke had no doubt that staying would have led to an unpleasant outcome.

Honestly, his own blade was all the reminder Luke needed of the role of power on Theos.

He didn't quite know whom Bellerophon was in this world, what he did, what he stood for, or why he'd been executed. All of it was a mystery. What he knew was that Zeus had struck him down and scattered his belongings to the corners of the world while he was at the moment of his apotheosis. What he knew was that the Seed in his soul hadn't protected Aeolus from death at the hands of Arke the paragon. What he knew was that Prometheus, whose blood ran through his veins, had been driven mad and condemned to eternal suffering.

Luke knew that while the path before him seemed clear for the moment, it was in truth far more treacherous than he could even begin to imagine. A single misstep and he'd be ripped apart.

So, he had to rely on the tools of past losers to succeed where they failed. To live where they'd died. To find peace where they had found insanity. It wasn't enough to keep killing things with his sword, harvesting stat points, and being led around the nose by the Seed. He couldn't rest on his laurels and fail. He wouldn't allow himself to be cast adrift in the Aether and be at the mercy of strange and cruel gods ever again.

That's why, instead of walking out of his room and eating breakfast—or whatever meal it was time for—with the warriors of the *Argo* or catching up with Lukeus and Rex, he munched on some jerky he kept in his storage ring and activated his bloodline.

He inspected himself for any sign of continued injury and smiled when he found none. Much to his relief, his metaphysical form was back to its old unballooned self, and its boundaries fit firmly within the confines of his skin. It showed no signs of ever having been stretched beyond recognition, and if Luke hadn't seen firsthand how bad it was when he had taken on the Hero-tier mana, he would never have believed he was injured in the first place.

I've definitely been out for a few days, then. Eh, I'll figure it out later. For now . . .

His focus drifted to the spell icon bobbing in a slow orbit around where his heart was.

Thankfully, the giant's Hero-tier mana had left the spell undisturbed. He had no reason to suspect that it would be damaged beyond the fact that his entire mana system had nearly burst. Which would have sucked. He was glad, though, to see that the worst hadn't come to pass and that the spell hadn't been lost amid the Seed's and Cybele's schemes.

He needed that spell. Without it, he wasn't sure he could win the tournament.

Foresight of the End was a scarily powerful and nigh-unstoppable ability, but it also shared many of the weaknesses of its less evolved versions. Foes that were invisible or not alive to begin with would still be out of Luke's grasp, just as they had always been. Unless, of course, he could hose them down with jets of unending fire, which would be an option as soon as he had endless iterations of the spell orbiting in his mana pool rather than the eleven uses of it he had now.

All right!

He clapped his hands and, falling back into the still-warm covers of his bed, he severed a blob of mana from his pool and went to work.

Slowly and intricately, he crafted branch after branch of the complex icon, once again gaining an appreciation of just how intricate the thing actually was. He held out as long as he could before the exertion of maintaining the mana outside his body became too much and his grip over his own mana became tenuous and then broke altogether.

Rubbing his temples, Luke fought off a wave of vertigo and watched as his mana fizzled away into nothing. Whatever quality it had that made the energy *his* was gone, and with it his ability to perceive it. Minus the headache, Luke was pleased with how well his first try had worked.

The spell icon had a hundred and three branches, and he had succeeded in forming seventy-two of them. The best he could do before was sixty-odd branches.

Honestly, it had gone better than Luke had anticipated, and he suspected his improved Arcana was to blame. Or perhaps it was something else entirely. His mana was much stronger than it had been in the holy land of Vulcan, but the concentration of mana in Sylcra was also just a mere fraction of what it was in the god's domain.

Or I'm just overthinking it, and I did better because I'm better rested and where I am and my Arcana have nothing to do with this.

Speaking of—

He opened his status and grinned at all those stat points just waiting to be spent. He was tempted to use them all right away, but after a brief moment of hesitation, he decided against it. He looked and felt fine, but flooding himself with that much mana so soon after his recovery seemed like a bad idea. It was better to trickle it in over the course of a couple days.

Seeing that Cybele hadn't cut him open when he had made the monumentally stupid decision to use the God Seed in front of her, being found out by anyone in Sylcra wasn't a big concern. Still, now that his judgment wasn't clouded by ungodly levels of pain, he decided that discretion was the better part of valor. It wouldn't hurt him in the long run, and drip feeding the points came with its own benefits.

The least of which were the better control over his power and the increased intimacy with how exactly the Seed strengthened him. Luke didn't think he would ever need to cultivate manually, and he doubted that he would ever be as good as the Seed at allocating mana, but it seemed prudent to better understand the process anyway. A windfall this big would only get rarer as he advanced his cultivation, and the chance to observe so many points being spent repeatedly over a short amount of time might reveal something interesting. Especially since the backlash from killing Hero tiers as a warrior felt so much worse than killing a Warrior tier as a mortal.

Seed or no Seed, I think harvesting the mana from a saint as a hero might even kill me. The stuff has to go through my body before my hacks can work their magic, and the difference in Warrior-tier and Hero-tier mana is too profound. If the trend continues and the power gap between tiers gets wider and wider . . . He sighed.

Not good, but it's also not going to be a concern for a while. Unless Cybele makes good on her promise, I doubt there are enough Saint tiers around for this to be a problem, anyway. Most likely, I'll end up having to clear out nests of Warrior-tier creatures for chump change, punch metal, and start benching mountains to cultivate.

He grinned and shook his head in amusement, imagining himself doing just that.

Shaking his head clear of his silly thoughts, he focused back on his status and began to spend his windfall. He started by adding two stat points to Agility and then cycled through the rest of his attributes one by one. Mana escaped the seed and, like a balm, spread waves of rejuvenating energy throughout his body, washing away pains and stress that he hadn't even known he had. With each point he felt better, and after the last point went into his Arcana, his dull headache faded just as quickly as it had come. His eyes widened in surprise.

This might have some potential.

Using stat points always felt good, but he hadn't really considered that they might be good for this kind of training. In fact, spending them in the middle of training was usually the worst time to use them, with the best time being at the start of the day, after his body had digested the previous day's gains over a good night of sleep. The purpose of training was to exert himself so that his body would seek nourishment from the environment and strengthen itself. Eliminating exhaustion in the middle of it was contrary to that purpose.

This, though, was different. Sure, he would miss out on a handful of points to his Arcana if he endured the pain, but adding a point or two after each attempt would speed up the process drastically.

And it's not like I'm hurting for points right now. The faster I can get this spell copied, and the more iterations I can make of it, the better. I want to be able to throw fire around like it's nobody's business. Hephaestus is going to regret not putting a limitation on spell use. Then again, he probably never thought someone could copy his work. He's also not above putting his hands on the scale if the last round is anything to go by . . . Eh, I'll see how it goes. Even if I can't use it at the tournament, endless fire is way too potent a power not to cultivate.

With stat points to ease the exhaustion and the experience gained from repeatedly making the same pattern with his mana over and over again, he began to make *real* progress copying the spell. The beginning stages, the ones he was most familiar with, he could almost manifest instantly, and the later stages were soon committed to memory as well.

Pretty soon it wasn't even a blob of mana he was starting with, but a half-formed spell. He had lost track of time and the number of attempts. It was only hours later, when he tried and failed to add another stat point to Arcana, that he roused from his trance. Inadvertently, he had raised his Arcana to nine hundred and ninety-nine, the limit of the Warrior tier.

"Shit." He scratched the back of his head. He didn't really mind that he had maxed out a stat, but he was annoyed that he had lost access to his instant headache cure. He didn't dwell on the feeling for long.

Luke had recreated a hundred of the hundred and three branches in his last ten attempts. The finish line was so close, he could practically taste it. Uncaring of his headache, he pressed on, and on, and on.

He pumped his fist in victory when he finally managed to recreate the hundred and first branch.

By the time he managed to create the hundred and second branch, he was so familiar with the structure of the spell that the blob he started with snapped the first dozen or so branches into shape on instinct alone.

Then, after twenty more failed attempts, he finally began to put the finishing touches on the last glyph on the last bra—

Someone knocked on his door, and the nearly completed spell broke into tiny fragments and faded from his vision.

"FUCKKKKKKKKKK."

"Luke! Is everything okay?" Rex yelled and barged into his room with Blinky draped over his shoulder and his features twisted in concern.

"I'm busy. Get out!"

Rex stood frozen. Slowly his gaze wandered from Luke's eyes to Luke's lap, where the blanket he was under was just slightly crumpled. Rex's face went beet red, and he slowly stepped back, nodded, and closed the door behind him and left.

"I didn't see anything!" Rex called out from the other side of the door.

It took every ounce of good sense and sympathy Luke had for Cyzicus not to stab the emperor's grandson then and there. Instead, he spent the next five minutes with his eyes closed in silent meditation to get his emotions under control before he once again separated a portion of mana from his pool.

One after another, the branches of the flame spell took shape in front of him. The hundredth. The hundred and first. The hundred and second. Then, finally, the hundred and third.

The moment the last glyph on the last branch took shape, the mana the icon was formed of glowed red and orange. Before Luke could make heads or tails of it, it slammed into his chest.

Focusing his sight inward, Luke's face split into a grin when he saw not one but two nearly indistinguishable spell icons bobbing in a lazy circuit around where his heart was.

Fuck, yeah.

Leaving the original spell alone, Luke focused his mana through the one he had made and laughed as it took on a fiery aspect.

Moments later, Luke was flying as fast as he could through the halls of the castle. The early-morning sun was filtering through the windows, illuminating the many paintings and statues beautifully littered about the place.

It was under that light that Luke sought out Rex and began hurtling balls of scorching fire at his feet. He deserved it.

CHAPTER 57

Oaths and Orbs

Sorry," Luke said quietly. His expression, his tone of voice, and even his posture were the epitome of sincere and utter remorse.

Clite glared at him.

Well, it was a long shot anyway.

"I'm *really* sorry." Rex bowed with his own apology. So low, in fact, that Luke suspected his nose might actually be scraping the ground.

Clite glared harder.

She was understandably angry. Luke and Rex's brawl had escalated more than either of them had anticipated. The fight itself remained good-natured, with both of them keeping sufficient control over themselves and their abilities to make sure no one got hurt and nothing too valuable broke. Really, it was just some good fun, and besides a few scorch marks, there was barely any damage. Even Blinky, for all her terrifying faults, caught on to the fact that neither of them was trying to actually hurt the other and had stayed docile throughout their battle.

Except the demon's mere presence evoked a certain sense of terror in those that beheld her. Normally, that wasn't a big deal. Everyone who was employed in Cyzicus's castle, from the lowest servant to the highest chef, was a cultivator. After months of exposure and many assurances from Rex and Cyzicus of the demon's good behavior, all the castle's residents had grown used to the dreadglare's harrowing form. Not comfortable, for that was likely impossible, but they knew enough, and had enough mana in their bodies, that they were fine. For the most part.

The problem, however, was that there were more than the castle's usual occupants present. The city had been shaken by the giant's assault, and while no lives had been lost, people were afraid. It wasn't every day that a skyscraper-size giant threatened to kill them all. So to calm his populace, Cyzicus had invited every mortal of some renown and all their friends to celebrate not only the giant's death, but the end of the tide. The best bakers, shoemakers, actors, and singers were all in attendance. Maybe if they weren't drunk, things would have gone better. As it was . . .

The mortals of the capital weren't prepared to handle Blinky.

To say the least, it caused a stampede. One that Cyzicus, at that very moment, was quelling.

It shouldn't be too hard. He has a bunch of warriors and he's their emperor. It sucks that I ruined the festival, though, Luke thought guiltily. Life on Theos was *hard* for people in ways that Luke could barely even begin to fathom. Being responsible for making it even marginally harder left a bad taste in his mouth. He felt like he had stolen something from them. Worst of all, he hadn't even gained anything but ill will for the act.

And just when I was about to ask Cyzicus for a favor, too, he thought morosely.

Talk about bad timing. I guess . . . I could ask Jason instead? Taking the Argo *won't be as fast as teleporting, but that might even be better, now that I think about it. Not the slow part, but the spectacle of it.*

The tournament is going to elevate my profile . . . a lot. I've already spilled the beans about my past, and Hephaestus literally knows everything he needs to know in order to find out that I have the God Seed if he ever chooses to investigate. Which means that I need to get rid of some loose ends. Preferably before I make myself even more famous. Which means dealing with Nefkha.

I wanted to ask Cyzicus to teleport me there, but if I can get Jason to take me there instead . . . the distraction of a flying ship above the society might be enough for me to find Nefkha and . . . not kill him. That's too much attention.

Murder isn't really a big deal in this world, but that doesn't mean that people won't ask why if someone suddenly gets decapitated. It's easy enough to answer that question when I actually have a reason I can share. Like, the tomb and Nafik or the Rebel. Literal cause and effect. No one will really feel the need to dig deeper. Someone can't, however, just die. Especially not one of the handful of warriors of a tiny sect. Besides, if the timing is too suspicious, they'll point fingers at the new people on the block, among which will be me. Theos is dangerous, but that doesn't mean lawless. That said, it's not like Arke is going to investigate every murder in the archipelago, but if I do go with Jason on the Argo *. . . No, it's too high-profile. It's not all of them, but enough of them have some sort of direct line to a deity, and who knows how big that club is and how much they gossip?*

At least I have it on somewhat good authority that Hephaestus is a recluse. Still, murder is out.

Meaning that either I have to frame Nefkha for something and take his life as justification . . . which seems kinda scummy. Or I can forgo that entirely and just get an oath from him.

Speaking of. Luke opened his status and scrolled through his inventory until he found what he was looking for.

Status | Skills | Quests | **Inventory**
Oath Orb
Tier—Saint

> A Saint-tier mana stone imbued with a binding contract between Cyzicus, emperor of Sylcra, and Luke, inheritor of Alexia. Breaking of the pact will inflict death onto Cyzicus, emperor of Sylcra. The orb is only binding to beings of the Saint tier or lower.

Just thinking of it brought to the forefront of Luke's mind the terms of the oath Cyzicus had sworn to him, along with another option.

It hadn't quite been apparent when the deal had first been struck, likely because Luke's mana hadn't been as heavy back when he was a mortal. But, just like the Mask of a Thousand faces, the orb had a little more depth to it than he initially thought it did. Namely, as the person Cyzicus had sworn the oath to, Luke had the option to absolve Cyzicus of it and, in doing so, free the orb to take on another oath.

Considering both his origin and the fact that the face he currently wore was fake and known to Hephaestus, anyone else the god had shared that information with, Spiros, and Arya, well, holding Cyzicus to the oath wasn't the assurance it had been. Too many people already knew Luke of Sylcra was the same person who had joined the Luminous Sky Society. If anyone went around asking about Luke and met Nefkha . . . it had the potential to end badly.

But I can fix that. If I can intimidate Nefkha into swearing to keep my secrets, then that will finally put an end to all this. He should be the only person alive who knows that I came back from the dead. Considering that he tried to hide my existence from Arke for his own gain, he also should have been smart enough not to spill the beans to anyone else.

Especially considering that he lost me. It's been long enough at this point that, even if he wants to turn me in to Arke, he'd implicate himself. That doesn't mean, however, that if someone else comes asking about me—someone who doesn't know the full picture—he won't tell them I came back from the dead.

Someone like Cybele, for example. Who likely knows that Arke was looking for someone who came back from the dead.

He suppressed a shiver at the mere thought of her knowing what he had.

Why is this sooo hard? At least Cybele is a goddess already. Which, worse comes to worst, means she has little to gain from the God Seed. She also probably has better things to do than to dig up my origins. I'm just a warrior, and she knows where to find me.

She's so much stronger than I am that she probably never even thought to use any kind of leverage. Honestly, what do you even need leverage for when you're a deity? The implication of that kind of power is enough of a threat.

"What were you two thinking!" Cyzicus yelled as he barged into the room.

"Umm . . ." Rex shuffled uncomfortably. Luke couldn't blame him. Cyzicus wasn't the type to show anger easily, making the times he did raise his voice a nerve-racking experience.

"It's my fault. Rex barged into my room at a . . . compromising time and I didn't realize the castle was full of mortals," Luke admitted.

Cyzicus stilled. "Compromising?"

"Uhhh." It was Luke's turn to shuffle uncomfortably as he considered what to say. His bloodline wasn't quite the secret the God Seed was, but Luke had kept it close to his chest all the same. Prometheus wasn't really a subject mentioned in any book he had read so far, and Luke didn't know how well his connection to the mad titan would be received. That said, it wasn't like he planned to keep his copies of the flame spell secret. He couldn't, really—they were too potent a tool to hide.

Luke wouldn't go around advertising how exactly he could make more copies of it, but even if someone did find out, it wasn't the end of the world. He hoped.

"I got a prize from the tournament, and I was just playing around with it," Luke said after a while.

"Oh." Cyzicus suddenly seemed less angry and more curious. "Something from the ring?"

"No, actually. I got this spell for completing the second round. It was only supposed to be good for a dozen uses, but I kind of figured out a way around that."

"A spell . . . fascinating. I've never been fortunate enough to acquire or craft one of my own." Cyzicus scratched his chin.

"Really?" Luke asked. "I didn't realize they were that special."

"Mmm-hmm, quite. Spells are imprints of a technique. I've heard some use them as means to train their juniors, but to even inscribe something like that into runes, the understanding you would need to have . . ." The emperor sighed. "It's not something just anyone can do."

"Huh." Luke activated his bloodline and inspected the icons orbiting in his mana pool with fresh eyes. He had known that spells existed before he had gotten one, but neither the descriptions he had read in Cyzicus's library nor the knowledge that came with the spell itself had mentioned how exactly they were made. Just that you needed a high cultivation level to do so. Luke had just assumed they were a higher form of talisman, and while that wasn't completely wrong, the knowledge of what a spell really was raised a few possibilities and even more questions.

If there was a way that he could learn a fire-based technique from the spell, it was much more valuable than he had thought it was. It also made the fact that he could copy it as easily as he had been able to with his bloodline a lot more interesting.

"Ahem." Clite cleared her throat and looked at Cyzicus meaningfully.

"Right, Rex! I've told you before, but if you're going to keep that demon, you need to make sure not to expose her to the mortals. Without mana in their bodies, they're much more vulnerable to her aura. If something like this happens again, you're going to have to go back to the Rising Sun Sect, or . . ." He pointed at Blinky and dragged his thumb over his throat.

Luke heard the emperor's grandson swallowing his spit.

"It won't happen again. Please don't make me go back there!" Rex pleaded. Cyzicus ignored him.

"Luke! It's good that you woke up. Taking that giant's mana was a risk, but not one that I can begrudge you. In your place, I would have done the same, and

I applaud your courage. You'll need every advantage to win the tournament. However, next time you intend to do something so reckless, please let someone know. This time, I managed to see your sword entering and leaving the giant's body, and we were able to administer some healing potions to you while you slept. Next time, you may not be as lucky."

Healing potions. What? With the one Cybele gave me, I shouldn't have needed another— Don't tell me he didn't see her and . . .

A pit formed in his stomach.

"How long was I asleep?"

Rex answered, "Thirteen days. We thought you might miss the Olympics."

Well, so much for going to Carim. They must have fed me so many potions that I went into a stupor again. Fuck.

No. No worries.

Sure, I have a pretty big loose end right now that I can't really do anything about. Yeah, someone can chase that thread and find my secret out. But, really, what are the odds? It's been two weeks, and no one has come knocking yet. I can wait a few days and deal with it after the Olympics.

Yeah . . .

Besides, the Seed's been quiet. I'm sure if it felt the need, it would have given me a quest. Right? Luke mentally poked the Seed.

It stayed silent.

He poked it again.

Nothing.

Relieved, Luke took a deep breath, ignored the feeling of impending doom, and met Cyzicus's gaze. "I need to look through your armory and get a full set of gear. Armor, shields, everything. They changed the rules a bit for the last round, and I'm spending every last merit point I have on your best stuff."

CHAPTER 58

The Hero's Vault

Cyzicus wasted no time in leading him to his personal stash. The massive and well-lit room underneath the castle was nearly empty save for a single storage ring floating next to a plain-looking podium. Before Luke could step inside, though, the emperor held out his hand and stopped him in his tracks.

"This is where I keep all my best stuff. Millenia worth of spoils and wealth. It's better guarded than near anything in the capital," he said, his voice uncharacteristically grave.

"You don't keep everything in your storage ring?" Luke asked.

"And give all my life's work to any fool who happens to kill me?" Cyzicus scoffed. "No, my ring just contains the essentials and some extra in case of an emergency. More than enough to help me survive even the most dire of circumstances, but not all my wealth. This, however"—he stretched his hand out toward the ring—"will go to my heirs. Even had the Rebel succeeded in defeating me and taken this castle, none of it would ever have been hers. The slightest movement beyond this step will teleport the ring away to Lord Hermes. He is oathsworn to safeguard and deliver its contents to the people I've entrusted them to on my passing." Then, before Luke could ask any more questions, a dagger appeared in Cyzicus's hands. He stabbed himself in the palm and let his blood drip onto the white marble floor.

Without a visible mechanism, the red seeped into the stone, disappearing without a trace. The sound of clanking metal echoed throughout the chamber, and Luke watched, stunned, as a veritable army of suits of silver armor shimmered to life in neat ranks around the ring, each of them armed with identical shields and spears. Suddenly, the size of the room made sense.

"Move," Cyzicus commanded, and instantly they parted. Stepping in perfect sync, they formed a straight path between them and the podium.

A hint of pride in his step, the emperor marched toward the ring. Feeling a mixture of anticipation and giddiness, Luke followed him, eager to see what Cyzicus had in store for him.

Luke already had a sizable collection of Warrior- and Hero-tier artifacts from killing the Rebel. Most of it was decent, but very little of it was what Luke would think of as high-quality. At least not anymore, knowing what he did about what was possible. He'd found Tyrisa's lack of wealth strange at first but reasoned that waging war against an entire island couldn't have been cheap. She had likely spent or given away most of her wealth to indulge her rebellion, however short-lived. Now that he saw this, though, he wondered if maybe she too had made arrangements with some god to pass her holdings down to her heirs.

Luke shook his head as row after row of empty suits of armor turned on their heels at his passing, each one ready to attack at a moment's notice in case he tripped some invisible alarm. He'd thought he knew what wealth looked like, but as they made their way past the ring's defenses, he realized he might have been too quick to jump to conclusions. Hero-tier cultivators lived for millennia. Cyzicus alone had lived longer than Earth's calendar had years. Much of that time was spent ruling what was practically an entire continent.

Of course he doesn't walk around carrying everything he owns on his finger.

Mind freshly blown, thoughts of what lay in that ring had his mind awash with ideas. Ideas he suspected would remain just that, as he doubted Cyzicus would give him a complete inventory.

Still, even among the same tier, there were differences in workmanship between artifacts. Which was what he was concerned with, and the reason Cyzicus had brought him here in the first place. Things like physical durability, mana efficiency, and the potency of abilities came down to the skill of the craftsmen who made the tool as much as, if not more than, the tier of mana that powered it.

Maximus was a great example of that. The sword was still a Warrior-tier weapon, but it had no problem slicing through Hero-tier flesh. Not to mention the host of other abilities it provided. The doubling of every stat, the intrinsic mana storage, along with the fact that it acted as a conduit of Luke's energy, made it better than any other Warrior-tier artifact Luke had ever heard of, let alone possessed.

Honestly, it was superior to most Hero-tier objects he had, too. Maybe not in every aspect—Maximus couldn't hold a candle to the Limitless Thunder Bow's sheer destructive power, for example—but it more than made up for it with its versatility and ability to harvest mana from the recently killed.

And while Luke carried little hope of finding anything even remotely as useful as his named and bound sword, he also knew that Cyzicus kept his best stuff out of his public merit exchange. Some of the items in there had been created by Cyzicus and were quite good, but most of it had been made and sold to the empire by warriors throughout the realm—warriors who had no hope of advancing to the next stage, had given up on their cultivation, and instead spent their time pursuing the crafts.

The artifacts they created weren't bad, per se, but they couldn't really compare to what Cyzicus could do, either. Not when the emperor had spent millennia honing his skills compared to their centuries, or more often decades. As for the contents of the ring, maybe some of them had been crafted by beings even higher than the Hero tier.

"So, what exactly do you need?" Cyzicus placed his still-bloody hand on the podium, and at the gesture, the ring flew off onto a finger on his other hand. Cyzicus dripped another drop of blood onto it, binding it to him so that he could access its contents.

"Umm . . . A full set of Mortal-tier armor. The best you have." The words had barely left Luke's mouth when the ring flashed and a mannequin, dressed head to toe in golden armor, appeared in front of them.

It wasn't the most ornate set Luke had seen, but it was regal. Lacking any sort of patterns or insignias, the thing almost looked more like the *Iron Man* armor than any he had seen on Theos before. Only the red cape and the Spartan-esque helmet set it apart from the stuff of comic books. Even its construction was so perfect that Luke wasn't even sure how he would go about getting into it.

But holy shit, this is awesome. I want it, I want it, I want it, he repeated over and over in his head. Outwardly, though, he remained stoic and eyed the suit of armor with a critical gaze.

Cyzicus quirked his eyebrow at that before shrugging. "I'll be honest, this isn't the most practical mortal armor I have. Truthfully, I'm not even sure a mortal could wear it. It's much too heavy. At your level, though, it shouldn't hamper your movements or slow your flight. It's enchanted with self-repair, environmental resistance, and durability. So it should offer adequate protection against the caliber of attack you can expect in the tournament. I wouldn't rely on it saving you from a head-on attack, though. No mortal armor will do that."

"Environmental resistance?" Luke asked.

"Heat won't cook you, the cold won't bother you as much, water will slide off, and lightning won't zap you quite as hard. It won't stand up to protracted energy attacks, though, so you'll need to dodge. The quality of the enchantments is about as good as you can get, but it's still a Mortal-tier armor set, so the amount of mana you can feed it without blowing them isn't that high. So watch out for that."

Luke nodded. "It's . . . nice. A little pretentious, though, don't you think?"

"HA," the emperor laughed. "You wield a golden blade. The time for seeming humble is long gone. Besides, a little ego isn't misplaced in those of us who dare reach for divinity. Cultivators are many things, but not humble. And at an event like the tournament, this much won't be out of place. It's not out of place on the battlefield, either, but you should wear something of a higher tier when your life's on the line."

Token resistance given, Luke nodded eagerly. "Sounds good to me. What do you have for Warrior-tier shields?"

The ring flashed once again, and a golden shield appeared in the air in front of them. Unlike the armor, though, it wasn't unmarked—a menacing lion head stared back at Luke, its mouth agape, seemingly in the middle of a roar.

"This one is decent," Cyzicus said, sliding his own hand into the grip. A moment later, a red bubble flickered to life around him, almost like he had activated a protective talisman. "The added coverage means it isn't as strong as if the entire defense was dedicated to the metal. The bubble can take one or two hits before it pops, but you can recharge it as many times as you want. It's . . . pretty mana-intensive, though, and the shield can't hold any, either. Something tells me, though, that that isn't going to be a problem for you."

Luke nodded. Mana, indeed, would not be a problem for him at all. His stats meant that he was sitting pretty close to the theoretical maximum of the Warrior tier when it came to his reserves. Reserves that were doubled thanks to his sword. Meaning that altogether, he should have more than twice the mana of everyone he would be competing against.

"Anything else?" Cyzicus asked.

"Yeah, actually. Do you have anything I can use in the midrange? Like a spear that shoots off energy blasts or something."

"What happened to the sword I gave you? That should serve you fine." Cyzicus frowned.

"I lost it," Luke lied. It had been in his inventory when he had killed the Rebel and had remained there when the others brought him back to the castle. He had wanted to use it more than once, but without a way to explain how he had recovered it, that had proven impossible. At least without exposing the fact that he had an inventory or something. The fact that Cyzicus didn't know he had lost it wasn't strange, though. Considering that his fiancée had just passed at the time, Luke would have been more surprised if he had noticed that Luke was walking around with one gold blade instead of two.

"Tch. That was a really good sword, you know? It may not seem like it, but making mana projections sharp enough to cut is hard. Doubly so when you want them to work with Mortal-tier mana."

"Oh . . . Don't you just need to enchant another sword the same way to get the same effect?"

Cyzicus looked personally affronted at that question. "No. No, you can't just squiggle the same lines on another sword and get an exact copy of a masterpiece. There're a million different steps you have to complete perfectly to get a result that good. If even one of them isn't performed with the utmost precision, the mana projection turns dull. Or maybe the distance it can travel before dissipating halves. Or maybe it doesn't contain enough *oomph* to actually cut anything thicker than a chicken's neck. I would assume that the fact that not everyone is carrying a weapon that versatile would clue you in to its true rarity."

Luke scratched the back of his head. His own knowledge of enchanting was nearly nonexistent, other than the fact that you carved glyphs into objects to do it. A consequence of everyone condemning any action that didn't improve your cultivation level. Wasting time on secondary pursuits while you hadn't reached the limits of your potential was practically sacrilege to cultivators. That, and plenty of people had weapons that blasted something out of one end. Thinking back, he realized sharp things were rare, but gouts of flame, lightning, bolts of force, and arrows were common enough. Still, there wasn't anything he could do about it now except feel glad that he hadn't actually lost the weapon and guilty that he had lied to Cyzicus about it.

Maybe I'll take a trip back to that castle and find it later. I'm going to outgrow it pretty soon, but maybe I can give it to some up-and-coming cultivator? Maybe my boots, too—it's not like I need them anymore.

And once this tournament is done, I should break the mold and really learn some of this stuff, too. With the Seed I can constantly improve my Arcana, so I'll never really hit my limit until I ascend. Which is going to start holding me back in other ways if I don't make the time.

Cyzicus stared at him a moment longer before shaking his head. The ring flashed one more time, though, and another golden blade, nearly identical to the one Cyzicus had given him all those months ago, appeared in his hand.

"Here. It's similar to the last one. More crude, but you'll find it a tad more powerful. Mortals won't be able to use it like you did the old one, but it won't be a problem for you."

"Thanks." Luke nodded gratefully, ultimately deciding not to point out that he had asked for a spear and not another sword. It was probably for the best, anyway—he was decent with a spear, but swords were practically his bread and butter at this point.

"Anything else?"

Luke shook his head. "I'm good for the rest. Thanks for all this," he said earnestly, even as his storage ring glowed and greedily squirreled it all away.

"Don't mention it. The reward I get for sponsoring you, even with your current rank in the tournament, is more than enough to pay for all your training and equipment. And, uhh, I'll say this now, because it won't mean much later. If you don't advance any farther in the tournament, don't feel guilty. I don't know what the earlier stages were like, but I've been around long enough to know that it's a miracle for you to have come this far. Those that do are usually either disciples of truly powerful sects, like Jason, or direct descendants of gods, wielding both destructive and powerful bloodlines and who knows what kind of techniques."

A vision of Theseus cutting down entire chunks of the forest with blades of water and Ella commanding constructs of rainbow light flashed through his mind.

It kinda was a miracle, wasn't it?

"Thanks . . . Hey, did you know I looked like Poseidon?"

"By look like, do you mean look nearly identical to him? If so, yes."

"Why didn't you tell me?"

"You mean you didn't know?"

"No."

"Strange, but it happens," Cyzicus said, leading him out the room.

CHAPTER 59

The Pregame

After a few hours of making as many copies of the flame spell icon as he could, Luke wandered into the throne room with his tournament token in hand. There was still an hour before they were set to depart, but the room was buzzing with activity.

Unlike the last time he had left, this was a much livelier affair. Earlier that morning, he had passed Clite all one hundred of his invitation tokens with a small list of people he wanted to invite, giving her free rein to hand out the rest at her discretion. Supposedly, she had given a few to Cyzicus's closest advisers and auctioned the rest for merit points. Considering his own unease around gods, he couldn't quite fathom why anyone else would *want* to be in a room full of people who could wink them out of existence, let alone pay for the opportunity. At the same time, his more rational self knew that not everyone had the God Seed planted in their souls, making them monumental targets for greedy paragons. No, most of these people would just have a good time and spend some time rubbing elbows with the rulers of the world, free of the fear of having their souls ripped apart.

I suppose that's a good thing, though. The Olympians might be near-universally disliked, but at least it seems that they don't have a reputation for needless violence.

"So, are you ready to win it all?" Jason asked moments after Luke stepped into the throne room, a wide grin on his face, a sway in his step, and a chalice filled with wine in his hand. Instantly, a hush fell over the crowd, and all of them looked at him. Right at him.

There are way more than a hundred people here.

"We'll see," Luke hedged. The older cultivator laughed out loud and, walking closer to Luke, wrapped an arm around his shoulder. Luckily, the crowd seemed to take that as a cue and returned to their own conversations.

"Don't worry too much. Win or lose, you'll walk away with a massive prize. Not as good as the *Argo* if you lose, but the prizes for the Warrior bracket are always powerful. Hero-tier items at the minimum, and often Saint tier."

"What tier prize is the *Argo*?" Luke asked, wondering what he would be missing out on by finishing second.

Jason laughed out loud. "Wouldn't you like to know . . ."

"I would, actually."

"Fine!" Leaning in to whisper into Luke's ear, as if everyone in the room didn't have super hearing, he breathed a single word into existence. "Herald. My boat's a Herald-tier artifact."

"Huh. Herald. I thought the last rank before god would have been more . . . poetic," Luke said.

Jason shrugged. "Herald tier, Demigod tier, Angel tier—it's all semantics and all equally made-up. The name isn't what matters; it's the power. It also changes by place. Older traditions use demigod, but it's kind of a mouthful, and not very accurate. Some people also confuse demigod with being the child of a god. The real demigods didn't like that all that much, so they started calling themselves something different. It makes sense; it's not like you can be part god. It's more of a do or don't thing, you know?"

Luke almost laughed but settled for a smile as he soaked in the new information. *So I was wrong, and Arke is an angel, sort of. The irony.*

"So you're kind of set with that kind of power, huh?" Luke asked.

"Not really. I'll need to make it to herald to unlock all the features, and I can barely even activate the Saint-tier wards at the moment. I can't attack with anything higher than the Warrior tier as long as I am one, too, so there's that. It's not like you win one tournament and the gods give you the power to dominate the world, you know?"

"I mean, kinda," Luke hedged.

"If you're a herald, you don't need a ship, trust me. You'd be able to destroy nations with the weight of your mana alone."

"Really? Does that happen often?"

Jason gave him an odd look. "It never happens. People who have that kind of power usually know better. If they don't, that's what the council is for. Lord Ares himself will come down from the mountain and swat you like a fly. Or so they say."

"What if Lord Ares is the one who wants to destroy a nation?"

"Gods can't, either. They all swore, um . . . oaths! The ones who didn't aren't alive anymore."

"Really?"

Jason shrugged. "It's what they say, but gods have a lot of leeway, and the exact terms of their oaths have never been made public, so no one who isn't a god knows for sure. No one even knows who they swore the oath to, either, so as far as I know, it's possible that none of them are bound anymore. But that's only if they even swore on a standard Oath Orb. I think they would have used something stronger than that, you know?"

"That's comforting."

"I take comfort in knowing that no country has vanished, out here in the sea or on the continent, for as long as Olympus has reigned and since Othrys fell."

The conversation stalled after that. It had gotten too heavy too fast to continue naturally, so Luke just patted Jason on the shoulder, leaving him to enjoy his drink, and went to look for Nel.

He hadn't talked to her in a while, as both of them had been fairly busy. Except when he finally spotted her, she was talking to Heracles. He got close enough to hear the son of Zeus, with too-pink cheeks, mumble something about good weather before Luke turned on his heel and walked away. There were a lot of horrific things about Theos, and watching a guy richer than sin making awkward attempts at flirting with a princess was one of them. Luke had long ago resolved that he wouldn't subject himself to that again, not unless he needed extra-strong motivation to meditate on his mana or something. The last time Luke had spent a significant span of time with the would-be lovers, he had found the trigger for his bloodline, after all.

That in mind, he made his way to Lukeus. He was always fun to kill time with.

The hour leading up to the tournament passed quickly, and before he knew it, the time to depart had come. Like every other time he had been teleported, the world flickered red and orange, and the next thing Luke knew he was once again back in the holy land of Vulcan.

All around him, people gasped in wonder as the rich mana seeped into their bodies and began to work its magic. Luke closed his eyes and let himself bask in the feeling. Then, on a whim, he circulated his own mana so that it would accommodate the mana of the holy land better and hopefully let him sneak an extra point or two out of the ordeal. It wasn't quite manual cultivation, as he wasn't forcing the mana into any single part and instead making it easier for him to soak up, but it was helpful, nonetheless. He wouldn't turn his nose up at a few free points, ever. Not when, just weeks ago, he'd had to spend hours in battle killing Warrior- and Mortal-tier giants for the same number of them.

I was gone for two weeks, most of which I spent sleeping. But damn, I really missed this, Luke thought moments later as he felt his Strength and Agility attributes tick up by a few points each. They would continue rising for a few seconds but taper off as his body got used to the higher concentrations of aethereal mana.

Had he not already maxed out Arcana and Constitution, those would have risen, too. He had initially planned to increase all stats to nine hundred and fifty or so with his windfall and a bit of hunting, but after getting a little carried away and maxing out Arcana when he was trying to recreate the flame spell, he had maxed out Constitution right after to get the most out of his mana pool.

It was probably better to be rounded out near the peak of the tier for the purpose of the tournament, but Luke couldn't bring himself to care. With his sword, he could always double an attribute far beyond what was normally possible for warriors if he needed to, and if that wasn't enough, a few more points would have hardly made a difference anyway.

Taking one last deep breath, Luke opened his eyes to a familiar sight. They were back atop the pyramid that had been the site of the second task. It was late in the evening, and all nine of Theos's suns were just setting below the horizon, casting a warm orange glow over the endless grassland that spread in every direction. In the sky above them, a few particularly bright stars were already twinkling.

Seeing the holy land like this made it seem infinitely more beautiful than the last time he had been here. Suddenly, Luke thought he understood why Hephaestus hadn't filled it with countless structures. There was something magical about the simple beauty of the endless sky and earth.

As quickly as it came, the moment passed when he saw the extraordinary number of people present. There were easily thousands of them, all packed onto the top of the pyramid that seemed a little too small to hold them. As if in response to Luke's thoughts, the metal beneath his feet hummed, and out of thin air floor space materialized around the edges of the pyramid.

With added room to stand, the crowd naturally dispersed into smaller clumps. Out of the corner of his eyes, Luke saw Heracles drag Nel toward Zeus. The god looked just like Luke had seen him last—like an older, bearded version of Heracles—and while nothing about his appearance particularly stood out among the crowd, people seemed to have almost an instinctive aversion to him. All of them gave him a wide berth without even realizing it.

Looking around, Luke quickly recognized the same pattern playing out all across the floor. Hephaestus he recognized almost instantly, and the god was not at all hiding his displeasure at having so many people around him. A ways to the left of him was another person people were giving a wide berth to, a tall and severe-looking man with hair and beard so dark that his pale face looked almost like the moon poking through a starless night.

Another man was the complete opposite and quite literally glowed in the night. His resemblance to Heracles, and his sunny smile, led Luke to believe he was looking at Apollo.

On the far side of the platform, thankfully far away from him, Luke spotted Cybele in the same form she had appeared in the last time they had met, a young blonde girl. Their eyes quickly met before Luke, fearing he might be forced into another conversation with her, nodded and started walking with feigned determination to the snack bar in the center of the room.

He wasn't hungry, but he reasoned that most people would be less likely to bother him if he looked like he was in the middle of something, and gods were people, too.

Spiros, however, wasn't most people.

"Luke!" he shouted at the top of his lungs and, ignoring the condescending looks everyone gave him, marched straight toward him.

Despite his general unease, Luke was happy to see him. He was reasonably certain that he would have passed, considering his quest was still active, but it was nice to have visual confirmation.

"Spiros. Nice to see you made it out okay." Luke grinned.

"Ahh, you know me. I always do what I have to do."

"Yeah, yeah. What about Arya? Did she get a scroll, too?"

"Obviously," Spiros said, and stepping beside Luke, he immediately started surveying the crowd. "After we sent you home, it was like a dam broke. Ten minutes in, we got attacked by this cyclops lady. I don't even know how she snuck up on us—she was like twenty feet tall. Being so big, though, Arya just threw her dagger at her, and you know how it is with her technique. We just waited a few minutes, and boom, we had a scroll."

"Hmm. Do you think Lord Hephaestus was working in the background? Keeping things fair, so that groups like ours fell apart and people had a fair shot instead of, you know, being destroyed the second they showed themselves?" Luke asked.

"It would be weirder if he didn't. Also, did you notice anything about the people who actually made it?"

"What do you mean?"

"Well, you, me, Theseus, and Ella. We all got the scrolls as a reward in the last round. That guy over there, I didn't see him in the forest, but I'm pretty sure he got one, too. That's like, five of the sixteen people. And exactly sixteen people got those scrolls."

"Arya didn't," Luke pointed out.

"Well, Arya's thing was better than a spell, so I'm not sure if that counts."

Is he just saying that, or does he not know spells are impressions of techniques?

"She got the fire in the bottle, right? I never asked, but what does it do?"

"It's this thing for alchemy. You're supposed to eat it, and it goes into your mana. After that, you can bring it out whenever you want. I have an aunt who has one; they're a big deal. If you feed the fire the right thing, it gets stronger. If you do it enough, they advance to the next tier, and you do, too. It's like, uhh . . . paying for your cultivation."

"That sounds incredible . . ."

"Eh. It's not as great as it sounds. I mean, it's pretty great if you're super rich, but finding stuff to keep feeding the fire is supposed to be really hard. My aunt's had hers forever, and she's still in their Hero tier."

"Still, if you get stuck at a level, it's nice to know that you can have another—"

Spiros started waving his arms wildly.

"ARYA! Over here!"

Luke winced as all eyes were once again pointed toward Spiros. Still, he was excited to see Arya again. Following his gaze, Luke looked toward her. A moment later, he regretted that he had.

Shit.

Danger detected.

The Seed, it seemed, agreed. Because a step behind Arya were a bunch of people Luke knew. Laxas, Ethan, Len, Elder Irila, and, most annoying of all . . . Nefkha.

Fucking hell.

CHAPTER 60

The Old Man

Arya and her entourage from the Luminous Sky Society walked toward him and Spiros, and Luke felt like his heart had crawled up his throat. Seeing Nefkha here inspired a sense of impending doom the likes of which he hadn't felt since Aeolus almost ate his soul.

But stay calm, Luke. The Seed hasn't offered me a charge yet, and I've gotten the warning that I'm in danger a million times by now. Besides, it's not like he's just going t—

Host in imminent danger.

Would you like to use a charge to escape?

Y/N

What. The. Fuck. Seed!?

It stayed silent.

Luke took a deep breath. Then he cursed Cybele for feeding him a Hero-tier giant and leaving him catatonic for nearly two entire weeks. He didn't *need* the points anyway. Not really. He cursed himself for not acting harder on his instinct and finding some way back to Carim so that he could swear Nefkha to secrecy like he'd wanted to. Cyzicus would have understood. He could have been teleported there, beaten the crap out of the old man, and been back in time for dinner. He was strong enough to do that, at least. Hell, he even could have used the mask to look like a completely different person while he went about it. He probably could have even soloed the entire society as he was now; there was a universe of difference between the quality of Carim's cultivators and him. They were all mortals anyway and led by nine below-average warriors. It was totally possible. A couple Hero-tier talismans, and—

He took another breath and hit the no button on his interface. Panicking and getting angry wouldn't help him. Neither would jumping the gun.

Like the last time he had declined the option to escape, the prompt disappeared, but in some recess of his mind, he could still feel the option. Unlike last time, he wasn't sure there was a way out of this. At the very least, advancing his cultivation wouldn't help here. Not that he knew how it would work out with the charge should he change his mind. The Seed had told him long ago that some beings could detect the use of the charges, and he would bet anything that there were a *lot* of them in the crowd right now. He had counted four gods, and likely many more that he hadn't seen were in attendance.

Nefkha took another step forward, and Luke's resolve to stay calm instantly shattered. He cursed the Seed for giving him the quest in the first place. Both the one for finishing second and the one that had directed him to kill the giant.

When he was finished with that, he cursed himself for thinking that Spiros would need help and exposing his identity to him and Arya, and for doing it in such a bumbling and incompetent way. He had been so scared of Hephaestus and trying not to let him, or them, for that matter, on to the fact that he had run intentionally, that he hadn't even sworn the two to secrecy.

Now, as they all strode toward him, he felt himself hoping beyond hope that neither Arya nor Spiros had said anything to anyone and that the Seed was just freaking out. However unlikely that was.

Because, surely, they read the clues on his face and his tone that day? Figured out that he was nervous for a reason beyond the fact that they'd caught onto his identity.

Except he knew even that was wishful thinking. Even if they didn't tell him anything, there was no guarantee that something wouldn't slip right now.

Nefkha might not have been a great cultivator, but he was bold, and he was shrewd. Luke didn't really know how long it had taken for him to arrive on Theos, how long it had taken for Arke to start the hunt, nor how long it had taken him to fully possess the body. But if he had a guess . . . an hour or less.

An hour, by which point Nefkha had not only discovered him, but made the determination to *not* turn him in to the all-powerful Olympian angel and instead extort him for his help for a matter in the future. All this after poking him a handful of times to make sure his method of possession was undetectable.

Honestly, Luke didn't have the slightest doubt in his mind that he would never, ever take the same risk. Had he been in Nefkha's shoes that day and he had found a man revived from the dead, knowing how strong the gods were, he would have turned the purported thief in and slept like a baby afterward.

Perhaps that could be attributed to the burden of his own knowledge. Luke knew too much about the gods. They were cannibals capable of capturing and eating souls of the dead. They could create and destroy entire worlds. Some guy who could punch hard and float really couldn't do anything against that kind of power.

Or, perhaps, Nefkha was just insane and cared nothing for the wrath of the gods or his own life. The man was old, and not just old, but old for a warrior. Meaning he had lived centuries. More than long enough to come to terms with his own death.

Luke took another breath and with an effort of will placed a figurative finger on top of the button that would activate the charge. Not pressing it just yet, but maybe it was good to keep his escape route at a hair trigger.

At the very edge of his vision, he saw something move.

"LUKE! You made it!"

"Wh—"

A moment later, a tangle of arms and a pair of pearly white wings slammed into him.

"Ella?" he said, peeling the girl off him.

"Who else?" She grinned and looked over her shoulder. "Mom, he's the boy I was talking to you about."

Oh, boy. How is this getting worse?

Spiros snickered beside him. Arya smiled in amusement. Nefkha perked up at hearing Luke's name, and Luke felt his gaze drift between the three of them. Luke could feel the gears spinning in the old warrior's head. Len, a step behind all of them, did the same, and then his eyes bored into Luke's. A moment later he made an O shape with his lips, traced a circle over his face, and mouthed the word *mask*.

Luke had never regretted saving someone's life more than in that moment. Never before had he better understood the phrase *no good deed goes unpunished*.

Before he could process any of that, though, a woman with rainbow-colored wings forcefully planted herself between him and Ella. Luke didn't have to be a genius to recognize that she was Iris, Ella's mom, and a goddess. One that did not look amused. Considering that her daughter was still attempting to wrap Luke in a hug . . . he honestly couldn't even blame her.

"What are you playing at, huh?" she asked, crossing her arms over her chest.

Fuck if I know, Luke thought miserably. *And what's with you playing the protective mother—weren't you supposed to be a deadbeat or something? And I'm not doing anything; she came up to me. I just gave her some pizza and had a conversation.*

"Peace, sister. You're scaring the child." A voice rang out from behind him. One that had haunted him as long as he had been on Theos.

"Arke." Luke stumbled back, bumping into Spiros in the way.

The Seed once again prompted Luke to use a charge. If using it didn't mean losing every friend he had made since he'd arrived on Theos, he would be bashing the button repeatedly. Because it would, though, he held off.

This is really bad. Like, terrible. Spiros, Arya, and Len know who I am. Nefkha is in the process of figuring it out. I can see it in his beady fucking eyes. Ella's mom thinks there's something going on between me and her daughter when there really isn't. Arke is glaring daggers at me. Likely not because she knows who I am, but because I freed Heracles.

All right.

That's not that bad. At the very least, I don't think anyone is going to murder me right this instant. And is that . . . yep!

"ARKE," Zeus yelled as he marched toward them. Lightning sparkled in his eyes and crackled over his wrist. "I won't have you bully those under my protection. Especially not when they are competing in this tournament."

Arke sighed. "I'm doing nothing of the like, my lord. My niece has struck up a *friendship* with our young friend here. I was merely introducing myself properly. As you're aware, our last meeting was less than ideal. After all, his actions allowed that despicable thief to escape."

"Your actions were unlawful, and they alone allowed this *mystery thief* of yours to escape. Had you followed the rules of conduct the council laid forth, perhaps that may have been different."

Luke risked a glance at Nefkha, only to see him staring back at him with a grin on his face.

Yep, he knows.

"Excuse me." Hephaestus cleared his throat and rose into the air. "I hate to interrupt whatever this is, but now that everyone has arrived, as the game master of this tournament, I'd like to get started."

"Our apologies." Zeus nodded toward him. "Please begin."

"Great. I'd like to begin by announcing the finalists. Arya of Carim, representing the Luminous Sky Society." On cue, the floor lit up underneath her, sending a beam of light shining into the sky. People clapped politely, and when the crowd quieted down, Hephaestus moved on to the next person on the list. Luke watched as, one by one, each of the finalists was called out. "Moros, son of Ares, representing Sparta. Spiros of House Paris, representing Mysiath. Theseus, son of Poseidon, representing Atlantis. Luke of Sylcra, representing Cyzicus. Ella, daughter of Iris, representing Iliad. Icarus of Athens, representing the Institute of Advanced Learning. Magnus of . . ."

Soon after his name was announced, Luke zoned out. He recognized some of the names while the rest were completely foreign. Any other time, he would be trying to piece together what he knew of each person's mythologies, but with his greatest foe standing only a few feet behind him and the only man in the world who knew his secret a few feet in front of him, he found it hard to focus.

He listened with half an ear as podiums erupted out of the ground and Hephaestus started listing the prizes. Places eight through sixteen would each get a Saint-tier shield personally crafted by the god, supposedly because staying alive was the most important qualification for becoming a god. Rank seven would get a pair of Saint-tier wings that boosted flight speed to a significant degree. Rank six would get Herald-tier gloves that quintupled strength when worn. Rank five would get a robe that massively increased Constitution. Ranks four and three would receive a customized manual made personally for them with instructions on how to increase their Arcana all the way through to the Saint tier. Rank two would get a deployable pocket dimension, equipped with its own garden and capable of hiding itself from anyone under the God tier.

"And finally, the winner of the tournament will receive—"

"Wait!" Spiros yelled, interrupting the god. "If I win, can I pick my own prize?"

"It's always something," Hephaestus mumbled under his breath. "What do you want?"

"I want to marry someone, and I was hoping you could help me."

"Sorry, kid. I won't force someone to marry you." Hephaestus rejected the proposal out of hand. "As I was saying, the prize for first place is—"

"Now, wait a minute." Zeus suddenly spoke up. "Let's not dismiss this without due consideration. Hephaestus is of course right, in that we won't force someone to marry you, Spiros. If you do win, however, I shall grant you this as a favor. If she or he is willing, I will arrange a meeting and put in a good word. Then, if, and only if, everything goes well and all parties are in agreement, I will personally officiate your wedding. Nothing more."

"That's more than enough. Thank you!" Spiros agreed right away. "Her name is Helen. She's your daughter." After dropping that bombshell, he bowed down to the king of the gods.

The room was already silent, but suddenly, the silence seemed deafening as they all waited for Zeus to respond.

To his credit, Zeus remained calm. Then, stiff as a board, he turned to a seemingly random section of the stage. "Helen. If this young man were to win this tournament, would you agree to a meeting with him, knowing his intention to wed you?"

The crowd, still silent, parted, revealing a woman who looked like she was in her early twenties, though Luke knew her to be a warrior in her forties. She was holding a half-eaten pastry and looked eerily like a deer caught in headlights. Luke watched in stunned silence as she finished chewing, swallowed, and then wiped the crumbs off her face.

"Sure. Spiros is a good kid, a little young, but if he's okay waiting ten . . . no, twenty years, then I don't see a problem," she said slowly.

"That's fine with me." Spiros grinned.

"Consider the matter settled, then. If you win the tournament, you can have a conversation with her in twenty years and I will be sure to give you my personal endorsement, whatever that is worth. Hephaestus, as you were."

"Wait a minute! That's my wife," someone yelled. "Helen! You're my wife. What do you mean, there's no problem?"

What the fuck is going on? Like . . . seriously.

Next to him, Ella looked to her mother. "Is this normal?"

Iris sighed. "Yes. Yes, it is."

CHAPTER 61

Hit the Fan

Luke didn't know what to think anymore. He'd always thought that his identity being exposed would be this massive, life-shattering, monumental moment.

The worst part was that it was. Just not at all in the way he'd envisioned it. He'd thought there would be a desperate struggle. A sinking realization that he would once again have to leave everything behind. Instead, he, Arke, and Nefkha were standing nearly shoulder to shoulder as the scandal of the ages shook Olympus.

It was humbling—a strong reminder that the world and its endless problems didn't always revolve around him. That other people lived, too, and caused problems, too, and other people could solve them, too.

In this case, it was Zeus doing the solving. Well, trying, really. Luke got the strong sense that the god was regretting ever entertaining Spiros's request.

"Okay. It seems that I was hasty in my actions. Helen, is this man truly your husband? If so, when did you get married, and why wasn't I informed?"

And the plot thickens.

"Well, I was twenty. Heracles had just been born, and you didn't seem to have time for anyone else. So I . . . It's not a real marriage, though. I just wanted to see if you'd even notice. I thought Menelaus knew that, too." She glared at him. "I haven't even seen him since it happened."

"Is this true?" Zeus asked Menelaus.

Menelaus looked absolutely miserable, but he nodded.

"Very well. In that case, as the king of gods, I hereby annul your marriage and state this matter concluded and this opposition void. Now, let us all get on with the tournament. Hephaestus, please proceed."

Hephaestus nodded. "Before I do, is there anyone else that would like to get anything out of their system? I'll warn you all now, if anyone, and I mean anyone disrupts it again, I will seek petty revenge for the next two thousand years." He looked around the room. "No? Very we—"

"I have something to say." Nefkha suddenly stepped forward.

A pit instantly formed in Luke's stomach.

"Who are you?" Zeus asked.

"My name is Nefkha. I know the identity of the thief."

Arke was on him the second the word *thief* left his mouth. The pressure of her aura billowed out uncontrollably, and instantly the Luminous Sky elder's face planted in the metal floor as she squashed him under the weight of her mana.

Well, it's happening, Luke thought, ready to use the charge at any time. If he was honest with himself, he had known since the moment he saw Nefkha that it was going to come to this.

"My lord, please allow me to take him away. This matter doesn't concern Olympus."

"Really? I seem to recall that you used your authority as an Olympian to command the islands of the Dolion to do your bidding, did you not? Let this man speak. Now," Zeus commanded. "Let us all learn the identity of this thief. Perhaps we might even learn what it was that he stole."

Arke stared at Zeus. Her wings slowly extended, and for a moment Luke thought she was going to do something. Maybe fly away, or perhaps just kill Nefkha then and there to hide the knowledge of the God Seed. Instead, she nodded slowly and stepped back, likely realizing that she was significantly outmatched. Zeus alone could easily defeat her, but with this many gods in the crowd, she didn't stand a chance.

Zeus smiled and knelt beside Nefkha. Then, prying open his shattered jaw, the god poured a healing potion down his throat. Luke winced as the old man's nose popped back into place.

"Speak. Tell us, who is this thief?"

"I just want to say something first. May I?" Nefkha asked. Rising unsteadily to his feet, he spat out three bloody teeth.

"Go on," Zeus said.

"All of you Olympian bastards can suck my dick," he yelled.

Oh, right. He hates them. It's why he didn't turn me in in the first place.

The king of gods summoned a rag, and wiped Nefkha's bloody spittle off his face. "I speak for all of us when I say this. I'm sorry you feel that way."

"No, you don't." Nefkha shook his head. "Your ilk never does."

"All right, that's enough. Clearly this man has some sort of grudge. I say we kill him and get this tournament over with."

"We're not going to kill him, Ares. The punishment for angry words isn't death." Zeus sighed.

"Why not? He's clearly not here to talk. I reckon he doesn't even know who this thief is," Ares drawled.

"Hmm. What do you say, Apollo? Does he know of the thief?" Zeus asked, not taking his eyes off Nefkha.

"He didn't lie," Apollo said. "He knows. Or thinks he does."

Huh. This could actually work.

"Well, you said what you wanted to say. Unless you have something more you want to add, I'd suggest you tell us of this thief."

"No. I've said what needs to be said, and I intend to keep my word," Nefkha said. Then, slowly turning around, he pointed his finger straight at Luke. "Luke. Luke is the thief."

"I didn't steal anything from Arke," Luke denied instantly.

"Apollo?"

"Both tell their own truth the way they have experienced it. Keeping that in mind, I'd say the old man believes what he says, but his belief is founded on false information. Luke would not be able to believe he didn't steal if he truly did."

"It can't be. I witnessed his resurrection myself. Arke told us that the soul of the man that had stolen from her had come to the archipelago."

"See, we should have just killed him from the start. He's senile. The kid shows no signs of corruption," Ares scoffed.

"Apollo?" Zeus asked again.

The god of truth shrugged. "He believes he has told no lie."

"Would you care to weigh in on this, child? Perhaps you could shed some light on why this man thinks you rose from the dead."

Luke considered his words carefully, acutely aware that he was balancing on a knife's edge. A single misstep, a single mistruth, and that would be that. This was his chance to escape suspicion forever. To clear his name once and for all. Or . . . he would be forced to use a charge in front of all of them and hide not just from Arke, but everyone. For once he used the God Seed to escape, there would be no hiding that he had it. Of course, knowing what he did, he knew the gods, while powerful nearly beyond measure, weren't omnipotent. There *were* ways to hide, and now that he had experience, Luke believed he could do a better job of hiding. He wasn't new to this world anymore. And yet, he still hesitated.

Apollo can't tell the objective truth. By his words, it's obvious that he can only tell I'm telling the truth because I believe I'm telling the truth.

I didn't steal the Seed. The Seed chose me after Arke tried to steal it from Aeolus. By right, it is mine, and you can't steal what's yours. That part is already covered, and it alone should wipe the suspicion off me.

So I guess the real question is what do I believe is objective truth that can also be used to convince them I'm innocent in all this?

Arya and Spiros shared a brief glance, and under the gaze of who knows how many gods deliberately walked to either side of Luke and stood shoulder to shoulder with him.

Luke remembered what he had told them in the empress's tomb about his past. He remembered that day he had spent on Al's boat after spending weeks traversing the wilderness. How easily everything had come to him because Max had grown up on a fisherman's boat, too. He remembered his thoughts, however hazy, when he killed the Rebel after nearly dying, and when he had named his sword. That Max wasn't just a name of his meat suit's last owner. That part of Luke *was* Max.

He felt, once again, the Seed's presence in his soul. Offering him escape, but ultimately leaving the decision up to him.

Taking a deep breath, he looked Zeus in the eye.

"My name was Max. I was born in a small fishing village in Carim. I don't know who my parents are, only that a fisherman found me one day, floating in the sea. He raised me from when I was a child to when I was a teenager. One day he had an accident at sea and died. Soon after that, debt collectors started harassing me and the fisherman's wife. She was old and suffering from heartbreak. She died. Soon after that, the debt collectors took everything I had and chased me out of town and into the forest. I don't remember how long I walked, but back then I was just a mortal. I was weak. I lost consciousness. When I woke up, I stumbled around a little. I cried. I had lost everything, and on top of that I was lost.

"That's when Nefkha found me.

"He was one of the first cultivators I'd seen. He appeared behind my back, floating in the air with his legs crossed. He asked me if I was possessing this body or not. I didn't really know how to answer him, and I was scared. He took my silence for an admission and continued to prattle on. About how the 'ruddy Olympians' were wasting his time. Of how he wanted to be left alone.

"Eventually he told me to join the Luminous Sky Society. Not having a place to go, I agreed and joined the society. When I got there, Arya showed me around. I met some disciples. Did my first mission to collect flowers with Spiros, his cousin, and his sister. We found this black snake that was worth a lot of money and killed it. I spent most of it on this golden sword I saw hanging on the armory wall.

"After that, I did another mission, this time to kill harpies with Arya, Ethan, Laxas, and some other guy. I forget his name. Then there was this expedition to go to the empress's tomb. I went there, learned some techniques. Killed a bunch of people. Awakened my mana. Mastered the techniques enough to be allowed to leave. I saw Len; he was bleeding out and his arm was infected. He wanted me to choose a healing potion as a prize, and he gave me a round rock-looking thing in exchange. I had a Warrior-tier healing potion, so I just picked something and gave him that instead.

"After that, some guy tried to kill me for a stupid reason. I took care of him and went to Sylcra. Fought some giants, met Heracles and the other Argonauts, some other stuff here and there. There was sweet cyclops named Sophia and some crappy Rebel. Now I'm here."

"So you really could be my brother! Dad, why'd you abandon him at sea?" Theseus jumped into the air and whooped. Luke hadn't even known he was there.

"I'm sorry?" Poseidon scratched the back of his head. "Stuff happens sometimes? I really don't know how I could have lost you at sea, son. I'll do better from now on."

Luke stared blankly at the god with his mouth slightly agape. He looked just like Theseus and, by that virtue, just like Luke.

What the fuck is he on about? How can he not remember if he lost a kid at sea or not? Like . . . what?

"Oh, sorry, I should have been more clear. I look like this because of a . . . mistake. The thing I took from the tomb was a mask, and when I used it, it did this. My original face wasn't as handsome. But yeah. I didn't steal anything from Arke."

Zeus scratched his beard. "Apollo?"

"It's true."

A weight lifted off Luke's shoulders.

"I guess that settles it. Nefkha, I know not your quarrel with Olympus. Knowing us, though, we likely did something that offended you, and for that I apologize. Being a god, being powerful, being old, none of it necessarily instills in us either wisdom or compassion. As such, I do not judge you for your hatred. However, I cannot in good conscience abide by the lies you have told us and yourself here today. Ares?"

The world blinked red, and the old man disappeared.

Just like that, huh.

Hephaestus clapped slowly. "Well, that was riveting. Luke, I give your story seven points out of ten. It reminds me of legends from ages past. Now, if there isn't anything else, can we please, for the sake of all that is just and holy, get on with the games? I realize that most of us are possessed of long lives, and some of us are immortal, but that is no excuse to waste time."

"I actually have a question, and I think after all this drama we all deserve an answer. What, Arke, was stolen from you?" asked Apollo.

"If I don't say?"

"You will speak, or you will die," Ares said.

"Ares! You are crossing the line!" Iris yelled.

"Am I? Last I heard, she's killed hundreds and extinguished the souls of hundreds more in this mad pursuit of hers. In the process, dragging our collective name through the mud. I say we deserve an answer."

"I propose we vote on it," Poseidon said.

"I second that motion," Apollo chimed in.

Zeus sighed. "All those who oppose this motion, say nay."

"Nay!" Iris yelled.

"All who are in favor, say yea"

"Yea."

. . .

"Yea."

. . .

"Yea."

One after another, the gods cast their votes.

Zeus sighed once again. "Arke. The council has spoken."

"I won't—"

A bolt of lightning shimmered to life in Zeus's hand. "I urge you to reconsider your decision."

"The God Seed."

A heavy silence settled into the throne room. Then it was pandemonium.

About the Author

Arthur Wordsmith is the author of the Theos series, originally released on Royal Road. He believes that books have the power to entertain, take people to different worlds, expand their minds, and connect them with their deepest selves. As a writer, he aims to create works of fiction that do exactly that. Visit his website at www.arthurwordsmith.com.

DISCOVER
STORIES UNBOUND

PodiumAudio.com

www.ingramcontent.com/pod-product-compliance
Lightning Source LLC
Chambersburg PA
CBHW030939120726
47906CB00002B/643